LETHAL KING

RUTHLESS DYNASTY BOOK 2

SASHA LEONE

Copyright © 2022 by Sasha Leone

All rights reserved.

No part of this book may be reproduced in any form or by any electronic or mechanical means, including information storage and retrieval systems, without written permission from the author, except for the use of brief quotations in a book review.

PROLOGUE
ROZALIA

11 years ago...

There he is again.

   No. Not 'he'. That isn't a man.

   It's a monster.

   For a split second, the violent storm raging outside stops dead, frozen still by a vicious streak of lightning.

   The jagged flash illuminates a horrifying scene.

   Endless black woods. Barbed-wire fences. Makeshift watchtowers. And at the center of it all, a mysterious figure.

   My heart pounds.

   The threatening silhouette stands on the scraggly lawn below, right at the forest's edge, unmoving—barely visible among the shadows.

   Where its face should be, I see nothing but a void. But I can feel its glare.

   I'm being watched.

   Sweat trickles down my forehead.

   The bars on my prison window suddenly don't feel so thick

and unbreakable anymore. Whatever that thing is, it could easily break through the rusted steel—I've never been so sure of anything in my entire life.

But who is it?

What is it?

Another one of Egon's guards?

No. I know all about those monsters. They don't go outside. Not alone. Not at night. And definitely not without their hellhounds.

But this thing—well, I don't know what this thing is.

A shiver washes over my skin. A tingle skates up my spine. An unexpected jolt of excitement rises through the horror. Dark fantasies billow through my mind like smoke.

Who knows, maybe this monster will tear Egon's monsters to shreds. Maybe this monster will save me from my nightmare.

Or maybe it will drag me into a whole new level of hell.

In the blink of an eye, the lightning strike vanishes. The world outside returns to its impenetrable shade of black. Still, I can feel the weight of that dark gaze lingering on me.

I've been spotted.

A clap of thunder scatters my thoughts. Its roar is so loud the house shakes. The window rattles. Sharp shards of rain chatter against the glass. The frame creaks against a howling wind.

Yet the rusted bars hold firm.

My chin drops to my chest.

I'm still trapped.

Somewhere in the distance, a tree falls, and the forest groans.

The gaze I'd felt lingering on me slowly dissolves, and I know that the mysterious dark figure has slipped away—if it was ever really there.

The next flash of lightning confirms that hunch. No dark

silhouette glares up at me. Whatever I thought I saw, it's gone, consumed by the stormy night.

Still, a chill remains on my skin—that is, until I feel a familiar warmth brush up against my bare shoulder.

"Willow..."

Wiping a bead of sweat from my forehead, I look over at the black cat. The last living ghost of my past life. A friend who's followed me to the edge of the world, and down into hell.

"Silly kitten," I mumble under my breath. "You should stay hidden."

But Willow doesn't heed my warning. No. All Willow ever hears is her own name. And when she hears her name, she does the only trick I've ever been able to teach her.

She comes to me.

Even through all of my gut-churning fear, I manage to find some comfort in her presence.

"I'm just like you now," I sigh, picking her up. But holding her in my arms is becoming more of a struggle every day. She keeps growing, and I'm practically wasting away. "An orphan. Only at least you're not a prisoner too."

Stroking her beneath the ear, I take one last look out into the stormy night. There's no trace of the heart-stopping monster. His presence has been swallowed up by the darkness, along with the little pinprick of hope he inspired in me.

There is no escaping this nightmare. Not if I want any chance at a future.

Willow purrs against my chest as I step away from the window and plop down on the edge of my allotted mattress, a stained white cushion that stinks of smoke and blood—or maybe it doesn't stink at all, and the scent of smoke and blood is the only thing I can smell anymore.

"I know it's cold outside," I whisper, using my free hand to wipe another bead of sweat from my temple. "But being cold is better than being trapped, right? My mom used to say—"

Before I can finish the thought, my withering heart twists in a painful convulsion, brutalized by the reminder of what happened to my parents.

It shrivels up even more at the thought of my dad... and what he did to cause it all.

Without warning, a flurry of brutal memories slash through my overheating mind.

Strangers. A truce. Broken promises. My village in flames. My family in ashes. My life in ruins.

My chest sinks inward—the pressure is enough to knock me out. It's not the first time this has happened, and when my eyelids flutter open again, I'm not even surprised, just drained.

I'm exhausted. But that doesn't mean I don't panic when I realize Willow is gone.

My hollow chest pounds.

Willow is all I have left. I can't lose her. I won't.

Snapping upwards, I fight through a pummeling headache and frantically try to find my cat.

"Willow!" I croak. My throat is so dry it hurts.

For a moment, nothing stirs. And then, just when I think all is lost, I see the curtain by the window stir.

Willow's black head pops out from behind the edge of the scarlet drape. A fuzzy black circle with two sharp ears and even sharper yellow eyes.

The sound of her name is too enticing to resist. She comes to me, and I gather her up in my arms and begin to cry.

"Don't ever leave me," I quietly plead.

Cold tears trickle down my hot cheeks. They mix in with the sweat that dampens my skin.

This place is becoming a furnace. Somewhere, someone has started a fire. I don't dare think about what they might be using as kindle.

So, instead of focusing on that horror, I force myself to concentrate on the black cat huddled in my arms.

I think about how strong she is, how loyal, how independent. I remember how I first found her, an emaciated kitten slinking along the back walls of my village, looking a lot like I feel now.

I recall how badly I wanted to take her in.

Mom wouldn't have it.

Black cats are bad luck, after all.

As if my luck couldn't get any worse.

Wiping at my tears, I remember how I would sneak out pieces of freshly caught fish to where I had last seen the tiny kitten, around the ancestral weeping willow that borders our village.

At first, finding the black spot among the tall grass was impossible—until I decided on a name and called it out.

Willow.

That's when she appeared. That's when I fed her. That's when I decided it didn't matter what mom said. This was my cat, and I was going to protect her.

Mom...

I hold Willow extra tight and remember how I grew with the kitten. Those are happy memories. The only ones I have left.

I do my best to focus on how my scraps of extra fish helped Willow grow from a scrawny kitten to an elegant cat. How, after only a few months, she didn't even need my scraps anymore. Instead, she started bringing me the leftovers of what she'd caught the night before.

Mice. Snakes. All types of pests.

I'd been so proud, and so hurt.

She didn't need me anymore.

Wiping back a tear, I do my best not to linger on the bad thoughts. I can't. Not at a time like this. It might kill me.

Willow grew into a strong young woman.

So can I.

It doesn't matter that I'm only eleven. That I'm up against unspeakable evil. That I've been taken from my home and locked away. That I'm surrounded by the monsters who stole me from my parents and burned down my village. That I have no one left but a black cat who should be anywhere but here.

If Willow can take care of herself, then so can I.

I only need some help—just a tiny bit. Someone to bring me scraps of freshly caught fish so I don't starve to death before I get a chance to rescue myself.

But who will do that for me? There's no one left…

My eyes snap open when I hear approaching footsteps.

Immediately, I'm back on my feet, desperately darting around the room, searching for a spot to stash Willow. But the cat is way ahead of me. Without making a sound, she squirms from my arms and drops to the floor.

"Hide!" I beg, careful not to say her name. If I did, she would only come running back to me. And I'm the last person any living thing should want to be near right now.

Obeying my order, Willow quickly disappears under the stained mattress.

My relief for her safety is quickly replaced by concern for my own well-being.

They're back.

The big bolt on the bedroom door is unlocked, and a cold gust follows my unwelcomed guests into the room. Two pale giants with bald heads and sunken faces. Their black eyes glare me down, and I do my best to return their contempt, if only to keep their attention off the black cat hiding beneath my discolored cot.

No one knows she followed me here. And no one ever will, I promise myself

"Come with us," the largest guard bellows. His paper-white skin glistens with sweat. The heat has only gotten worse. It feels like this whole place is about to burst into flames.

But there's nowhere else to go.

"Now, girl!" the other echoes.

He takes a threatening step forward, and I instinctively flinch away. Fear grips me like a noose. I know who they're taking me to see.

Egon. Their boss.

He's the man who bought me from my father. The man who turned his back on my village, then had his men burn it to the ground.

The man who dragged me here.

He's already killed everyone I've ever known or loved. He's made me an orphan, a prisoner, a ghost.

I may only be eleven, but it already feels like I'm dead.

What more could he want from me?

"Are you deaf?" The big ogre shouts.

"Grab her," his partner commands.

I want to turn away and run. But there's nowhere to go, and if I try to hide, they might find Willow. I won't let that happen.

So, instead of delaying the inevitable, I let the monster's icy grip dig into my flesh. He yanks me forward, and I'm hauled out into the hallway. I try not to look back over my shoulder. *Willow is safe*, I tell myself. They can't know I have anything left to live for. There's no doubt in my mind that they would kill that too.

"He said to meet him in the library," one of the men grumbles as I'm pulled towards a rickety flight of stairs.

Loose floorboards creak under our feet. Dust shakes from the ceiling. Wallpaper sags and peels. Even the cracked windows are foggy from the growing heat.

Before coming here, I'd never seen a house this big, or this dilapidated. It's a perfect setting for my nightmare. And the deeper we descend into its rumbling belly, the hotter it gets.

"In here, girl."

Suddenly, the ogre leading me along stops. With a single shove, he sends me tumbling through an open doorway.

I'm immediately hit by a wall of insufferable heat. It's the kind of heat that makes your eyes water and your throat burn, and my vision blurs as I trip into a hellish room.

Even through the tears, though, I can make out the intense orange glow raging out from the massive fireplace ahead. The scorching fire is so intense it seems to bleed through my skull and grab hold of my swollen brain.

My tears quickly evaporate.

This is the belly of the beast. This is hell. And there's no turning back.

I can feel the two ogres standing firm behind me, guarding my only exit.

"Come here, girl. Come stand beside your king."

The new voice is one I instantly recognize.

Egon.

The man who took everything from me.

"Don't make me ask twice," he warns.

"Go!" A large pair of hands shoves me from behind, and I'm pushed further into the depths of hell.

"There you go," Egon taunts, his voice hardly distinguishable from the crackling firewood.

I can sense his frigid presence as I trip over towards a giant crimson sitting chair. The tall back could almost be mistaken for a throne, if it wasn't peeling, just like the wallpaper outside.

"How are you feeling?" he asks, when I catch myself.

His face is hidden behind the melting seat. I don't dare look or respond. Not that I could, even if I wanted to. The air in here is too thick. Too suffocating.

I can't breathe.

"Answer me, girl. Or I'll kick you into the fire to join your parents."

If my heart were anything more than a shriveled husk, his threat might hurt more. But there's nothing left there.

Well, almost nothing.

"I hate you," I rasp.

The voice is barely mine, and it's accompanied by a sliver of rage so sharp I can't grab hold of it. I've never felt anything so powerful before.

It almost scares me.

"What was that, *girl*?"

Desperate to feel something more than endless grief, I wrap myself around the jagged rage and squeeze, impaling my common sense.

"I hate you!" I yell through the liquefying air.

The burst is followed by a flurry of coughs. Each one hurts my empty chest more than the last. But before I can fall to the dusty floor and give up, a long hand flashes out and catches me by the hair.

"That's a shame," Egon chortles, pulling me back onto my feet like a rag doll. "Because we're stuck together. That is, unless I can find you a suitable groom."

His dirty nails are so sharp they nearly slice through my hair as I'm turned to look into the overflowing fireplace.

Flames lash out like furious souls, desperate to eat my tears and claim my empty insides. I can practically hear them begging me to join them.

I refuse.

"What do you say to that?" Egon taunts, rattling me for good measure. "How would you like to be used in that way? Married off to one of the other slum lords for a portion of his land? You would fetch a high price, to be sure. Especially after we put some food in you."

Every cruel word is numbing. Yet no matter how grim my future appears, I can't think past the flames.

Something tells me I won't survive the night.

Do I even want to?

Do it for Willow.

"And if they think you're too scrawny to bear children, I'll just show them this picture of your mother—a promise of what's to come. You have the potential for beauty in you, girl. But with how you look now, it will take a good salesman to convince anyone of that."

Out the corner of my water-filled eye, I catch Egon pulling something out of his breast pocket. Even through the crackling flames, I can hear it crunch beneath his careless fingers.

Somehow, I instantly know what it is.

The sharpness of my anger steepens, becoming even more desperate as I crank my neck towards the demon.

But my gaze doesn't fall onto him. Instead, I only see the crumpled-up photograph in his hand.

It's the only picture ever taken of my parents. A memory from before I was born. A keepsake they got on a rare trip into town, the day after getting married.

It always hung above our stove. Now, it sits in Egon's greedy hands.

"Mom!" I croak, impossibly sad.

I miss her so much.

"Your mother isn't here," Egon spits. Crushing the photograph in his fists, he shoves it back into his pocket. Then, he twists me back around to face the flames. "She's in there. Along with your father."

With a vicious jerk, Egon shakes the tears from my eyes and the sweat from my brow so I can see what he means.

There, in the center of the flames, surrounded by glowing red wood and black ashes, is something formerly human. Something charred and shriveled and dark.

A body.

The shriek that rips from my throat sucks all the sound from the room. No matter how hard I cry or struggle, nothing seems real.

This is a nightmare. It has to be.

But the longer I'm forced to stare into the fire, the clearer it all becomes. There's more than one body in the fireplace. More than one melting face.

This is all too real.

"Recognize anyone?" Egon's voice slithers through the air like an icy snake, echoing against the glowing embers and peeling furniture. "Your father double-crossed me, girl. Your whole village did. Even after we agreed to exchange your life for my protection, they banded together and tried to take you back."

Wrenching me closer to the cremator, Egon forces me to stare at the black and melting faces.

"Without my protection, this is where you end up. Betray me and be thrown to the flames of hell."

His words echo around my hollow insides like a single stone. It's the final blow. Just like that, the last bits of who I once was go up in smoke. That innocent little girl is dead. An empty body is all that remains.

Egon can threaten me with hell all he wants; it won't make any difference. I'm already here.

"Boss!"

An outside voice invades the eerie silence that engulfs us. It's a voice that's filled with panic, and it's accompanied by the savage barks of Egon's killer hounds.

"So, he's finally here," Egon grumbles, knowingly.

Is that fear I recognize in his voice?

No. It couldn't be. What could scare a man like this?

Suddenly, I remember what that flash of lightning revealed to me earlier.

The black figure.

The faceless void that stood deathly still against the rain and the wind, and looked up to my window. Who looked up at me.

That monster wasn't one of Egon's. I could feel it.

Egon's fingers unfurl from around my hair, and I drop to the steaming floor like a brick. The contorted wood smacks against my bare knees, sending a ripple of pain up my legs.

But I don't care.

A pinprick of hope has been nailed into my empty chest.

Maybe this monster will tear my monsters to shreds. Maybe it will save me from this nightmare.

Maybe I wasn't so foolish, after all.

Before that pinprick of hope can grow any brighter, though, I feel the weight of Egon's giant body rise up behind me. Then, I feel his sharp fingers wrap around my little wrist.

"Come with me," he starts. But we're both slippery with sweat, and the moment he pulls me back onto my feet, I yank myself away.

Then, suddenly, I'm running.

My knees pulse with a savage heat. My thighs are cold and numb. Still, they somehow manage to carry my heavy body forward as I race past the distracted ogres at the doorway.

"Grab her!" I hear Egon shout, but his voice quickly trails off into the distance.

Yapping hounds replace his barking orders.

Turning a corner, I spot a shadow struggling to keep his beast under control as it lunges uncontrollably at something I can't quite see.

A flash of fear bashes down my resolve as I turn and start to run the other way.

I need to get out of here. This is my chance to escape. Whatever is happening, it's given me an opportunity.

But then I hear something that stops me dead in my tracks.

The vicious barks of that ravenous hellhound spiral into a flurry of terrified whimpers. The man who was holding it back screams, and his deep voice shatters into a high-pitched wail that's so shrill it stings my ears.

Then, they both go quiet. Quiet enough that I can hear their blood splash against the peeling walls.

Suddenly, the burning air is filled with something more terrifying than suffocating heat.

The stench of death.

Somewhere ahead, another set of brutal barks turn into the witless whimpers of a dying animal.

My pinprick of hope fades. This new monster is no better than the others. It kills animals.

But instead of feeling fear, my mind snaps onto what I have hidden beneath my mattress upstairs.

Willow.

She'll be devoured too.

Even as terror threatens to drag me through the floor, I find my aching knees pumping towards the staircase. But I can hardly find my way through this twisted maze, and sweat mixes in with my tears until I can barely see anymore.

When I turn the next corner, something heavy catches my foot, and I fall to the floor. But I don't stop to check what just slowed me down, not even as I desperately crawl through a pool of crimson blood and push myself back onto my feet.

Only one thing matters.

"Willow!"

My voice cracks. My shriveled heart pounds. My lungs burn. My legs turn to lead. But when I finally see the stairs up ahead, I only run harder.

In the blink of an eye, I'm up them.

More screams crawl through the chaos below. More barks turn into terrified whines. More blood paints the peeling walls.

I ignore it all.

Finding my room, I burst inside and slam the door shut behind me.

"Willow!"

My shriveled heart catches in my throat as I desperately scan the room for the black cat.

It feels like an eternity before I spot her fuzzy face and yellow eyes. There's no time to bathe in any sense of relief. Almost immediately, something heavy crashes against the bedroom door.

The force sends me flying forward, and my cheek crashes against the wall.

I don't stop to fight the pain. Instead, I grab the only chair in the room and drag it over to the door. Setting it up under the handle, I try to buy myself some time. But the second I have it in place, the knob starts to rattle.

Someone is trying to get in.

Turning around, I spot Willow on the window sill. If she's scared, she doesn't show it.

I decide to do the same. It's a split-second decision, but it saves me from getting lost in the fear of what's to come as I race towards the window.

Squirming my scrawny arms through the bars, I desperately feel for a latch on the frame. I already know it can open. It's how I first let Willow in, back when she initially showed up.

But I'm drenched in sweat. My eyes are blurry with tears. Each one of my fingers feel like it weighs a thousand pounds. And then there's that pounding at the door behind me. Each knock sends a dreadful shockwave blasting through my throbbing skull.

"Got it!"

Even with everything going wrong, it only takes a single positive to spike my pulse.

The window unlatches. And when I pull the frame up, a cold gust of sharp rain comes rushing directly into my face.

It might as well be heaven.

But then I remember what I have to do, and my empty stomach drops.

I'm not going to be able to escape through this window. The slits in the bars are too thin even for me. But Willow can easily make it.

She can escape. She can be free.

She just has to do it without me.

"Go!" I order, pointing out into the stormy night.

The pounding on the door has momentarily stopped, but it's quickly replaced by the deafening crackle of something I recognize all too well by now.

Gunshots.

"Willow!" I beg, more afraid for her than for myself.

But the stubborn cat only knows one trick, and it's to come when her name is called.

Her soft fur blocks the harsh wind as she nudges up against my cheek. I can't help but push back into her comforting warmth.

Then, the gunfire stops, and I know there's no time for a tear-filled goodbye.

"You have to go," I quietly choke.

Digging my palms into Willow's fur, I try to push her away. She pushes back.

I push harder, and those sharp yellow eyes tilt in confusion.

"It's for your own good," I whisper, barely able to get the words out. "Please, Willow…"

The sound of her name only draws her closer.

Behind me, I hear the chipped wood of my bedroom door crack. A rush of hot air spills in.

I feel Willow's soft fur one last time.

"I'm sorry," I whisper.

My shriveled heart shatters into a thousand tiny pieces.

Closing my eyes, I force Willow through the bars. Then, I push her off the ledge.

My heart falls with her, disappearing into the stormy blackness below. But unlike my heart, cat's always land on their feet

—at least, that's the best I can hope for. Not that I'm given any time for hope.

My bedroom door explodes, and the heat from the hellfire below crashes into my back. It's a scorching wind that even overpowers the frigid gust blasting in from the open window.

The stench of death overpowers me. The presence of evil destroys whatever hope I had left.

I fall to my knees.

"Rozalia Dorn?"

The voice that calls my name is softer than I expected; so is the hand that falls onto my shoulder.

But when my eyelids flutter open and I look up, I see no softness on the face that greets me.

Still, I somehow instantly know it's the same face I spotted in the strike of lightning earlier—only now, it's not shrouded in darkness.

Though, I wish it were.

The stranger's pale skin is deeply stained with dark crimson blood. A fresh, pulsing gash slashes through his eye—claw marks from one of the dogs he just slaughtered.

His black hair drips with scarlet-shaded sweat. He reeks of death. I can feel the evil that surrounds him. It's the same evil I felt when I saw his black figure watching me from outside.

"Who are you?" I hear myself rasp.

Despite all the darkness surrounding him, I'm not scared.

What could this monster do to me that hasn't already been done?

"My name is Dragomir Raclaw," he replies. "I'm here to save you from this nightmare."

"I don't need anyone to save me," I stubbornly cough, hanging my head. But it's just instinct, a personal little eulogy for Willow. She only needed a few scraps of fish to survive. The rest she did on her own.

Why can't I be more like her?

"Very well," Dragomir responds. "Then I am here to teach you how to conquer this nightmare. All you have to do is come with me. Deal?"

The hand on my shoulder turns over—an offer of assistance. There are no scraps of fish on his fingers, but his words are filled with promise.

Somewhere downstairs, a wall crumbles. This building is condemned. But that doesn't mean I have to be.

Is this how Willow felt when I first found her?

My dashed pinprick of hope suddenly glints, reborn somewhere deep in the blackness of my hollow soul.

I don't know this man, but the hope is addicting.

Reaching up to my shoulder, I place my heavy hand in Dragomir's palm. His skin is rough yet welcoming. For a moment, he carries the weight of the world for me.

Someday, I'll repay him, I promise myself.

"Deal," I whisper.

"Good girl."

Pulling me onto my feet, he slashes something across the bars of my cage. Just like that, the rusted steel severs, clanging to the floor like plastic toys.

I'm free.

"Thank you," I mumble, hardly able to process what's happening.

"I'm sure you'll find a way to repay me."

Those callous hands lift me onto the window sill. Cold wind pounds against my damp skin. Harsh rain wipes away my sweat and my tears.

I look for Willow.

But the black cat is nowhere to be found.

Please be alright.

"Where are we going?" I ask.

Dragomir climbs up onto the window sill behind me.

"Home."

Wrapping an arm around my waist, he blocks off the suffocating heat of the burning mansion.

I take a deep breath of fresh air.

So does he.

Then, we jump.

1
RIAN

Present day...

"What the hell is that?"

My simmering headache flares up. This is the last thing I need. Another surprise.

"I believe it's a cat."

Sharp yellow eyes glare at me from behind my uncle's tattooed forearm.

"I know that," I grumble. "Why the hell did you bring a cat to my coronation?"

Before he can answer, one more surprise pops out from behind his broad shoulders. The tuff of auburn hair is unmistakable.

Mel.

My little sister.

"Technically, it's still a kitten," Mel casually corrects. "So be nice."

She's not supposed to be here. Hell, my uncle Maksim isn't either. I've put out a strict 'no visitation' order to my men.

"What the fuck is going on?"

My frustration immediately turns to my uncle. In response, the cat cuddled against his chest curls its back. My hackles rise too.

As if I wasn't jumpy enough already.

"Let's not raise our voices," Maksim insists, holding the kitten tighter.

"Yeah, your *majesty*," Mel joins in, wiping a bead of sweat from her pale forehead. "Be quiet, or you'll scare your subjects."

"What. The. Hell. Is going on?" I repeat, ignoring my sister's attempt at banter. "What is that thing doing here? What are *you* doing here?"

Maksim and Mel both share a side-eyed glance. Neither of them seems particularly bothered. It's infuriating. Don't they understand why they can't be here?

"You want to answer first or should I?" Maksim asks.

"I'll go first," Mel shrugs. Turning her hazel eyes to me, she blindly scratches the black furball's forehead. It seems to calm the creature down but it does nothing to help ease my concerns. "I'm here because it's my big brother's big day. The day he's crowned king of our mafia empire. Anointed ruler of the underworld. Named boss of the Kilpatrick–"

"Enough," I interrupt. Pinching the bridge of my nose, I clamp my eyes shut. "I get the point. But you weren't invited."

My headache worsens.

"You think that would stop me from sneaking out to be here for you?"

"It's not safe."

With that, Mel's gaze slides from me over to our uncle. "You hear that, Uncle Maks? There he goes again. A king who doesn't trust his people."

"I'm not king yet," I remind her. Stepping forward, I plant two fists into the hard oakwood of my desk. The black cat hisses.

"Stop. You're scaring the poor thing," Mel coos. Reaching out, she urges Maksim to hand her the kitten.

He complies.

"Be careful," he quietly mutters, as if Mel isn't the gentlest creature either of us knows.

"I will be," Mel assures him. As expected, she coddles the little black ball, and it immediately sinks into her loving arms, hackles dropping.

But mine stay raised.

A fearsome pulse is pounding behind my skull. My fingers curl and uncurl as I consider the true consequences of what's happening.

We've been compromised.

"I trust my people," I insist, grimacing. "To an extent. But there isn't anyone I trust more than myself. And I didn't have time to plan the security for tonight's ceremony. Not with everything else going on. That's why I didn't invite any family. To ensure their safety. To ensure *your* safety."

"I'm sure your men have done a good job," Mel naively suggests. Bending her neck, she nuzzles her nose against the precious package in her arms.

"Have they?" I question. "Because it seems like there's already been a breach."

Mel lifts her eyes back up at me. But before she can respond, Maksim steps in.

"You put your men in a tough spot," he explains. "Do you know how hard it is for them to say no to your father's daughter, to *your* sister?"

"Is it harder than doing their job?"

"Apparently so."

"Hey, that's not fair," Mel pushes back. "No one let me in here. I had to sneak through security, just like anyone else would."

"Shit," I curse. "That makes it even worse. Maksim, tell the men my coronation is canceled. If Mel can slip through the perimeter, then there's no telling who else could."

"That's insulting," Mel quickly snaps. The cat stirs in her arms, but my sister quickly pats it down.

Still, those sharp yellow eyes stay fixed on me.

"Is it?"

"Uncle Maks, back me up," Mel pleads. "You know better than anyone just how slippery I can be. Remember when you used to babysit us?"

"All too well," Maksim huffs, shaking his head. "No matter how well I boarded up your crib, you always ended up downstairs again. I'm still not sure how you did it."

"See. I'm more than just your little sister, Rian," Mel says, turning back to me.

"You're an artist," I remind her.

"An escape artist," she smirks back. "You know I can't be contained."

"Is that why you really came here? Just to prove you could?"

"No," Mel says. "That's not why I'm here. I'm here because I wasn't going to let anyone else give you my gift." After a split-second of hesitation, she gives her furball a gentle kiss; then, she hands it back to Maksim.

"It could have waited until afterward."

"No. It couldn't have. I might have painted over it. You know how I am."

"You only ever really finish a piece when someone physically takes it from you," Maksim confirms. But I already knew that. "It's hard to believe you would willingly give one away."

"It's a special occasion," Mel says, shooting me a stubborn look. "So, stay still and look after the kitty. I'll bring it in."

"Mel, we don't have time for—"

"Stay!"

Turning her back on me, she skips towards the office door before disappearing into the hallway.

I take a single step after her. The cat hisses.

"Let her go," Maksim mumbles. "Don't get distracted."

I stop. But my headache doesn't. Neither does the bubbling fury heating up my gut. It feels like a thousand needles are pricking at me from every angle.

If I'm not careful, I could lose control.

"What the hell is going on?" I ask my uncle. "How did she really get in here? Did you help?"

"I haven't had the time to help anyone with anything lately," Maksim quietly responds. "You know that. For the past month, I've only had one mission."

"And that's why I have a bad feeling about today," I remind him. "Your mission has had nothing to do with security at this ceremony. We've had to delegate that responsibility to others. I don't trust others. I trust myself. I trust you. And I trust Dad. That's all."

"I understand," Maksim replies. "Your dad used to be the same way. So did I. But we learned."

A heavy silence momentarily fills the space between us at the mention of my father.

"How is dad, by the way?" I finally dare ask.

I've been trying not to think about it. But there's no ignoring the issues rumbling outside of these fortified walls.

"He's proud of you," Maksim notes. "This is a brave thing you're doing. For him. For the family. For the empire."

"It's my duty."

"You could have refused."

"No. I couldn't have." Shaking my head, I turn to gaze out of my office window.

Ancient vines crawl over the glass, obscuring the view outside, but I can still see what awaits me on the carefully manicured lawn below.

It makes my headache even worse.

Strangers. A crowd filled with them. Their low incessant chatter creeps up through my brick walls.

Sure, I know each face by heart. I can recite the family lineage of each Italian Don. I can tell you how many kills each soldier has; how much dirty money every crooked businessman brings in. But they make me feel nothing.

When I look at them, I feel frigid. Ruthless. Distant.

Without my family in attendance, this coronation is nothing more than a cold formality—and an unnecessary one at that.

We all know who's king now.

Me.

But Dad insisted I go through with this charade. He told me how honored my esteemed guests would feel to be part of my historic ascension. How this gesture would help me win them over.

But I hardly care about big picture shit like that. If I had a choice, I'd be in the streets right now.

I like to feel the heat of my smoking gun. I want to see the steam rise from a fresh kill. I need to hunt, to personally beat my enemy into the ground. Even if that's not what a king does.

"A man as powerful as you always has a choice," Maksim tells me.

A deep breath fills my lungs. A sneer twitches my lips.

"You're right," I grumble. "My choice was simple. Abandon my family in their time of need, or step up to the occasion and become what I was meant to be."

"A king."

"A king," I quietly echo. "But I'm not ready to be a king."

"Agreed."

Maksim's harsh claim whips me back from the window. Usually, my uncle isn't so direct. It catches me off guard.

"So, what the hell am I doing here?" I ask, trying to hide the offense I've taken to his remark.

"You're being brave… and stupid, as usual."

"Would it be smarter to abandon my duties?"

"It would be smarter to concentrate on one thing at a time."

Holding the restless kitten close to his chest, Maksim steps forward.

"That's what I'm doing," I lie.

But there's no fooling the seasoned consigliere.

"Do me a favor," he calmly responds. "Look back out that window, and tell me what you see."

"Strangers," I immediately huff.

"Rian."

"Fine." Cranking my neck, I stare back out through the tangled vines.

The sight below angers me.

This day should be shared exclusively with those I'm closest with. Family. Friends. Mentors. Instead, those I love will have to be broadcasted in, all because I've been preoccupied with a problem I can't bring myself to pass on to anyone else.

Her.

My fists tighten.

"So, what do you see?" Maksim repeats, turning my focus back onto what's in front of me.

"I see fat selfish men and their greedy plastic wives."

"And in the far corner, by the tall hedges?"

Fuck.

"Goddamnit, Uncle Maksim."

He knows me too well. And he understands exactly what I've been purposely trying to avoid ever since we first opened the gates out front.

Maybe it's part of why I'm so jumpy today. And it's not just because of my security concerns.

There, huddled like cattle in the corner of the garden, are about a dozen women. Daughters of the Italian dons. The best they have to offer. Their white dresses stand out against the green shrubbery like flowing candles.

Not a single one of them looks comfortable. And not a single one of them should be. Everyone knows why they've been brought here today.

To entice me into marriage.

To seduce me into picking them.

"How the hell am I going to marry any of those women?" I growl, hating that my cock is already starting to swell at the sight of some of them. It's been so long since I satisfied that urge. Too long. "They've been brought here like cattle. The last thing I need is another set of eyes looking up to me for guidance."

It doesn't help that the Italians have been dragging their asses lately. Instead of doing their jobs, the greedy bastards are putting all their energy into winning the Rian Kilpatrick's bride sweepstakes. It's making them sloppy. And that's dangerous.

It's why I'm trying to force myself to make a decision. The sooner I get this over with, the better.

"Is that why you're starving yourself?"

"Excuse me?"

Turning back to Maksim, I try to gauge how much he knows. But his dark eyes are indecipherable.

"There are some things a man should never withhold from himself," he hints. "Some desires that can break even the strongest king if bottled up for too long."

"Who told you about that?" I sneer. "Was it Branko? I swear to—"

"It wasn't any of your cousins," Maksim assures me. "They didn't need to tell me. I know you all too well, nephew."

"Fuck." This is the last thing I want to discuss with my uncle. A vow of celibacy is a personal matter—hell, I shouldn't have told anyone about it in the first place. "What the fuck does that have to do with anything?"

"Let's count out what you have on your plate right now," Maksim replies. He starts before I can stop him. "One. You're trying to hunt down the woman who threatens your family. Two. You're trying to take over for your father as he deals with an issue that could destroy our empire. Three. You're trying to force yourself to pick a bride, even if it's the last thing that should be on your mind right now."

"A king needs a queen," I remind him, loathing the truth of it.

How many times have I heard that in the past few months?

"A king needs to be in control. And a man who's desperate to satisfy his primal urges is not a man who's in control—of himself or others."

"If I'm not desperate for a woman, then how else am I going to force myself to do what needs to be done?"

"You don't need to do anything right now but walk downstairs and accept the crown."

"I need to do my duty!" I boom, the weight of my responsibility cracking ever so slightly. "I need to do it so that dad doesn't have to deal with the stress of an unstable empire. So that he can concentrate on his problems while I solve mine. So that my sister, my cousins, and my aunts and uncles can sleep easily at night, knowing that I have everything under control."

"When's the last time *you* had a good night's sleep?"

"A king never rests."

Maksim only sighs at that claim. "You have so much to learn, my—"

"Hey, thanks for your help, guys!"

Mel's tiny voice cuts through the thick air like a knife.

Unfurling my fist, I run a hand through my hair and watch as my little sister waddles back through the doorway, her slight body almost entirely covered by the backside of a massive canvas.

"We'll talk about this later," I mumble to Maksim.

He bites his tongue, then hesitantly nods, all while stroking a gentle finger over the kitten's forehead.

"Hold this thing, will you," he asks. "I'll help your sister."

Before I can refuse, the tiny puff of black fur is pushed over my desk, towards me. Maksim is already turning to help Mel when I reluctantly reach out and take the thing. "What the hell am I supposed to do with this?" I grumble, grabbing it by the scruff.

"Love it," Mel orders from behind the canvas.

Maksim helps her set it down as I lift the kitten and turn it around.

To my surprise, it doesn't hiss at me. Instead, those big yellow glare past me, towards the vine-covered window. It already looks fed up with all of this shit.

"You and me both, little fella," I mutter.

"It's a girl," Mel is quick to point out.

"What did the Italians name her again?" Maksim asks, resting a steadying hand on top of Mel's gift.

"The Bitch," my sister sneers. "Excuse my language, but those people are fucking barbarians."

"That's no way to talk about our allies," I reply, unable to hold back my smirk.

At least we agree on one thing.

"Your brother's right," Maksim echoes. "No matter what you think of them, we need to keep the men downstairs happy. The basis of our entire east-coast operation relies on their local connections and day-to-day labor."

"They're the ones who need to keep us happy," Mel snips back, disgusted.

"You're both right," I acknowledge. Staring down at the kitten, I give it a quick look-over. "So, I gather this thing is supposed to be a gift from one of the dons?"

"Not a gift," Mel hisses. "A sacrifice."

"A sacrifice?" I repeat, momentarily confused. Then, it all clicks into place.

Those fuckers.

"I overheard Don Sabatino bragging about it," Mel snarls. "The drunkard told everyone how he planned to drag the poor thing into your throne room before the ceremony. When you arrived, he'd make his toast, a solemn vow to help destroy all of your enemies—including the one who's been causing you the most trouble lately."

"Rozalia Dorn," I growl.

My heart clenches with rage at the mere mention of the vile woman. To my disgust, something else stirs as well. Something below my waist. Something big and wild.

My pants tighten, and I bite down hard on my tongue.

Fuck. Maybe this was a mistake.

"The Black Cat," Maksim nods.

"So, they went out and found a literal black cat to butcher in front of me?" I grunt, shaking the blood from my cock.

Forget about her. Today isn't about what she's done. And it definitely isn't about how you'll make her pay. Focus.

Maksim just shrugs. "I guess so."

"And they thought that would impress me?"

"Your guess is as good as mine."

The rageful spite filling my heart turns outwards. Those pigs are on my property right now. Drinking my wine and eating my food.

They're too scared of Rozalia Dorn to help me find her, but they'll slaughter an innocent creature and pretend it's the same thing.

Disgusting cowards.

"I had to rescue her from their greasy little fingers," Mel says. "I knew you wouldn't want to see that."

"You were right."

With more care than I'm used to showing, I gently place the cat on my oakwood desk.

But inside, I'm a chaotic mess.

"What else do the Italians have planned for today?" I ask. "And how the hell was I not told about this in advance?"

"It definitely isn't a good sign that no one notified you about it," Maksim agrees. "That means the men in charge of planning today either didn't know, or they obeyed the Italian's order to keep it a secret from you. I'm honestly not sure which is worse."

"After I'm crowned, there's going to be a reckoning," I rumble. "This organization needs to be shaken up, from top to fucking bottom—but all of that will have to wait until after the ceremony."

"So, you will go through with it, after all?"

"Of course he is," Mel announces. "My brother isn't afraid of anything or anyone."

The kitten on my desk wobbles on unsure feet as I brush the back of my fingers along its side. The rage in my chest has leaked into my gut, but I don't let it extend to my limbs.

Control yourself, Rian.

"I'm going to get this stupid coronation over with," I say, looking over at Maksim. "Then, I'll have one less thing to worry about. And the less there is on my plate, the better. Right?"

"Is it worth the risk?" Maksim questions, always the devil's advocate.

"That depends on what's at stake.". Sliding my hand under the kitten's belly, I scoop it up and present it back to my uncle. He takes it. "Bring Mel home. Take the cat with you. If something happens here today, I'll be able to take care of myself. But I'd rather not have two innocent creatures to look after."

"Hey, I'm not that innocent," Mel protests, her voice conveniently cracking halfway through the claim.

"Please. You're by far the most innocent twenty-three-year-old I've ever met," I counter. "And believe me, I mean to keep it that way."

"We all do," Maksim confirms.

"I think that says more about the company you keep," Mel huffs.

"Perhaps," I admit. "But that's all the more reason to keep you away from me and my company."

Mel's shoulders drop as she slowly realizes there's no changing my mind. But she's not done with me yet.

"Fine. I'll leave. But only if you let me show you your gift first."

"Deal."

Maksim is right. I need to get all this shit off my plate. But I can't do it all at once. If I want to succeed, I'll have to take this journey one step at a time until I've crushed the entire world beneath my feet.

"Good, because I wasn't planning on leaving until you saw it," Mel discloses. "Uncle Maks, help me turn it around."

Maksim doesn't hesitate. Juggling the cat in his left arm, he uses his right to help my little sister flip the canvas. The thing must be heavier than it looks, because it takes the aging musclehead a few deep grunts before the painting is properly situated.

It's well worth the wait.

For a moment, I'm awe-struck by what I see. And slightly confused.

I know Mel's work well. She's so talented at painting realistic portraits and landscapes that we used to hold family contests to see who could guess which image was her work and which was the photograph she used as inspiration.

But this is different.

This piece is far more abstract. And even though I'm immediately struck by the beauty of it, I can't help what comes tumbling out of my mouth.

"What is it?"

That's the wrong thing to say, and I immediately know it. But I don't get a chance to correct myself.

"It's you," Mel pouts.

It only takes that simple hint to illuminate some meaning in the chaos-covered canvas. Sure enough, I can make out flashes of my wild dirty blonde hair jutting across the tarp. Two splashes of ocean blue must be my eyes. That sharp white arrow my jawline. Below that, broad contours melt into a mess of hard lines and freeform figures. Bright colors clash against one another before somehow bleeding perfectly into something new.

"It's…"

It's mesmerizing. I just don't know how to describe it exactly. Art is so far from my comfort zone. Show me a complex computer program or a mysterious line of code and I'm in heaven. But this? Shit, what do I say?

"It's alright," Mel sighs. "You don't have to like it."

The chatter bubbling up from the lawn below seems to grow as I try to ignore everything except what's in front of me.

Screw my coronation, my baby sister needs some encouragement.

"No. It's amazing. I'm just not used to seeing this style from you."

"I thought I'd try something different for such a special day."

"It's perfect. Maksim, put it in the throne room on your way out. Call some men if you need help. I want my guests to see my sister's masterpiece."

"You really like it?" Mel asks.

"I love it," I promise.

But I can tell she doesn't quite believe me. I'm just a simpleton, after all—a brutish mobster with an unusual knack for technology. Nothing in my DNA suggests I could appreciate such abstract beauty. But I do. I'm just finding it impossible to describe how.

"Thanks," Mel whispers, her shoulders rising and falling in a faint shrug.

Fuck. This day just keeps getting worse.

Just like that, my headache returns with a vengeance.

"I swear, this is—"

Before I can finish cursing, the faint sound of hurried footsteps yanks my attention away from my sister and towards my office door.

Almost immediately, I'm overcome by a primal instinct. My fingers snap back into fists. My hackles rise again. Blood rushes into my ears, muffling the world. I reach for the gun tucked beneath my belt.

Maksim feels it too. In the blink of an eye, we're both in front of Mel, blocking her from any potential harm.

No one's allowed up here, and the only two people who could peacefully break that order are already next to me.

Behind us, the black cat hisses.

"Who is it?" Maksim booms.

Cocking his gun, the experienced killer takes a steady step forward. I'd join him, if I weren't already pushing Mel further back from the open doorway.

"What's wrong?" she asks. Her voice is hushed, but I can tell she doesn't quite understand what's happening.

This is why I didn't want her here. Mel isn't made for this world.

"Stay quiet," I grunt. "And get ready to run if I tell you to."

"What about the kitten?"

"Sir!" A new voice creaks through the hallway just as Maksim lunges outside to greet it.

"What the fuck are you doing here?" he barks. "You were told not to disturb us." But even as he lowers his gun, my tensed shoulders don't drop.

Something is wrong. I can feel it.

Lifting an arm, I hold Mel back.

"I need to speak to Mr. Kilpatrick."

The voice is faintly familiar. It's one of my men, I'm sure.

"Whatever you want to say to him, you can tell me," Maksim tells him.

"Let him in," I call out, fingers still wrapped tightly around the handle of my gun.

Maksim hesitates. A rare instance of disobedience. But when his intense eyes turn back into the room, and his gaze drifts over my shoulder, I understand why.

He wants to protect Mel.

Whatever we're about to be told, it can't be good news. No one would dare disobey us for the sake of good news.

On another day, I might wait until Mel was safely ferried out of the room before I let any bad news slip through these walls. But Maksim's words of wisdom have stuck to my pounding skull like shrapnel. One step at a time.

"Be quick about," Maksim tells the messenger, stepping aside.

Keeping his eyes peeled on our new guest, my uncle allows him to step into the office. Sure enough, it's one of my men—a battle-worn Irish enforcer.

The blood rushes from my ears, but I stay tense.

The chatter outside is louder than before. Much louder.

"What the fuck is going on?" I growl.

"There's something you need to see," the man pants, half out of breath.

Even through the red scars and black tattoos that slash across his bearded face, I can see the terror in his eyes.

The fucker is pale as a ghost.

"What?" I demand to know. "Fucking tell me already."

"It's the Black Cat, sir. Rozalia Dorn. She's here."

2

ROZALIA

"Showtime."

Tytus' voice is giddy with excitement. Hell, I don't blame him.

How often do you get to crash a king's coronation?

"I'm guessing that means everything's in place?" I ask, swallowing the last bits of my dessert.

"Yeah, obvio—wait a minute, are you eating?"

"I might have swiped a slice of cake," I shrug, licking the frosting from my fingertips.

"Just a slice?"

"Okay, maybe the whole thing. Hey, I'm PMSing over here, give me a break."

"Too much info, Roz," Tytus grumbles, but I can practically hear his smirk.

He lives for this shit.

So do I.

"Pussy," I playfully respond.

"I'm not the one PMSing."

"Could have fooled me."

Wiping my glazed fingers off against a black drape, I stare

down through a vine-covered window and drink in my view of the chaos unfolding below.

Those idiots. Already running around like headless chickens. And all it took was a single holographic image of me.

Who knew I was that terrifying?

"Do you just want to keep talking, or shall we set this place on fire?" Tytus asks.

"Light the match, baby."

"As you wish."

The sound of Tytus flipping his switches and clicking his buttons is music to my ears. The symphony blends in perfectly with the rising panic bubbling up from below.

For a moment, I can't help but pause.

That's me down there, causing all this mayhem. A perfect double. Black pixie cut, red lipstick, green eyes glowing against my pale-ass skin. The only difference between me and that thing is that I'm filled with blood and guts. That thing is just a bunch of lights. An illusion. But fuck me if it isn't a sexy illusion.

Sure, maybe I went a little overboard on the contours of my body. Perhaps my cheekbones aren't quite that sharp, or my tits exactly that perky. But I wanted to remind the future king what he's been missing out on.

Gone are the days when he sends others to chase me down. That charade has gone on for long enough. I'm sick of killing fresh-faced recruits. I want a man. I want the king.

After this, he won't have any choice but to chase me down himself. Then, I'll get exactly what I want.

"Lights. Camera. Action."

Tytus hardly even lets himself finish before setting off the first smoke bomb. It ruptures through the chaos below, slowly blocking out the sun with its long tentacles of hazy goodness.

"The smoke is a little thick, don't you think?" I tease. Pushing the cake aside, I zip my backpack halfway open and stuff a slice inside. Then, I sling the strap over my shoulder and head for the door.

"What, afraid I'm doing my job better than you're doing yours?"

"Oh, honey," I sigh. "That will never happen. Just flip on that radio switch in your dirty van and listen in. I bet you a million dollars they still think that hologram I cooked up is the real thing."

"Up that bet to two million and you have yourself a deal, little sister."

A crackle of static accompanies Tytus' offer. He's already turned the radio on.

"Aren't you already running low on your part of the inheritance?" I taunt, sliding my switchblade out of its ankle holster.

"I don't see how that's possible," Tytus huffs. "I'm still trying to count how much we actually have."

"Run out of fingers?"

"I ran out of fucks."

We share a little laugh as I creak open the bedroom door. Footsteps charge down the hallways outside. Orders are being barked from the floor below. A pleasurable tingle washes over my skin.

I can smell their fear.

"This is what they get for fucking with Gabriel," I snarl.

"This is only the start," Tytus assures me. "Wait. Fuck."

"What?"

"You were right. Our radio just picked up on a conversation between Maksim Smolov and the king himself. Sounds like they actually do think it's you up on that stage."

My adrenaline-swelled heart freezes for a second at the mention of that fucker.

"He's not king yet," I sneer, ignoring my chance to gloat. "And if we have anything to say about it, he won't ever be."

"Well, then you better get to the throne room quick.

Because Rian just ordered Maksim to take Melina Kilpatrick there for safekeeping. If you don't beat them to the punch, you might have to go through that old wolf to get what we came for."

"I can take him."

"Maybe. But I'm not ready to take that risk. I'm coming in. At the very least, I can distract him for a little bit."

"Have all the smoke bombs already gone off?"

"Yep. And the big finale is all ready to drop. We just have to wait for the clock to run out."

"Is the cattle still in place?"

"The Italian dons couldn't give less of a shit about their daughters. They're all still huddled in the corner of the lawn, scared shitless."

"I almost feel bad."

"Don't act like that wasn't your idea in the first place."

"True," I admit. "But just imagine Rian Kilpatrick getting married before he can come after me. Unthinkable."

"You're obsessed."

"And you should be too. Remember what he did to our brother."

"Gabriel is—"

Before Tytus can finish, he's cut off by a flurry of gunshots. The crackle cuts through the cacophony outside. A wave of palpable panic follows closely behind.

"The idiots are shooting at a ghost," I can't help but laugh.

"I guess you were right. That little hologram is believable."

"And you doubted my skill."

Reaching around into my backpack, I pull out a pair of sunglasses. The bedroom I've been hiding out in is quickly filling with smoke. Shit is getting dark. But I don't have to be blind.

"I guess I might have downplayed yours a little bit, too," I return. "The smoke is working like a charm. Alright, you earned it. Come in from that cold van and have your fun. But be quick about it. The old wolf needs to be distracted."

"As if I need your permission to have fun."

All I can do is roll my eyes before our communication goes dead. Pressing a finger against the temple of my sunglasses, I initiate the thermal imaging feature.

Just like that, I can see through the hazy smoke. My fingers tighten around the warm handle of my switchblade.

It's showtime.

With one last short breath, I slip out into the hallway and make my way toward the throne room downstairs.

As if on cue, a raucous chorus of footsteps starts to pound up the stairwell ahead. The red and yellow figures turn towards me just as I'm able to stick my back against the nearest wall.

The smoke works like a charm. I might as well be invisible, and I sit tight as they pass—until an uncontrollable urge takes hold of me.

If I wanted to, I'm sure I could blame it on my hormones, but I'm hardly thinking that far ahead when I dig my nails into the last red blob's thick wrist and yank him back from the safety of his group.

The fucker must be a foot taller than me, but it hardly matters. I've tackled worse. All it takes is a foot to the back of the knee and he's on the ground. He doesn't even get a chance to scream. I shove the tip of my switchblade through his beard, directly into his throat. Nothing but blood rushes from his parted lips.

Still, the thud of his big body hitting the ground is enough to catch the attention of his friends.

"What the hell was that?"

"Where's McGrath?"

"Over here!" I shout, deepening my voice as much as I can.

"Fuck. It's her!"

I can't help but laugh as they fumble with their guns and

start blindly firing in my direction. But they only hit their friend's corpse. I'm already long gone, flying down the smoky steps of this mansion's main spiral staircase.

"She's getting away!" I hear one of them shout from back around the corner.

That's right, chase me, you idiots. See how that turns out for you.

"I'm in."

The moment I hit the bottom of the steps, Tytus' voice appears in my ear.

"That was quick."

"Just because I'm big doesn't mean I can't move fast."

"I'm sure you hear that from your lady friends all the time."

"Hey, at least I'm getting laid."

"Only because you're a manwhore," I snip back, trying not to let on how much that comment actually bugs me.

PMSing can be a bitch.

"Guilty as charged," Tytus chuckles. "Oh shit, I think I see them."

"Who?"

"Maksim Smolov… and Riana's little sister."

"Stay away from her," I immediately order. "She's a last resort."

"Come on. I'll give her back," Tytus promises.

"Enough, Tytus. Stay focused. Distract those two. I'm almost at the throne room."

"Fine."

Once again, I'm cut off from my adoptive brother. To my surprise, his absence sends a subtle gust of loneliness rustling through me.

For better and for worse, I'm alone now.

Hell, other than the thugs upstairs, I haven't encountered much resistance at all. It's not exactly what I was expecting—or even hoping for. But that's fine.

Plenty of blood will still be spilled.

Up ahead, I spot the entryway to my destination. The throne room.

Technically, I haven't been inside yet, but my ghost has. One of Tytus' little birdies managed to sneak a hologram disc of mine into the stately manor last week. It's how we were able to sketch out our own digital blueprints of this secret Kilpatrick alcove. It's how we managed to embed Tytus' smoke bombs into the walls. It's how we were able to plan our little ambush.

It's also how I'll leave my final message to Rian Kilpatrick after I've disappeared with his crown.

"Get down!"

Even though I've never met the man in person, I still recognize Maksim Smolov's voice up ahead. It rages through the smoke, quickly accompanied by a deafening round of gunshots.

Tytus must be here.

There isn't an ounce of concern in me for my adoptive brother. He can take care of himself almost as well as I can.

Almost.

"Good luck," I silently smirk, my hand falling onto the ornate doorknob of the Kilpatrick throne room. "Try not to hurt the girl. I wouldn't want this to get any more personal than it already is."

Even as I say it, part of me knows that's a lie. I do want this to get more personal. It might be the only way to get my reckless little lion back on my tail.

Pushing on the handle, I take one last look around to make sure I'm not being followed. I'm about to enter the most dangerous section of our little plan.

There's only one way out of this room, after all. And I'm standing in it. If my enemies find out that I'm here before I can leave, then they might just be able to trap me. And I've long since promised myself I won't ever allow myself to be trapped again. Not for long. Even if it means death.

"... What the fuck?"

I've barely even had time to finish my scan of the hallway before something completely unexpected brushes against my ankle. A pistol immediately replaces the switchblade I've been holding.

But I don't shoot.

Is that...

A little red blob has stopped some five feet from me, frozen in fear. It takes me a second to recognize the strange figure, but by the time I do, it's the least of my concerns.

A new round of shouts have filled the smoky air. More men are approaching from where I just came—back up for Maksim and the Kilpatrick princess.

Really, all I'd have to do is step inside the throne room and close the door and I'd easily avoid them. But something nails my feet into the ground.

That little red blob frozen in the chaos.

It's a kitten.

I saw it earlier. One of those disgusting Italian dons was holding it by the scruff and waving it around like a fucking white flag. The sight made my blood boil. Luckily, Melina Kilpatrick managed to do something about it before I could blow my own cover—it's part of the reason I decided to forbid Tytus from taking her.

Someone has to protect the cat, after all.

But I guess Melina isn't strong enough to protect such a precious little package. Luckily, I am.

I'm still staring at the tiny furball when Maksim's backup arrives. My mind is quickly made up.

Four shots rip from my silver pistol. Four heavy bodies hit the ground. The kitten's hackles rise as I race forward to grab it.

To my surprise, it bites at my fingers as I try to pick it up.

"Fuck. This is for your own good," I hiss back.

Forcing it into my arms, I carry us both back to the throne room. It will be the only safe spot in this entire mausoleum.

But the kitten doesn't seem to agree with how I'm holding it. One last nip makes me place it back down on the floor, but only after I shut the heavy throne room door behind us.

We're quickly sealed in, isolated from the violence outside. Only muffled pangs of the chaos seep in through walls. Otherwise, all is silent.

"We're safe now," I whisper, my voice quivering ever so slightly.

Maybe it's just my hormones, but I'm actually hurt at the kitten's response to my help. A whole tsunami of repressed memories threatens to crush me as those little paws scurry away, deeper into the throne room.

My unsure feet carry me forward. There, in the center of the room, is what I came for.

Rian Kilpatrick's crown.

Forget the cat, I tell myself. *They've never been anything but trouble for you. Focus on what you really want.*

But that line of thought only sends a sharp pain through my hollow chest.

What do I really want?

"Fancy seeing you here."

Rian Kilpatrick's voice might as well be a burning whip—I can practically feel its hot leather wrap and my wrist as I'm yanked around.

Sure enough, the Irish lion steps out of the shadows, gun already drawn.

We both ignore the hiss that comes from the ground as he steps toward me. Every hair on my body rises.

"Pull the trigger and see how fast I do the same," I warn, not daring to raise my gun quite yet. I've underestimated this man before, and it bit me in the ass. Hard. I'm not doing it again.

"A quick death would be too easy for you," he spits back.

"What a coincidence, I was about to say the same about you."

"How convenient."

As if by instinct, we both start to circle each other. Each step is a careful ballet. One wrong move and it could be our last.

"You wanted me to overhear you on the radio," I quickly realize.

"No. I didn't," Rian furiously admits. "But it only took a minute to realize that you must be listening in."

"You sure are perceptive."

"You sure are in a load of shit."

My hackles rise even higher. He's not wrong.

How am I going to get out of this one?

Shit. My only option is to bluff.

"I'm pretty sure that smell is just coming from you."

Rian doesn't take the bait. Those ocean blue eyes stay fixed on me. They're filled with hate.

I return the favor.

"You're surrounded. We have thermal cameras here too, you know," he says, tapping at his temple. My glasses suddenly feel clunky. I take them off and throw them aside. "From what we can see, it's just you and your brother. That was a foolish move. You should have brought back up. What happened to that army you stole from Gabriel?"

The mention of my brother's name is nearly enough to set me off. But instead of giving into the hate and the grief, I force myself to latch onto something else. Something far more helpful.

Hope.

Rian just fucked up. He let his position slip. I already knew about his thermal cameras. What he clearly doesn't know is that I've already hacked into them.

Okay, maybe I'm not so fucked, after all.

It would only take a single command for my program to initiate the virus I've already installed in his software. I wouldn't even have to press down on my earpiece, and a hundred red-hot ghosts would appear on every Kilpatrick thermal camera. They'd think I brought an army with me.

Fuck. For someone so brilliant, Rian Kilpatrick sure seems clumsy today.

"We didn't need an army," I say, suddenly remembering something else, too. "Not with how quickly you're running this empire into the ground. Two people are all we need to get what we want."

Slowly, I start to lead us both towards the shelf where I know my hologram disc has been stashed.

"And what do you want? To steal my crown? Is that all?"

"Isn't it enough?" I stall.

All I have to do is get close enough.

"I'll still become king."

"In name, sure. But what about in truth? Who would respect a king whose crown was stolen before he could put it on his head?"

"I'm not going to have to worry about that," Rian sneers. "And neither will—"

"Wait," I interrupt. Pretending to hear something, I look towards the door. Once again, Rian doesn't take the bait. But he doesn't have to. His silence is enough. "A *ghost*?" I tease.

This time, I can't help my smirk.

But Rian isn't fooled. He recognizes a keyword when he hears one.

"What the fuck was that?" Rian growls. "What did you just do?"

"Nothing."

My hologram discs are silent, but I can practically feel the vibrations as it turns on just behind me.

Then, as if by design, a holographic image flickers around me.

I hold my breath.

This is the moment of truth. Rian needs to buy that I'm not actually here. Otherwise, I'm fucked.

"You've got to be fucking kidding me," Rian barks, those delicious red lips of his twisting into the meanest snarl I've ever seen. "You sent in a hologram?"

My heart jumps for fucking joy.

He's buying it. He's actually about to fucking fall for my bluff.

"Nice to see you finally catching on, big boy," I taunt. "And to think, I once thought you were almost as smart as me."

In response, the fearsome lion tightens his grip around his gun. "Want to see how fast I really am?"

"I'd rather you take it slow," I smile. "Otherwise, you'll just be shooting blanks at a ghost."

Now that I'm back in the driver's seat, I can actually stop to appreciate that gorgeous fucking face. The impossibly deep ocean blue eyes. The thick, wavy dirty-blonde hair. The sharp lines of his flexed jaw. The massive size of his clenched fists. The darkness and the power in the black tattoos that crawl up his neckline and under the cufflinks of his navy suit.

This is the closest I've ever physically been to him.

He smells like fresh earth and burning wood.

My shoulders furl as all types of dirty thoughts wash through my hormone-addled brain.

"Where the hell are you?" Rian demands to know. But I'm not one of his subjects. He doesn't rule me.

"Outside," I casually lie. "Right by those pretty little brides of yours. I'm about to turn their white dresses red. Then you won't have any more distractions left. You'll finally be able to come chasing after mama again."

"You wouldn't fucking dare."

"Watch me."

As if on cue, the kitten I dragged inside decides to throw a fit.

With an air-popping hiss, it jumps onto the mantle where Rian's crown is proudly displayed, knocking the glorified hat off its stand.

It's just enough of a distraction. Those sharp ocean blue eyes are momentarily torn away from me, and I take the opportunity to reach up and press down on my earpiece.

"Lights!" I shout.

In the blink of an eye, the throne room goes completely dark.

"Fuck!"

The lion's roar is so loud it pricks at my skin—and makes my toes involuntarily curl. But, otherwise, I remain completely still.

He fell for it.

Rian's cursing follows him as he turns his back on me and storms away.

My fingers tighten around the handle of my pistol. He's defenseless. I could finish him right now.

But I don't raise my gun.

No. I won't have it end like this. Especially not if there's any chance I hit that cat with one of my bullets. One way or another, I'm going to win it over.

Rian, on the other hand, needs to suffer a whole lot more.

Up ahead, I hear the heavy sound of the throne room door being opened from the inside. Then, it slams shut.

For a moment, I'm almost sad to hear him go. But that disappointment quickly gives way to an explosion of adrenaline.

Now is no time to be humble. What a fucking performance. Shit, someone needs to hand me an Oscar. But I guess I'll take the lion's crown instead.

"Lights," I whisper, keeping my finger pressed on my earpiece.

Sure enough, the lights flicker back on.

My heart momentarily stops. Rian's crown isn't on its mantle. Neither is the cat.

But then I see the little black fuzzball flash across the room, and my gaze falls on the toppled crown. It lays on its side, hardly any more glorious than an ordinary baseball cap.

What a perfect image.

I can only hope it's prescient.

Without wasting another breath, I scoop down and pick up the bejeweled crown. It's lighter than I thought it would be, and it fits perfectly inside my backpack, squished right next to the cake.

Good. That will make it easier to carry the cat.

"You're coming with me," I insist, spotting the little black void cowering in the corner. "I promise to protect you from these Irish devils."

Either the fuzzball is too tired to resist, or I'm already winning it over, because the poor little thing hardly puts up a fight as I bundle it up in my arms.

"A girl," I note. "I wonder what I should call you?"

No. No names. Not yet. Don't get attached, Rozalia. Not again.

Just like that, a repressed sadness threatens to send me through the floor.

Trying my best to ignore it, I look back over my shoulder. The hologram disc is hidden well enough that it would be impossible to find... unless you were looking for it. And I'm sure Rian will be.

That's good too. I want him to find it.

I've already left a little breadcrumb in the hardware. An irresistible treat that should lead him into my next trap. Hopefully, it will be our final encounter.

The thought sends my heart racing. And a flicker of rage cuts across the pit of grief in my gut.

Fuck my stupid hormones for making me attracted to that vile monster. I'll have to nip that shit in the bud. Because there's still so much to take from the lion who helped steal my brother away from me. And I won't stop until I've taken everything. From him. From his family. From the world that's tried to destroy me.

I'll conquer this darkness. I fucking swear it.

But first, I'm going to conquer him.

3

RIAN

"You've got to be fucking kidding me."

The blood is so thick it weighs down my hair like lead, practically blinding me. My suit is soaked through.

My rage is infinite.

I took the fucking bait—even if it wasn't for the reasons Rozalia Dorn was hoping.

"Tell me that's not human blood," I hear Mel gag.

"It's not," Maksim is quick to assure us both. "If I had to guess, I'd say it's pigs blood."

"That hardly helps."

Lifting my gun into the air, I fire. One shot. Two shots. Three. It doesn't matter. Even through all the blood, I can sense that the shadow I saw hovering over the lawn just moments ago is gone.

"A fucking drone," I curse. "They brought a blood-filled drone to my fucking coronation."

The crimson liquid pools at my feet like molasses. Each step I take feels heavier than the last. This shit is humid and sticky. I'll be cleaning it out of my hair for the next week.

"Well, at least you get to look like a hero in front of the Italians," Maksim points out, trying to find a silver lining.

Looking back over my shoulder, I spot the cowering silhouettes of the women I just saved from this disgusting fate.

Some of them are openly weeping. A few look like they're passed out. Others just stare blankly ahead, pristine white dresses fluttering like ghosts in the thinning smoke.

This is the first time I'm getting a good look at them. And even through the thinning smoke, it's immediately apparent that not all of them are women. More than one are clearly just girls. Underage pawns dragged here by their greedy fathers.

Fucking barbarians.

"Is everyone alright?" I ask, wiping smoke away with my hand.

But that only reveals more of me to them, and I can't imagine it's a pleasant sight. It's not like I'm the picture of holiness on a good day. Covered in blood, I must look like some demon that just crawled straight out of hell.

Hopefully, that will convince these girls to run far away from me—not that they have much choice in the matter.

"Don Kilpatrick! I saw everything. You saved our girls. Thank you! Thank you!"

Don Sabatino's greasy voice is the last thing I want to hear right now. It slithers through the haze like a pitiful snake. That asshole is already on my shit list for his attempted stunt with that kitten.

"Where the fuck were you?" I snap, turning to him in all of my blood-soaked fury.

The chubby don flinches against my anger. "I... I... was trying to secure the perimeter," he stumbles.

"And what about your daughter's safety?" I ask, pointing back to the shaken group of girls. Blood drips from my outstretched finger.

I need a fucking shower.

"I... I thought they would be left alone. Surely you were in more danger than them."

Even through the clearing fog, I can practically see the shit on his nose. The pathetic ass-kisser.

"Take your daughter home," I spit, turning my back to him. "Everybody get the fuck out of here!"

At the sound of my roar, all the spineless guests still hiding in the bushes suddenly bolt upright, desperately scrambling over one another to act like they're doing something now that the danger is over.

It only makes my hate all the stronger.

"Rian, are—" Mel starts to call to me, but before she can continue, I reach out and grab her wrist. We need to get out of here. "Hey, ow! That hurts."

"Sorry," I grumble, letting go of her. "Follow me. Maksim, you too. Gather information from the men. I want a full fucking diagnostic."

"Yes, sir," Maksim nods. "But I can probably already tell you everything."

Mel struggles to keep up as we burst back into the house.

My embarrassment grows hot as the smoke clears from the hallways.

Bullet holes riddle the dark wood paneling. Lamps and busts and paintings lay on the floor, cracked and strewn about in the unnecessary panic.

Those two made complete fools of us.

"This is what I get for trusting security to anyone but myself," I growl.

"I didn't think it would be this bad," Maksim agrees. "Fuck. I wish I could have been here to help."

"I should have known better than to go through with it," I respond. "At the very least, we should have used this opportunity to set a trap. It would have been so easy. She was five feet from me, Uncle Maks. Rozalia Dorn. The Black Cat. I fucking had her. Right in the palm of my hand. If there was a plan in place, I could have ended this all right here. Instead, I've spent the last month letting myself get distracted."

My rage flares as we approach the throne room. But so does something else. Something wholly unwelcome.

My cock is starting to swell again.

It doesn't matter that I'm drenched in blood; that I'm so angry I could tear this place down with my bare hands; that I'll never entirely trust my subordinates again.

In the back of my mind, all I can see are those emerald green eyes; those plump red limps; that hour-glass figure.

My nails dig deep into my palms as I stop just before the door. Before I can fall any deeper into my lustful trance, Mel runs into my back, and I'm temporarily snapped back to reality.

"Oh no!" my little sister gasps. "What do you think happened to the kitten?"

"Fuck the cat," I say. "We've got bigger problems."

I didn't see Rozalia leave with my crown. But I know both are long gone.

Still, I can't help but wonder where that little kitten has run off to. Really, I should be thanking it—because If it hadn't appeared out of the shadows back there, I might never have broken out of the trance Rozalia put me under. Shit. I was almost considering doing something stupid—not that I didn't anyway.

I let the Black Cat go.

On purpose.

It was either that or pinning her against the wall so she could feel how hard I was.

Fuck.

At first, that hologram bullshit nearly had me fooled, but there was one thing Rozalia couldn't hide with technology. And it quickly became clear that I wasn't dealing with a ghost.

My cock could sense her warmth. I could smell her spicy scent...

And then the kitten knocked my crown from its stand, and a little blood rushed from my swollen member and back into my brain.

Mel was still out there in the chaos.

By then, I'd already figured out that Rozalia had come alone—well, figuratively. There was no army backing her up. Only her adoptive brother. But that didn't mean my little sister was completely safe.

Maksim could only do so much against a bull like Tytus. And I'd left him to do it alone when I'd suddenly realized that Rozalia might try to beat us to the throne room.

So, I ran ahead and planted a few special parting gifts into the jewels of my crown. Then she came in, and I lost track of time.

That chaotic kitten helped me remember what my real duty was.

To protect my family.

By the time I got back to Maksim and Mel, though, Tytus was already gone. I didn't mind. But that didn't mean I could rest. There was still Rozalia's threat. The poor girls huddled on my lawn outside.

She'd promised to paint their white dresses red.

No matter how much I loathed the idea of marrying one of them, I couldn't let that happen. Not if I wanted to contain the shame of what had already happened today.

So, I raced out onto the lawn, just as the shadow of a giant fucking drone appeared above the smoke.

Whatever it was carrying was quickly dropped.

I only had time to tackle my potential brides out of the way. Most of the blood got onto me. Their virgin dresses remained unblemished.

But the same can't be said for my reputation.

Placing my bloody hand onto the ornate door handle, I try to calm myself with a deep breath. But all I taste is blood.

"Rian, are you alright?"

Mel's tiny voice might as well be coming from the bottom of the ocean. Still, I'm brought back to earth when I feel the warmth of her hand on my blood-caked shoulder.

"I'm fine," I insist, shrugging her away. "Go wash your hands. We still don't know what's in this shit."

"I'm not worried," Mel whispers. "Not about the blood, anyway."

"You don't need to worry about anything," I tell her, pushing open the door. "That's my job. You stick to your art."

"My art..." Mel mumbles to herself, before a realization sends her into the air. "My art! Your gift! We left it behind. Maksim, where–"

"Don't worry," Maksim echoes my sentiment. "I'll get some men to find it. That thing is heavy. I'm sure it didn't go far."

"I hope not," Mel mutters.

Their conversation continues behind me as I step into the throne room alone.

Somehow, I can still smell her. A spicy rose scent that singes the tip of my tongue. It's part of why I wasn't completely sold on her hologram trick—though, I wouldn't put it past a woman like that to build a perfume dispenser into one of her contraptions.

Rozalia Dorn. Fuck. For as frustrating as she is, I won't deny her twisted brilliance.

My cock is already swelling again when I feel Maksim step into the room behind me.

"I guess we didn't make it on time," he says, his words drifting towards the empty mantle where my crown once stood.

"Or maybe I wanted her to take it."

"Does that mean you got to put your tracking device on it?"

"More than one. Sure, she'll find most of them. But if she

misses even a single sliver, then I'll know exactly where she and Tytus are hiding out."

"And if she wants you to come after her?"

"Then she'll get her wish."

Brushing past the empty mantle, I make my way to where the Black Cat stood. Her lingering scent intensifies. So does my erection.

It sends a shockwave of shame crashing through my pounding chest. That shockwave is quickly followed by a flurry of red-hot desire.

Thoughts of revenge fill my racing mind.

Rozalia's punishment will be severe...

Before I can plunge too deeply into those dark fantasies, a new set of heavy footsteps comes barreling into the room.

"Sir, the premise is clear. There's no sign of any more intruders. We seem to have chased them all off."

I immediately recognize the voice. Ian McQuade. One of the men who was supposed to be in charge of security for today's event. He doesn't sound nearly as fucking devastated as he should be.

Shit, I swear I even detect a tinge of pride in his voice—like chasing off those two hyenas was such a big accomplishment.

Doesn't he know how badly he's fucked up?

"There were only two—" I bark, whipping around. But as I do, something on the shelf catches my eye. It's just the faintest glint, but it's enough to turn my attention away from the man in the doorway.

"Give me your update. I'll pass it on," Maksim tells McQuade, sparing me. Together, the two men disappear back into the hallway.

I wait until I'm alone again, then I reach for the suspicious glimmer. At first, I don't feel anything—just smooth wood. Then, the tip of my bloody finger brushes over a subtle bump. I click down.

The wood cracks and splinters. Slowly but surely, a metal tick appears. I dig it out of the wall and hold it to the light.

"How the hell did you get in here?" I mumble under my breath.

My lips twist into a snarl.

There are only two possible answers to that question, and neither of them bode well for me.

Treachery or incompetence.

Fucking hell.

Some king I am. I haven't even been crowned yet, and my reign is already falling apart. If I want to survive this mess, I'll have to do something seriously drastic.

"Find anything interesting?"

When I turn around, Maksim is there again. Over his shoulder, I can see Mel talking to McQuade. She's clearly trying to describe her painting to him. But finding that giant canvas is the least of my worries.

"Nothing I didn't already know was there," I tell my consigliere. "Gather the men outside. Tell the guests to stay."

"Understood," Maksim nods. "What are you going to do?"

Keeping the silver tick tucked tightly beneath my fist, I turn back towards the doorway. Blood drips from my knuckles. And my hair. And from every inch of my drenched suit.

Yet all of that blood pales in comparison to the blood raging through my veins. My forearms flex. Every last muscle in my body clenches.

My cock is rock hard.

Fuck. It's so swollen I'm worried it might leak. I can still smell her. That spicy burning rose. It's driving me crazy.

It needs to be taken care of. Everything does.

"I'm going to have a fucking shower," I announce. "Then, I'm going to come back downstairs and do what I should have done long ago."

"What's that?" Maksim asks.

"Take control."

You should have left me alone while you had the chance, kitten. Now, there's no going back.

You're mine.

Hot water batters down on me from above. Thick rivers of blood swirl down around my feet. The shower drain is already clogged. I'm slowly boiling alive in a pool of my own failure.

But I don't give a shit.

All I can focus on is my hand.

It's wrapped around the base of my swollen cock. Every inch of me shakes with desire, screaming for just one stroke.

Those lips. That body. I want to let myself imagine all the dirty things I could do to them. To her.

But my brain refuses. I don't deserve any relief. No pleasure. Not after what happened today. What I *allowed* to happen.

Fuck. I'm already done blaming others. I've accepted responsibility. This was my fault. And it's up to me to fix what was broken.

My reputation.

Because if I don't, it's not just me who will pay. It's my entire family.

One grunt at a time, I pry my fingers off my pulsing shaft. It twitches in the hot air, desperate to be touched again. I don't give in—even if all I can think about are Rozalia's thick red lips wrapping around my girthy head.

Fuck. Stop it!

Making a fist, I punch the faucet. The water stops. The steam settles. I open the shower door and storm out.

A draft of crisp air blows in from the open bathroom door. I let it wash over me.

For a moment, my raging erection finally calms. My obsessive desire temporarily cools along with it. Grabbing a towel, I make my way back into the bedroom, towards the desk by the far wall.

There's something else I should be focusing on.

In the middle of the table, splayed out on a white cloth, is the silver tick I found earlier.

My men can wait. So can my cowardly guests. I'm not going anywhere until I have something to say to them. And something tells me this taunting piece of technology will give me exactly what I want.

Answers.

First, I just have to dissect it.

Reaching into the top drawer, I find my incision scalpel and a fiberoptic wire. The little black cable is so thin it could be a strand of hair, but it's filled with more high-end circuitry than some computers.

Slicing open the back of the silver tick, I slip the wire inside. Then, I get up from my chair and find my phone. It's over by one of the bedside drawers.

There are already a dozen missed calls showing on the screen, and even more texts are waiting to be seen.

I ignore every last one.

The outside world can go to hell. So can all of my duties. I've tried watching over my empire from a gilded throne. It didn't work out.

Now, it's time to get my back to my roots.

It's time to hunt.

Rozalia Dorn has chosen to play a dangerous game with me. She won't like where it ends up. I promise.

Sitting back down at my desk, I get to work. First, I set up the wireless connection between the fiberoptic cable and my cell phone. After a few false starts, the screen finally fills up with a tableau of delicious data. Then suddenly, it all vanishes.

My phone vibrates with an incoming call.

I freeze when I see the caller ID. It's from the one person I can't ignore.

My father.

Fuck.

"Hello," I answer, swiping aside the call screen to look back at the comforting mosaic of raw code and tangled data.

"How are you doing?" Dad asks.

Static cracks behind his voice, a by-product of all the protective measures I've put into place to disguise our communications.

"I'm fine," I grumble, curling the fiber cord up the tick's spine. "How are you?"

"Rian."

"I promise, I'm fine," I lie.

"It's alright not to be fine."

"Well, that will be good to know in the future, when I'm not fine. But right now, I'm guts deep in a piece of technology I've never seen before. And you know how happy that kind of shit makes me."

"A piece of technology the Black Cat left behind?"

"Yes," I reluctantly admit. "A silver tick."

"Pets tend to do that."

My steady fingers pause at the word pet. For a moment, my fading rage flares up again, and a red-hot image appears behind my aching skull.

Rozalia Dorn. On all fours. At my feet. Gagged and bound in a leather leash.

"Fuck..." I grumble, stomping my heel into the ground to divert the blood rushing into my growing cock.

I should have jerked off in the shower—whether I deserved the relief or not, it doesn't matter. I need to stay focused.

"Find anything interesting?" Dad asks. He doesn't sound nearly as bothered as he should be.

"Not yet," I admit. Scrolling the tip of my finger along my phone screen, I search for a clue. "But I'm looking."

"And your men are waiting," he reminds me.

"So, you've already talked to Maksim..."

"He gave me the rundown of what happened today. All in all, it doesn't sound so bad."

"You weren't the one drenched in pig's blood."

"I've been drenched in a lot worse," Dad chuckles.

The lightness in his voice makes me second guess the heaviness in my own. Why isn't he taking this as seriously as I am?

"How's everything going over there?" I ask, hoping that maybe it's because he has some good news.

"Still preparing for war," he sighs, dashing those hopes. "Figuratively, of course. The US government is too strong to take on in any kind of physical battle. But legally, they are bound by a tangled web of rules and regulations. We're using that to our advantage. Who knows, maybe they'll get frustrated enough to give up."

"You know that won't happen."

"No harm in hoping," Dad says, and I can practically hear him shrugging. "But you're right. This isn't just another money laundering scheme or extortion plot. They want blood. Payback for what they think we did to Congressman Olsen's daughter, and revenge for what one of our new members actually did do to Senator Polanski's son."

The reminder is like a thick rope around my throat.

"Has Maksim still not been able to confirm who kidnapped and killed the Congressman's daughter yet?"

We didn't have the time to go over the details before this morning, but if there's anyone in our organization who could figure this shit out, it's Maksim.

"I think we all already know who it was," Dad responds. "The problem is finding evidence. Until we do, the feds will keep trying to pin it on us."

"Just another reason why I need to go after the Black Cat myself," I growl. "If anyone knows where Drago Raclaw is, it's her."

"Does that mean you're going to abandon your kingly duties?"

"She threatened our empire, Dad. Isn't it my duty to wipe out a threat like that?"

"Not personally."

"I'm never handing off my responsibilities again," I snap. "That's what I did for today, and look where it got us."

"A good king must pick and choose where he puts his foot down."

"I choose her throat," I blurt out, immediately regretting it.

My anger mixes with shame as I try to focus back on my data.

"Rian," Dad's voice suddenly becomes more rigid. "Remember what happened the last time you got this obsessed with catching a little mouse."

The legs of my chair scratch against the floor as I push myself up from the desk.

"That wasn't a mouse," I sneer down at my phone. "That was a rat. A whole fucking swarm of them."

"You didn't have any proof. We still don't. It's why we had to send you away. Do you think I wanted to temporarily exile my own son? Fuck no. But we had to wait until the heat died down from your wild rampage. Well, it finally has. You're home, and you have the freedom to do whatever you want. Don't you want to keep it that way?"

"I've learned my lesson," I huff.

"I don't think you have. Because it sounds like you're ready to dive head first into another foolish venture."

"Capturing the Black Cat is not a foolish venture."

"It is if it means ignoring all of your other duties."

The headache I'd had earlier this morning returns with a vengeance as I force myself back into my seat.

"How the hell did you handle having so much on your plate for all those years?" I ask, pinching the bridge of my nose.

It feels like the world's caving in around me.

Dad sighs. "There's only one way, Rian. And it's by taking on each problem as it comes, one step at a time."

"There are so many fucking problems."

"Then start combining your solutions. That's what I used to do. Hell, it's what I still do to this very day."

"How the hell am I going to do that?" I grumble. "My problems are all so fucking different. The Black Cat; those slimy Italians and their daughters; your court case. I've got an empire to secure, a crown to recover, and a marriage to arrange..."

Grimacing, I force myself to sit up straight and stare down at my phone again.

To my surprise, something has changed on the screen.

The code, it's re-arranged itself.

"That's for you to decide," Dad says. "It's your kingdom now, after all."

"What the fuck..." I curse, leaning closer to the screen.

"Is everything alright?"

Just like that, the code switches again.

Something clicks.

"Can I call you back? I think I just found something."

"A solution or a distraction?"

Wrapping the edge of the thin wire around my finger, I wait for the code to re-arrange itself again. The second it does, I pull. The silver tick is gutted. The data on my phone screen pixelates, then freezes.

"I fucking found you," I sneer.

There, hiding just behind the code, is a tiny IP address. To an average person, it might not seem like anything more than an insignificant set of numbers. To me, it might as well be coordinates.

This is how I'm going to find her.

This is how I'm going to make her fucking pay.

My fists clench and my heart jumps as I stand back up from my chair.

"Rian. Don't do anything you might regret. You can't ignore one commitment for another anymore."

Dad's words of warning make me pause. But not because I take them to heart. Instead, I suddenly have another idea—a way to appease both my father and my obsession.

A combination of all my commitments into one cruel act.

The thought hits me like a sledgehammer.

... Do I dare?

"Don't worry. I won't. I've been listening. And I've just had a thought that might solve all of our problems."

"Want to fill me in?"

"Of course, I'll need your blessing after all."

That leaves my father momentarily speechless.

"Rian, what are you going to do?"

"I'm going hunting," I tell him, biting down on my tongue. "And when I return, I'll have destroyed our most dangerous enemy. And captured myself a wife."

The static crackling seems to intensify as my father tries to make sense of what he just heard.

"A forced marriage..."

I can't help but smirk.

"Taking Rozalia captive would essentially neuter Tytus. There's no way he would dare attack us if it could harm his sister. That takes care of the biggest threat to our empire. But it might also force the Italians to actually get off their asses for once, because they couldn't just keep throwing their daughters at me anymore. They'd have to work for my favor, just like old times. Hell, it might even draw Dragomir Raclaw out of hiding.

The only obstacle would be catching her, and I just found out how I might be able to do that."

It would also allow me to break my vow of celibacy, I think. *But that's beside the point.*

"Interesting," dad mumbles. "There's actually another possible benefit. Has Maksim been keeping you updated on his mission? Just last week, he told me about something that might make your proposal even more successful…"

"Do tell."

"Talk to your uncle about it. He knows more than I do. And I shouldn't get too involved. Not yet. Not with the feds watching. But this plan of yours might just work."

"I'll make it work," I assure him, knowing fully that I don't actually plan on it.

I've just thought this shit up as a way to ease my father's mind. He has enough shit on his plate already. Because one way or another, I'm going after Rozalia Dorn.

I will capture her. And the threat of marriage will keep her and her brother in check while I secure my empire. It should also get the Italians working again.

By the time Dad finds out what's really happening, I'll have everything under control, and he won't have to worry about a thing.

In the end, I'll choose to marry whoever the fuck I want to marry. But that's a long ways away.

For now, my vow of celibacy will remain in place. This time, though, it won't be until I can stand to choose a wife.

It will be until I've captured my personal plaything.

"Shit. This is why I was so confident you'd make a good king, Rian. Always thinking. I'm proud of you."

The sincerity in Dad's voice almost makes me feel guilty. But I quickly pry out that weakness.

I know what needs to be done. There's no room for sentimentality.

"Save your pride for when I've wiped our enemies from the face of this earth."

"... Or married them," he laughs.

"It will be a hell of a wedding."

But I don't picture wedding bells or white dresses or sweet vows in my future. All I can see is Rozalia Dorn kneeling at my feet. Naked. Begging for mercy.

She won't find any.

"Good luck, my boy," Dad says, and I hear someone calling for him behind the static.

"Same to you."

"Try to keep me updated."

"I will."

"Long live the Kilpatrick empire."

"Long live the Kilpatrick family."

With that, our call ends.

I immediately screenshot the IP address on my screen. Then, I call up Maksim.

"Is everyone still outside?" I ask.

"Yep."

"Good. Because I have an announcement to make."

4

ROZALIA

"I know it's in here somewhere."

Riffling through the cabinets as quietly as possible, I try to find what I'm looking for. But I'm not having any luck. And I'm running out of time.

It's a peaceful Sunday afternoon in the countryside, which means the owner of this idyllic little cottage should be waking up from her nap anytime now—I'm not trying to speed up the process by making a bunch of noise.

Unfortunately, the kitten has other ideas. Her meows rise up from her spot on the countertop, each louder than the last.

"Give me a second," I mumble. "The old lady loves her tuna. There's got to be a canister or two stuffed away in the back."

"Try the third cabinet from the left."

Babcia's unexpected voice twists me around. Instinct makes me reach for my knife. But that kind old sagging face immediately drops my guard.

"You should be napping," I tell her.

"And you should be out looking for a nice man to settle down with," she waves me off.

Her frail voice creaks with the floorboards as she shuffles into the kitchen.

"If only you knew," I smirk. Sliding across the counter, I open up the fabled third cabinet from the left. Sure enough, a leaning tower of tuna cans is tucked in the back corner.

"Who's this precious little thing?" Babcia asks.

When I look back over my shoulder, I find the old Polish grandma gently brushing the black kitten. The tiny creature is a lot more welcoming of her than she has been of me.

"It's my prize," I mutter, disappointed.

"Living things aren't prizes," Babcia tsks. "What is her name?"

"I haven't thought of one yet."

"Well, I have. Welcome to the family, *Kaja*."

"What family?" I huff.

Using my switchblade, I open up the kitten's lunch. To my surprise, the black furball slinks out from under Babcia's fingers and makes a beeline for the food.

"Ah, she's a survivor," the old polish grandma acknowledges. "Just like you."

I'm about to brush off her remark when I'm suddenly ambushed by a flood of heavy memories.

A starving kitten. Scraps of fish. A melting cage. A brutal choice. A false savior.

"Animals require food," I grumble, shaking my head.

"And what do you require, my dear?"

"A babysitter."

"For this sweet little creature?"

Babcia's kindly voice brings me back to the present.

"If you wouldn't mind…" I whisper, a pulse of guilt pounding through me. Babcia doesn't deserve my attitude.

"Of course not, dear. I will treat her as I treat you. As if she is my own granddaughter."

"I hope she treats you better than I do."

"Impossible," Babcia laughs. "Unless the kitten will also pay off my debts and buy me a cozy little cabin by the cliffs?"

"Well, I mean, I did find her at a king's palace," I shrug. "Who knows how much she's worth."

"A king's palace," Babcia smiles. "How magical."

The grandmother I never had sighs as her sparkling brown eyes trail off into some fairytale.

I take the opportunity to jump forward and plant a kiss on her wrinkly forehead.

"You're sweaty," I notice. "Do you need me to fix the AC again?"

"Heavens no, dear. I'm just old. Truth be told, I'm glad my sweat glands are still working."

A light laugh putters from my lips.

On the counter beside me, little Kaja nibbles away at her breakfast.

The small slice of domesticity is a far cry from the recent events of my life. It makes me glad I found Babcia when I did. Otherwise, I might have spiraled out of control after we lost Gabriel.

Gabriel.

"I can't wait until I'm old," I announce. "No more stupid mood swings. No more endless cravings. Look, Babcia, I'm sorry about being moody, it's just—

"Woman problems," Babcia knowingly nods. "I know all about them—or I used to. You take care of yourself. Come back tonight; I will have some pierogis ready for you and that brother of yours. *Kaja* will be well taken care of."

My stomach rumbles at the mere mention of her famous pierogis.

"I'm not sure tonight works," I reluctantly admit. "But if all goes well, Tytus and I will be treating you to a feast soon."

"I can't wait."

Kaja meows, and I get a whiff of the tuna on the counter.

Fuck. I'm already starving again. It feels like I've grown a second stomach.

"Mind if I raid your fridge?"

"Someone needs to eat that food."

Twirling on my tiptoes, I pull open the fridge door and scan the insides. Sure enough, there are all sorts of delicious treats.

"Are those cabbage rolls?" I ask, reaching into the back.

"Only a couple of days old," Babcia confirms.

"Perfect."

Shrugging my backpack to the floor, I zip it open and nudge aside the crown to make room.

That's when I see something I had nearly forgotten about.

"There's some Hunter's Stew in there too," Babcia says. "Bring it to your brother, please. I know it's his favorite."

"He has more than enough to eat," I chuckle, jumping to my feet. "But you are all skin and bones, Babcia. Here, this is for you." Curling my hand, I scoop out the discarded slice of cake I had stolen earlier. "I know it's a little squished, but I'm sure it's worth a small fortune."

"It's that rich, huh?"

"Dessert made for a king."

"Then maybe I'll sell it, buy you something nice."

Grabbing a plate from a bottom drawer, I place the mushed slice down and try to mend it back into shape.

"If you're having money problems, you come to Tytus and me," I say.

"I'm just joking, dear. It's only been a few months since we met, and you two have already taken care of me plenty. Now, it's my turn to return the favor. And I'll do that the only way I know how. With food."

"I wouldn't have it any other way."

The cake crumbles against my touch, and a pretty little melody suddenly appears in my earpiece. It's Tytus' ringtone.

Giving up on the cake, I use my hands to hang up on him.

It's better not to answer any calls while I'm here, just in case someone is listening.

"I have to go," I say, gently clicking the fridge door shut. "Take care of yourself and Kaja. I'll see you both soon."

Licking the frosting from my fingers, I go to pet the hungry kitten. But she slinks from my touch.

My heart drops an inch. But there's no more time to waste. I've felt worse pain. Picking up my useless organ, I figuratively stuff it in my backpack, right between Babcia's cabbage rolls and Rian Kilpatrick's tracking-device-covered crown.

I can't help but laugh to myself as I give Babcia's sweaty forehead one last kiss, then bound out the back door.

There's no way the lion thought I wouldn't be able to spot and demobilize every last one of his beacons. It only took the trip up here to scramble the lot of them. And that was while I was trying to win over that stubborn kitten.

Hell, the only reason I even bothered to destroy the pathetic little devices was so he wouldn't be able to track my movements to Babcia's place.

Who knows what a monster like him would do to a little old lady like her. The Irish have no respect. No common decency. No regard for a person's age. It was clear enough on the faces of those poor girls he'd herded like cattle in the corner of his lawn. Half of them looked like they were still children. Fuck. If I'd known how young they were beforehand, I might have called off our pig's blood finale. But by the time I saw those fresh virgin faces, it was too late.

That blood was meant for the greedy women who were trying to steal my plaything away from me. Not for little girls who had no other option but to be there.

My lips twitch into a sneer as a very personal rage flickers up inside of me.

I fucking hate men who use little girls like pawns. Those barbarians are going to pay.

And it all starts with their supposed king.

Rian Kilpatrick.

He'll find the IP address I left for him in my hologram disc. And he'll come precisely where I want him to come.

In my pussy.

The flash of heat that accompanies that unexpected thought is nearly enough to stop me in my tracks. An intense pressure in my core follows closely behind.

My toes curl, and my fingers clench into fists.

Stupid fucking hormones.

Furious at myself, I whip out my switchblade and slice a very fine line against the back of my ring finger. It's no bigger than a papercut, and it immediately starts to bleed like one.

I suck up the blood and then spit it onto the gravel.

Slowly, the unwelcomed arousal seems to leak from the nearly invisible wound. So does my anger. It's an old Polish tradition that supposedly rids oneself of corrupted blood.

It's one of the few things I remember about my mother. She used to do it. Sometimes, I'll do it when I'm overwhelmed.

Stop getting stuck in the past, Rozalia.

Pulling down my sleeve, I let my black turtleneck soak up the rest of the blood. Then I look over my shoulder.

Babcia's cottage is long gone.

It's time to call Tytus back.

"Is this the infamous Black Cat?" he quickly answers. "Crown burglar? Hologram model? Pig's blood aficionado?"

"No."

"Okay, then you must have the wrong number. Bye."

The line goes dead, and I can only roll my eyes as I wait for the jester to call back. It doesn't take long.

"Was that worth it?" I ask, already fed up with his antics. Clearly, he's still reeling from the high of our successful caper.

"I thought you might need some cheering up."

"Cheering up from what?" I play dumb. There's no way I'm getting into a conversation about PMSing with my brother.

"Oh shit, you really haven't heard, have you?" The sudden seriousness in his voice makes me pause.

"Haven't heard about what?"

Tytus hesitates to respond.

"I really don't want to be the one to break it to you," he says. "But I guess I'm all you've got. Shit. What the hell were you doing on your trip back? You're usually listening to the Kilpatrick airwaves. That's what I was doing—even as I prepared for my big meeting with our new associate."

Fuck. Our new associate. I completely forgot about that shit.

"I wanted to take a break from those pigs," I spit. "Plus, I had some debugging to do on the crown we stole. Tell me what you heard."

But I already have my phone out, and I'm searching through a long list of hacked email accounts and texts for any hints.

Interestingly enough, I almost immediately stumble upon a name I've been trying my best to ignore.

"Dragomir," I hiss.

"What? No," Tytus quickly replies. "Why the fuck would you think this has something to do with Drago?"

Clicking on the text, I scroll up on my phone screen to the source of the information.

"One of your little birdies put a listening device in Rian's guest bedroom for me. I'm looking at a voice-to-text transcription of a conversation that was held there a few hours ago."

"Between who?"

"I'd have to listen to the audio."

"Well, listen to it later. As far as I know, the coward is still in hiding... or dead. I don't care. He's not worth our time anymore. But something else is. What else do you see?"

My finger glides across the screen as I search for more keywords. One of the programs I've installed in my spy software picks up on predetermined words of interest, then highlights them for me.

"Dragomir. Italians. Dad…" My stomach drops. "Marriage."

"That's what I was talking about," Tytus confirms.

My vision suddenly goes blurry. A fist of dread punches me square in the gut.

"Who the fuck is getting married?" I snap, desperately trying to see my screen through the black spots invading my eyes. "Fuck. Tytus. Don't say it's Rian. The whole point of our stupid ambush was to draw him away from the safety of his empire, not entrench him within it. He's the weak point in that entire operation. A reckless hot-head. The only one of his countless aunts and uncles and cousins who would even think of breaking from the group to do something so foolish as chase me. We saw it when he killed those union reps and got exiled to the west coast. We were trying to replicate that. It's why we added the pig's blood. It's why we chose to take his crown. To maximize his embarrassment. To force him to choose to chase after me instead of marrying one of those Italian child brides."

I'm just rambling now. The world feels like it could collapse in on me at any moment.

I was so confident this plan would work. But was I just blinded by my desire to be chased by those haunting blue eyes?

"Child brides?" Tytus asks, confused.

Through all the haze filling my head, I remember that he never got a good look at the cattle.

"Never mind that. Who the hell is getting married?"

"Rian Kilpatrick," Tytus says.

"To who?"

"… To you."

Just like that, the world freezes.

The Sunday afternoon sun goes dark. The soft breeze stops blowing. Birds stop chirping. My lungs stop working.

"What the fuck did you just say?"

"I'm just the messenger," Tytus insists. "Rian Kilpatrick is the one who wrote the decree. After we left, he made his guests stay behind. Then, he made an announcement. You two are to be wed—by force, if necessary."

The stillness surrounding me erupts.

"He fucking said that?"

"I have the recording, if you'd like to hear?"

"No. I fucking would not."

Ripping my knife back out, I plunge the bloody blade into the nearest tree.

"Is he insane?"

"Yes. And that's why we did what we did. This is the response we wanted, Roz," Tytus cautiously reminds me. "Now, he'll have to come collect his bride."

"I'm nobody's bride."

"And you won't ever have to be. Because before he can force a ring around your finger, we'll put a bullet between his eyes."

But imagining Rian's ocean blue eyes turning white doesn't calm me down. "A quick death is too good for him."

Ripping my knife from the tree, I begin to carve an *X* into the bark.

How the fuck did he know? Nothing else he could have done would have bothered me as much as this.

Long ago, I promised myself I would never become an unwilling pawn in anyone's quest for power ever again. It's why I broke away from our adoptive brother, Gabriel. It's why I forsook my adoptive father, Dragomir. It's why I'm so desperate to destroy the largest mafia empire in the world and claim its power for my own.

Because the only way to protect yourself in this world is by crushing everyone else beneath your feet.

I'm going to grind Rian Kilpatrick into dust.

"Hey, I agree. A quick death is too good for him," Tytus says. "That's why I'll let you have your fun before we put him in the ground."

"Before *I* put him in the ground," I correct him. "He's mine."

"Alright. Fine. I'll just be your backup. But take this for what it is, Roz. Good news. From what I've heard, he's coming for you himself, just like we wanted."

The reminder snaps some sense back into me.

"I need to get back to the lair," I think out loud.

Rian has probably already found the IP address hidden in my hologram disc. He can't be allowed to reach my trap first.

Pulling the blade from the tree, I get ready to run. But before I can even take my first step, the phone in my hand starts to violently vibrate.

"What is that?" Tytus asks.

"A warning," I grumble, looking down at the note flashing on the screen. "One of my tripwires has been activated."

"What does that mean?"

"It means he's here."

"Fuck. Want me to come over?"

'No," I snip. "Stay away. This is between me and my new fiancé."

"Fine. But I'm delaying my meeting with our new associate, just in case you need my help. I'll be on standby." There's no point in arguing. Tytus can be just as stubborn as me. "Make that Irish fuck regret the day he dared propose to you."

Fucking hell. I still can't believe he's done that. What an infuriating piece of shit.

My fingers clench into fists as I think of what I want to do to that man.

Then, suddenly, the memory of his scent overrides my senses. Fresh earth and burning wood. It lingers like a ghost, haunting me from afar.

That fucking fragrance caught me so off guard. It was the first time I ever got close enough to smell the man. And for a second, I'd only wanted to close my eyes and breathe in more.

That won't happen again. This time, I'll be ready. I know his stench. It needs to be destroyed.

"I'll show the lion what it's like to be prey," I hiss.

"Good luck."

"See you on the other side."

The second I hang up on Tytus, I start sprinting. The tripwire Rian just set off is far enough away from my base that I'll have some much-needed time to prepare, but only if I hurry.

Because I need to prepare. Everything needs to be just right. I'm about to come face to face with the lion again.

This time, though, there won't be anything between us. No crown. No cat. No hologram. No surprises—not for me, at least.

Just hate... and a raging desire that I might just use him to satisfy—whether he likes it or not.

Let the games fucking begin.

5
RIAN

Everything is quiet.

Too quiet.

Even the long dark forest that surrounds this crumbling gothic castle has stopped creaking and rustling. No birds chirp. No squirrels race up trees at the sight of me. I don't hear the babbling of a brook, or the distant sound of falling branches.

It's like I've entered a dead space.

I can't help but wonder if the place came like this, or if the Black Cat made it this way. Not that it matters. It's not going to be quiet for much longer.

Tightening my grip around the handle of my gun, I scan the overgrown lawn ahead. There must be more traps hidden in the weeds. The little tripwires I found set up around the perimeter were so easy to evade that I'm starting to worry this might not actually be the trap I'm hoping for.

Instead, I might just be in the wrong spot.

And that would be almost as embarrassing as losing my crown on my coronation day.

Fuck.

The flicker of rage that follows that thought reminds me

why I'm here. Gone are the days where I listen to my advisors; if I'm going to rule a kingdom, I'm going to have to listen to something stronger. Something far more ruthless.

My heart.

And my heart says hunt. It says capture. It says devour.

It's time to end this.

Reaching into my pocket, I shove aside my pulsing phone and pull out a black rubber ball. It only takes a little squeeze to activate the hardware inside, and when I throw it into the weeds at my feet, it shakes and rattles until a wave of nearly invisible red-light washes from its seams.

For as eager as I am to repay the Black Cat for what she's done to me, I'm equally as cautious. I will not be embarrassed again—even if I've already had enough time to second guess my rash decision.

No. Fuck that. You've made your choice. Follow through with it.

That inner voice gets louder as my little black ball picks up on a few tripwires hidden around the ancient property. With a quick whistle, I recall the device to my hand.

"Good job," I mumble, patting it like a pet before stuffing it back into my pocket.

Rozalia Dorn thinks she can outsmart me. She thinks she can lead me into a trap and dance over the bars of my cage. She thinks I'll let her do it.

She's going to learn what happens when you corner a lion.

Putting away the black ball, I take out my pulsing phone and double-check the signal it's tracking for me.

Sure enough, the black arrow on the screen points straight ahead, into the dark and dilapidated woodland castle.

"You better be here, kitten. And you better be ready."

It barely takes any effort to dance around the snares and tripwires. When I'm about halfway across the overgrown lawn, I spot the first security cameras. Two of them are fixed into the faded grey bricks of the old castle's west tower, while three more crawl up the side of the eastern wall.

To my delight, they aren't mobile. And I easily figure out how to crawl between their blind spots.

Before long before I'm at a dusty back door. The chipped wood and rusted metal hardly puts up a fight as I wedge my switchblade between the hinges and push.

With a deep groan, the door pops open, and I'm given my first look at the insides of my enemy's lair.

And what a fucking lair it is.

Shit. I don't know what I was expecting. Maybe a deceptively well-decorated interior, or at least a half-hazard attempt at comfort. Rozalia is a woman, after all, and all the women I know enjoy some level of luxury.

But the inside of the castle is the furthest thing from luxury.

It doesn't look like the Black Cat has put any work into making this place feel like a home. Instead, the place feels more like a museum.

It makes the hairs on the back of my neck stand up. My grip tightens around my gun.

With a sneer plastered on my lips, I move forward.

There's no going back. I've made my announcement. Delivered my intentions to an attentive empire. Bended the truth for my father and anyone else who trusts me. I've given in to my most primal desires and dropped everything to go hunting.

I *will* be dragging Rozalia back to my kingdom. There's no question about it. The only obstacle is catching the elusive Black Cat.

But my prey is somewhere nearby. I can literally smell her. It's how I'm certain this is the right place.

I knew that IP address wouldn't let me down—even if it was clearly left there on purpose.

That spicy rose-infused scent is baked into the walls. It's subtle, but not subtle enough to ignore.

Hell, she might as well be right in front of me again. My cock reacts, engorging until it's practically a third leg.

This time, I don't dismiss the feeling. Instead, I let it drive me forward.

You'll satisfy this hunger for me, kitten. And I'll make sure you do it in the most shameful way imaginable.

Stale water drips from the ceiling as I find a stone staircase. The walls seem to close in as I ascend them, but each step I take causes my vibrating phone to pulse harder.

It's locked on to a purposely subdued, but still strong digital signal. One that I found with the help of that hidden IP address. My best guess is that I'm headed toward the room where Rozalia keeps her security equipment.

If I can get there without being detected, then I can hack into the system and take control of it for myself. With that, I'll have eyes watching the insides of her little lair.

Hopefully, that means I'll be able to see her before she sees me. But even if she gets the first jump, I've brought a few surprises that not even the Black Cat can counteract.

Pushing my way out of the claustrophobic stone staircase, I come to a tight hallway. The stone walls are lined with dark moss and black cracks. My phone begins to beat like a pounding heart.

I'm close.

I let my thumping phone lead me to the end of the hall. There, a heavy door awaits. Taking a shallow breath, I press my ear against the peeling wood.

Through the dripping water and ringing silence, I can just make out a familiar buzz. The hum of technology.

I'm in the right place.

With one last check, I make sure my gun is locked and loaded. Then, without further ceremony, I kick down the door.

I'm not exactly sure what I was expecting, but somehow, it's exactly as I imagined.

The wall ahead is covered to the ceiling with screens, each filled with a different video feed. Just in front of that, silhouetted against the white, flickering lights, is a tattered red chair, fit for a long-dead king.

Its tall back reaches up into the darkness above. From behind, It's impossible to see if anyone's sitting in it, but I quickly find its reflection in the monitors.

Empty.

Perfect.

Keeping my gun primed, I turn around and carefully shut the door behind me. When the splintered wood clicks shut, the wall next to it rattles ever so slightly. That draws my attention to the empty bookshelf in the corner of the room.

That might be a good spot to set up some of my own equipment.

I'll get to that next.

First thing's first, though.

As a safety measure, I pull out my little black ball and place it at the foot of the door, so that its near invisible red light can monitor the hallway outside while I get to work.

I also reach into my back pocket and pull out a repurposed lip balm container. The waxy homemade solution sticks to my skin as I dab the tip of my index finger across the top.

"Now, all I have to do is find you."

Turning my attention back towards the flickering wall, I sit down on the ragged throne and begin my search for a hard drive.

It's not difficult to find, and I've already placed my flash drive into the USB port when I spot movement on one of the screens.

"What do we have here..."

Just above, on the fourth monitor down from the ceiling, something catches my eye.

Before I can make out exactly what it is, the image wobbles

and distorts. Then, everything slowly materializes back into focus.

That's when I see her.

The prey I came here to hunt.

Rozalia Dorn.

She wanders into the frame with her back to the camera, but I can immediately tell it's her. She's still in that tight black turtleneck from earlier. It hugs her curves like a fucking dream as she struts towards a bed.

A grunt leaks from my twisted lips. The adrenaline pumping through my veins involuntarily redirects to my cock.

And that's before she even starts to undress.

"Don't you dare," I grumble, shifting in my seat as the Black Cat slowly unfurls before me.

It only takes me wanting to get a better view to realize how grainy the footage actually is. In fact, every screen on the wall looks like it's being recorded on an outdated device—not that I care to look at any other screen. The entirety of my attention is fixated on one singular image.

Still, I find myself cursing the low quality of the video feed as I mindlessly lean forward.

I thought you could afford better than this, kitten.

"What are you doing?" I hear myself groan. It's like I can feel myself losing control in real-time. But there's nothing I can do to stop it.

With an elegant shrug of her long slender shoulders, Rozalia twirls out of her tight black top. The sight of her bare back makes me stiff. A bouquet of colorful tattoos fills up the pale, toned canvas. A single bleeding rose rides up her spine, flowering just under her nape.

My swollen cock twitches. I follow the dark green stem down her backside as she bends over and starts to pull down her leggings.

Just like that, the rhythm of my pounding switches beats.

The gun in my hand just barely dangles from my fingertips. My jaw has dropped. My tight pants strangle the thick beast growing beneath my beltline.

I should have jerked off before coming.

Fuck.

I'm transfixed.

But I only get a glimpse of Rozalia's lace panties before she pauses. It's like the air is sucked out of this damp room.

"Don't stop," I quietly order.

As if she can hear me, Rozalia glances over her shoulder. That fucking face. It makes my heart jump. And combined with the sight of her toned ass, I just can't control myself.

My gun dangles from my limp right hand as the fingers on my left move to free my throbbing cock. The subtle sound of my zipper unwinding cuts across the quiet room.

Ahead, on the grainy screen, Rozalia considers whether she should continue or not. To my delight, she decides to keep going.

"Good girl."

Those tight black leggings slip down her soft pale thighs until I can see every last inch of her.

Well, almost every last inch.

"Now the panties," I mindlessly whisper, completely lost to a primal lust.

My fingers squeeze around the base of my engorged shaft. A deep, addictive warmth washes up from below my waist.

I'm even more tempted to start stroking than I was in the shower.

I'm nearly about to give in when the Black Cat straightens back up. But that's all she does. For what seems like an eternity, she just stands there, staring at something just out of frame.

Then, without warning, she turns her head around. Just her head. Slowly, that sharp jawline comes back into the frame. So do those plump red lips and perfectly sculpted cheekbones.

Even through the grainy feed and warped coloring on the screen, those green eyes shine.

When they land on me, my jumping heart stops dead.

A cool breeze trickles along the backside of my neck.

"What are you looking at, kitten?" I whisper.

Forcing myself to lean even further forward, I meet the Black Cat's intensely capturing gaze.

It's only when I get close enough to the screen that I see the subtle smirk lifting the corners of her perfect lips.

She's smiling.

At me.

Fuck.

Does she know I'm here?

Before I can react, I feel the cold steel of a sharp blade press against my throat.

"Drop your gun, big boy."

The Black Cat's hot breath washes against the back of my ear as the warmth of her body suddenly engulfs me from behind.

"What the—"

"Ah ah ah," she taunts, cradling the bottom of my Adam's apple with her blade. "Let's not get excited—or, at least, let's not get any more excited than we already are, huh?"

I can feel those sharp green eyes stare down from over my shoulder. My hard cock rises out from my unzipped crotch like a girthy mast. It's unavoidable.

I've been caught with my pants down. Literally.

"If you're going to cut my throat, you better be quick about it," I growl, my hackles rising. "Because if you give me even an inch, I will—"

"You're not in any position to make threats," Rozalia interrupts. "Now, do as I say. Drop the gun. If you don't, I'll make all that blood in your cock spill from your throat."

Rage, lust, and shame batter against my insides as I realize I have no choice but to obey. With a vicious snarl, I let my fingers go limp. My gun clanks against the metal-sheeted floor below.

How the fuck did she get in here without my little black ball picking her up?

"I meant the other big useless thing you have wrapped between your fingers," Rozalia teases.

"Either one would destroy a fragile little thing like you," I snap back.

"Wouldn't you just love to destroy me?" I can hear the smirk lifting her juicy red lips. It's the same smirk still staring up at me from the now frozen security feed.

"It's a fucking recording," I grumble, coming to the realization far too late.

"Well, aren't you the boy genius everyone says you are."

"If I'm a boy, then you're nothing but a baby," I foolishly bite.

"Well, I'm definitely not a baby, am I? I guess I'll have to remind the authorities to try you as an adult when I bring you in for voyeurism."

"You better charge me with something a hell of a lot more serious, because if I ever get out of prison, you're dead."

"It's hard to take you seriously when you still have your hand wrapped around that tiny plaything of yours."

Even as she plays with me, I can hear the faintest gulp slither down Rozalia's throat. Her breathing is jittery.

The top of her hand brushes against the stubble on my jaw. Her warm skin makes my hard cock even harder.

"This tiny thing would tear you in half," I growl.

"I'd like to see you try."

In the blink of an eye, Rozalia pirouettes around the chair. Suddenly, she's straddling me, knife still pressed against the most tender part of my throat.

"What the fuck are you doing?" I bark as my knees dig into the soft flesh of her perfect ass.

"Oh, was that not an invitation?" she leers, her snatched waist framing my rigid cock.

The glowing screens silhouette her mouth-watering body as I struggle to control myself. I heard her loud and clear. One wrong move, and all the blood in my cock will come spilling out of my throat.

I don't doubt that someone like Rozalia Dorn would kill someone like me without hesitation. But what she'll actually do next is impossible to tell.

"What the fuck do you want?"

My question seems to intrigue her. The plumpest part of her ass sinks into my thighs as she subtly bites down on her lower lip.

That's enough of a hint for me to pick up on.

No fucking way.

"What are you willing to give me?" she asks, her voice filled with a faux innocence.

"A head start."

That draws a laugh from her pretty red lips.

"I'm not running anymore," she tells me, her blade pushing half an inch deeper into my throat. "But I'm not about to chase either."

"Then what are you going to do?" I ask, knowing full well what I want her to do.

My cock is ready to explode. It's been so fucking long since I let myself get this close to a woman. It doesn't matter that I'm not in this position by choice.

I want her.

I want her to rip off those black leggings and impale herself on my cock.

"I'll tell you exactly what I'm going to do. I'm going to take," Rozalia explains. Leaning in nice and close to my ear, she takes a soft breath.

My entire body twitches.

"You don't have the guts," I dare her.

"I'd rather feel you in mine."

I can't help the deep groan that rumbles up my captive throat when Rozalia bites down on my earlobe.

Then, her hips start to sway.

There's no room for shock in my lust-addled mind.

My throbbing cock spasms, and I can feel the pre-cum pooling out from the tip of my engorged head.

"Then do it already," I grunt.

Without thinking, I unwrap my fingers from around the base of my cock. Rozalia doesn't stop me, and I grab onto her leggings, right between the legs, unchallenged.

Then, I pull.

A high-pitched gasp escapes her throat as I rip the material to shred, creating a gaping pussy hole for me to fuck her through.

"You animal," she rasps.

Before I know what's happening, she's taken my cock in her free hand. The touch of her fingers is electrifying, but it doesn't compare to the heat of her soaking cunt as she presses me against her pussy lips.

"Is this what you came for?" she asks, each breath short and raspy. "Or did you just want to watch and jerk off from afar, you creep?"

"You're the one who recorded the video," I grumble.

"Just for you, my king."

King.

The reminder of what she's done cuts through me like a knife. But my lust is just as strong as my hate.

Rozalia doesn't stop me as I clamp both of my hands into her ass.

"I'm going to make you fucking pay for that," I growl.

Jerking her up and forward, I find her freshly exposed hole with my bulbous head. Then, I pound upwards.

The slick walls of her tight little cunt immediately wrap around my cock. Gritting my teeth, I push through the tension, slathering myself in her juices, doing my best to reach her guts.

"Fuck," we both gasp at the same time.

She feels fucking incredible. Mind-blowingly good. I only want more. I need more.

Fuck everything else.

All that matters is using her tight little body to make myself explode.

To Rozalia's credit, even as I pound her into oblivion, her blade doesn't budge from my neck. Not as she quietly gasps and whimpers. Not as she starts to sway her hips again. Not as her breathing becomes short and raspy.

She's here for this, just as much as I am.

"Make me pay harder," she chokes, confirming it all.

At that, I feel her free hand wraps around the back of my head. Her fingers curl into my hair. She holds on for dear life as I continue to jackhammer her tight little cunt with all my pent-up desire.

"I'm going to break you, kitten."

Shoving my hand under her black turtleneck, I grab a palm's worth of her impossibly soft, perky tit. Between my rough fingers, I can feel her hard nipples. I pinch down on them without mercy.

"Holy shit," she cries, her back arching as her neck snaps downwards.

Her black hair covers my eyes, blocking my vision. But I don't need to see to understand what's going on.

We've both lost our damn minds. And it's fucking ecstasy.

I can feel Rozalia's racing heart running wild behind her chest. I can feel each shallow, jittery breath she takes as my thrusting cock inches deeper and deeper into her guts. I can feel it when she decides it's not enough anymore.

Her swaying hips stop dancing and start battering back

down onto my cock. Every savage thrust is filled with infinite hate and endless desire.

The warmth of her cunt, the heat of her breath, and the cool danger of her sharp blade pressing against my throat makes me tense up.

The explosion starts somewhere deep in my core; all of this time, it's been building, lifting and falling like growing waves against a jagged cliff. But suddenly, the cliff crumbles, and the waves are unleashed.

"I'm going to cum," I growl.

"Oh, no you don't," Rozalia hisses. Digging her nails into the back of my skull, she tries to keep me in place. "Not before I do again."

"Again? You selfish bitch, you've already cum?"

"Shut up," she rasps. Steadying herself against me, she stops pounding her hips up and down and starts to thrust back and forth, bending my cock in a way that brings me even closer to the edge.

But for some reason, I try to hold out.

It doesn't take long before Rozalia's whimper-filled breathing crescendos. Her limbs tremble. Her tight cunt clenches around my thick cock.

She holds me there for a moment, then just like that, she goes limp.

"Fine. Now you can cum," she sighs, her entire body slouching.

At that, she lifts her hips in an attempt to escape my cock. But I don't let her go. Digging my fingers deep into her tit and ass, I haul her back down.

"You aren't going anywhere," I tell her. "Not until I'm done with you."

"You'll be fucking done, alright," she hisses, pressing the blade deeper into my throat… but not before turning it around, so I'm only choked by the dull side.

She doesn't want me to stop.

Rozalia Dorn wants me to fill her up, and I refuse to let her leave without a limp and a mark. She may have gotten the jump on me, but I'll fucking explode in her.

She'll be washing my cum out of her guts for the next week.

"Stay still," I demand.

Ignoring her blade, I unhand her tit and her ass, and instead wrap my arms around her tiny back. With an urgent desperation, I cage her against my body and start to thrash upwards.

There's no control in my movements. No grace. No calculation. My mind goes blank with a primal lust as I savagely search for the relief I've been starved of.

I find it deep in Rozalia's cunt.

Like a matchstick to a fire, her guts set me off. My throbbing cock erupts, and several months' worth of cum rockets into her cunt.

"Holy fucking hell," I shout into her chest, my words muffled by her heaving breasts.

I don't stop pounding her until there isn't a drop left in me. By the time I'm done, there's more cum in her than there is left in me.

"Shit..."

For a moment, neither of us move. We don't dare speak. The only sound is the heavy panting of two exhausted animals. It echoes around this damp, dark room like a hypnotic beat.

Then, I hear Rozalia mumble something I can't quite make out. With one last hard push against my throat, she tries to climb off me.

I don't let her.

"Un-fucking-believable," she hisses, turning her blade back around so I can feel the sharp side again.

But her disgust only affords me a moment of clarity.

What the hell did we just do?

Before I can consider that travesty, though, I remember what I have smeared against the tip of my index finger.

I needed to get this close to her. But fuck if I knew it was going to happen like this.

"You know you like it," I growl, shoving a cupped hand beneath her exposed pussy.

She sighs, momentarily closing her eyes.

Perfect.

My index finger finds her dripping clit, and I'm able to spread just enough of the waxy coating through her soaking lips before she slices a warning across my throat.

"We're done!" she croaks.

I don't test her any further. Letting my hands drop, I hardly move as she pushes herself off me.

Blood trickles down my throat. I've been cut enough times to know it's nothing serious. But I still stare at her like she just tried to cut my head off.

"What are you looking at?" she sneers. Even silhouetted against the glowing lights of the flickering monitors behind her, it's clear that Rozalia's pale cheeks are flushed with a subtle pink shade.

She's flustered.

Well, so am fucking I.

"I wonder what the authorities would take more seriously," I recall, watching as Rozalia looks down at her crotchless leggings in semi-disbelief. I can already see my cum leaking down the inside of her thighs. "A peeping tom or a rapist?"

"You weren't raped, you pig," Rozalia spits. Bending down, she picks up my gun and points it at my head.

I bite my tongue. But I can only do that for so long.

"Did you hear me consent?"

"I heard your cock fucking squeal for more."

"I'm not sure the authorities will buy that."

With a deep snarl, Rozalia pulls her new gun away from my head... and aims it down towards my softening cock.

"We both know there are no authorities in our world." Leaning down until her lips nearly touch my ear, she pauses for a second. "There is only power. And right now, I hold all the power."

"You won't use it," I call her bluff.

Shoving the barrel into my crotch, Rozalia makes sure I understand how real her threat is. "Want to dare me?"

"I'd rather keep my dick."

"There's the boy genius."

Pressing her nose against my temple, Rozalia makes sure I feel the electricity in her lips as she grazes them against my ear. I remember the feeling of her teeth digging into my flesh. A warm shiver runs down my spine. Then, I feel her finger tap my temple, replacing her nose as she slowly lifts my gun back to her side.

"So, what now?" I ask.

Her footsteps are almost entirely silent, but I can still hear them subtly fade as she slowly starts to back away.

"Now you leave me the fuck alone."

"You know I can't do that."

"Then I guess you'll have to keep chasing me."

I don't even bother turning around to watch her go. I know she's still pointing that gun at me, and I'm sure she won't hesitate to use it, no matter what weirdly intimate shit we just shared.

Instead, I look up at the monitor she used to trick me. The one with the recording of her undressing. It's gone black. In the screen, I can see the reflection of what's going on behind me.

Rozalia is almost entirely invisible. Her stupidly beautiful face floats like a porcelain mask in a pocket of darkness by the far corner of the room.

A stone drops in my gut.

Because that's when I realize how she got in without being

detected by my little black security ball.

There's a fucking hidden doorway behind the bookshelf.

Why the hell didn't I check for a fucking hidden doorway?

You're getting sloppy, Rian. And stupid.

All I can do is stew in my self-loathing and watch as Rozalia takes one last long look at me. Our eyes meet. I spot a familiar confusion in her emerald green gaze. It's the same conflict raging inside of me.

We both enjoyed that way too much.

I'm not even worried about the fact that I came in her. There's no chance a woman like Rozalia isn't on some type of contraceptive.

"You better not get pregnant," I sneer anyway.

"As if I'd ever let that happen," she hisses back.

Then, just like that, she's gone, her pretty porcelain face engulfed by the darkness. The hidden door is pulled shut. The bookshelf clicks back into place.

It's like she was never even here.

But I can still smell her.

Fucking hell.

My first instinct is to shove my cock back into my pants. But it's not entirely soft yet, and the memory of what just happened is already making me hard again.

But there's no point in staying here to jerk off. And there's no use in going after her. This is Rozalia's domain. I'll just get lost in the maze.

And I refuse to get lost again.

The next time we see each other, it will be on my turf and on my terms.

Lifting my hand to my face, I look at my glistening finger. Most of the wax has been rubbed off.

Good.

That means it's all on Rozalia.

I've marked her. Now, there's no fucking escape.

It may have cost me my dignity, but I've finally trapped the Black Cat.

Let's see how she likes being toyed with.

I won't be so gentle.

6

ROZALIA

No matter how hot the water gets, his stench still clings to me.
Rian Kilpatrick.
Me.
We fucked like animals.
And it was amazing.
The hate he pounded me with sent shockwaves through my body. The way he forced me to take every last inch of his huge cock made me cum harder than I ever have before. Not once. Not even twice. But three fucking times.
What the hell was I thinking?
Steam swirls around me as I slam a fist against the porcelain wall.
That was stupid. So fucking stupid and naïve and dangerous. I should have killed him—and as long as I did, it wouldn't have mattered if I'd done it before or after I used that cock to satisfy my reckless hormonal urges.
But I chickened out, flustered by my own conflicted satisfaction. Now, the lion is still alive, and I can't stop thinking about how I want more.
I need more.

I need him.

Chasing me. Fucking me.

Devouring me.

Stop!

With a brutal yank, I nearly tear the shower faucet out of the wall. The water is so hot I can feel my organs cooking. Yet not a single ounce of dirt seems to wash down my tainted skin.

I'm filthy. And I'm covered in *him*.

Fresh earth and burning wood.

The stench haunts me like a fucking ghost.

Hell, even back in the castle, when I hid behind the bookshelf, listening to the lion order around my recording from his shabby throne, I could smell him. How? I don't fucking know.

Before he'd arrived, I'd sprayed enough of my perfume around the fake security room to disguise my eventual approach.

He wouldn't be able to smell me coming. And he didn't. But all that time I was waiting, I could smell him. I could crave him.

His fragrance seeped through my perfume, through the thick brick walls, behind my skin. Now, I'm worried I might never be able to get rid of it.

"Fuck this," I curse out loud.

Slapping at the faucet again, I turn off the shower and storm out into the bathroom.

The chilled tiles hardly do anything to wake me up. Half of my mind is still lost in a hazy dream state of lust and hate. The other half is full of self-loathing.

My thighs clench as I remember how good that thick girthy cock felt writhing up into my cunt. How it felt like Rian might actually puncture my guts and disembowel me right then and there.

He hates me so fucking much. But I've never been with someone who wanted me as badly as he did. Even as he fucked my brains out, and I pounded back down onto his swollen shaft, I could sense the difference. I've been fucked before, but never like that.

The specialness clashed with the hate in an addictive cocktail.

I might as well be fucking drunk.

Or, worse, hungover.

My skull gently throbs as I roughly dry myself off with a towel and wash my hands in cold water—anything to keep them from wandering back below my waist.

Anything to keep myself from falling back into that wild trance.

Fuck.

Rian Kilpatrick saw me at my most vulnerable.

My enemy. My hunter. My prey.

He saw how I cum. And then he saw how flustered I was that I had cum.

There was no other option. I couldn't kill him. All I could do was get the fuck out of there and drag whatever was left of my dignity behind me.

But even as I clicked the bookshelf door shut and raced down the cold dark steps, I couldn't shake his heat.

Rian's scent followed me. His cum trailed down the inside of my thighs. I couldn't help myself. I reached down and scooped some up with my finger.

I tasted him.

And he was fucking delicious.

"Stupid fucking hormones," I grumble to myself.

Raging back into my bedroom, I find the new outfit I had ripped out of my closet when I got home. The turtleneck and legging I had worn earlier are already nothing more than a pile of ashes. I set that shit on fire as soon as I had the chance.

He. Tore. A pussy hole in my leggings.

My toes curl. A heavy pressure threatens to take hold of my core. My hand wanders down my flat stomach.

I can't help but wonder if I could still taste his cum on my cunt...

No!

My other hand slaps away the treacherous one. I drape myself in heavy cloth.

Rian Kilpatrick isn't just some good fuck you can lead around on a wild goose chase. He cursed you to a fate worse than death or abstinence.

He wants to marry you.

The reminder is well served. A sneer twists my face as I force away any thoughts of enjoyment or pleasure.

Then, my bedside drawer rattles, and my attention is turned further from my shame. My phone is ringing. I quickly grab it, desperate for a distraction. But when I recognize the number, I decide I'd rather be alone.

I'm in no mood for Tytus' banter. I'll find out how his little meeting went later.

I need to get some food in me.

Stomach rumbling, I push my way downstairs and towards my kitchen. I already know my fridge is nearly empty, but when I open it up, I'm met by a nice little surprise.

I'd forgotten about Babcia's cabbage rolls.

God bless that woman.

Ripping them out of the fridge, I start to gorge. But even as I satisfy one hunger, another remains stubbornly in place.

Rian fucking Kilpatrick.

How does he seem to know all of my weak spots?

My heart wilts as the obvious answer presents itself.

Gabriel.

My other adoptive brother.

The traitor.

He fell in love with Rian's cousin. He abandoned us to join Rian's empire. He started a new family with the Kilpatricks.

A family I may have threatened... but only because he destroyed mine by leaving it.

You don't have a family! A cruel inner voice reminds me. *Not even Tytus. He's not your real brother. There's no blood relation. Babcia isn't your grandmother. Drago wasn't your real father. In the end, everyone will leave you, and you'll be all alone.*

Good.

That's what I want.

Long ago, I swore an oath to myself. Never again would I be used by the wicked and the powerful. Not if I had anything to say about it.

And it turns out, I have a lot of fucking say about it.

I don't have to be a damsel or a pawn or a captive or a bride.

I can just be me.

But it took a lot of suffering to figure that shit out.

Hell, it's one of the only good things to come from my relationship with my adoptive father. Dragomir Raclaw. If he taught me anything, it was how to just be me. He showed me how to survive without the help of others.

And then he taught me never to trust anyone either.

Not even him.

Another *traitor*.

Babcia's cabbage rolls are almost completely gone when my phone starts buzzing again. A full stomach helps clear my hazy mind. Even my frustrating horniness is finally beginning to fade as I give in and answer Tytus' call.

"Are you alright?"

"Why wouldn't I be?" I huff.

"You usually don't ignore my calls."

"Who said I was ignoring your calls?"

"Well, if you weren't ignoring my calls, then that must mean you were busy with Rian Kilpatrick. I didn't expect it to take so long. Does this mean he gave more trouble than you were expecting?"

Just like that, my full stomach seems to empty, and a gaping hole appears in its place. A hole that only a lion's cock can fill.

How dare he remind me of that fucker.

"Hardly," I snap. "I made quick work of him."

Lies.

"He's dead?" Tytus asks, full of skepticism.

"No," I angrily admit. "But I wasn't planning on killing him right away anyway."

"And why was that again?"

"Because I haven't had my fun yet."

"Ah yes... you maniac," Tytus chuckles. "Well, don't have too much fun. Our new associate wants Rian Kilpatrick dead just as badly as I do."

"You met with him already?" I ask, suddenly wondering how long I was actually in the shower.

"Just a quick phone call while I waited for you to finish your thing."

"You didn't have to wait for me."

"I don't have to do anything. But I told you I'd be waiting around in case you needed help. So that's what I did. Now that you're safe, I can proceed with the real meeting."

"When and where?" I ask. Without food to distract me, I can feel my mind already begging to wander back to what happened earlier.

"You want to come?" Tytus sounds surprised. "I didn't think these kinds of meetings interested you."

"They don't, but I have nothing else to do."

"Shouldn't you be preparing for your next encounter with that Irish plush toy of yours?"

The hole in my stomach spreads to my chest as I consider Tytus' question.

"No," I respond, shaking my head. "He's not worth my time."

That's only half a lie. The truth is, a part of me is disappointed with how easy it's been to get the upper hand on the notorious Rian Kilpatrick. So far, he's barely even put up a fight. I was expecting more.

Hell, maybe that's why I let him live—because of the hope that he might regroup and provide a better challenge.

Or maybe I'm just a horny, hormonal bitch who doesn't know what she wants right now.

Oh, you know exactly what you want.

Food and cock.

"It's probably better to be safe than sorry, you don't think?" Tytus urges. But he and I have always been different in that regard. Tytus is a chess player. Always planning two or three moves ahead. It's why he set up this meeting with a potential new ally.

I, on the other hand, like to improvise. My traps spring on me just like they spring on my victims. Instantaneously. Once I have the idea, I get to work. Then, I wait for the bell to ring, and I pounce.

"I'll come up with some other lure for the lion later," I insist. "Tell me where and when *our* meeting is."

Tytus sighs.

"Alright, I'll send you the coordinates. Don't be late."

"I bet I'll get there before you."

Before he can argue, I hang up.

Then, I get busy.

There's no point in sitting around thinking about Rian Kilpatrick—not about how to lure him into another trap; what I'll do to him once he's captured; how his cum nearly ruptured my diaphragm; how his stiff cock felt in my tight cunt, how I'm already desperate for more…

Fuck off.

Tossing my phone onto the mattress, I storm over to the closet and try to busy my mind with another task.

What will I wear to this meeting?

Not another fucking black turtleneck, that's for sure. I don't need to blend into the darkness. Instead, I need something that will draw the eye of our potential partner.

Leander Onasis.

A few weeks ago, Tytus sent me a write-up on the guy. I quickly followed it up with some research of my own.

As far as I can tell, he's a typical trust fund kid playing with family money. Other than that, one thing quickly became abundantly clear. The thirty-two-year-old billionaire is a veracious playboy. He owns more clubs than most people have fingers and toes.

But I guess that wasn't enough.

The brat must have gotten bored with his luxurious lifestyle. Now, he wants to dip his feet into more dangerous waters.

Apparently, his family used to have mob ties.

He wants to rekindle them.

We've promised to help.

On one condition.

My phone buzzes loudly from back on my mattress as I shuffle through my closet.

Which one of these outfits will help me wrap a Greek billionaire around my little finger? Something flirty? Something dangerous?

When my eyes fall on a copper mini silk slip dress, I realize that my best bet is probably to go with something that has a little bit of both.

The skimpy dress is easy enough to get into, and when I check my reflection in the closet's body mirror, a single unwelcome question flashes across my mind.

Is this dress skimpy enough to make a lion jealous?

The answer is a resounding yes.

Even if Rian never knows what I wore and who I met, I find myself desperate to do something I'm sure he would disapprove of.

The Irish king seems like the possessive type, after all.

In my mind, this will be another small victory. A way to erase the vulnerability he pounded into me earlier. A way to claim back some agency, even if I already feel like I'm in complete control.

Fuck. This asshole has me chasing my own tail.

No. Don't give him the credit. It's the hormones.

With a shake of my head, I try to rid myself of the man. I'll get back to our lust-infused game of cat and mouse shortly. But I need a break from those maddening blue eyes. A reprieve from that massive cock and those strong rough hands.

But there's no fooling myself, and even as I strut back to my phone and take note of the coordinates Tytus' has just sent, I know there's no forgetting Rian Kilpatrick.

His fucking scent still clings to me.

The best I can do is use my body as it was meant to be used.

To get what I want.

Power.

"What the hell is that?"

Tytus seems unimpressed by my reaction. Retracting his phone, he pinches the screen, zooming in before shoving it back in my face.

"How's that?"

"I'm still not sure what I'm looking at," I grumble.

"It's a painting, dummy."

"I know it's a fucking painting," I snap.

As if I'm not already on edge enough. Between my wild hormones, my shameful encounter with our fiercest enemy, and my completely inappropriate choice of dress, I'm in no mood for Tytus' shit.

Old men have been staring at me since I walked in here. I have a deep desire to kill them all.

But Tytus doesn't give up.

"What do you think of it? Gorgeous, right?"

"It just looks like it's a bunch of lines," I mumble, crossing my arms. I want to cross my legs too, but then I'd be flashing half the restaurant.

That's exactly what they want.

Pigs.

Fuck. What the hell was I thinking, wearing this skimpy shit? I'm practically a sitting duck. If a fight breaks out, I won't be able to do anything without showing the world my lace panties.

Fumes blow from my ears as I sink down into my cushioned seat, furious that my little hormonal plan to make an unaware Rian Kilpatrick jealous has already backfired.

Idiot.

And, by the way, no fight is going to break out, dummy. This isn't that kind of meeting. Look at this fucking place. It might as well be a ballroom!

"Those aren't lines," Tytus corrects me. "They're brush strokes. Masterfully placed."

"Who cares," I huff, scanning the crowd for any signs of potential trouble. But my stupid brain is right. The only criminals here are white-colored ones. No fight is coming. Even if I already want to smack our potential ally for being late.

"People with taste care about artwork this good," Tytus beams.

"As if you have any taste."

"How do I survive with the company I keep?" Tytus smiles, shaking his head. Pulling the phone back from my face, he admires the photo a little bit longer. "Maybe I should just kidnap the Kilpatrick princess, so I can have someone who really appreciates great art."

That spikes my fucking interest.

"What the hell does Rian's little sister have to do with anything?" I say, sitting back up straight.

"This is an original Melina Kilpatrick," Tytus grins, tapping a thick finger down onto his phone screen. "And now it's mine."

"You stole a painting from the coronation?" I ask, flabbergasted.

"It was heavy, but I managed."

"Why?"

"Because it struck me."

"Well, you strike me as stupid."

"Says the woman who wore a dress she can't fight in."

"Watch me kick your ass."

"I'm sure our dinner guests will enjoy the show."

"Bastard."

But Tytus is already off me and back onto his phone.

"Look at that use of color," he mumbles. "Exquisite. Genius, really…"

"Can you focus?"

"No," Tytus chuckles. "Believe me, I'm trying very hard not to take our new friend's tardiness as a sign of deep disrespect. The painting is the only thing keeping me calm…"

"We should leave," I say, staring out over the dining hall.

Glistening gold chandeliers hang from high vaulted ceilings. Everything is covered in white silk and cloth. The people here look like they either just came from a board meeting or a boat house.

It sends a chill skating up my spine.

I don't belong in a place like this. Even with all of the money I've come into, this type of company feels far too foreign. Too cold.

This is not home.

"We'll give him ten more minutes," Tytus shrugs.

"Waiting is a sign of weakness."

"It's a sign of patience and security. We don't have anything to prove to this man."

"Then why wait for him?"

"Because we need what he has—especially after what happened to our army. We need—"

"Shush," I hiss, furrowing my brows. "Don't talk about that. Not in public."

Tytus may be a tactical genius and a master at rigging all sorts of physical traps, but he's never fully understood technology, not like I do.

Listening devices, bugs, wiretaps, they hardly concern him. So, It's up to me to watch out enough for the both of us. And that includes reminding him to shut up when he wants to start talking about a sensitive subject, especially when we're out in public.

Anyone could be listening.

"Fine," Tytus shrugs. "But—"

This time he interrupts himself.

We both feel the same thing at the same time. Our attention snaps towards the front door of the fancy restaurant.

"That's him," I mumble, spotting the tardy billionaire. "Finally."

"Our newest ally has finally arrived," Tytus confirms.

"He'll only be our newest ally if I don't kill him first."

Putting his phone away, Tytus stands up and nods toward our approaching guest.

"Trust me, Roz. We'll get more out of him than he could ever dream of getting out of us. I've plotted everything out to a tee. Just behave for a bit, alright?"

"We'll see," I complain. Still, I stand up beside him, lowering my dress a tad at the sight of what's coming.

Leander Onasis is easy to spot through the crowd of old men and women. And it's not just because he's joined by a half-dozen bodyguards.

His impeccable beige-colored suit floats through a sea of black and white. His smooth olive skin, tanned golden, contrasts the wrinkled gazes that have been leering at me. His understated jewelry glimmers beneath the chandeliers.

I can see the blue of his eyes before he's even halfway across the room. His beard is well manicured. His hair looks like it was cut five minutes ago.

He is absolutely not my type.

If he had been on time, then maybe I'd have tried to hide my disdain for a bit. But the bastard is late. And I'm sick of all these old men staring at me like I'm the reason for their next divorce.

I give one particularly bold pensioner a look of pure death before turning my frustration back on the approaching billionaire.

"So sorry I'm late," Leander offers when he arrives at our table.

His bejeweled hand reaches out in greeting. Tytus takes it. I only look at the jewels he's carrying.

The old street rat in me wonders how much I could sell those puppies for. They'd definitely be easy pickings.

"Bad traffic?" Tytus asks, gesturing for Leander to sit down across from us.

"Bad business," he replies, looking over at me. I provide a curt nod in response. Nothing more. "Had to ax a few of my subsidiaries this morning. They weren't performing as well as I had hoped."

"Let's hope we never have to say the same about our partnership," Tytus says.

"Yeah, let's hope," I finally join in, my words laced with venom.

But my attitude only makes Leander smile. Those greedy blue eyes slowly crawl over my body before jumping back to my face.

"I've heard a lot about you, Ms. Dorn," Leander says, reaching his hand out to me.

"Sit down," I respond, taking a seat to show him how it's done. "You're late."

"My apologies," Leander nods, retracting his hand. Looking back over his shoulder, he gives another short nod. His security team quickly disperses into the background. "You two must know how much work it takes to run an empire."

"That's why we like to get our work done on time," Tytus explains, subtly jumping to my defense. "It saves a lot of pain."

He's better at being passive-aggressive.

"Of course. It won't happen again. Perhaps a gift will excuse my tardiness." Lifting a hand to his ear, Leander motions for someone to approach.

From over his shoulder, I see one of his beefy security guards take the cue.

I immediately tense up.

"No surprises," I warn our guest.

"Not even pleasant ones?" he smirks in response.

Before I can answer, a strange sensation pulses up from between my legs. A flash vibration that seems to be coming from somewhere deep inside of me.

It's completely unexpected... as is the strange warmth that follows it.

"Is everything alright, Roz?" Tytus asks.

The shock must be evident on my face, because both men at my table are glaring at me.

"I'm fine," I assure him, trying to keep my brows from furrowing.

What the fuck was that?

"Shall we continue?" Leander asks, his gaze dropping back down my body.

I'm mid-way through a sneer when the strange sensation

returns. This time, though, it's not just a flash. A full breath goes by as something rattles between my legs.

An unexpected gasp rips up my throat.

It feels so... good. In the weirdest fucking way.

But it's definitely not worth the looks I'm getting. And I have to bite down on my tongue to keep myself from jumping off my seat.

Leander gives me a curious look, until his bodyguard taps him on the shoulder, and his attention is ripped away. He turns his ear to the man, who hands him a manilla envelope. The two exchange a whispered conversation as Tytus leans over to me.

"What the hell is going on?" he quietly asks.

"I don't know," I hiss under my breath. "Where the hell is my phone?"

Looking down, I subtly spread my legs, half expecting to see my phone down there. But I already know I didn't bring it with me. All I have is my earpiece. And while it will occasionally vibrate, that only happens in my fucking ear.

"I'm pretty sure you didn't bring your phone with you," Tytus confirms. "Want to take a step outside? I can handle this."

"No," I stubbornly insist, still trying to figure out what the hell is happening. "I'll—"

Once again, I'm interrupted by the strangest fucking sensation.

This time, the vibrating is so intense that I can't help but jump up onto my feet. But the vibrating doesn't stop when I'm standing. In fact, that only makes it worse.

My thighs clench, and my stomach flexes. Whatever this is, it almost feels like it's coming from inside of me.

"Excuse me," I mutter. Shuffling out from behind the table, I try to make a swift exit, but the vibrating is too intense.

Each step requires a very concentrated effort, especially as the vibrations start to cause a warm tingle to wash up from between my legs.

"Is everything alright?" Leander asks.

I hear him stand up from his chair.

I turn my back from the table.

Then, I feel Tytus' hands on my shoulders.

"What's wrong?" he asks, concern bubbling through his voice.

"Nothing. I'll figure it out," I whisper. "Finish the meeting. I'll call you if I need any help."

My breathing deepens. To my horror, the vibrations seem to open up a familiar pressure in my core. My hands clasp together.

"Are you sure?"

"Yes!" I gasp, louder than I wanted to.

My eyelids flutter as I realize what's happening.

I'm having a fucking orgasm.

But how?

Why?

It doesn't matter. I feel Tytus' hands on my shoulder. My adoptive brother is the last person I want to be touching me while I cum. Slamming my eyes shut, I shake his hands from me and start to run for the back entrance.

I can feel all the old judging eyes following me. I can sense Tytus' concern and Leander's confusion. It's embarrassing, and by the time I burst outside, not even the cool alley air can calm the shameful heat burning through my cheeks.

"What the fuck is wrong with me?" I sputter, my knees clanking together as another warm, ecstatic wave washes through me.

"You're such a naughty girl."

Rian's voice cuts through my hazy confusion like a scythe. Immediately, I reach for my gun. Even through my confusion, it easily comes out of its hidden upper thigh holster.

But when I force my eyes open and point my gun, all I see is a dirty alley wall.

My back furls as I desperately try to find the source of that fucking voice. But there's nothing. And the vibrations haven't stopped. My heart is thumping like a drum. My pussy is already soaking wet.

It feels like some invisible machine is playing with my clit.

"Show yourself, you fucking coward!" I pant, trying not to pass out.

"Or what?" The familiar voice teases.

I can't tell if I'm imagining it or not. Rian's voice sounds like it's coming from directly in front of me. But he's not there.

Until he is.

The holographic image takes a second to form, but when it does, there's no doubting who it is.

Even through the orgasmic haze building inside of me, I can make out those ocean blue eyes.

Fuck. They're so much more striking against Rian's pale skin than they were against Leander's over-tanned hide.

"Whatever you're doing, stop it!" I beg, my voice crackling.

"What's the magic word?"

"Stop fucking playing with me," I demand, pointing my gun at him. But we both know it's pointless. Even if he was actually there, my grip is too shaky to aim properly.

"Doesn't feel too good, does it?" he taunts. "To be used."

"No. That's the fucking problem," I hiss. "It feels fucking amazing."

An ear-rupturing orgasm is building inside of me. But before it can reach its peak, the vibrating stops.

I fall to my knees, scraping my skin against the hard pavement below.

"That's all I wanted to hear," Rian says, his voice crackling against some distant static. Wherever he actually is, it's far away from here. "Payback's a bitch, isn't it?"

"You're a bitch," I spit, head hanging as I try to gather my breath. But shots of warmth still spasm through my body.

"Who's acting childish now?"

"What. Did. You. Do. To me?" I heave.

The cold steel of my gun handle feels so heavy against my trembling fingers.

"I marked you," Rian explains. "But only because you let me."

Forcing my neck to straighten out, I look up at the cheap rip-off hologram fluttering before me.

"You did a shit job of copying my technology," I spit.

Rian smiles.

Are those fucking dimples?

"Not bad for a few hours' work," he shrugs. "But that's not even the best part. I—"

"How did you find me?" I interrupt. "I know for a fact that I covered my tracks."

"You sure did," Rian nods. "Under normal circumstances, finding you would have been a real challenge. But I couldn't let my bride run too far from me. How would it look if you were late to our wedding?"

"I swear to fucking god." Rational thought momentarily leaves my mind as I lift my gun and fire three quick shots at the hologram.

The bullets ricochet off the alley wall.

My ears start to ring.

"Easy there, cowgirl," Rian chuckles. "You're not in any state to run from the cops."

"You better tell me what you've done to me," I demand, internally begging he doesn't start the vibrating again.

"I already told you. I marked you."

"With what?"

"With a failed project."

Rian is smiling again. Those blood-red lips curl up in the corners, revealing the subtlest dimples. How did I never notice those before? I've stalked him closely enough that I should have already known.

But here I am, playing catch up.

Now, he's in the driver's seat.

"I bet you have a lot of failed projects," I snip.

"Only a few of which are ever true failures. Take this tracking device, for example," he says, pointing down between my legs. "A soluble wax-filled nanotechnology that can dissolve into any liquid—whether that be water, booze, tears, cum..."

The revelation hits me like a mack truck.

"You put a fucking tracker in my pussy?"

"No," Rian shakes his head. "I only just glazed your clit with it. An untraceable coating that's seeped into your very flesh. The problem is, I've never had the time to perfect the concoction. At certain frequencies, the minerals inside start to vibrate. Knowing that, I can make them pulse at whatever rate I like... or whatever speed you'd enjoy the most."

Suddenly, I feel a soft buzz return between my legs. My heart jumps in a panicked response, and I scramble onto my ass in a futile attempt to push myself away from the devilish image.

"You asshole," I grumble, terrified at how vulnerable I am right now—yet oddly impressed with his ingenuity.

... And somehow strangely aroused.

"You aren't the only genius in the underworld," Rian replies. "And you definitely aren't the only monster."

"What the hell do you want?" I ask, feeling the hard brick of the alley wall hit my back. There's nowhere to go. I'm trapped.

Fuck.

"I want my crown back," Rian states. "Oh, and apparently, your brother took one of my sister's paintings. I'd like that back, as well."

Fucking Tytus.

"And if I refuse?"

"The consequences won't be so bad," Rian smirks. "Just a lifetime of this."

The soft buzzing between my legs begins to amplify. The pressure in my core swirls as I reach down to my pussy in a pointless attempt to stop the orgasmic torture.

"Stop!" I plead, my voice frustratingly shaky.

"As you wish."

To my surprise, the vibrating stops. I'm given a second to breathe.

"I'll get your sister's painting," I relent. "And I'll tell you where to pick it up. But only if you tell me how to get rid of this stupid fucking torture device."

But Rian isn't done playing with me yet.

"Well, either I can provide you with the recipe and the ingredients to safely dissolve the nanobots, or I can give you that solution myself when I pick up the painting AND my crown."

A strange desperation kicks up inside of me at the thought of giving everything back so quickly.

I worked so hard to have him chase me.

Could I really throw it away before I truly get what I want from him?

"Even if you don't provide the recipe, I'm sure I can figure it out myself," I promise.

"I don't doubt you could," Rian bites. "But even if it only took you a few hours to figure out the recipe, it would still take a week to mix it all together properly."

"I'd do it in three days."

"Oh, but what a long three days those would be."

With that, the vibrating starts again. My toes curl so sharply I start to get cramps in the soles of my feet. But that doesn't stop the pressure in my core. It builds and crackles and whirls as my thighs clench and my fingers spread, and jagged breaths rip from my throat.

It feels so good I could cry.

Fuck. I haven't felt this helpless in so long.

It's awful... and dangerously addicting.

"Fine," I whimper. "I'll bring both."

My voice is so shattered that I don't think the cruel lion can even hear me.

Yet, to my surprise, the vibrations slowly ease. By the time they stop, my body is shaking enough to pick up the slack.

Warm shivers take hold of me. All I can do is stare at the ground, hair covering my face, and breathe.

"Good girl," Rian says. I want to grab a fistful of rocks and throw it at him, but I'm too weak. "Now, pick yourself up and go back inside. You deserve a nice dinner. On me."

Before I can spit at him, the metal door I burst out of earlier is flung open.

"Roz!"

Tytus covers me with his massive body, and I collapse into him as I try to make sense of what just happened.

"Do you see him?" I croak.

He helps me to my feet, and when I finally pick my head back up, I see what I already suspected.

Nothing.

Rian's rip-off hologram is long gone.

"See who?" Tytus asks, looking around.

"Never mind," I whisper. Shockwaves of warmth still tremble through my body, but I try my best to breathe them away.

"I'm going to call a doctor," Tytus says.

I grab his wrist before he can grab his phone.

"No. I'm fine. It's just woman problems."

"This doesn't look like any woman problem I've ever seen."

"That's because you're a guy," I remind him. "I just had some bad cramps. Let's get back inside."

"Are you sure?" Tytus asks, propping me up with his shoulder. "Leander brought us some pretty big news. I don't know if you're in any kind of shape to handle it."

"Big news?"

Hating the weakness that has taken hold of me, I snort out a strong breath.

What could a man like Leander possibly bring us that we don't already know or have?

"Yeah, he said he was thinking of holding onto it until we were officially partners, but he wanted to make up for being late. So he's giving it to us now."

"Giving us what?"

For a moment, Tytus just pauses. His big silver-blue eyes look deep into mine, trying to decipher what the real problem is. But I'm an expert at hiding my true feelings.

He doesn't get the truth.

"Tell me," I demand.

Tytus gives in.

"It's our dear old adoptive Dad," he sighs. "Roz. Drago is back. And Leander says he can take us directly to him."

7

RIAN

The video loop starts again, and I sink deeper into my chair.

My fingers are already wrapped around my swollen shaft. But I don't stroke. Hell, I hardly need to do anything.

The satisfaction pours out of me.

Up on my laptop screen is possibly the best video I've ever recorded. The quality is clear. The cinematography is stellar. The subject is perfect.

In full 4k, I watch Rozalia Dorn crumble to the alley floor for the seventh time in the last hour.

Her entire body trembles, and my cock can feel each subtle movement. It's like she's back on my lap, thrusting up and down.

Still, this is somehow better. This time, I'm in complete control. And we both know it.

In a way, It's almost uncomfortable.

Almost.

I never thought I'd see Rozalia so close to breaking. Fuck. I'm shocked she didn't. Usually, when someone is pushed to the edge, they jump. Either that, or they go limp and fall.

But even as the Black Cat begged for freedom, she never gave up.

I may not have physically been in front of her, but it felt like I could sense her determination.

It was perfect.

She was perfect.

I wanted her to struggle. And she gave me exactly what I wanted.

"One more time, kitten," I grumble.

Tightening my fingers, I strangle my cock until it's red and angry. Pre-cum leaks from my bulbous head. The video loops around to the start, back to when she first burst out into the alleyway.

I couldn't have planned it any better.

Sure, my hologram was rudimentary compared to hers. But my setup was not. A million-dollar drone hovered two hundred feet above that stuffy restaurant, undetectable to the naked eye. It projected my image down into the alley like a dream, all while recording every last second of the delicious encounter.

Before that, I used the drone's thermal imaging to watch as Rozalia and Tytus waited for their guest to arrive.

The identity of that guest is still a mystery to me—no name was ever mentioned—but I can't imagine it will take long to figure it out.

The fucker waltzed into that high-end restaurant like he owned the place, and with a dozen bodyguards in tow too. I can't imagine he's exactly discreet.

I've already put Maksim on the task. My consigliere needed something to do while he took a break from his other mission.

I could have helped. But I'm busy.

Up on my screen, Rozalia falls to the alley floor again. Her tight little dress rides up her perfectly toned thighs, exposing her hidden holster.

My cock twitches.

"Who did you dress up for?" I wonder out loud.

To my chagrin, a pang of jealousy appears deep in my chest. It's the same pang of jealousy I felt when I first saw what she was wearing to her little meeting.

It's an outfit made to seduce.

My grip tightens around the base of my throbbing cock.

"You forget who you belong to…"

I'm going to find the man she dressed up all pretty for, and I'll make her watch as I show her what happens when she ignores me for someone else.

Cracking my neck, I feel my gaze drift over to the remote I have sitting beside my laptop.

How many times have I made her cum so far? Three? Four times?

And yet she's only made me erupt once.

We'll have to change that.

Gritting my teeth, I pry my fingers from my cock and reach for the remote. At the top of the device, above the frequency dial, are the coordinates to Rozalia's location.

Hopping back onto my laptop, I minimize the video and type the coordinates into my mapping program.

My prey waves hello in the form of a blinking red dot.

"There you are."

I'm already reaching for my cock again when a knock at the door momentarily shifts my attention away from the screen.

"Who is it?" I boom.

Reluctantly tucking my cock away, I stand up.

"Maksim."

"Give me a sec," I grumble.

Leaning back, I close my laptop. Then, I take a quick look at my reflection in the nearest mirror. My pupils are clearly dilated, but other than that, I don't look like I've spent the last hour locked in a room watching what amounts to homemade porn.

Still, Maksim seems to spot something in me the second I open the door. "You're in a good mood," he notes.

"Says who?" I challenge, quickly walking past him to hide my smirk.

He doesn't know where I've been or what I've been up to. I doubt anyone but Rozalia knows. And that's just fine. This part of her humiliation is just for me. The fake marriage will be what shames her in front of the world—even if I'm still not sure exactly how I'm going to pull that off.

Still, the self-doubt that has been growing in me like an infection since my coronation is slowly starting to fade. My confidence is returning. So is my taste for domination.

I've still got it.

And that's bad news for Rozalia Dorn.

"I assume that means you've been in contact with the Black Cat?" Maksim asks, striding right up next to me.

"She's currently under my control," I confirm.

"You've captured her?"

"Something like that." This time, I don't even try to hide my smirk. But I do reach down and shove aside my cock as it throbs at the memory of Rozalia's fiery warmth.

"Does that mean you've retrieved the crown? Your father's been asking after it."

That surprises me.

"Really? Dad cares about that stupid thing?"

"I don't think he cares about the physical object itself," Maksim says. "More what it represents."

"And what does it represent?" I ask, already knowing the answer. Just like that, a crack appears in my mending armor.

"Respect. Authority. Control."

My fists clench and my good mood sours as I'm forced to remember how my game of cat and mouse with Rozalia isn't isolated from the rest of the world.

All of my old problems still exist.

"Does that mean we're having trouble with the Italians?" I ask, dreading the response.

I still haven't followed up on their reaction to the coronation. Hell, I hardly even waited around to see what anyone thought of my announcement to marry my sworn enemy.

It must have really pissed some of them off. But I didn't give a shit. Only one thought occupied my mind.

Revenge.

Now, I finally have my first taste of it. Rozalia has been forced beneath my fist. And even if she isn't broken yet, I know it's only a matter of time.

But then what? I go talk the Italians down from the roof? I set up shop in some stuffy office? I become a wise and distant king who leaves the fun shit to everyone else?

That doesn't sound like my idea of victory.

Fuck.

"The Italians are fine," Maksim assures me. "At least, they are for now. But you know them. If there's one thing they respect more than respect itself, it's power. And your power was tested at the coronation."

"I'll have to schedule a meeting with the four families," I grumble, already dreading it.

There's no fun in the diplomatic side of ruling.

"It might be best to meet them individually," Maksim suggests. "A show of respect and appreciation for all they've done."

"They're doing less by the day," I snip, remembering how Dad and I went over the numbers before he relinquished his crown to me.

The Italians were performing at an all-time low. Their production numbers were in the dirt, and they didn't seem interested in picking up the slack—at least, not while my father's future was in turmoil.

Disloyal bastards.

"Maybe you can motivate them to do more."

Maksim is being insistent. That must mean this shit is important. And as much as I hate to take time out of my day to meet with people I have no interest in, I understand that I've already taken far too many liberties in my young career as a supposed mafia king.

"Fine. Put it in my schedule," I relent.

"Very good," Maksim nods, clearly pleased.

"Now, tell me why you knocked on my door."

"Ah, yes. You have two special guests here to see you—well, three. Actually, four, if you count Don Sabatino as special."

"I don't," I growl.

"Alright. Then let's get that meeting out of the way first."

"Who said I was going to meet him?"

Maksim just sighs.

"Rian, listen to me. Now is not the time to be testing the loyalty of your subordinates. They were all there when your strength was tested. They saw how your power was attacked. They know you aren't interested in forging a stronger alliance through marriage. They've heard about how your crown was stolen…"

"My crown wasn't the only thing stolen that day," I blurt out, before forcibly settling myself. I don't want to talk about my failures anymore. But there is something else on my mind. "How is Mel doing, by the way?"

"She's fine. Upset but fine. Would you like to stop by her guest room on the way downstairs? It would probably do her some good."

For a moment, I hesitate. But not because I don't want to see my little sister.

Mel is high on the list of people I've disappointed the most. And I was waiting until I had her painting back before going to her. But a thread of guilt pierces my chest when I realize how distant I've been acting.

She doesn't deserve that.

"Yes," I nod. "Let's go see her. I have good news."

"You found it?"

Mel's eyes light up when I mention her painting.

But that doesn't make me feel any better. In this world, nothing is done until it's done, and I haven't gotten shit back from Rozalia yet.

"I did find it," I tell her. "Now, I just have to pick it up."

Mel's hope momentarily flickers as she realizes what that means.

"Won't that be dangerous?"

"Danger is my middle name," I try to smile.

"No. Your middle name is Maksim," Mel giggles.

Her light laugh helps ease my tension, if only for a moment.

It also helps remind me of what's most important in all of this.

My family.

Mel must be protected at all costs. It's why I strongly 'suggested' she stay in my compound until I'd managed to diffuse the situation with Rozalia and Tytus.

"And what a handsome middle name that is," Maksim joins in. "Really, I don't know why you choose to go by Rian instead."

"Oh no, that would be too confusing," Mel playfully waves him off. "And since you're the original, we'd all have to call my brother Maksim Two. Or maybe Maksim B. What do you think, Rian, which would you prefer?"

I can't help but laugh. With all that's been going on, it's nice to see that the most innocent member of my family hasn't been too negatively affected—even if she is essentially a temporary captive here.

I won't let that last for long. I'll get her painting back, and then I'll hang it somewhere everyone can see.

"I think you need to start painting again," I joke. "Otherwise, you might go crazy."

"Hey, I'm not arguing with you," Mel acknowledges. "But the studio you're setting up for me in the basement isn't ready yet."

"Can't you work in your room?"

"I've tried," she shrugs. "But it's not the same. You know, I could always just go back to my place. At least during the day. My studio there is perfect. And you can send all the security you want."

"Out of the question," I quickly respond, careful not to be too stern. "It's too dangerous right now."

"Yeah, ok…" Mel sighs, and I can't quite tell if she's playing up her disappointment for sympathy points or if she's actually that bummed. "Does this mean I'll have to delay my apprenticeship too?"

Fuck. I had completely forgotten about that.

"When is that again?"

"It's supposed to start during the fall semester. So, in like four months."

"I'll make sure this is over before then," I try to assure her.

"You swear?"

"Did I stutter?"

Reaching out, Mel extends her pinky finger to me. For as innocent as she is, there's no denying that infamous Kilpatrick stubbornness.

So, instead of fighting it, I wrap my pinky around hers and tug.

"I promise."

It's not a promise I'm sure I can keep. But how could I say no to my baby sister?

"Rian." Maksim's hand falls on my shoulder. "We should go see Don Sabatino."

"He can wait a little longer," I tell him, my finger dropping from around Mel's.

"Apparently, he's starting to get agitated."

Looking back over my shoulder, I see Maksim checking his phone. Someone downstairs must have sent him an update.

"The bastard should be grateful he was even let in here," I sneer, remembering what he'd tried to pull at my coronation.

But Mel is way ahead of me. Jumping to her feet, she straightens her arms and forms two tiny fists at her sides.

"What is he doing here?" she demands to know, cheeks reddening. "Wait—do you think he found the kitten?"

Glancing over my shoulder, I look to Maksim for an answer.

He gently shakes his head.

"I've sent some men out to look for the creature," he tells us. "Don't worry. I'm sure it's fine."

"And what if she's not?" Mel questions. "There are plenty of stray dogs out there looking for an easy meal. And there are even more cruel humans looking for something innocent to take advantage of."

The darkness in Mel's words concerns me. It's not like her to be so stark and hopeless.

"There's no point in getting all worked up over it," I say. "It escaped in a nice, wealthy neighborhood. No one there would even think about hurting an innocent cat."

"Doesn't Don Sabatino have a house in the neighborhood?" she reminds me. A subtle sneer scrunches her button nose.

"If he did anything to that cat, I'll make him pay for it."

But all this talk of the cat has my mind begging to return to the last time I saw it.

In the throne room, face to face with the woman who has since fallen to her knees for me. And cum all over my cock.

In the blink of an eye, I can almost smell Rozalia's spicy scent in my nostrils. I can also feel the remote in my pocket.

I want to be back in my room, watching that video—or better yet, I want to be out chasing my prey. Caging her. Playing with her.

Making her pay.

Fuck.

Pinching the bridge of my nose, I try to force away all those dirty thoughts.

I'm in Mel's room. This is a place of innocence. My dark fantasies don't belong here.

"Tell the men to hurry with Mel's studio," I tell Maksim. Turning from my sister, I march for the door. "Up the reward for whoever finds the cat. Set up my meetings with the heads of the Italian families. Tell Don Sabatino I'm on my way down."

"You got it," Maksim nods.

"Mel, try to be patient. Please…"

"Wait!" Mel calls after me.

I stop in the doorway.

"What is it?"

"Don't up the reward for whoever finds the cat…"

That request confuses me, and I turn back around.

"You don't want them to find it?"

"No, I do. It's just… well, Maksim knows."

Those big eyes look over to our uncle.

He just shrugs.

"The men I've tasked with finding the creature keep bringing strays back here," he explains. "Some of them aren't even black."

"What the hell are we doing with all of those cats?" I ask, confused.

"They're in the basement," Mel tells me.

"It's part of the hold-up with her studio," Maksim confirms. "The place is crawling with furry four-legged creatures."

I can only shake my head in disbelief and wipe a hand down my face.

"What kind of fucking organization am I running?"

"We could always expand into the animal patrol sector," Maksim smirks.

But I'm quickly losing my patience.

"I don't have time for this shit. Mel, if you can't paint in your room, then I'll give you something else to do. Figure out this cat problem. Take charge of your studio. You have my permission to order the men downstairs around, but only as it concerns this project. You're still to stay here until I get everything under control. Understand?"

"Yeah, sure…" she mutters.

This time, when I turn around, I don't let anything hold me back.

"I'll let everyone know about Mel and the studio," Maksim says when he catches up to my side.

"You can do that later," I tell him. "Right now, you're coming with me. We're going to meet that bastard Sabatino."

"This isn't happening," I growl. "Not right now. Not ever."

Adriano Sabatino has hardly even opened his mouth yet, and I can already tell what's going on.

He's brought one of his daughters along with him. One of his clearly underage daughters.

And he's trying to pawn her off on me.

I'm not having it.

"We didn't mean any disrespect," the greedy Italian cowers. "I just thought you might like to meet Adriana. Since you weren't able to at the coronation. You know, because of—"

"Enough," I roar.

But I quickly regret my outburst.

The teenage girl hiding behind her father was already terrified when I stormed down the stairs. Now, it looks like she's on the verge of tears.

It makes me want to pin her father against the wall and pound some sense into him. But that would only make everything worse.

None of this is her fault. And she doesn't deserve any of my ire. But her father is striking a fucking nerve—of course he named his daughter Adriana. The egotistical son-of-a-bitch.

"Don Sabatino, why don't you and Adriana come with me," Maksim steps in. "I'll accompany you back to your car. Anything you want to tell the king, you can tell me."

"Are you serious?" Adriano looks like he's just been slapped across the face. "We came all the way out here for—"

"You live down the street," I interrupt, remembering what Mel said. "If you want to set up a meeting to discuss business, then Maksim will be happy to set something up. Otherwise, we're done."

"This is business," Adriano foolishly pushes.

"No. it isn't," I sneer, getting up in the stubby Italian's greasy red face. "Your daughter is none of my business, and she shouldn't be a part of yours. Protect her, Adriano. That's your only job as a father."

"I—" It looks like Adriano is about to say something he might regret. Thankfully, he thinks better of it. "I will schedule another meeting with you."

"Good."

With that, I turn and march away.

Snapping my fingers, I order Maksim to join me.

"You two," Maksim quickly points to a pair of guards standing watch in the hall. "Escort Don Sabatino and his lovely daughter back to their car. Make sure they get home safely. Understand?"

"Yes, sir!"

"That didn't go well," Maksim notes when we turn the corner up ahead.

"You should have warned me about his daughter," I grumble. "That shit disgusts me."

"My mistake," Maksim admits. "I'd forgotten."

"The great Maksim Smolov forgot something?" I'm genuinely shocked.

But he only shrugs. "I guess I'm just that excited about your two special guests. Actually, wait. No. It's three now. I keep forgetting."

A smile crosses his weathered face.

"Whoever it is, they better make up for that bullshit."

"They will," Maksim hints. "Would you like me to spoil the surprise?"

"I'm done with surprises. Tell me."

"It's your cousin. And her husband. And your nephew."

I stop in my tracks. But I don't know whether I should be enraged or ecstatic.

"Why the hell wasn't I told they were coming?" I ask.

"You've been busy."

A tinge of regret juts through me at Maksim's remarks.

What else have I missed while I've been away?

"They shouldn't be here," I mumble. "It's too dangerous to travel right now. Especially with an infant in tow."

"I believe Jakub would be considered a toddler by now," Maksim corrects. "But they didn't travel from the west coast. At least, not since your coronation. They were already in town for the ceremony. It was supposed to be a surprise. But when you sent out the order to stay away, they respected your decision. They've been staying up at your family's place in the Catskills ever since."

"Fuck," I curse, wiping a hand down my face.

Part of me spikes with joy at the opportunity to see my

cousin and my nephew again. It's been too long. But another part dreads the reunion.

And it's not just because I have little to show for my absence.

My cousin, Bianca, is married to the man who used to work with Rozalia and Tytus.

Gabriel Reca.

Their adoptive brother.

I've been meaning to talk to him about his former ragtag family. But the opportunity just hasn't come up yet.

And I'm not sure I want to bring it up. How am I going to pay attention to him when I could be playing with little Jakub or catching up with Bianca instead?

There's only one way to find out.

"Take me to them," I hear myself say.

"Right this way."

Leading me around another corner, Maksim stops at the library door. Immediately, I go to open it up. But my hand freezes on the handle.

From the other side of the door, I can hear the sound of a laughing baby. It's followed by Bianca's trademark giggle.

The innocence is palpable.

Do I really want to drag them into my mess right now?

I'm not given a choice.

It's like the three of them can sense I'm here. And before I can pull the door open, it's done for me.

Just like that, Gabriel Reca stands in the doorway. Big and tall and dark. He's a man I've fought to the brink of death. A man who I've tortured. A man I've hunted.

A man I've welcomed into my empire... and my family.

"You look like hell," he smirks.

Like it's instinct, our hands grasp around each other's wrists for a firm shake.

"That's because I've actually been working," I shoot back.

"You wish work was as hard as raising a child."

"I really don't."

"Rian!" Bianca's voice is as sweet as any melody. And when she comes racing up for a hug, even her possessive husband steps aside.

"Glad to see Gabriel hasn't ruined your spirit yet," I play, allowing myself to hug her back.

"Only corrupted it a bit," she giggles.

I can't help but roll my eyes. The last thing I want to hear is how some guy has corrupted my cousin—even if he is slowly becoming a real friend. And she is already a complete badass.

"How are you?" I ask.

"Pretty good. Missing the west coast. But obviously it wouldn't be smart to travel right now."

"You've done dumber things," I note, gesturing over to Gabriel.

"Well, yeah, obviously," Bianca laughs. "But I'm a mother now. I have to be responsible."

"Speaking of my nephew..."

"Of course."

Letting go of me, Bianca leads the way to the stroller.

Little Jakub's smile immediately melts my cold heart and brightens the entire room. He's got his father's green eyes but his mother's auburn hair—a perfect mixture of Irish, Italian and Polish genes.

His stubby arms reach out to me, and I pick him up.

"How's my favorite nephew?" I ask, bouncing him against my chest.

"He's your only nephew," Bianca playfully reminds me.

"For now," Gabriel adds.

The implication nearly knocks me off my feet.

"... Does that mean?"

"We're pregnant," Bianca beams.

"Still not sure if it's a boy or a girl yet," Gabriel says.

"What are you hoping for?"

"A healthy baby," they both agree at the same time.

"Of course."

For a while, everything is fine in the world. I rock Jakub in my arms and catch up with Bianca.

Then, I feel Gabriel's hand on my shoulder. It's heavier than the mood in the room. I know what he's going to say before he even opens his mouth.

"Hey, look, I'm sorry about the coronation," he starts.

"Don't be. Shit happens. Now it's time to clean up the mess. Are you willing to help?"

"What do you need from me?"

"Inside information."

I catch the slightest bit of hesitation in Gabriel's sharp emerald green eyes as he purses his lips.

Still, he provides a dutiful nod.

"I'll tell you what I can."

"Good, because we'll need every last advantage we can get."

"Is it that bad?" Bianca asks.

"No. In fact, I should be picking up my crown from Rozalia sometime tomorrow. But there are other issues."

"Like what to do with her," Gabriel somberly acknowledges.

"And Tytus."

"What about their army?" Bianca points out.

"That's one of the things I wanted to ask your husband about."

"I never got to see it," Gabriel reminds me.

"No one has," I return. "That's what's suspicious."

"You think something's wrong with their army?"

"I don't know. But I overheard a conversation between Tytus and Rozalia recently. And when Tytus brought up their supposed army, Rozalia hushed him awfully quickly."

"Something must be wrong," Gabriel mumbles, unable to

keep the concern from his voice. "I know it's not my place to ask. But... how are they?"

"They're fine," I respond. Patting my nephew's back, I hold back a sneer. "In fact, just last night, they treated themselves to a nice expensive dinner."

"Does it sound like they have any regrets?" Bianca joins. "Maybe they'll turn a new leaf and actually take us up on the original offer to join us..."

"No. There's no going back now," I say, careful not to pass on my anger to Jakub. "Or did you forget about how Rozalia threatened your newborn son?"

"It was unforgivable," Gabriel admits, a fierceness piercing his sadness.

Placing Jakub back down into his stroller, I run a hand through my hair.

"It would just be nicer to use their talents instead of destroying them," Bianca speaks for her husband.

Oh, I'll use her plenty.

"They've made their bed. Now, I'm going to make them sleep in it."

Gabriel and Bianca share a troubled look before accepting my declaration.

"It's the only way," Gabriel nods, before forcing a subtle grin. "I mean, unless you end up falling in love with your new bride."

His smile makes me roll my eyes again. Still, my fists clench at my sides.

"I thought an announcement like that might draw her out into the open," I explain.

"Maybe," Gabriel sighs. "But it could also backfire spectacularly. Rozalia has a troubled relationship with marriage..."

"She's been married before?" I ask, shocked. My fists tighten. An unwelcomed shot of jealousy rips through my chest.

"Hell no," Gabriel eases my concerns. "But that doesn't

mean brutal men haven't been trying to trap her like that for the entirety of her life. "

"I'll be the one who succeeds," I grumble.

To my surprise, it actually sounds like I mean it.

But I can't possibly, right? The whole forced marriage idea is just to ease my father's concerns.

I don't actually want to marry the Black Cat.

I want to end her.

"Then you might not have to kill her," Gabriel says. "Because forcing a ring onto her finger and submitting her to a life of captivity and servitude could break her spirit beyond repair."

I swear I hear the ruthless killer's voice crack ever so slightly.

"That seems dramatic," I huff.

Gabriel shrugs. But it's a heavy shrug. A sad shrug. "Like I said, Rozalia has a troubled relationship with marriage."

"Tell me everything," I snarl.

A sliver of sympathy has invaded my gut. I want to get rid of it as quickly as possible.

The truth can't be that bad.

"How long do you have?" Gabriel asks.

Reaching out, I pull up the nearest chair and point for him to sit in it.

Bianca takes the cue and goes to tend to Jakub.

"Until dawn tomorrow. That's when I'll meet her next."

"No, you won't be meeting Roz," Gabriel says, shaking his head. "At least, it won't be the Roz you think you know. She's not who you think she is, Rian. Not entirely. There's more to her than meets the eye. And I worry that pulling back the curtain might hurt you more than it helps."

"How could it possibly hurt?"

"Because it might make you realize she's an actual person, and not just your prey."

Gabriel's words make me pause. But only for a moment.

"I'll be the judge of that."

"Alright," he says, taking his seat. "I'll start at the beginning."

8

ROZALIA

"I'm not getting on that fucking boat."

My thighs are still sore from the thrashing they took in the alleyway. My mind is on the verge of shattering.

At any moment, the vibrating could return.

There's no way I'm willingly giving up any more power.

Not even if it means losing out on Leander's gift.

Drago.

"It's a yacht," Leander casually points out. "Well, technically, it's classified as a super-yacht."

"I don't care what it is," I tell him. "You didn't say anything about a boat."

"That's because it's not a boat," he repeats, agitation rising. "It's a—"

"Is Drago on board?" Tytus interrupts, trying to cool things off between us.

"No," Leander responds, wiping the frustration from his over-manicured face. "But I was going to take you to his hideout."

"Why don't you take the yacht," Tytus compromises. "Lead the way. We'll follow behind in one of those motorboats."

Pointing down the dock, Tytus draws our attention to a row of speedy-looking vessels. Each one has the Onasis name engraved into the starboard.

"Have you ever driven one of those things before?" Leander asks, intrigued.

"I'll figure it out." Before Leander can respond, Tytus starts walking away. "Have someone bring us the key," he says, looking back over his shoulder. "And please don't make us wait around again."

"What a fucking mop," I grumble, catching up to my adoptive brother. But even as I scurry behind him, my arms stay straight.

It's impossible to get comfortable. Fuck. I almost want Rian to just pull the trigger already. At least that way, I can force myself to fight through what's bound to happen.

The waiting is so much worse—especially considering how frustratingly good the tremors can feel.

"A mop is a good description," Tytus agrees. "But only because we can use that empty head of his to help clean up some of our problems."

"We don't need him."

"That's not true, Roz," Tytus sighs. "And you know that just as well as I do."

"Fuck."

We're only waiting at the motorboat for a few minutes before someone arrives with the keys.

In that time, we carefully watch Leander board his massive super-yacht. The discussions he has with his crew strike me as suspicious, and I don't like that another dozen or so bodyguards have shown up to protect him. But Tytus is right. We don't have much of a choice.

We need a new army, and fast.

And Leander is the only billionaire stupid and shallow enough to give one to us.

"I can probably drive this thing better than you," I note, watching as Tytus studies the controls.

"I'm not sure I trust you to do anything right now," Tytus mumbles back. Sticking the key into the ignition, he turns on the engine. "You know, what with your woman problems and all."

I hardly even hear him.

For a split second, I'm engulfed by a blinding panic.

The vibrating is back.

Gritting my teeth, I grab onto the driver's seat and try to muffle the scream that tears up my throat. My legs start to tremble so hard my knees clank together.

I feel Tytus' hands on my shoulder, and I desperately shake him off. I am *not* having an orgasm while he touches me. No fucking way.

Turning my back on him, I bend over the stern and clench my eyes shut.

And then, just like that, the vibrating stops.

"Ok, fuck this. Roz, I'm tired of playing around. What the hell is going on?"

"Cramps," I croak, wrapping an arm around my stomach.

"I've known you for eight long years, and I've never seen you react like that to cramps."

"Start the boat," I demand.

"I just did, and it set you off like a grenade."

A stone drops in my gut as I realize that what I just felt wasn't from the shit Rian rubbed onto my clit.

It was from the boat.

I'm losing my fucking mind.

"No. Sorry. I'm milking it. Tell Leander to cast off. We need to see Drago."

"You're in no state to see Drago."

Twisting around, I stare daggers at Tytus.

"Do it!"

It feels like I'm coming undone. Between my hormones, Rian's mind games, Leander's shit, and the fact that we're supposedly on our way to see my missing adoptive father, I'm ready to fall apart.

I hate how quickly the tables have turned. Just yesterday, I felt like I could conquer the world by myself.

Then, I got too close to my prey. I gave into my urges and sat on a thick juicy cock I shouldn't have even looked at. I came and opened myself up to a man who took advantage of it.

It wasn't the first time I'd done something so stupid. But it was the first time my mistake was ever that intimate.

Fuck. He came inside of me.

Thank god for contraceptive injections.

"Please, Tytus," I beg, softening my voice. "We need to see him."

I can tell Tytus is just as desperate to confront Drago as I am, because he only hesitates for a second before turning around.

"Fine."

This time, I prepare myself for the rumbling engine. Still, I can't help but flinch when the boat starts to rock.

Up ahead, I see Leander's yacht pull out. The billionaire's bright suit glares against the setting sun as he waves us forward.

Tytus follows after him.

Instead of looking ahead to where we're going, I turn my back to everything and glare at our wake.

Stupid girl. Look what you've gotten yourself into.

Before I take a seat, I slip my phone out of my back pocket.

The signal scrambler I've attached to the case is still glowing, blasting out a uterus-shriveling amount of radiation. For the time being, Rian shouldn't be able to track us. At least, not accurately.

The risk of radiation poisoning will be well worth the few hours of privacy. Not that I'm completely safe. If Rian checks to see where I am, and can't find the signal, he's going to punish me.

A warm tingle runs up my thighs. Dread empties my gut.

I look up to the sky.

A foolish part of me thought my scrambler might make the pleasure the vibrations caused a lot less enjoyable.

But now, I highly doubt that.

Clenching my fists, I try to calm myself.

The lion will pay for the pain he's caused me. And the pleasure too.

But first, I need to do something I promised I'd never do for anyone ever again.

Submit.

That's the only way to get rid of this stupid shit he's stuck to me. I've already tried to concoct a solution of my own, but nothing seems to mix just right, and I'm not about to lather a bunch of chemicals on my clit in the hopes that one of them works.

Fucking hell.

Closing my eyes, I try not to think about just how much control that man has over me right now.

When I open them again, the sky has darkened a shade.

"Did I fall asleep?" I mumble to myself.

Rubbing my eyes, I turn around and face forward. Leander's yacht fills up most of the skyline. But behind it, I can just make out the silhouette of a growing island.

"I think that's it," Tytus shouts through the roaring engine.

My heart clenches.

Drago.

The coward's been hiding ever since we broke free from his grip. I wonder if he knows we're coming?

I hope he does. And I hope he dreads it.

We're deep into dusk by the time we pull up to a shabby dock. Just down the row, Lander's opulent yacht stands out like a sore thumb. But it doesn't appear like there's anyone around to notice.

It's quickly clear that this rocky island is abandoned.

"Where are we?" I ask, still slightly groggy.

"Hell if I know," Tytus says. Tying the boat up, we both walk down the dock towards Leander.

He's surrounded by a group of his bodyguards. An uneasy feeling appears in my gut. But I'm not sure if it's from suspicion or seasickness.

"I don't like this," I say, brushing the back of my hand against my thigh holster. My gun is still there, locked and loaded. But that doesn't mean I'm in any state to use it.

All it would take is one single vibration during a shootout, and I would be a sitting duck.

I fucking hate this.

"Let's stop here," Tytus suggests. Slowing down some thirty feet from Leander and his men, he takes out his phone. "Take yours out too. Look up our coordinates. Figure out exactly where we are."

"I can't," I quickly realize. Pulling out my own phone, I gesture down at the mini nuclear reactor attached to my case. "I brought this along to scramble any potential followers. But it means I can't get a good signal either."

Tytus recoils at the sight of the thing. "Looks excessive. And dangerous."

"It is," I grumble. But Tytus can't know the truth. "No one is allowed to know where Drago is but us."

"And apparently Leander."

"Someone better be ready to tell us how this little partnership came about, because if they don't, this island might just become a graveyard."

"Agreed," Tytus nods. "Now, let's find out what Drago's been up to."

The living arrangements are much more modest than I was expecting.

For some reason, the idea of Drago living in squalor for this past year doesn't fill me with any sense of satisfaction. Not like I thought it would.

Instead, there's a sadness to it all.

I can't help but remember back to when we first met. When he saved me from an unspeakable fate. His words gave me hope. His determination helped me push aside the darkness and strive for something greater than victimhood.

We were supposed to rule the world together.

Now, it looks like he's living in an isolated cave, all alone.

Our family has been shattered.

But I still carry that dream with me.

I just don't need him to fulfill it anymore. I don't need anybody.

Right?

"If you'd be so kind as to wait here for a moment..." Leander says, asking for permission before he turns to leave.

Water drops from the cave ceiling. A soft howl blows over us.

Tytus nods before I can respond with disgust. "Go ahead. But don't be long."

"I would never dream of making my partners wait twice," Leander tries to charm, a sickly smile lifting his glass cheeks.

It doesn't work on either of us.

Still, he doesn't hesitate to make his way to a depression at the far end of the grotto. Four black-suited security guards follow him. Eight stay behind.

More water drips from the ceiling, splashing down into the small green body of water beside us. Giant stone daggers jut out of the rocky walls.

We all wait in tense silence as Leander and his men disappear.

I'm not sure what to expect.

Part of me is hoping that this is an ambush. Any excuse to let off some steam... and avoid confronting the man who's caused me so much pain.

But another part of me needs to see him again.

I need to look in his face and remember that he's just a man—someone I can kill.

"No fucking way..." Tytus growls, spotting the shadow up ahead before I do. "It's actually him."

We both tense up as footsteps echo through the oceanside cave.

Then, without further ceremony, Drago appears.

At first, it's like seeing a ghost. He's so thin and frail that I can almost see through him.

A long scraggly beard drags down his chin. A wiry head of hair drops like wet drapes along the side of his emaciated face.

He looks more like a castaway than the fearsome dragon I remember.

But there's no mistaking that face. And when my former savior steps into a beam of moonlight, I can't help but tremble.

The claw marks that cross his cheek are as deep and as red as ever. His dead eye is paler than the moonlight. His skin is paper white.

It's him.

"My children..."

My mouth opens. A certain word desperately wants to drift out of my lips.

Dad.

But it all gets stuck in my throat.

I'm speechless.

Tytus, on the other hand, is not.

"So, you're working with the Greeks now?" he accuses, steam rising from his breath. "Always the opportunist."

To my surprise, Drago doesn't respond with anger. Instead, those bony shoulders drop, and a heavy sigh escapes him.

"We've always done what we need to in order to survive."

"The point of this was never just to survive," Tytus reminds him. Stepping forward, my protective brother tries to block me off from the disturbing sight. "It was to thrive."

Peeking under Tytus' arm, I catch something unexpected. A small smile lifts Drago's sunken and scarred cheeks.

"And you two have done so well," he practically beams. "Even Gabriel has—"

"Don't you dare talk about Gabriel!" I rasp. My voice echoes around the hollow cave, building in emotion with every iteration. No one speaks until it fades away. And then it's me who breaks the silence. This time, I can only manage a whisper. "It's your fault he's gone."

Stepping back, Tytus rubs a comforting shoulder against me.

"It is my fault," Drago agrees. "Everything is. I'm… I'm sorry."

Who is this pitiful old man? His passiveness is infuriating.

"Broken," I sneer. Pushing Tytus aside, I take my own step forward. Drago doesn't budge. "You're just a broken old man."

"You're right."

"And I suppose you called us here to fix you up again?"

"No," Drago says, shaking his head. "I wanted to make it all up to you. I want you to live the life I promised. I want—"

"Your promises were all lies!" I explode. Everything is catching up to me. To my horror, I feel a hot tear trickle down my cheek. I don't wipe it away. "You have nothing to make up for. There was never anything real to break."

"I broke your trust."

"You never had my trust," I lie.

"Rozalia, I—"

"No. Don't call me by my name. You don't deserve it. You don't deserve me. All you ever wanted was to sell me off, just like everyone else. From the moment you tore me out of that burning mansion, all you wanted was to use me. Use my body to build your empire. Use my gender to form alliances. The only thing you didn't want to use was my mind. And guess what? It's why you failed."

I feel Tytus' hand fall on my shoulder. But his touch doesn't calm me down. Instead, it only reminds me that Drago has also failed two others. And he's driven one of them away forever.

"I know," Drago admits. "It's all true. I've had nothing to do but remember and regret. I've been a fool."

"I could have saved you a lot of suffering and told you that a year ago," I spit.

"I wasn't wise enough to listen back then."

"Wise enough? How old are you? Fucking eighty? The time has passed. If you weren't wise enough last year, you'll never be."

That's all I can take.

Turning my back, I storm back towards the cave entrance, only stopping halfway because I can't bear to leave Tytus behind.

Tytus.

Fuck. He was right. I'm not in any kind of shape to be at this meeting. Even if my brother doesn't know exactly what's going on, he's seen what it's doing to me.

I'm falling apart.

That's one thing Drago and I both have in common right now—though I wish we didn't.

"What do you want?" I hear Tytus ask from behind me.

"I want to help," Drago's feeble voice returns.

"And how are you going to do that?"

"He already did it," Leander steps in. I don't turn around.

Instead, I stare out over the ocean. Moonlight sparkles over the water. The world feels empty.

"How so?" Tytus returns, filled with skepticism.

"By recruiting me."

That's enough to spin me back around.

"So you aren't providing Drago to us," Tytus sneers. "He's provided you to us."

"Something like that," Leander chuckles. "But he's also providing me with something."

Those lifeless blue eyes glimmer in the moonlight, glowing as they set themselves on me.

I freeze.

"What?" I manage to choke.

"You."

Tytus is the first to rip his gun out. I'm not far behind. But my hands are still shaky and limp. The steel feels like a hundred-pound weight as I try to aim it.

"So it's a fucking trap," Tytus roars, pointing his barrel at Leander.

I lift mine towards Drago. But my arm is already shaking.

"No, please. My son. It's not," Drago begs.

Every last one of Leander's guards have also whipped out their guns. Half are pointed at Tytus, and half are directed at me.

Cold sweat drips down my forehead, replacing the hot tears.

"Think of it more as a partnership," Leander steps in, sounding awfully confident for the only person without a weapon.

Waving his hands, he tries to get his men to lower their weapons. Only a few of them comply.

"I'd rather think of it as your death sentence," Tytus growls, straightening his gun.

That only draws more attention to him. The men who had lowered their weapons retrain them onto Tytus.

"I'll slaughter all of you," I hiss.

"Come on now, I can't be that bad," Leander smirks. "Listen, a marriage would only combine our wealth and power. I have an army too. Together, we can kill Rian Kilpatrick and take control of the American underworld. Then, we'll be unstoppable. Hell, I might even accept a divorce after certain terms are met…"

My skin crawls at the implication. A furious fire flares up inside of me.

Why are all these greedy fucking men only ever interested in marriage? Have I not made it clear that I'd rather slit their throats and mine before I submit like that?

Leander doesn't even know me and he's already trying to cage me for life. Fuck. At least Rian has had the common decency to work for it.

"No one gets to kill Rian Kilpatrick but me," I snarl.

"Alright, then I'll kill that traitorous brother of yours. Gabriel. Call it a bonus."

That nearly makes me pull the trigger. But before I can do anything stupid, Drago seems to come to life.

"That wasn't part of the deal!" he shouts, turning to Leander.

To his credit, the spoiled Greek billionaire actually looks mildly shocked.

"My mistake," he says, taken aback. "I thought you weren't on the best of terms with him."

"That doesn't mean you get to kill him," Tytus barks.

"Then I won't. Not that I would have personally anyway." The asshole has the gall to check his spotless nails.

Imagine me marrying a man like that. No amount of money or power would be worth it.

Dread and sadness and anger swirl around inside of me as I prepare to fight my way out of this.

Then, like a sudden nightmare, I feel something that makes me instantly drop my gun.

"Roz?"

The first vibrations make my vision blurry. And I can only barely see Tytus checking on me with quick glances over his shoulder. He can't look for long. There are too many guns trained on him.

"Rozalia? What's wrong?" Drago's voice is also filled with concern.

The strength of the vibrations increase.

"I…" I need to get out of here.

Without even bothering to pick up my gun, I turn around and bolt.

I don't know where I'm going—Tytus has the keys to the boat, and we counted at least a dozen more of Leander's men waiting behind on the yacht when we left—but it doesn't matter. I need to leave. Flee, while my legs will still carry me.

I will not be shamed like that in front of my brother. Not in front of Leander either. And definitely not in front of Drago.

Rian must be trying to find out where I am. He must have seen that my signal was scrambled.

He's punishing me.

"You asshole…"

My thighs clench and my core flexes as dreadful waves of heavy warmth crash over me.

Hot tears of frustration return to my cheeks. They mix in with the cold sweat, blurring my vision even further.

Then, I slip.

It only takes the smallest puddle to send my feet flying up into the air. A split second later, my back slams against the hard rock below, knocking the wind out of me.

But my punishment isn't over with yet. The path is on a

slant, and I desperately reach out for something to grab onto as I slide towards the waves crashing below.

I don't find anything.

Before I can scream out, I'm engulfed by the ocean. A fistful of salt water rushes into my open gullet, filling up my lungs until it feels like I'm going to explode.

Then, everything goes black.

9

RIAN

She's late.

Clenching the remote, I dare myself to turn the dial all the way up to ten. It would be a fitting punishment.

But something stops me.

I can't help but remember what Gabriel told me last night. Rozalia isn't who I think she is.

He was right. My perception of the frustrating Black Cat has changed—if only slightly.

Still, that doesn't excuse her for standing me up.

She'll pay.

Just not right now.

"I don't think she's showing up," Maksim crackles over my earpiece.

"No shit."

The first bits of morning light are seeping in through the holes that line the pockmarked tin roof above my head.

This old warehouse is filled with spiderwebs and bloodstains—countless shady deals have gone down behind its condemned walls, but it doesn't look like anything will happen here today.

Fuck.

"Where the hell is she?" I grumble.

It's not like the Black Cat to shy away from a confrontation—especially if showing up means freeing herself from someone else's control.

Do I not know her as well as I think or do, or is something wrong?

Shit. Part of me almost wants to be concerned. Is she alright? Has something happened?

Before that weakness can get too strong, though, reality slaps me across the face.

She's your enemy. Act like it.

Still, even as I turn towards the only door in and out of this place, I can't help but focus on all of the reasons Rozalia might have stayed away.

Maybe she's already found an antidote to my wicked trap. Maybe she's still flustered from our last encounter.

... Maybe she's pregnant.

My eyes roll at the mere thought of that last possibility.

There's zero chance. I remember the words she hissed at me from the darkness of that security room.

As if I'd ever let that happen.

She's on some kind of contraceptive. At the very least, she must have cooked something up after our encounter—or just gotten her hands on some ordinary plan B pills.

Neither of us were thinking straight in that dark, screen-lit security room. But there was nothing stopping us from coming to our senses afterward.

My fist clamps down tighter around the remote.

This time, though, it's not because I'm thinking about turning the dial way up.

It's to keep the blood from rushing into my cock.

There's ignoring how good she felt. And there's definitely no denying how badly I want more.

Last night, after I'd dealt with all the shit a king has to deal with, I went back to my room and sat down at my laptop again.

That video loop filled up my screen. I barely even had to touch my cock. Just the memory of how those trembling thighs felt straddled around my waist brought me so close to heaven that I could taste it.

But tasting just wasn't enough anymore. At one point, I laid the remote back out in front of me and started to turn the dial to match the looping video.

The idea of having so much power over such a strong woman made me climax. And even after I'd stained my carpet with cum, I kept the dial turned up, just to assert my domination over her.

But it must not have worked. Because the Black Cat is a no-show.

Maybe she's just angry at me. That, or something is wrong.

There is another possibility, though. One that I don't even want to consider...

"Are you sure she got your message?" Maksim asks.

He doesn't know the exact details of how I've been controlling my nemesis. But I've given him hints, and he knows enough to understand how perplexing her absence is.

"I'm sure," I growl. "Maybe she's with that new friend of hers."

A pinprick of jealousy grows inside my chest, and I decide I've done enough waiting.

With one last look around the shabby warehouse, I head to the door.

"If she is with the man from the restaurant, then that's her mistake," Maksim reminds me. "We should be getting info on that fucker any second now. He'll lead us right to her."

My uncle has put some of our best spies on the case of figuring out who Rozalia and Tytus' fancy dinner date guest was.

About two hours ago, they got their first clue. They've been following that thread ever since, promising to update us as the information becomes available.

"Whoever he is, I'll make sure to pay him a nice visit."

Shoving the remote back into my pocket, I pull out my phone and push my way outside.

It's a beautiful calm morning. But I don't sit around to smell the flowers. I'm immediately nose deep in my phone, re-checking the signal on Rozalia's tracking device.

It's still scrambled.

My pinprick of jealousy shivers into another momentary bout of concern.

Something feels off.

In order to scramble a tracker as strong as the one I've stuck in her, she'd need to be carrying around a miniature nuclear reactor's worth of radiation.

It's not safe to keep that on you for this long.

But shit, maybe that's her preferred birth control method.

Still, something tells me there's a more nefarious reason behind her efforts.

Either that, or it's not her blocking me off.

Whatever the case, one thing's certain.

Whoever's keeping me from her is going to pay.

"Just got a name," Maksim's voice becomes clearer as I approach his position at the head of our dockside convoy.

"Read it to me," I demand.

Rolling down the tinted window on his black escalade, my uncle leans out so he can be heard over the growing sound of squawking seagulls.

I rip my earpiece out and listen carefully.

"Leander Onasis. That's who Rozalia and Tytus met at the restaurant."

"Who the fuck is Leander Onasis?"

"Greek Billionaire. Trust fund extraordinaire. Investor.

Tycoon. All of that bullshit. To be honest, the name is oddly familiar…"

"Doesn't sound like someone Rozalia and Tytus would be meeting."

Maksim just shrugs. "We put our best men on the job. They seem pretty confident that this Leander Onasis is our guy."

"Well, then let's confirm it. You drive."

Stepping into the backseat of Maksim's escalade, I pull open a cover on the backseat headrest, revealing a built-in desktop. The Bluetooth connects to my phone's keyboard, and by the time Maksim has pulled off the docks and onto the highway, I've compiled a massive file on this Leander fucker.

A quick keyword search finds something that I already suspected.

"He's former mafia," I grumble.

Ahead, in the driver's seat, Maksim perks up. "I knew that name sounded strangely familiar."

"You'd heard of Leander before?"

"Not Leander. No," Maksim shakes his head. "But his father… Stravos, I believe—yeah, Stravos Onasis, he used to run a small family of his own. An offshoot of the Greek mafia. If I remember correctly, the Greeks call those factions 'Oikos', and they're kind of like what the Italians are to you. Ask your cousins. Stravos was semi-famous in the underworld for being one of the first crooks to go fully legitimate."

While Maksim talks, I furiously type away, double-checking every word.

"You're right," I tell him, confirming the story through pieced-together articles, police reports, and business documents. "Why the hell did he go straight?"

"For the same reason your father did," Maksim explains. "Because rich businessmen don't have to worry about jail time —but even the wealthiest crooks always have a target on their backs."

"My father isn't afraid of jail," I snap, suddenly remembering all the shit Dad is going through.

I've been trying to keep it in the back of my mind because there's nothing I can do for him right now. Not on that front. But it's hard to forget. And it's even harder to keep myself from jumping to his defense.

"No. He isn't afraid of jail," Maksim agrees. "But believe me when I tell you there's nothing your father fears more than the thought of his children being locked up in some cage. He would do anything to prevent that from happening. Anything."

"And look where that got us," I murmur.

Maksim sighs.

"It could still all work out. Your father's a smart man. And obviously, there's a template he can follow. Look at Leander. A billionaire. I imagine it's all clean money too. If he and his father can do it, then why can't you and yours?"

"I can't imagine Stravos was trying to go clean while under federal investigation," I remind Maksim. "Plus, going legitimate is the last thing I want to do. The mafia is my life. And I wouldn't give it up for all the clean money in the world."

"I know," Maksim nods. "It's where we both belong. Your father too. He was never set on destroying this part of his legacy, only masking it. You understand that, right?"

"Of course I do," I sneer, hating that my almighty father is in such a vulnerable position. "But there's nothing we can do about that now. Our job is to maintain control of our dirty dealings. And there's nothing dirtier than whatever Rozalia and Tytus are up to."

"And what do you think they're up to?"

"I don't know," I confess.

"Do you think they could be trying to go legitimate?"

"There's no fucking way."

I hadn't even considered that option.

With a quick flurry of typing, I try to find out if Leander

Onasis has any remaining criminal connections. But no matter how wide I cast the net, I don't see anything that would suggest he does.

"Well, if they're not trying to go legitimate, then that means Leander must be trying to go dark," Maksim remarks.

A quick peek at the man's net worth makes that assumption seem absurd. It would be insane to risk all that money and influence to get back into the criminal world.

"Why the hell would he do that?" I ask. "Especially after his father clearly worked so hard to get out of the underworld."

Maksim doesn't seem to have a direct answer for that.

"If I remember correctly, Stravos Onasis dead, right?"

"Heart attack," I quickly confirm, looking up his obituary. "What does that have to do with anything?"

"Not much," Maksim acknowledges. "But perhaps father and son didn't share the same vision for the future."

The implication is clear. But the reasoning still remains murky.

Before I can dig any deeper into that mystery, though, a notification pops up on my screen.

One of my programs has made a connection.

Clicking on the link, I'm led to a map.

My stomach drops.

Rozalia's scrambler may be strong enough to keep me from knowing her exact location, but it only works to an extent.

My tracking signal is powerful enough to still give me a sense of what area she's in. And as far as I can tell, she's currently in roughly the same region she was in last night—somewhere up north, near the water.

Her hazy tracking cloud seeps into the ocean, like she's camped out somewhere along the shore. By now, I could have easily sent a hundred men to sweep the area. But I haven't seen the point. She was supposed to meet me this morning, after all. And why wouldn't she? I'd promised her freedom.

Now, I'm wishing I'd sent those men up north—if only to catch her in the act.

Because she wasn't the only subject of interest down by that part of the shoreline last night.

My program has picked up on the geolocation history of a yacht registered under Leander Onasis' name.

He was there with her.

He might still be.

The coincidence is too great to ignore.

Any bit of concern I'd had for Rozalia is eviscerated by an eruption of red-hot jealousy.

Did she run to him?

Was he watching as she squirmed against my rising dial? Did he hold her as she begged for more? Did he get to taste her cum?

The idea is infuriating. Even if I'm well aware of the absurdity of it all, I can't help the rage that flows through my veins.

With a few clicks, I find a mansion on the beach that's also registered to Leander Onasis. It's not far from where his yacht is moored.

I'm betting that's where he spent the night.

It better have been the best night of his life.

Because I'm going to make sure it's his last.

"Head north," I growl to Maksim, sending him the address. "We're going to pay our new friend a visit."

"Yes, sir."

For the first time since our chase began, I find myself hoping that Rozalia isn't where I think she is.

Because if she is, there's no telling what I'll do.

She's mine, you bastard. And I'm willing to fight to keep it that way.

I might also be willing to do something far worse...

10

ROZALIA

The moment my eyes rip open, I swivel around and reach for the knife I keep tucked beneath my pillow.

But it's not there. And before I can realize why, a blinding headache bursts out from behind my skull.

"Fuck..." I groan, slamming my head down into the pillow.

The scent in the linen is unfamiliar. Harsh almost. There's a salty thickness to everything. It reminds me of the black waves that swallowed me up.

My stomach drops as I remember what happened.

I drowned.

Did the ocean spit me back out?

How the hell am I still alive?

I don't have the strength to dig too deeply into those memories. Instead, I focus on taking deep breaths. The pain ravaging my head is like a crown of thorns, tightening every time I move. I just want to sink into the soft mattress and close my eyes again.

Then, I feel a giant presence approach from my bedside.

Headache or not, I pull out a clenched fist and prepare to defend myself.

But that just makes everything so much worse. And it only worsens as I try to fight through the throbbing ache and stare down my visitor.

I don't need to see clearly to instantly recognize the shape leaning towards me.

"Take it easy, Roz. It's just me."

That's Tytus' voice. And I recognize the comforting weight of his heavy hand as he softly pushes me back down into the soft mattress.

"Where am I?" I croak. My throat is bone dry.

"You're safe."

"Where. Am. I?"

Tytus sighs against my stubbornness, and I know I'm not going to like his answer.

"We're at a mansion on the beach."

"Who's mansion?"

"Leander's."

It only takes that name to overwhelm me. A flood of recent memories crash around inside of me.

A cursed reunion. An expected betrayal. A cruel trap. Vibrations. Hard rock. Cold water. Salty darkness.

My thighs clench.

This nightmare isn't over. I'm in the belly of the beast. And Rian's contraption still clings to me like a ball and chain.

"I'm leaving," I cough.

But when I try to sit up, Tytus effortlessly pushes me back down again.

"You aren't going anywhere."

"Like hell." Curling onto my back, I try to roll off the other side of the bed.

But the act only makes my pounding headache explode, and I'm quickly sent falling to the floor.

"Stop it!" Tytus orders.

His heavy footsteps crack against the floorboards as he races around the bed to pick me up.

"Leander wants to marry me..." I remember out loud. "And Drago wants to help him do it. I have to get out of here."

"You don't think I've been grilling those two relentlessly for the past six hours?" Tytus asks, clearly offended. "You're safe here, Roz. I would never make you stay anywhere you weren't safe. Even if this place is surrounded by Leander's bodyguards, they aren't here to keep us in. They're here to—"

"I've been out for six hours?" I interrupt, shocked.

"You've been out for longer than that. But I wasn't going to start interrogating anyone until I was sure you were out of harm's way."

"Why did they let you live?" I ask. "We were already outnumbered, but when I ran away, you were all alone..."

A strike of guilt cuts through my aching chest.

"It didn't matter. If they had tried to stop me from going after you, I would have killed them all," Tytus snarls. But his anger doesn't last; it slowly turns into something far less energetic. "If I had gone down that path, you might not be alive."

"You came after me," I realize. "You pulled me out of the water. You saved me."

"Not just you," Tytus mumbles, shaking his head.

My brows tent and a painful flash tears through my skull.

"What do you mean?" I ask, confused.

"I didn't think the old man had it in him," Tytus shakes his head. "And I guess, in the end, he didn't. But you should have seen Drago, Roz. It's like he knew you were in trouble. None of us moved when you ran out of the cave. Not at first. We were in a showdown, after all. But then something in the old dragon snapped. He raced by me like a shadow. At that point, I didn't even care about Leander's security. I went chasing after him. By the time I got to where you'd fallen, he'd already jumped into the water and dragged you up from the seabed. But he couldn't get you out any further than that. He was too weak. And both of you were about to fall back beneath the waves when I jumped in."

Those waves crash against the inside of my skull as I try to remember any of that. But all I see are stars and darkness.

"Drago saved me?" I gulp, still tasting the frigid seawater.

"That's right."

"And you saved the both of us?"

"I did my best."

My heart drops at the implication.

"… Does that mean…"

Tytus' dark eyes go wide as he realizes his mistake.

"No. Drago is fine," he quickly assures me. "Well, he's not fine. The man has health problems. But they have nothing to do with the gallon of seawater you both inhaled. He's been up and about for the past six hours. I've made sure of it. He had a lot of questions to answer."

Scrunching my nose, I force myself up straight. With Tytus' help, I manage to sit down on the edge of the bed.

"Tell me all of it," I insist. "Tell me what bullshit he's fed you."

"I think it's best if he tells you himself," Tytus exhales. I'm only now noticing how exhausted he looks.

"I don't want to talk to him."

"You should. The man isn't who you remember. He's changed—I'm still trying to find out if it's for the better."

"Men like that don't change," I spit, my voice trembling ever so slightly. "You heard him. I'm supposed to marry Leander. Even after all this time, he only sees me as a helpless little girl. A pawn. He's the same thoughtless manipulator he's always been."

"I think his intentions may be different this time," Tytus tries to explain. But he stops himself before he can go any further.

We both hear the knock at the door.

I've already learned my lesson—no quick movements. So, instead of turning around, I look up at Tytus.

His face tells me everything I need to know.

"Who is it?" he booms.

"Me."

The voice is so meek and small I almost don't recognize it.

"We're not ready for you yet," Tytus barks.

"Is... Is she alright?" Drago asks.

"I'm fine," I hiss.

Wrong move. My eyes clamp shut as I'm hit with another strike of pain.

"Rozalia, I'm sorry. None of that was supposed to happen, not like it did. I—"

"Save your apologies for someone who gives a shit!" I curse, not caring how much it hurts.

Drago needs to hear my rage.

He needs to feel my wrath.

Reaching out, I grab Tytus' sleeve.

"Let him in," I demand. Pulling myself onto my feet, I wobble for a moment before falling back down onto my ass. "Fuck..."

"Are you sure?"

"Yes."

Tytus cranks his neck, ready to fight for me, as we both share a long look.

I nod up at him, and he reluctantly nods down at me.

"Fine," he says, walking back around the bed. "Do you want me to stay here while you two talk?"

"Stay close," I ask him. "But I want to speak to Drago alone."

"I'll be in the hallway."

With that, the door to this unfamiliar bedroom is pulled open.

At first, I don't turn around. I just listen as Tytus gives Drago a mumbled warning.

I only turn around when the door clicks shut again.

Sure enough, there's Drago.

He looks even worse than he did in the cave.

The man who once terrorized entire criminal empires might as well be a ghost. There's hardly any muscle left on his once impressive frame, and the last bits of color on his pale face are all concentrated on the deep red scars that claw across his dead eye.

"How are you feeling?" He asks when the silence draws on too long for his comfort.

"Better than you look."

"That's not saying much," he chuckles.

A raspy cough quickly follows.

"I heard you saved me."

Crossing my damp arms, I try not to think about how close I was to dying.

Fuck. If I had gone out like that, I might have killed myself.

"No," Drago says, dropping his head. His thin strands of hair still look wet, and they fall over his face like curtains as he stares at the floor. "Tytus saved you. I only made things harder on him because he decided to save me too."

"I wonder why he did that," I sneer.

"I wondered the same thing."

When Drago steps forward, I instinctually reach down to where my thigh holster would be. Obviously, it's gone.

"Where's Leander?" I demand to know.

That slimy asshole was so smug about everything last night. I don't care how he can help us anymore. As far as I'm concerned, he's my enemy.

"He's decided to give you some space," Drago quietly explains. "We both agreed that things didn't exactly go as....

desired. And that was our fault. I should have known better than to spring that all on you, Roz. I'm sorry."

"Stop fucking apologizing, you creep," I rasp.

My headache takes a backseat as I force myself onto my feet. It takes a second to adjust, but this time, I manage to fight back the stars and stay standing.

Drago opens his mouth, but stops before he can apologize again.

"Understood," he says.

But that's just as infuriating.

"What the hell happened to you?" I ask, heart suddenly racing. "Is this what happens to dragons when they're cast aside?"

"This is what happens to a man who's lost everything."

"Pitiful," I huff.

My headache is slowly evaporating against my fiery disgust.

To think, I once looked up to this man.

"Agreed," Drago exhales. "It is pitiful. But it's what I deserve for failing my children."

"We were never your children."

Somehow, that's what finally shocks some life back into Drago.

A red fire rises in his eyes as he glares me down.

"Wrong," he says, a familiar sternness returning to his gruff voice. "No matter what happens, you four will always be my children."

My racing heart stops.

"Four."

There's no way he just brought those other two up.

"No matter how your relationships have changed, you four will always be my children."

"Krol is dead," I quickly remind him, unsure how to feel.

Krol.

How quickly I'd wiped that fucker from my mind. It's only been a year, and I've already convinced myself he never existed.

Fuck. Just the thought of him makes my skin crawl. He was despicable, even by mafia standards. And I'm glad Gabriel managed to wipe him from the face of the earth.

It was the last good thing my long-lost brother ever did.

But I never knew Drago thought of Krol as his own child—even if I knew that's something the snake always wanted.

"No, he's not quite dead yet," Drago whispers, shaking his head. "Just like Gabriel isn't completely lost. There's still hope. Hope that we can all reunite and take what's ours. Together. That's why I partnered with Leander. That's why—"

"What the fuck are you talking about?" I croak, emotions suddenly clogging my throat. "You really have been living under a rock. Krol fell into a black pit. He's dead. Gabriel is married. He has a child. A kingdom. He's lost. There's no coming back for either of those fuckers. You're delusional, old man."

"Krol isn't dead…" Drago repeats. "Not yet. I can save him, but only with Laender's help…"

I don't know what to think. It feels like I'm sinking into a fevered nightmare.

"You've gone crazy," I grumble, wishing that Tytus has in here with me.

Tytus.

He must have heard this same spiel from Drago. Why didn't he seem as disturbed as I feel right now?

There must be more.

"Losing everything will make any man go a little crazy," Drago admits.

"There's no one to blame but yourself."

"I know. But that only makes it all so much worse." Rubbing the backside of his hand against the broadside of his scarred cheek, Drago takes a deep, raspy breath.

"So, live with it. And stop trying to drag us back into your miserable life."

"That's not an option," Drago sighs. "I can't rest until I've made it up to you. To your brothers. To our family."

"We were never a family," I spit. "And you proved that time and time again by choosing yourself over any of us."

"I was foolish."

"You still are foolish. And you haven't learned a thing. I should kill you right now for trying to marry me off. Last time you made that mistake, I almost did. Now, I'm regretting that show of restraint."

"This time is different from all the others," Drago tries to explain. "This time, I wasn't being selfish. I'm trying to look out for you, Roz. I'm trying to—"

Before he can finish, I've darted across the room and landed an open palm against his emaciated cheek.

The force of my slap sends his thin neck snapping aside, and for a split second, I almost worry that I've decapitated the bony bastard.

But then he spits blood onto the carpet and straightens himself back out, and any concern I'd had for him evaporates against my indignation.

"Who the hell do you think you're trying to fool?" I bombard him, already dizzy from the effort. "You literally just told me how you needed Leander's help for some weird twisted fantasy you have about Krol. What does that have to do with me? I'm not a little girl anymore, Drago. You haven't saved me from anything in a very long time. I'm not under your spell anymore. Do you think you can trick me just because you look different? Because you look weaker? How could any of this shit be beneficial to me, huh? Fucking tell me."

Grabbing his jaw, Drago tries to click it back into place.

"I'll tell you," he mumbles, the flame in his eyes calming as he looks past me. "But, first, I need one last favor from you."

"No. Fuck you."

Dropping his shoulders, Drago seems to finally accept that I'm not his little pawn anymore.

It only took him eleven years.

Still, he doesn't give up.

"It's nothing serious," he gently explains. "But I don't want Leander to hear what I say next."

That's when I realize he's searching the room for listening devices.

I know I shouldn't fall for his games, but I can't help the frustrated curiosity bubbling up inside of me.

"Where's my phone?" I snarl.

"In the bedside drawer, I believe," Drago gestures.

Still wobbly on my feet, I turn around to fetch my phone. Sure enough, it's in the bedside drawer. To my surprise, it's been turned off, almost like someone decided to respect my privacy.

The nuclear-powered scrambler, on the other hand, is still running at full steam—probably because no one knew how to turn it off.

Even though I can practically feel the radiation leaking from its pores, I decide to keep it on for a little bit longer. I'm in no shape to face off against Rian right now. And I'm sure he's desperately trying to reach me.

He'd better be.

Turning my phone on, I find a homemade scanner app. It only takes a single click to send a soft red light pulsing out from the camera slot. I paint the walls with its crimson spectrum.

When I'm done, the results pop up on my screen.

"We're in the clear," I huff, unimpressed.

"Good," Drago nods, a hint of strength returning to his withered voice. "Then I can tell you the truth."

"I'm listening," I insist, doubtful that there's anything Drago could say to change my mind—about him or his insulting plan.

Still, part of me is desperate to be proven wrong.

He is the man who raised me, after all.

"Leander is—"

Drago doesn't get a chance to finish.

Before the first word is even out of his mouth, an all too familiar sound rips both of our attention over to the bedroom window.

"Was that a gunshot?" I ask, stunned.

Another crackle slashes through the silence.

My hackles rise.

This time, there's no pause between the first shot and the second. Chaos erupts. Somewhere outside, it sounds like a bomb goes off.

Fuck.

My legs begin to tremble. And I can't tell if it's because I'm weak or if the vibrating has started again.

Either way, my heart drops.

It doesn't matter.

He's here.

Rian is here.

I'm not ready to face him again. Not after what I've been through. And definitely not with Drago around.

The bedroom door bursts open.

Tytus already has blood in his eyes.

"We have company."

11

RIAN

It's immediately clear we're not dealing with mobsters.

The fuckers fight too clean, too tightly. They might as well be a royal guard. Practically toy soldiers compared to the animals I've brought with me.

It's disappointing.

Whatever army these men are a part of, it's not the one Rozalia and Tytus supposedly have control over.

I'm sure of it.

These are just run-of-the-mill bodyguards—eye candy to help an insecure billionaire feel safe and look tough.

Well, he won't be feeling safe now. Not if he's in that house. We've already upended the driveway and shattered all the windows.

And we're just getting started.

Each time Leander's bodyguards try to form a protective perimeter, we cut through them like a savage machete. And by the time I manage to massacre my way through the corpse-covered driveway, to the back of the beach house, the sand is already drenched in blood.

I add to the flood.

"These must be Leander's men," Maksim points out as I pick off the last of them. His voice crackles over my earpiece. A few quick gunshots erupt on his end. "They're weak."

Back by the front, I hear another one of our grenades go off. The stone driveway must be completely destroyed by now.

Lifting my gun, I put a bullet in a body flailing down by the shoreline.

"That begs the question," I grumble, turning back to the beachfront property. "Why the fuck would Rozalia and Tytus want to align themselves with someone this weak?"

On the second floor of the opulent beige mansion, a window breaks. I only see the glint of a rifle's scope before I hit the deck.

A round of bullets rip over my head. I roll through the blood-soaked sand, avoiding their trail.

"Do we have anyone inside yet?" I ask, finding cover behind a small pile of fresh corpses.

"Not yet. Whoever is protecting the foyer has a better shot than any of the poor saps outside."

Rozalia. It must be.

And even if it's not, I'm willing to take any chances.

My plans for her don't involve a funeral.

"Remind the men that we don't kill women. If a single bullet comes anywhere near Rozalia Dorn, there will be hell to pay."

"Understood," Maksim listens. "I'll hold down the fort out front then. Are you going to sneak in the back?"

Another flurry of bullets rip into the dead bodies protecting my position. Blood and guts spurt into the air as the morning seagulls squawk above.

"I'm going to need a distraction," I explain. "Draw all fire towards the front. Can you do that for me?"

"Consider it done."

I don't concern myself with what Maksim is going to do. He

has my trust. Reaching into my pocket, I pull out another round and load it into my gun.

I'm ready to fight my way into that house. But before I can, something happens. Something that stops the chaos in its tracks.

An odd stillness takes over the beach—even the bullets coming from the second-story window stop.

"What's happening?" I ask, pressing down into my earpiece.

"I don't know," Maksim responds. "I haven't done anything yet."

"Why did you stop firing?"

"Because they did."

"That's not a good excuse, I—"

"Oh shit," Maksim interrupts.

That's a rarity for him.

"What?" I demand to know.

"She's here."

My racing heart freezes.

"Rozalia?"

"The one and only. And she's waving a white flag."

I'm immediately suspicious.

"That doesn't sound like the Black Cat to me."

"Well, why don't you come around and see for yourself, then," Maksim insists. "I'm staring at her right now."

"Where is she?"

"In the window by the front door. She must have ripped up a bedsheet or something, because that's literally a white flag in her hand."

My grip tightens around the handle of my gun.

"Send some men to my position, out back. Now," I order.

"How many?"

"At least half. I have a bad feeling about—"

Before I can finish, something suspicious catches my eye.

Every curtain on every window in the house seems to flutter backward at once.

"Did anyone just open up the front door?" I ask.

"No. Why?"

That sly fox.

"I'm going inside. She's escaping."

Throwing caution to the wind, I bound over my protective pile of corpses and make a beeline for the mansion's backdoor.

I'm not greeted by any more gunfire. But that only heightens my suspicion.

"I've sent the men around back. What's going on?" Maksim asks. "Talk to me."

"Come in the front door and see for yourself," I tell him, bursting in through the back door.

Sure enough, the place is a ghost town.

"What about Rozalia?"

"That's not her."

Moving as fast as I can, I try to find a set of stairs leading down to the basement. I already know there is one. Fortunately, it's not hard. An intense draft whips up from a dark, half-open doorway just around the corner from the living room.

"What do you mean that's not her?" Maksim asks, confused. "I can see her with my own two eyes. Does this mean you want me to engage?"

"Do whatever you want, just don't hit me," I say.

"Rian, I don't understand—"

"It's a fucking hologram," I bark, descending the dark staircase. "A distraction. Someone just opened up a doorway, probably to an escape tunnel. I saw the curtains being sucked towards it. Whoever's here, they're about to get away."

But it's no secret who's trying to escape.

Rozalia.

No one else would use a hologram. No one else could.

"You're telling me the place is empty?"

"No," I clarify, remembering the rifle upstairs. "Who knows what kinds of traps have been set. Send half a dozen men in. Tell them to be careful. They have my permission to shoot whatever moves."

I'm not concerned for my prey's safety anymore.

Now, I'm just angry.

Furious.

... And ecstatic.

Rozalia isn't hurt. She's not in danger. She's not dead.

She's just stubborn.

Our little game can continue.

"Understood," Maksim responds. "I'll go in with them, just to make sure."

"I have another job for you," I stop him. Shoving aside some ammo, I pull out my phone and increase its signal. Then, I send an encrypted code to Maksim's phone. "Follow the signal I just sent you. You'll be my eyes above ground. And my last resort. Bring some explosives. Get ready to use them. On my word, you're going to set them off."

"Rian, what's happening?"

"I'm hunting."

I'm unable to control my smirk. Even as I descend deeper into the unknown, all alone, I feel a new energy come over me.

This is fun.

I'm in my element. I have my advantage. I'm closing in on my prey.

The fear I'd had earlier—that this game of cat and mouse might have already come to an end—has been eviscerated.

The Black Cat isn't so easily beaten.

But that doesn't mean I'm not about to break her.

When I hit the last step of the basement stairs, I replace my phone with Rozalia's remote.

The dial turns up to ten. My cock swells.

I lick my lips.

"You're punishment has only just begun, kitten."

Through the darkness ahead, I swear I hear the faintest echo of a yelp.

It's her.

Keeping the remote grasped in my hand, I chase after the sound. It leads me to a rickety hatchway. The thing has barely been closed, and a stale breeze lifts from its uneven edges.

For such a nice house, this sure is a shit escape route.

It only bolsters the mystery behind Rozalia's choice in partners even more.

Why Leander?

Maybe she just likes him better than you.

Lifting my foot, I send a strong, angry heel down into the wooden square. It shatters beneath my weight, revealing a ladder.

My gun leads the way. And I climb down with only one hand, ready for an ambush—not that I'm exactly expecting one.

Rozalia isn't trying to catch me. She's on the run.

It's like I can taste her fear in the dry air.

Whatever Rozalia was doing here, it definitely wasn't waiting for me. This ambush caught her by surprise.

Maybe the vibrations are driving her mad.

My smirk falters a little at the thought.

That would be too easy.

I want to see her shatter in person.

The second my feet hit the last rung of the ladder, I hear another faint whimper echo through the tunnel. It's followed by a frustrated screech.

That's right, kitten. I'm inside you. There's no escape.

"Maksim, can you hear me?" I mutter as quietly as possible.

"Loud and clear."

"Do you see my signal?"

"Yep."

"Good. Follow it. And have the explosives ready."

"Copy that."

The tunnel is deep enough that I can't hear anything above ground. Dim, flickering yellow lightbulbs sway from the dirt ceiling as I race ahead, gun drawn and ready to fire.

To my surprise, the underground tunnel doesn't stretch out in a straight line. Instead, it slowly begins to wind like a snake. For caution's sake, I have to slow down around every new corner.

Even if this isn't a trap, there's no way Rozalia isn't beginning to feel cornered. Who knows what she'll do to keep me from catching her.

Slipping my way past a stretch of hanging lightbulbs, I steady myself before a sharp turn ahead. But it's not because I'm extra wary.

A new scent has joined the moldy underground air.

A spicy rose fragrance.

My eyes momentarily shut. A deep breath fills my lungs.

She's close.

Then, as if to further confirm it. I hear a voice.

Her voice.

It's too lost in the twists and turns of the tunnel to hear clearly, but there's no mistaking it.

My heart lifts… then falls into darkness.

Another voice joins Rozalia's. A deeper voice.

I don't recognize it. And my first instinct is to snarl at the thought of who it might be.

Leander.

Who else would it be?

This is his house, after all. The house my black kitten ran to when she couldn't handle me anymore.

My grip tightens around the handle of my gun.

I'll make her watch as I tear him apart.

Somehow, I manage to stay in control of myself as I edge

closer to the voices. It doesn't sound like they're moving. Not fast, at least.

I decide to play with them.

Rozalia's remote in hand, I turn down the dial until it's almost off.

"We're not going anywhere without you," I clearly hear a man's voice state.

It's strangely familiar.

"Fuck. It stopped," Rozalia mumbles.

My heart starts to pound in anticipation. My half-hard cock starts to grow again.

She's so close.

"What stopped? Roz. Fucking tell me!"

I don't even turn the final corner before I realize it's not Leander's voice I'm hearing.

That's Tytus.

Fuck.

I wasn't expecting him. But I'm not exactly disappointed.

With him here, I can kill two birds with one stone.

"It's nothing," I hear Rozalia stubbornly insist. "It's just these fucking cramps. Let's get the hell out of—"

With an uncontrollable smirk lifting my lips, I turn the dial back up. This time, though, I stop halfway.

It should be enough. Enough to momentarily incapacitate her. Enough to shame her. Enough to arouse her.

The idea of making the Black Cat cum in front of her own brother is strangely arousing.

Such a naughty girl.

"Fuck!"

The helpless rage in Rozalia's roar fills the tunnel.

I take it as my cue to reveal myself.

"Hands off the girl."

Tytus is trying to help Rozalia off the ground when he turns to see my gun trained on him.

His dark eyes momentarily go wide with shock before settling into an unadulterated rage.

"You..."

He's already reaching for his gun when I fire a warning shot at his feet. The blast rips through the tunnel like thunder, leaving behind a sharp ring.

We all wait for it to fade before anyone says another word.

"Don't do anything you might regret," I warn him.

But Tytus doesn't seem to be listening. Instead, something seems to click behind his fiery eyes.

"What the fuck have you done to my sister?"

"Nothing she didn't want," I smirk.

"You fucking asshole," Rozalia hisses.

She's still on the ground.

"Help your sister up," I tell Tytus, urging him with the barrel of my gun.

Tytus hesitates to comply. But when I don't budge against his fiery glare, he eventually rips his attention from me to his sister.

"Are you alright?" he asks Rozalia, helping her up.

"I'm fine," she lies. Her knees are practically clanking together.

I bite my bottom lip, remembering how those thighs feel wrapped around my cock.

"No. You're in trouble, little lamb," I taunt. "You missed our meeting this morning."

"What meeting?" Tytus asks, turning to Rozalia before she can answer.

"I never agreed to any meeting," Rozalia snarls, clearly trying to keep her discomfort from showing—and hide any pleasure she may be feeling.

"What you agree to doesn't matter," I remind her. "I'm in control."

I don't even need to lift the remote gripped in my left hand. Rozalia hears me loud and clear.

"Give it to me," she demands.

Pushing herself off Tytus, she clumsily stumbles forward.

"I have something even better," I playfully suggest. "It's in my back pocket. The solution to all of your problems."

Rozalia stops dead in her tracks.

"You have the antidote?" she whispers, a desperate innocence smothering her anger.

"Will someone tell me what the fuck is going on?" Tytus shouts.

"Your sister belongs to me," I explain. "Or didn't you hear? We're to be married."

That nearly sets the man off.

Somehow, he just barely manages to control himself.

Still, the thick underground air crackles with intensity. Tytus stares down the barrel of my gun like he's ready to do something stupid.

But before he can, something stirs behind him.

"She's not yours to marry."

The voice is like broken glass. It's harsh and disjointed and eerie. But no matter how jarring the sound is, nothing prepares me for the face that accompanies it.

It's like seeing a ghost.

No. Not a ghost. A demon.

To my utter shock, Dragomir Raclaw slips out of the darkness behind Tytus.

I can't believe my eyes.

He might as well be a walking corpse. His pale skin is practically translucent beneath the bulb swinging above him. His arms are thin, bony, and covered in worn tattoos and faded scars.

His dead eyes are sunken and empty.

But the gun he has pointed at me is held with a strength that can't be ignored.

I'm so stunned, I hardly even react as Tytus takes the opportunity to rip out a gun of his own.

All of a sudden, I have two weapons directed at me, and they're both wielded by notorious killers.

There's nowhere to run for cover.

Fuck.

"What the hell are you doing here, coward?" I sneer at Drago. My feet dig into the ground as I prepare for the fight of my life.

"Making up for lost time," the ghost responds.

With that, Drago clicks down on his safety, ready to shoot me where I stand.

There's no way I can beat both of them to the draw.

So, I do the only thing that can save my life.

I turn my gun on Rozalia.

"Easy there, cowboy," I threaten. "Let's not turn this tunnel into a graveyard."

Neither of these fuckers need to know I'd never pull the trigger. I just need to buy a little time.

I just need Rozalia to get a little closer.

"I dare you," Tytus growls.

"Double-doggy dare?"

"This isn't a fucking joke."

"Did I say it was?"

To my surprise, Rozalia lifts a shaky arm, blocking off Tytus' barrel with the back of her hand.

"Turn it off," she tells me. "Turn it off and we can all walk out of here alive."

Her voice rattles ever so subtly. But not even that clues Tytus in on what's really happening. How could he know?

He looks just as pissed off and confused as ever.

"I'm not leaving without my bride," I reply, not budging.

"I'm not yours," Rozalia sneers.

"Is that because you already belong to someone else?" I accuse.

"No one owns me."

"What about your new friend Leander Onasis?"

I try my best to keep the envy out of my question. But I worry it's all too clear.

"No. One."

"I'm not buying it. Why else would you be at his house?"

"You don't know anything," Rozalia spits.

"That's not true," I say, shaking my head. "I know how to free you from those cramps of yours..."

Rozalia must truly be desperate, because she easily takes the bait.

"Tell me," she demands, stumbling forward some more.

Tytus twitches behind her. "Roz. Stop. I don't know what's going on. But he's goading you. Don't get too close."

"I know what he's doing," Rozalia says, her sharp green eyes zeroing in on me. "But I need what he has."

"It's right here, baby," I smile.

With my left hand, I pat down onto my pocket, implying that I have the antidote stuffed down there, right beside my cock.

"I'm going to butcher you," Tytus growls. Still, he doesn't dare move an inch as Rozalia strays further away from him.

He doesn't know I won't shoot her. And that might just save my life.

"Watch your mouth," I snap back at him. "You're speaking to your future brother-in-law."

"You're going to regret those words," Drago says, speaking up again. "I'll make sure of it."

"You aren't doing shit," I lash out. "Why don't you run and hide again. Coward. Just like you did the last time one of your disciples was in trouble."

To my surprise, Drago's gun dips slightly at the dig. The fire in his dead gaze wavers.

"You've seen Gabriel…" he mutters. A heavy sadness takes over his bony shoulders. "Is he well?"

If I was smart, I'd take advantage of Drago's lapse. Hell, I should massacre both him and Tytus right here and now.

But I don't do that. Instead, I feel the need to defend my brother-in-law.

"Gabriel is thriving," I tell him. "No thanks to you. Or either of you." My eyes dart between Rozalia and Tytus. "You two had your chance to join our empire. But you spat in our faces. You threatened my family. Now, you're going to pay for it."

Trying to hold onto that rage, I take a subtle step backward, hoping Rozalia will follow me.

Just a few steps closer, kitten.

I try to concentrate fully on her as she silently obeys my wishes. But even as she complies, something else comes rushing out from the back of my mind.

Gabriel.

Just the mere mention of his name brings me back to our discussion in the library.

He told me all about Rozalia. About her tragic and brutal past. About her nightmares. And about her dreams.

He wasn't lying when he said it would change how I saw the Black Cat even if I'm trying to treat her the same way I always have.

With contempt.

But Gabriel was right. She's not who I thought she was. Not as cold or heartless. And not as impenetrable either. She's far more damaged than I could have ever imagined. More fragile.

Last night, I went to bed dreaming about her.

This morning, I woke up with the most dangerous thought I've ever had.

I can fix her.

But only after I break her.

That's the mindset I brought into our meeting at the warehouse. Oh, how quickly I lost sight of that desire. When she didn't show up, my empathy was devoured—replaced by something far more primal.

I was pissed, and my original instincts returned.

All I wanted was to hunt again.

Not fix. Or break. Or mold.

Just hunt.

But now she's right in front of me again.

I've caught up to her.

AND I can't help but remember the brutal past Gabriel revealed to me. The horror of it.

The hope.

Rozalia doesn't want to get married.

And neither do I.

Maybe, just maybe, we can chase each other forever.

Or maybe, she's already decided to marry someone else.

"Roz. Stop!" Tytus' roar breaks me out of my trance.

But Rozalia isn't listening. The Black Cat is slowly approaching me, just like I want. Her unsteady feet curl into the ground as her desperate eyes search for what I've promised.

A cure for her captivity.

"I can fix you," I whisper, taking another soft step backward.

"Give it to me," she rasps. "I know you have it."

"I'll give you what you want…"

When she's nearly close enough to grab, Tytus drops his gun and springs forward. But I'm closer to Rozalia than he is, and before he can get anywhere near her, I pounce.

Rozalia hardly flinches.

My gun presses against her damp forehead. Tytus is forced to drop to the ground.

"Stop it."

Her voice is so faint I hardly hear it.

But I can see her bottom lip quivering, and the water building in her beautiful green eyes.

The sight sends a pulse of guilt pounding through my chest.

I know what you've been through, kitten. But it's not over yet.

Reaching out, I take her by the wrist and twist her into my body.

My gun brushes against her temple for a split second, before I turn it on Drago.

He's the real monster here. Not Tytus. Not Rozalia. Not me.

It's him.

Gabriel told me all about the greedy dragon.

He's the one who's made Rozalia's life so hard.

"Drop the gun," I demand.

I can feel the faintest vibrations shaking through the meat of Rozalia's ass. It makes my cock swell, and my eye twitch.

That must make me look even more unhinged than I actually am, because Drago only hesitates for a second before complying.

When his gun dips, I push my lips into Rozalia's ear.

"The remote is at your feet, kitten. Pick it up," I whisper. "Turn it off… or turn it up. Whatever you want."

I help her bend down and pick up the very device that's been torturing her. When it's in her grip, she immediately turns the dial down. But not all the way.

I can't help but smile.

I knew she liked it.

"Give her back," Tytus growls. He's still on the ground, knees dug into the dirt. Sand seeps from his clenched fists. Fume billows from his ears.

It looks like he's about to explode.

You'll get your wish in a minute.

"You," I say, suddenly remembering one last important piece of information. "Return my sister's painting."

Tytus' dark eyes burn with a vicious hatred.

"... Or what?" he snarls.

"Or you'll never see your sister again."

"Your entire empire will crumble," Drago croaks.

But his shattered voice has lost its power. I can see now that he's just a broken old man.

"Not before you do." Looking up at the lightbulb swinging between us, I take one last deep breath. "Maksim. Now."

My consigliere must have sensed that I was getting ready to give the order, because I hardly even have time to jump back before the first blast goes off.

The ceiling of the tunnel cracks, and an avalanche of debris comes tumbling down.

"What the fuck..." Tytus grumbles.

"Again!" I shout.

This time, I wrap a tight arm across Rozalia's chest and turn us around. When the second blast shakes the walls, we're already running back down the winding path.

Behind us, I can hear the tunnel implode, shutting us off from Tytus and Drago. That was the plan. But it was supposed to stop there.

Instead, a heavy roar fills the darkness.

"Stop!" I shout over it.

But Maksim must not hear me, because a third blast soon follows.

"Fuck."

The tunnel starts to collapse.

All we can do is run.

12

ROZALIA

I'm still trying to figure out exactly what happened when I hear a door click open.

"Fuck off," I rasp.

Dust and debris fall from my hair as I rattle my chains. The bed posts I'm tied to sway against my effort, but they don't give in. I know they won't. It doesn't stop me from putting on a show.

I'm pissed, and Rian needs to know it.

Because even if he doesn't respond to my demand to fuck off, I know it's him.

Who else could it be?

Out of all the fuckers in the world, there's only one who could have started the series of events that led me here.

He's the fucker who led an ambush into Leander's mansion. The one who followed us into the secret underground tunnel only Drago knew about. The one who pulled me away from Tytus. Who ordered some kind of explosive to go off. Who suffocated me with his body as the tunnel collapsed around us.

He's the same fucker who yanked me out of the rubble,

shoved a black bag over my head, then pushed me into a car and sat beside me in silence as we drove far away from the beach.

Far away from my brother.

I can smell Rian's earthy scent.

I want to be sickened by it.

But I just can't find the strength.

Hell, something inside me is almost glad not to be alone anymore. I've been waiting in this bed, all chained up, for what feels like hours now. And all of that time, I've been desperately trying to fight away a mountain of dread.

I'm worried sick about Tytus. Fuck. To my irritation, I'm even a little concerned about Drago.

Did they escape the tunnel too? Or are they still buried beneath the carnage?

My heart sinks.

I hate that I actually care about Drago's fate.

But not as much as I hate that I don't want to flinch away from Rian's earthy musk as he approaches—even if it's only because I know he'll momentarily distract me from my own dark thoughts.

"Will you leave me the fuck alone?" I blindly lash out.

"Unlikely," the lion says. With surprisingly tender hands, he slips the black bag off my head.

For a moment, I'm stunned by an influx of light.

But I can still spot a shape standing beside me. His shape.

"You killed them," I spit.

Despite how dry my throat is, I still manage to gather some saliva. It smacks against Rian's chiseled cheek.

Slowly, he comes into view. And I watch with disgust as he lets my saliva slowly drip down his jaw.

He doesn't wipe it off right away. And when he does, it's very slowly.

The animal.

"They're fine," he grumbles. "They killed about a dozen of my men in their escape."

A momentary wave of relief washes over me.

It's soon replaced by a molten anger.

"Good. I wish they had killed you too."

"No, you don't," Rian shakes his head. "That's an honor reserved for you, and you only."

"If I weren't shackled to this bed, I'd bestow that honor upon you right now."

My chains tighten as I continue to test their strength. But we both know it hardly matters how strong they actually are. I'm still so weak. My head throbs with a dull ache. My lungs burn. My limbs are so sore I almost feel like cutting them off.

Dead weight, the lot of me.

"I'm sure you would," Rian acknowledges.

With the back of his wet hand, he wipes off what remains of my saliva against me. A warm tingle crawls over my skin, bursting out from the point of contact. Rian's rough hands are even warmer than I remembered.

I hate that I don't hate that he just touched me.

"Hands off, creep," I hiss. Lunging forward, I try to bite him. But I don't even get close. My restraints are too tight.

The failure is all it takes for the claustrophobia to start settling in. My reality is bleak. I'm completely trapped. Utterly at the lion's mercy—even more so than before.

Still, an unwelcomed pressure follows the fear. My toes curl, and a bolt of self-loathing flashes through me.

Rian's wearing a tight white shirt and loose grey sweatpants. The shirt shows off his muscle-bound body, hiding just enough to tease what he looks like without it. His pants hardly hide a thing.

I force myself to look away. But the image doesn't vanish from my mind. Neither do the fantasies. The best I can do is blame it on my hormones and hope I don't do anything stupid.

Don't give in.

"Where's my crown?" he asks. His ocean blue gaze ventures up my neck, pausing at my lips before settling on my eyes.

"At the bottom of the ocean," I bluff.

Leaning forward, Rian nearly brushes his nose against the tender skin beneath my ear. Then, he inhales. Deeply.

My shoulder blades furl. A jittery sigh escapes my throat.

"Is that why you smell like the sea?"

"I smell like the sea because you almost got me drowned," I tell him, deciding not to hold anything back. "Those stupid vibrations made me lose my fucking mind. It made me sloppy, and I fell, ok? Right into the fucking ocean. And I would have died too, if it weren't for my brother saving me."

"Just your brother, huh?" Rian's voice is filled with suspicion.

But that suspicion is lined with something else. Something far more lethal.

Is that envy?

An involuntary gulp worms down my throat. It joins the frustrated fury seething from my lips.

"What the fuck is that supposed to mean?"

Those deep blue eyes study me for what seems like an eternity before he stands up straight again.

"It means I know about your friend Leander Onasis," he says.

The girthy veins on his thick forearms flex. Another shockwave pulses out from the pressure growing in my core. Desperately, I try to writhe away any arousal.

There's no use.

"Leander Onasis isn't my friend," I snap. Chains rattling, I make a big show of how pissed off I am at the implication. But really, I'm just trying to hide my growing arousal.

"So, he's more than a friend?" Rian sneers.

His big hands curl into tight fists as he turns around. His

broad back looks like it could block out the sun. But the sight doesn't leave me feeling cold.

Fuck. If anything, I'm about to overheat.

Why is this so hot?

"The second you let me out of here, he's a dead man."

That piques Rian's interest.

"You'd take the time to kill him when you could be killing me instead?"

"There's time enough to kill you both," I shoot back.

"And you'd let him be your first?"

Rian's words send a warm wave pulsing out from the pressure in my core. I can't help but remember what he did to me in that lonely old castle; what I did to him.

I impaled myself on his massive cock.

He erupted inside of me.

Closing my eyes, I try to fight all that away. But when I open them again, Rian has turned back to me. There's no ignoring the giant bulge swelling beneath his grey sweatpants.

The outline of his juicy cock is nearly enough to make me drool.

"I've killed far too many men to have him be my first," I swallow. "And I've fucked even more."

In the blink of an eye, Rian has sprung forward and wrapped his huge fingers around my tiny throat.

"You fucked him?" he growls, blue fire raging in his furious gaze.

I spit right between those gorgeous blue eyes.

He doesn't even blink.

"No. And I never would," I snarl. "How fucking dare you accuse me of something so disgusting."

My indignation seems to calm him. But that strong grip doesn't ease from around my throat.

"What we're you doing at his beachside mansion?" he asks, his blood-red lips so close to mine that I can taste them.

It occurs to me that, for all we've already done together, we haven't even kissed yet.

"I was dragged to Leander's McMansion after you nearly drowned me," I explain, forcing my gaze away from his lips. "I didn't have a choice in the matter."

"Where is he?"

"I don't know."

"Were you meeting with him before you almost drowned?"

"That's none of your business."

"You are my business, kitten," Rian growls. His fingers press deep into my throat. The pressure is strangely intoxicating.

But not nearly as intoxicating as that word.

Kitten.

I've never been called that before. To most, I'm the Black Cat. A grown-ass woman. A Fearsome killer. *The* femme fatale.

But kitten?

I should spit in Rian's face again.

Instead, I want him to dominate me.

The thought is so shocking that I'm momentarily stunned into submission.

"I'll talk," I finally choke, not wanting him to unhand me quite yet. It's a confusing feeling, but there's no denying the electric warmth washing up from between my legs.

I'm already wet.

"Go ahead."

I shake my head as far as it will go. "I'll talk if you give me what I want."

For a moment, Rian pauses.

I can't help but wonder if he knows what I want, because I sure as hell don't.

To my disappointment, he drops his fingers from around my throat. It's not until I'm free that I realize just how light-headed I was getting. I can't help but hope that it's the reason for some of my insane thoughts.

A flurry of shallow breaths rip up my throat.

Rian stands up.

"You want this, don't you?"

My heart jumps when he reaches into his pocket. That bulge is bigger and more prominent than ever. But he doesn't grab onto his swollen cock.

Instead, he pulls out a tiny vial.

I stop breathing.

"… Is that…"

"The cure for all of your problems," he nods.

The chains holding out my ankles stretch as I unconsciously try to cross my legs. But I can't pull them close enough together. My legs remain open.

There's nothing stopping Rian from staring down at my leaking cunt. There's nothing stopping him from tasting what he's done to me.

Even through my black leggings, I can tell he sees my arousal. My toes curl as I picture him ripping me another pussy hole.

"Are you going to give it to me, or are you just going to stand there?" I snap, tired of waiting.

The double meaning in my demand isn't intentional, but we both know what's about to happen.

There's no stopping a runaway train—or a hungry lion.

He can do whatever he wants to his captured kitten.

"Answer my question, kitten. And I will give you exactly what you want."

My teeth dig into my bottom lip as a burning breath fills my pounding chest.

"What was your fucking question again?"

"Were you with Leander before you almost drowned?"

There's no doubt in my mind he already knows the answer.

My concern is that I'm in no state to reveal any kind of

secrets to him. If I open the floodgates now, I might not be able to shut them again. Not until he makes me cum.

I've gone feral.

"Yes," I reluctantly admit.

My outstretched arms are starting to get sore. But I don't want to be untied.

I've met my match.

And I want him to prove that he can do whatever he wants to me.

"Good girl," Rian praises. Stepping forward, he unfastens the seal on his tiny vial. "Now, tell me why you were with him."

The treachery I faced in that island cave is the last thing I want to revisit right now. But it's not like I have a choice.

My body wants to give in to Rian Kilpatrick, and my mind doesn't want to fight it.

I've never felt this way before. It's terrifying. And exhilarating.

"He wants to team up with us to take you down," I tell him, arching my back as he sits on the side of the bed.

His body is so big and powerful it collapses the mattress. If I wasn't bound to the bedposts, I'd roll right into his gravitational pull.

Instead, all I can do is wait as he studies my body, open vile held between his thick, coarse fingers.

"And why does he want to take me down?"

"I don't know," I admit. "We haven't gotten that far yet."

Rian's lustful gaze pauses at my chest. I remember how those powerful hands of his felt on my tits.

"I believe you, kitten," Rian nods. Bending down, he presses his cheek against the base of my stomach. My entire body convulses. He smiles. Those goddamn dimples tug at my chest. "If you want, I can administer it myself."

The lion swirls the vial just above my belly button.

"Do I have a choice?" I gulp.

"You could always do it yourself. But I won't allow that to happen under my supervision. If that's what you want, it will have to wait until I release you."

"You're going to release me?" I gasp.

A light shiver of disappointment creeps up my spine.

"I haven't decided yet."

Fuck.

He's playing with me. If I want to keep my sanity, I'm going to have to make the first move.

"Do it then," I demand, staring up at the ceiling.

"As you wish."

My stomach caves in as Rian's hot fingers slip beneath the waistline of my leggings. His cheek lifts. Then, he tears my pants down my ankles.

A gasp rips up from my lungs. My hands instinctively rush for his hair, but the restraints pull me back into place.

Rian doesn't stop. The stubble around his jaw brushes against the insides of my thigh as he tips the vial over, letting a single drop fall onto my soaking clit.

"It needs to be rubbed in," he tells me.

The flat side of his thumb presses down onto my swollen nub.

"Do you like the way that feels, kitten?"

"Yes," I rasp, unable to help myself.

"Good. Because I'm not stopping."

Leading me in circles, Rian baths me in another few drops of the vial. It might as well be lube—not that I need it. I've never been so wet, except maybe when he fucked me.

"Oh my god."

My entire body trembles as Rian gently pinches my clit between his fingers. He rubs, pulls, and plays with me until I can't see straight anymore.

"Let's see if I can make you squirm even more," he whispers.

With one last dip of the vial, he empties the contents onto my begging cunt.

The substance is warm and gooey, and a sweet scent rises from between my legs. Rian spreads it out with the palm of his hand. Then he reaches into his pocket and pulls out a remote. Even through my blurring vision, I can tell it's not the same one he teased me with in the tunnel.

It doesn't matter. When he turns up the dial, the vibrations start all over again.

"You said you would stop that!" I croak, twisting against my restraints.

"I will, kitten. I will. This is just so you can go out on a high note. I never meant for this to hurt you. I'm sorry that it did."

Rian's fingers slide down my clit and enter my cunt.

"You almost got me killed..." I wheeze, fighting through the wonderful pressure.

"That's not how you were supposed to get to heaven," he says. A second finger enters my slick hole. The vibrations increase. My cunt trembles. I'm on fire.

"I don't belong in heaven," I tell him.

"No. And neither do I. But that doesn't mean we can't taste it from our place in hell."

The rest of his fingers slam into my pussy and his face falls back onto my stomach.

The pressure in my core is so intense I could implode, but when I feel the tip of Rian's thick wet tongue lash across my clit, it only gets better.

"Holy shit," I heave, hardly able to take it.

"You taste so fucking good, kitten," Rian growls in between his big, wet slurps.

It feels like I'm being eaten alive. The lion has caught me. I'm his dinner.

And it feels fucking amazing.

"I'm going to cum," I rasp.

Rian's hand pumps through me with increasing ferocity. His fierce tongue only adds to the pleasure. When his lips close in around my clit, it's game over.

He sucks me up.

I cum for him.

"Fucking drown me," he demands, pushing his face deeper into my soaking cunt.

My restraints twist and shake as every inch of me spams with pure ecstasy. Rian's teeth graze against my swollen nub, and my entire body jolts into him.

The world goes white. I'm blinded. All of my dread and anger and fear vanish.

For a moment, there's nothing but ecstasy.

Then, just like that, it's done.

"Fuck," I sigh, my head falling back against the mattress.

I'm dragged back down to reality.

Rian stands up, and I see him wipe his lips as he finds the vial and stuffs it back into his pocket.

Pre-cum stains the inside of his grey sweatpants. I can still see the thick outline of his engorged cock. It's just as big and hard as ever.

I'm already ready for round two.

"Is that all you've got," I ask, trying to sound tough, but my voice is just as shaky as the rest of my body.

"I did what I said I'd do," he growls.

Only then do I realize the vibrating has stopped.

My heart sinks.

"I don't believe you," I test, unsure how to feel about it.

I gave myself to him, and I did it because he could take me.

But now he's just going to give me up?

"Try it for yourself," he says. Pulling out the new remote, he throws it onto my still heaving chest.

"You'll have to untie me first," I remind him.

That makes him smile again. The dimples are back.

Fuck.

"I don't think you're quite ready for that yet," he says. "Especially now that I can't track you."

Reaching down, he grabs the remote, careful to press his palm down on my hard nipples before he lifts the device to my face.

"You mean *you're* not ready to untie me yet," I charge. "You want more of me."

Without acknowledging my accusation, Rian turns the dial up and down.

I feel nothing.

"See. You're free."

"Could have fooled me," I say, pulling at my restraints.

"You still have some more questions to answer."

"Well, let's get it over with then."

Rian isn't taking the bait. He just shakes his head and turns away.

I guess it's hard to take me seriously when my pants are down around my ankles and my arms are tied up above my head.

But that doesn't mean his flippancy doesn't immediately enrage me.

"Where the hell are you going?" I ask, watching in horror as he moves towards the bedroom door.

"I'm going to get something to eat," he says, patting his flat belly.

When I look at him, I can't see anything except the giant outline in his sweatpants.

"You're not fooling anyone, you creep," I sneer. "If you wanted to pretend like you don't want more, then you should have worn some darker pants."

"Who says I'm done with you, kitten?" Rian smiles. "I'm just going to refuel."

With that, he opens the door and steps out into the hallway.

"Wait!" I call after him.

"What?"

The orgasm he just slurped out of me is slowly starting to recede. My arms are beginning to ache again. So is my head.

But none of that compares to the emptiness in my stomach.

Fuck. When's the last time I ate?

I've been through so much lately that not even my hormones have been able to pry me away from it all.

"Bring me some food," I whisper, hating how desperate I sound.

"I'll bring you something better than that," Rian nods, grabbing his crotch.

"You bastard," I sneer. But even as hate fills up the emptiness inside me, so too does a new wave of arousal.

My ass lifts off the mattress. My toes curl.

I remember how that giant outline felt when it dug deep into my guts.

"I hope that throat of yours opens wide, kitten," Rian says, turning back around. "It will have to."

When he shuts the door on me, I want to scream. But I know there's no point. I might as well save my energy.

He's not done with me yet.

And I fucking hate how much that excites me.

What the hell have I become?

13

RIAN

I have to tuck my erection beneath my beltline just to keep anyone from seeing—not that the pre-cum stain isn't clear enough on its own.

My grey sweatpants have been marked from the inside out. But I don't even bother to stop and change them. These pants are only going to get dirtier.

I'm not done using Rozalia yet.

No matter how guilty a small part of me feels for caging such a wild animal, my primal side won't even consider the thought of letting her go.

The Black Cat is mine. Finally.

And all it took was a few explosives and nearly being crushed alive in a landslide I created.

Worth it.

Licking my lips, I turn into the kitchen and head straight for the fridge. But nothing inside looks even remotely appetizing.

What could taste better than Rozalia's cum?

I can only imagine one thing.

Her submission.

Fuck.

She practically begged for me to eat her out up there. The way her body squirmed, the way her chest heaved and her plump thighs clenched. It made me ravenous.

When I first laid my head down on her flat stomach, I thought I was making a mistake. It's never smart to turn your back on someone like Rozalia. But it quickly became clear that there was a way I could control her.

With my thumb. All I had to do was press down on her clit; lead it in circles; suck it up with my lips, then clean it off with my tongue.

She was so wet I nearly drowned.

My stomach rumbles as I search through the overflowing fridge. Out in the living room, I hear a few of my men talking. It sounds like they've brought one of the guard dogs inside—presumably to keep it out of the hot sun. Usually, I'd go say hello; get a few good pets in. But not today.

Lifting my shirt, I wipe some of Rozalia's leftover juice from my glistening lips. No one needs to know what we've done. No one can even be allowed to guess. This is between her and me, and no one else.

"This will do for me," I grumble, spotting a big juicy rotisserie chicken in the back of the fridge. "Now, what would a submissive little kitten crave after an encounter like that?"

If it were any other woman tied up in my room, I might search for some kind of soup or salad. But despite Rozalia's slender frame, I can't picture her daintily slurping up some meatless meal.

And the last thing I want is for that pretty little body to waste away into nothing. She needs to be able to fight back as I take her again, and again, and again...

This rotisserie chicken might just work for the both of us.

"Got anything in there an old man might be able to nibble on?"

Maksim's voice carries over the fridge door.

"Doesn't look like there's any porridge left," I play along. Lifting myself up, I drag my meal out and slam the door shut.

"Just as well. Probably wouldn't hurt to lay off the calories," Maksim chuckles, slapping a wide hand against his stomach.

I've seen him shirtless before, and I know how modest he's being. Not even my father is as ripped as my Russian uncle. The salt and pepper wolf is still a beast to be reckoned with. If anything, he needs more fuel to satiate his tireless work ethic.

But to Maksim, he's just an older version of his younger self. And from what I heard, his younger self was nearly invincible.

"If you do that, you're going to end up looking like Drago," I point out. "He was practically a corpse."

"Well, that's a good deterrent," Maksim acknowledges. "But the bastard can still fight like hell."

He's not wrong.

"What's the casualty count up to?" I remember to ask, still pissed off about how we let those two escape.

Stuffing the chicken into the microwave, I put the heat on high and lean against the counter. My erection is still as strong as ever, but I figure some bad news will help calm it down.

"Two more men died at the hospital," Maksim grunts. "For a total of fourteen dead."

"And how the fuck did a half-dead corpse manage to kill fourteen of our men?"

I'm angry about the losses on our side, but not devastated. I've lost plenty of men before. And those who died knew what they were signing up for. It's just a shame they had to go out like that.

"He had help," Maksim reminds me. "Tytus might be one of the most vicious fighters I've ever gone against."

That's not a lie either.

"And he wasn't just fighting for his life," I recall, shaking my head. "He was fighting for his sister's safety."

"Well, he failed at that, at least," Maksim nods.

"But only because you and I were there," I point out, a sudden ache pounding through my skull. I know a stress headache when it's coming. "Fuck, how are we going to run an empire when we can't trust anyone but ourselves?"

"It's not easy," Maksim is quick to teach. "You have to pick and choose who to trust. Carefully."

"That sounds like a lengthy-ass process," I grumble.

"You can't rush it," Maksim agrees.

"My enemies won't just wait around until I'm ready to face them."

"That's why we stagger their attacks."

"And how do we stagger their attacks?"

My uncle's eyes drift up to the ceiling, and I'm quick to understand his implication.

We have a hostage now.

A dangerous, beautiful, frustrating captive.

Tytus wouldn't dare attack us if there was a chance Rozalia could be hurt.

I'm not so sure about Drago.

"Just because Tytus may be momentarily neutered doesn't mean our other enemies are," I point out. "Gabriel has already told us about Rozalia's strained relationship with Drago. And now we've got this Leander fucker to worry about too."

The microwave beeps, and I turn to take out the hot meal.

"Speaking of Leander…" Maksim grumbles. "I've been following up on him. But he's harder to find than expected."

"Don't you have another mission to focus on?" I note.

Rummaging through a cupboard, I find a big glass pitcher and fill it up in the sink.

"I've put that aside for the time being," Maksim says, pausing for a moment before continuing. "There's nothing more important than securing your bride."

The reminder is like a punch to the chest, and the pitcher in my fingers shakes ever so slightly as I squeeze down against the handle.

"Of course," I growl.

Fuck. I keep forgetting about that little white lie. This game of cat and mouse is so exhilarating that everything else seems to fall to the wayside. When I'm hunting Rozalia, she's not the woman I publicly proposed to. She's my prey.

That's all she is.

… Right?

"It's a smart move," Maksim assures me. He must sense my hesitation, but I can't imagine he sees through my bullshit. Not quite yet. "Even if the Italians aren't happy about it."

For once, the Italians and I are on the same page—even if it's for entirely opposite reasons.

"Fuck the Italians," I curse. "You were going to tell me something about Leander. Where is he?"

To my surprise, Maksim shrugs.

"I don't know. It's like he disappeared. Up until last night, his movements were relatively easy to track. But every path I've followed since then has led to a dead end."

"How far could you have possibly searched already?" I ask. "The man is a Greek billionaire. He probably has countless luxurious hideaways spread across the globe."

"And we have countless spies and contacts spread out right alongside him. But every spy I've sent to one of his properties has come back with the same response. Nothing."

"He must be scared."

"Wouldn't you be?"

"You mean if I was a coward?"

"Precisely."

Setting down the filled pitcher, I clench my fists.

"I'm sure my new captive knows where to find him."

"And if she doesn't want to tell you?"

"Then I'll tear it out of her."

Maksim responds with a knowing smirk. "Are you going to eat that whole chicken by yourself?"

"I didn't say I'd starve the answer out of her," I snarl back. "She's going to have to look good on our wedding day."

"Do you want me to call a priest?" Maksim calls my bluff—though I'm not sure if it's on purpose or not. "Perhaps we can threaten her with an early ceremony. I know a particularly—"

"One step at a time," I interrupt.

But a knot has already appeared in my gut.

How far am I willing to take this charade?

The answer fluctuates by the hour. Hell, yesterday, when we were racing towards Leander's beachside property, I was so encompassed by jealousy that I momentarily convinced myself to actually go through with that stupid plan.

Anything to keep her out of the hands of some other man.

Fuck. I was on the brink of madness. And what happened next didn't help.

The Rozalia I found down in those tunnels wasn't like the one I'd come to hate.

She was so vulnerable. So desperate.

She had changed—or maybe I was just finally seeing the girl Gabriel told me about. The scared little kitten running from all sorts of evil men.

In that moment, I wanted to fix her.

"Keep looking for Leander," I tell Maksim. Picking up the warm chicken and the cold pitcher, I head back upstairs.

"I will," Maksim assures me. But before I can leave the kitchen, he stretches out his arm, stopping me. "There is one lead on Leander."

Raising my brow, I allow myself to take the bait. Still, I don't hesitate to call Maksim out on it.

"If I didn't know any better, I might think you were trying to keep me away from my new captive."

Maksim keeps his steely gaze fixed ahead, but I can tell he's already seen the stain on my crotch. He's too perceptive not to have noticed.

If I had to guess, he's probably concerned I'll get lost in that bedroom and never come out.

Well, he's not wrong to worry. But I still have a half-chub, and nothing except some very pertinent information is going to keep me from going upstairs.

I promised to fill Rozalia up. One way or another, I'm going to fulfill that promise.

"I've come across the name of a man who might know where to start looking for the Greek billionaire."

"I'm listening."

"Flavian Baros," Maksim says. Taking out his phone, he brings up a file on the screen. "Infamous socialite. Big-time club-owner. Notorious pervert."

"Seems like the kind of company billionaires keep."

"Apparently, Leander likes to host large-scale orgies at extremely private locations. Secret residences that he's paid to keep off the records. I've looked into how we might go about finding one of these residences, and that one name kept popping up. Flavian Baros. Apparently, this creep is the one who arranges these orgies for Leander. Every guest is blindfolded and privately driven in. Everyone except the man who organizes them all."

"Flavian Baros," I mutter, repeating the name.

It's a slippery name. A greasy name.

I'm sure we'll get along famously.

"I haven't sent anyone after the man yet, because I wanted to give you first dibs."

"Well, I appreciate it," I say, before pushing out into the hallway.

"Does that mean you don't want to interrogate him yourself?" Maksim calls out after me.

"I didn't say that," I shout back. "Just give me twenty

minutes... maybe thirty."

With that, I turn up the stairs, juicy chicken in one hand, ice-cold water in the other.

But no matter how hard my stomach rumbles, there's no ignoring the fire growing in my chest.

The uncontrollable envy is back. It spreads across me like a forest fire, blocking my peripheral vision as I storm down the hallway towards the room where my captive is held.

By the time I get to Rozalia's door, my mind is made up.

I'm going after this Flavian fucker myself. But only because he'll lead me to Leander. And if there's one thing I'm more obsessed with than stamping out any threat to my empire, it's making sure everyone in the underworld knows what's mine.

Whether she likes it or not, Rozalia belongs to me.

And the idea that another man could be after her makes me go nearly blind with rage.

It doesn't matter that I'm disgusted by the very idea of marrying her—even if only as a political tactic. She's still *my* prey.

Setting down the glass pitcher, I reach into my pocket and pull out a key. It unlocks the door, and I'm already pushing it open with my ass when I reach down for the pitcher.

It nearly gets me killed.

The second my fingers touch the glass handle, a rope of wound linen wraps around my throat. My Adam's apple is nearly crushed against the force, and I'm pulled backward.

"You bitch..." I curse, not needing to see my attacker to know who it is.

Somehow, Rozalia has gotten out of her restraints. I should have expected that. Fuck.

Before the bedroom door can slam shut behind us, I smash the pitcher against the inside of the frame. The glass shatters in my hand, and a rush of blood immediately starts gushing from the wounds.

It's a small price to pay. A sharp shard remains gripped between my fingers. I have a weapon now.

I swing the makeshift blade blindly behind me, but Rozalia only pulls down tighter on my noose. When I try to twist around, I feel her feet dig into my back.

She's riding me like a fucking bull.

"Die, you piece of shit," she hisses into my ear.

I go to stab her in the eye, but she's quick, and I only end up grazing my own cheek.

The crackle that escapes her is almost as infuriating as the thought of her doing this to another man.

"What's. So. Fucking. Funny?" I choke out.

With all of my strength, I turn my back to the nearest wall and throw myself against it.

I can hear the wind being knocked out of Rozalia's lungs as she's slammed against the hard surface. Somehow, though, her grip doesn't loosen.

I guess she's not so fragile, after all.

"Bastard," she wheezes.

"Bitch," I retch back.

Leaning forward, I gather enough momentum to shover her back against the wall. The ceiling shakes, but the cloth stays wrapped tightly around my throat.

I'm starting to see black spots.

No. I won't fucking go out like this.

"Listen carefully," Rozalia rasps into my ear. "These are going to be the last words you ever hear: this is what happens to any man who tries to marry me."

My face is on fire. My heart pounds against the inside of my chest. There's no room for lies or half-truths anymore.

"I don't want to fucking marry you," I croak. "And I never did."

To my surprise, that's what finally eases her grip.

The lapse only lasts for a split second, but it's enough.

Shoving my glass shard beneath the slightest opening, I begin to cut the cloth from the inside out.

"What the fuck did you just say?" Rozalia asks, still seemingly starstruck.

"I said. I. Don't. Want. To. Marry. You."

With blood gushing down from my neck, I call on all my strength and push.

It's enough to send the glass shard cutting through the thick wound fabric strangling me.

I fall to the floor, gasping for air. But there's no time to rest.

Spinning around, I catch Rozalia's wrist right before her nails can dig into my eye sockets.

"I'll never marry anyone," she screams, her bright green eyes wild with bloodlust. "Let alone someone as despicable as you."

"Are you fucking deaf?" I growl. With a firm twist, I whip Rozalia onto her back and roll on top of her. "I don't want to marry you, idiot."

She flails wildly under my grip, but it's no use. Even with all the blood dripping from my hand and throat, I still easily overpower her.

"Liar!" she wails.

There's a pain in her voice that cuts me harder than any glass ever could.

I can't help but remember what Gabriel told me. About how she was sold to protect her family. About how it didn't matter. About how she lost everything at such a young age.

About how she kept losing everything.

"I swear to god, if you don't calm down…" I growl.

Still, the glass shard slips from my hand. Instead, I find myself wrapping a bloody palm around her throat.

"Kill me?" Rozalia spits. "Is that what you want to do? It's always the same with you men. First, you want a wedding, then, if you can't get that, you want a funeral. Well, go ahead, put me in the ground, you fucking—"

I shut her up with a kiss.

I don't know what I'm thinking. Whether I'm delirious from blood loss or a lack of oxygen, it doesn't matter. My mind is blank as I shove my lips against Rozalia's and hold them there until she stops struggling.

Even through the metallic tinge of blood, I can taste her rosy perfume.

It's intoxicating.

I become ravenous.

"I don't want to kill you," I grunt into her mouth. "And I don't want to marry you either."

"Then what the hell do you want?" she softly cries, clearly just as confused as I am.

"I want to fuck you."

14

ROZALIA

Even through the blood, I can taste his earthy musk. It seeps through my lips and down into my core.

Those ocean blue eyes glare down at me with a look I've never seen before.

I don't know what the hell to make of it.

I don't know what to make of *this*.

All I know for sure is that I want to feel him inside of me again. I *need* to feel him inside of me.

Rian's stiff cock presses down onto my stomach as he holds my face between his bloody fingers. A crimson waterfall slowly drips from the mark on his neck.

I want him to kiss me again.

But I won't admit it. I can't. Not ever.

"So do it then," I croak. "Fuck me."

Rian doesn't wait around for clarification. His fingers fall from my throat, and he palms my breast with one hand while shoving the other beneath his beltline.

"I thought I ripped these off of you," he grunts, his thick finger finding my swollen clit one more time.

"I put them back on," I rasp.

"After you escaped your chains..."

"You should have known they couldn't hold me."

"That's right, kitten. I'm the only one who's allowed to hold you."

With that, Rian slips two fingers straight into my soaking hole. I gasp as he begins to ruthlessly pump. In and out. Back and forth. Fast and slow.

He reaches so far deep inside of me I can practically feel his fingers curl around the intense pressure in my core.

When he squeezes, I'm sent flailing again.

But he's right. The lion can hold me down all he wants. I'm no match for his physical strength. All I can do is squirm under his powerful body as he fist fucks me to oblivion.

"Keep going," I breathlessly order.

He obeys, and the pressure in my core cracks. My mind goes blank, and when I come back down to earth, I'm immediately sent into the throes of my next orgasm.

"What were you planning to do, little one," Rian growls. "I have men surrounding this entire property. You wouldn't have gotten far."

"I would have killed them all," I manage to whisper. "And then I would have run far away from your corpses."

"... Right into Leander's arms?"

My reaction to Leander's name is stronger than I could have expected. But when I lift a tired arm to strike Rian with, he easily pins it back down to the floor.

"Fuck that asshole," I curse.

"No," Rian shakes his head. "I'm the only one you're allowed to fuck."

His hand pulls out of my pussy, and a cold empty gust rushes between my legs. This time, when I lift my one free arm, it's not to strike the bleeding lion. It's to grab onto him, so I can pull him back onto me.

But I don't have Rian's trust, and he quickly pins my bicep

down with his knee. Then comes his other knee. It falls over my other bicep.

The giant beast straddles me, staring down from his throne over my heaving chest. The pressure of his powerful body sitting on my tiny body nearly makes me shatter.

But I force myself to look up into those ocean blue eyes.

"What? Do you want me to beg for it?" I spit.

He only smirks down at me. Those dimples deepen, and my stupid heart stirs.

"You mean more than you already have?"

"Stop fucking teasing me," I demand.

With all of my remaining strength, I push my ass off the ground. Somehow, I manage to gather enough momentum to wrap my ankles around Rian's bleeding throat from behind.

Reaching up, he grabs my feet. But he doesn't push them away. Instead, he opens up his glistening lips and shoves my toes deep inside his mouth.

A furious heatwave crackles over my skin. A deep gasp gets stuck in my throat. I cum. Hard.

His tongue swirls around each and every one of my toes as he slurps me down. My body shakes and shivers. I'm contorted like the fucking handle of an umbrella. Stretched thin. But I've never been more consumed by pleasure.

Then the massive bulge in his grey sweatpants shifts, and that big cock falls onto the tip of my chin.

I can't help but open my lips and take a gentle bite down on his bulbous head. Even through the thick material covering it, I can taste the fleshy thickness.

"Take off your pants," I command, my voice broken and filled with a shaky desire.

Finally, Rian pushes my feet away from his face, and my ass comes tumbling back down to earth.

"Whatever you say, kitten," he growls.

His knees slide down from atop my arms, only to be

replaced by his feet. I don't complain, because when he stands upright, those stained grey sweatpants quickly drop down from around his waist.

They fall onto my face, and I'm temporarily blinded, but I don't mind that either. Rian's musky scent is stronger than ever before, and it seeps deep into my nostrils as I feel his underwear drop down onto my face as well.

Then, it's his shirt.

My racing heart starts to pound as I realize I've never seen him completely shirtless before. My back arches and my ass lifts into the air.

Rian rips his pants from my face. When I look up, all I see is him.

There is no room. No cage. No white walls or windows.

Just a beast of a man, naked and bulging with muscles. His dark tattoos are stained with blood. His giant cock swells out from his thick and sculpted thighs, eclipsing his face.

My hips thrust up towards him. My cunt leaks like a fucking fountain. My nipples are rock hard.

"Do it," I whisper. "Fuck me!"

Rian huffs like the alpha lion he is.

Then, he turns around. His powerful ass and chiseled back flex as he bends over and grabs my ankles again.

My shoulder blades furl and unfurl as I'm twisted into a pretzel. By the time Rian turns back around, my feet are at my ears, and my leaking cunt is stuck up in the air, presented to him on a fucking platter.

"How much do you think you can take?" he asks, his deep voice getting deeper.

Those ocean blue eyes wash over me like a stormy sea.

"All of it."

"Don't shatter on me, kitten."

A primal snarl twists Rian's gorgeous face as he places a

bloody thumb at the base of his swollen shaft, tipping down his hard cock so it's aimed directly at my pussy.

"Don't tell me what to do," I croak.

"No," Rian says, shaking his head. "I'll tell you exactly what to do." With that, he squats down and impales me with his giant cock. "Take it. Take every last inch of me. Take it, baby girl."

He doesn't wait for my response, and I don't get a chance to give one.

Like the animal he is, he starts to fuck me without mercy. The cheeks on my upturned ass quickly turn raw against his savage power. He pounds down with a flurry of furious thrusts, threatening to snap my spine in two.

But I do as he says.

I take it.

Gritting my teeth, I feel the intense pressure in my core grow to an overwhelming level.

Before I can burst, though, my newly freed arms lift off the ground. It's pure instinct, because my mind is completely empty, but I don't even try to stop myself.

Open palm and all, I slap Rian against the face. First, my hand smacks against his right cheek. Then, his left.

He grunts in response, but that's all he does. There's no slowing down. No dirty talk. Just outrageous desire.

His cocks digs so deep into my pussy that it feels like it could pop out of my throat. It's hard to breathe. And even harder to imagine that this is the man I just tried to kill.

Fuck. Just a few minutes ago, we nearly ended each other forever. Now, a new life is taking hold of me, and it's thriving up from somewhere deep inside my cunt.

It's rapturous. And the hate in each of Rian's thrusts sends a searing shockwave rippling through my body.

"I'm going to fucking cum, kitten," he growls.

I slap him again.

"Don't you dare," I threaten.

But Rian just repeats his claim.

"I'm going to fucking cum."

I go to slap him again, but this time he catches me by the wrist.

"You can't stop me, Roz."

My hand is slammed against the ground as a deafening roar escapes Rian's lips. His neck bends upwards, revealing the cut on his throat, and the red burn mark around his bulging Adam's apple.

The sight only brings me closer to the edge.

I did that to him.

That big powerful beast was temporarily at my mercy. Just like he was in the security room. Just like he will be again.

Submitting to him can feel fucking incredible. But there's nothing quite like twirling this lion around my pretty little finger.

I'll get there again. And if I have to bend to his will a few more times before that, then so be it.

I won't complain.

My neck snaps back just like his as the pressure in my core cracks. Rian's thrusting cock throbs between my tight slick walls. He swells with anticipation.

I explode first.

Then, it's his turn.

Stream after stream of thick cum shoots into my pussy. I slap him again, but this time, I don't let my hand fall away.

Instead, I grab a handful of his thick, dirty blonde hair and hold on for dear life.

My toes curl beside my ears and my back extends and everything erupts in a fiery flash of searing ecstasy.

I struggle not to froth from the mouth as Rian pounds every last drop deep inside of me. But even when he's empty, he stays embedded inside my pussy.

"I hope you learned your lesson, kitten," he grumbles, finally unsheathing from me.

"What lesson?" I quietly croak.

Standing up, Rian finally lets my ass fall back to the floor. Still, he looms over top of me. Cum drips from the tip of his wet cock. His perfect body is stained in blood.

"That there is no escape," he says, glaring down at me.

My heart sinks.

"You called me, Roz…" I suddenly remember. "Just now, you—"

"Get up," Rian interrupts. Reaching a hand down, he offers to help me up.

But I don't take his offer.

Instead, I gather a deep breath and roll onto my side. I'm surprised that Rian lets me push myself up. But the second I'm back on my feet, he grabs my arm and starts to lead me to the bathroom.

"What are you doing?" I ask, still half-lost in a state of lustful shock.

"I'm going to clean you up," he says. "You're a mess."

"You're one to talk."

"That's why you're going to clean me up too."

Stopping outside the frosted glass of a tall shower, Rian lets go of me. I don't have the energy to do anything but watch as he turns on the water.

"Are you coming in or not?" he grunts.

The steam grows as he steps behind the frosted glass. For a moment, I don't move.

My mind scrambles to make sense of everything. But through all the chaos, one thing seems to stand out.

He called me Roz.

I don't know how to feel about that.

Only my closest friends have ever called me Roz. Rian must have picked it up from Gabriel.

My heart sinks.

Thinking of Gabriel reminds me of all I've lost.

And that includes Drago.

Fuck. Where has he been all of this time? What has he been up to? I didn't think I wanted to see him again. I didn't think I'd ever want to. But now, I'm not so sure.

How much more could I lose?

My adoptive father is still out there. And for some reason, Tytus trusts him.

I need to find out why.

But how the hell am I going to do that if I can't even escape Rian's grip?

Hell, do I even want to escape his grip?

Fuck.

I must be going crazy, because a sharp conflict rises inside of me as I remember what kept me from killing the lion.

Those bedsheets were pulled so tightly around his throat he could hardly talk. I was so close to ending him.

Then he said those magic words.

I don't want to fucking marry you.

It was like he reached into my chest and clamped his fingers around my shriveled heart.

He's the first man with any power to ever say something like that to me. And the declaration shocked me so badly I let the bedsheets go limp in my hands.

He took full advantage of my lapse.

Next thing I knew, he was fucking my brains out. The next thing I knew, I was loving it.

"I won't ask you twice, kitten." Rian's deep voice drifts out from behind the shower's billowing steam.

My toes curl.

My heart flutters.

He doesn't want to marry me.

So, why the hell do I suddenly want him more than ever?

15

RIAN

I don't take my eyes off her.

Not as she washes beneath the hot water. Not as she steps out of the steam and dries herself off with a towel. Not as she picks up her stained rags from the floor and gently puts them back on.

Rozalia is hypnotic. And it's not just that I'm still ravenous for her body. There's something else.

Something more personal. And more dangerous.

Something I can't quite explain.

Fuck.

I called her Roz.

It just slipped out. I still don't know why, but I've been trying to figure it out ever since I dragged her into the shower.

I've only ever heard two people call her that. Tytus and Gabriel. Her two adoptive brothers. They're the closest thing she's ever had to family.

But what am I to her?

The thought is too dangerous to contemplate. And so are the implications

I am not developing feelings for my enemy. I refuse to.

But when Rozalia clasps her hands together and looks down to the floor, my stone heart flickers.

How could something so corrupt suddenly look so innocent?

Is it the wet hair?

... Or the red marks I've left on her wrists...

No. It couldn't be the latter. She's already done the same thing to my throat.

So why do I feel like a monster?

"What the hell am I going to do with you?" I grumble out loud, gathering my own clothes.

For the most part, Rozalia hasn't been returning my constant gaze. Ever since we got in the shower, she's been trying to look away. But I catch her giving me a quick side glance as I slip my shirt back on.

"You could always let me go," she snidely suggests.

A small bucket of relief pours over me at the snarky comment.

She's not completely lost. The Black Cat I first became obsessed with is still there, burning away.

Still, it's hard to say exactly how hot her fire is burning. There's so much conflict raging behind those beautiful green eyes.

So, I decide to test her.

"You know I can't do that."

"You can do anything you want," Rozalia says, turning her back on me. "You're the almighty king, after all."

"And you're just an upstart street rat."

My insult has the desired effect, and Rozalia quickly comes twisting back around.

"This 'street rat' has caused you more trouble than the rest of the underworld combined."

I only nod. "And that's why I can't let you go."

"You can," she repeats. "You just don't want to."

"In my world, there's no difference."

Brushing past her, I make my way toward the blood-splattered doorway. Crimson marks stain the walls. A thousand glass shards litter the ground. In the middle of it all sits our upturned lunch.

"It's gone cold," I note, picking up the rotisserie chicken. "But I keep the floors clean. And it's the best you're going to get."

Ripping off a chicken leg, I toss it at my confused captive. Her reflexes are still sharp, and she easily catches it.

"How do I know this isn't poisoned?" she asks. But I can tell she's just being stubborn.

My Black Cat is desperate to eat. She just needs an excuse.

I give it to her.

"This is how you know," I grumble. Tearing off the other leg, I start to chow down. Savory juice dribbles down my chin, but I don't give a shit. I'm starving. And I know Rozalia is too.

"That doesn't mean there isn't another one of your twisted tracking devices baked into the skin," she sneers. "You could fit a billion nanobots into this piece of meat alone."

"I'd only need a dozen to track you," I taunt.

"And I'd only need one to end you."

I can't help but chuckle. "I don't doubt it. That's why I would never give you access to any kind of technology. Not in a million years. Hell, I left you alone for fifteen minutes with a pair of restraints and some bedsheet, and you nearly killed me."

"I should have taken the time to unbuckle the chains," Rozalia mutters.

Then, to my satisfaction, she finally bites down on her chicken leg. It eases my nerves a bit—especially as I fill my empty belly up right alongside her.

"Why didn't you?"

"I didn't think I'd have the time. It looked like they were fastened to the bedposts with bolts."

"They are. You made the right choice."

"Obviously not," Rozalia mumbles through a full mouth. "You're still alive."

"If you'd actually wanted to kill me, I'd be dead right now," I note.

She lifts a curious eyebrow. "What makes you think I didn't want you dead?"

"I never said you don't want me dead. But I don't quite believe you want to kill me yourself."

"Keep telling yourself that."

"I'd rather hear it come from your mouth."

When I step forward, Rozalia instinctively retreats.

"Don't fucking test me," she hisses.

"Easy there, kitten," I say. "I was just going to offer you some more chicken."

Lifting what remains of our legless carcass, I silently urge her to eat—even if I'm not entirely sure why. She'd be so much easier to deal with if she were constantly on the brink of starvation.

But I don't want to see her half-starved.

I want to see her satisfied.

"Toss it this way then," Rozalia finally accepts. Like a true barbarian, she tosses her half-devoured bone onto the floor so she can hold the rest of the rotisserie in her hands.

For a moment, I just watch her snap away at the meal. The savagery of her appetite is almost impressive, and I can't help but remember how good those glistening lips felt pressed against mine... or imagine how good they would feel wrapped around my cock.

Fuck. I can't believe I kissed her.

It was only to shut her up, I tell myself. But the truth is much simpler than that.

I kissed her because I wanted to.

In that moment, it's all I wanted to do.

"Feeling better?" I ask, just as Rozalia rips the last bits of flesh from the bony carcass.

"Much," she grumbles. "Maybe now I'll finally have the strength I need to properly kill you."

"Touch me again and see where that gets you," I smirk.

To my surprise, Rozalia's pale cheeks redden ever so slightly. Throwing the scraps of her meal to the floor, she tries her best to look away from me.

But there's no escape.

I take another step forward.

"You know this means nothing, right?" she says, still averting her gaze.

"What means nothing?" I play dumb. My cock is already begging to be back inside of her.

"The sex. The games. That... that fucking kiss."

"I never said it meant anything."

"I'm just trying to make sure you don't catch feelings."

I nearly choke on my own spit.

"Why? Are you afraid to hurt me?" I taunt, trying to play off how close she is to hitting a nerve.

I take another step forward, and Rozalia retreats further. But her back quickly reaches the wall.

"I'm not afraid of anything," she postures. "But I sure don't want to be stuck in here with a madman. And who knows how crazy you'll get if I hurt your stupid little feelings."

"Oh, I've already lost my mind," I chuckle.

My full stomach helps lighten my mood. Still, I can't shake the intense feeling that something has changed between us. Something big.

"Clearly," Rozalia huffs. "Because I could have sworn I heard you say you didn't want to marry me—yet you recently made a very public announcement saying the exact opposite."

Biting down on my tongue, I remember how that confession likely saved my life. It was only when I admitted that I didn't actually want to marry her that Rozalia finally allowed her grip to loosen.

But how much do I reveal to my enemy?

Lifting my bandaged hand to my neck, I feel the deep marks she's left around my throat. It's like an inverted collar. Strangely enough, I'm not completely offended. Hell, I'm not even that pissed off.

She earned it.

"You answer my questions, and I'll answer yours," I tell her.

"I don't negotiate," Rozalia spits. But her back is literally up against the wall. And as I continue my slow approach, there's nothing she can do but look up at me with a conflicted hate burning behind her perfect green eyes.

"I'm not negotiating, kitten. I'm telling. You're in no position to negotiate."

"Stop calling me kitten," she demands.

In response, I reach over her shoulder and splay my hand out across the wall—my forearm brushes against her cheek. I can feel the air thicken.

Every part of me flexes, ready to pounce in case my Black Cat tries something.

"You play along, and maybe I'll grant your wish... kitten."

With that, I lift my other arm up, caging her between my forearms. Now, her only way out is through me.

Fuck. I almost want to dare her to try something—any excuse to throw her back onto the floor and have my way with that tight body.

"Be careful, cub," Rozalia snarls. "I'm not one of your child brides. I'll bite back."

Leaning into her ear, I let out a shallow sigh just so she can feel the heat in my breath.

"I hope you bite hard," I whisper.

I can practically feel the electricity pricking her skin.

For a moment, I just pause there, inches away from her cheek. When I finally do pull back, it looks like Rozalia wants to bite my face off. I stare down at her like I want to return the favor.

Whatever's changed between us, it hasn't ruined the most important part of our dynamic: the taste for each other's throats. And that's good. Because I'm not finished with our little game of cat and mouse yet—not that I'm entirely sure I'll ever be.

"Go ahead, ask me anything," Rozalia finally relents, after our stare-down becomes too much for her.

I don't waste any time.

"Are you on birth control?"

I might as well have slapped her across the face.

"You think I'd ever even get close to you if I wasn't?"

"What does that mean?" I poke.

Her offended cheeks flush ever so slightly. That porcelain skin pinkens. I can't help but sniff in a deep breath of her coveted shame.

"It means I know how men like you are," she snips. "Pigs. Greedy fucking vermin who only want one thing."

"And what's that?"

"Me."

I snort. "How modest of you."

At that, a slight smirk finally appears on Rozalia's perfect lips.

"Can you blame me? I'm being hunted by a king, after all... and he's left his entire empire behind just to follow me around."

"I haven't left anything behind," I tell her. Running the back of my hand up Rozalia's wrist, I wait until she tries to pull away. When she does, I grab her. "You're in my domain, kitten."

"Let go of me," she hisses.

But she's hardly putting up a fight. If she truly wanted me to unhand her, I'd be eating a headbutt right about now.

"What kind of birth control?" I ask, tightening my grip.

"An injection."

"And how long does this contraceptive last?"

"Six months."

"How long ago did you take it?"

"I take it every six months, on the fucking dot—whether I'm being chased by a mad king or not."

"How many men are you sleeping with?" The jealousy in my question is impossible to filter out.

"Fuck men."

"No. You are only allowed to fuck one man. Me. Now, tell me who else you've slept with."

"Why? You want to fuck them too?"

"I want to kill them."

Rozalia tries to pull out of my grip again, but I don't let up.

"Be my guest," she sneers. "While you're out chasing ghosts, maybe I'll get a chance to finally breathe."

"You're telling me a beautiful young woman like you isn't having any sex?"

"I don't have time," Rozalia responds. "The only men who cross my path are the ones I kill."

"Have you killed Leander?"

This time, when Rozalia tries to pull away, she's not just doing it for show. But it doesn't matter how much effort she puts into it, I'm still far stronger than her.

"Leander is nothing to me," she rasps.

I push her against the wall.

Her perfect tits press into my chest as I hold her in place. My cock is already rock hard. I want more of her.

And she wants more of me. Even through the fabric of her black top, I can feel how perky her nipples are.

But before I'll allow myself to taste more of her, I need to get some answers.

"If Leander is nothing to you, then why did you dress up all nice to meet him? Why a fancy restaurant and not some back alley?"

"Because billionaires don't meet in back alleys," Rozalia snidely responds, her green eyes glimmering an inch away from mine.

"I met you in a back alley," I remind her.

"Who the hell do you think you're talking to? That was a hologram. *My* hologram. You weren't there."

"I was in spirit," I play.

With that, I push myself off the wall. Still, I keep Rozalia's arm gripped tightly between my fingers.

"You have no spirit," Rozalia huffs. "You're a soulless monster."

"Just like you?"

"... Just like me."

Rozalia's sharp gaze falters, and when her head drops, I finally let go of her arm. But only so I can pinch her chin.

"We're not so different," I say, lifting her head back up.

"Stop torturing me."

"Only when you stop liking it."

"You're such an asshole," she mutters.

Those green eyes flutter onto my lips.

I desperately want to kiss her.

"Your turn," I say instead. "Ask me a question."

Rozalia hesitates. I can see the gears turning in her eyes.

"What do you want with me?" she finally asks.

"I want to play with you," I respond, lifting my thumb up her chin, I push into the bottom of her plump lower lip.

"Stop bullshitting me," she orders, shaking me away. "Tell me right now, why did you tell the world you wanted to marry me?"

"I thought it might piss you off enough to make a mistake," I half-admit.

There's no point in telling her the entire truth—about how I thought it might help ease some of my father's concerns. She won't buy that.

"That's it?" Rozalia asks, flabbergasted.

"I also thought it might help draw Drago out of hiding," I shrug.

Rozalia's scrunched face goes limp.

"Drago..."

"How long have you two been back together?"

Rozalia's attention momentarily slips into some dream world.

I have to rattle her back awake.

"What's wrong?" I ask.

"Drago... he just showed up out of nowhere" I can feel her legs tremble as she remembers something deep and dark.

My free hand clenches into a fist.

"What did he do to you?" I growl.

"... He tried to set me up with Leander," she blurts out.

My heart sinks beneath a landslide of rage.

"As a business partner?" I hope.

"No," she mumbles, softly shaking her head. "As his bride."

I nearly erupt.

I'm so fucking furious that I even let go of Rozalia. But before I can turn away, her nails dig into my forearm.

"You really don't want to marry me?" she asks, her green eyes glimmering as she holds me in place.

Suddenly, I'm not so sure. In this fiery moment, it feels like I'd do anything to keep her from falling into someone else's hands.

Then, something clicks. And I know precisely what Rozalia wants to hear.

The truth.

"Not in a million years."

The thick air sizzling between us seems to momentarily pause as we stare deep into each other's eyes.

Then, without warning, a new life comes over my dazed captive. In the blink of an eye, she's lifted her left hand and slapped me across the face.

But her fingers don't leave my cheek after they've made contact. Instead, she digs them into my skin and pulls me forward.

The passion in her kiss is so unexpected I almost freeze up. But this shit is too hot to ignore. Any hesitation is quickly melted away.

Still, I've only barely started kissing her back when she pushes away again.

"This doesn't mean anything," she mumbles, wiping me from her lips with the back of her hand.

I pretend to do the same. But really, I just press the taste of her deeper into my mouth.

"I wouldn't have it any other way," I agree.

Shaking off her temporary lapse, Rozalia takes a deep breath.

"Do you have any more chicken?" she asks.

"I'm sure I could find some," I respond, studying her carefully.

What's happening behind those pretty green eyes?

"I believe in you," she says.

Clearly, she wants me to leave.

Too bad.

"You tell me where Leander is, and I'll get you some more food, kitten."

Rozalia's cute little button nose scrunches back up into a sneer.

"How would I know where that fucker is?"

"You seem like the type to track the movements of your business partners."

"I'd only met him once before..." she starts, before catching herself. "Twice. And the second encounter made it clear that he wasn't interested in being my business partner."

"Because he wanted to be your husband..."

"I'll show him what happens to men who try to marry me."

My Black Cat's slender fingers curl into fists, and her green eyes sharpen. She's ready to kill.

Fuck.

Seeing her so angry and vengeful is such a turn-on—not that I wasn't already hard. It almost doesn't matter that she's pissed off at another man.

Almost.

"From experience, I'd rather not let you do to him what you've done to me," I half-smirk—the other half of my face twists in a scowl.

In response, Rozalia almost lets herself laugh.

"Watch your mouth," she huffs.

"Or what? You'll kiss it again?"

This time, she actually does laugh. But it's a villainous laugh, the kind that would send shivers down the spines of ordinary men.

Thankfully, I'm no ordinary man.

I fucking love the sound of her evil cackle. It makes my stupid dead heart sing.

My half-scowl turns into a full smile.

"So you really don't know where Leander is, huh?" I ask, trying to ignore the light feeling in my hard chest.

"No. Not that I would tell you if I did. That bastard is mine to kill—same goes for Drago."

"What would you say if I told you I knew how to find Leander?"

That draws a curious look from my Black Cat.

"Lead you to Leander? Has the coward already gone into

hiding?"

"He's surprisingly good at it," I nod.

"And you're looking for him?"

"I can't let him go around thinking you belong to him."

"I don't belong to anyone."

"Wrong, kitten. You belong to me."

My claim sparks something feral in Rozalia. She lunges for me. But I'm ready for her.

Still, the moment my fingers close in around her wrist, she ducks and spins, taking out my shins with a hard kick.

Somehow, I manage to keep her firmly in my grasp as I fall to the floor. Rozalia is pulled on top of me. And we wrestle across the floor until I'm on top of her.

"I thought you said you'd stop calling me kitten if I answered your questions," she pants, her white cheeks filled with color.

"You're right," I puff. "I'm sorry... *angel*."

"Fuck off."

Wrapping her leg around mine, Rozalia gathers enough leverage to flip me onto my back.

For a moment, I'm so shocked I just let her hold me down.

Then, I just start to laugh. I don't even try to wrestle her back down. She's earned the chance to be on top of me... for now.

"At least angel is more fitting than kitten," Rozalia mumbles, shaking her head to hide the small smile lifting her perfect lips.

She likes being on top.

But does she like it better than being under me?

"Shortened for fallen angel, of course," I say. "It's hard to believe, but even I know you used to be innocent."

It's only supposed to be a joke, but I can't help but remember what Gabriel told me. His stories drift over our heads like a dark rain cloud.

Rozalia was once an ordinary girl—until that life was brutally stolen from her.

A heaviness crushes our playful mood. I regret bringing it up, even before Rozalia responds.

"You've been talking to Gabriel," she sneers, the subtle smirk wiped from her face.

When she tries to push herself off me, I wrestle myself back on top of her.

"He had a lot to say about you," I say, wishing I could extinguish the horrors of her past. Wishing I could fix her.

But I know that kind of wish comes at a price.

Without those struggles, she wouldn't be the Black Cat.

She wouldn't be *my* Black Cat.

Would I still be obsessed with her if she was just like every other girl?

"All lies," Rozalia spits.

"They must have been," I agree, studying her carefully. "Imagine you being innocent."

When she tries to wrap her leg around mine again, I slam my knee into the ground and spread her thighs out. She's not tricking me twice.

"What about you?" she asks, spite lashing from her perfect lips. "Was the great Irish lion ever innocent?"

"No," I shake my head. "I was never innocent. But I wasn't always so great."

"You still aren't."

"Maybe you're right..."

Those stunning green eyes glare up at with me with all the hate in the world. But unlike before, that hate doesn't burn alone anymore. It's joined by something else. Something I can feel, but can't quite describe.

"You've made so many mistakes," Rosalia whispers.

My nose hovers an inch above hers. Our lips practically touch. I can taste her hot breath.

"You're the biggest one."

"No," she says, a darkness coming over her. "You weren't on the west coast because of me."

My chest tightens.

How does she know about that?

A barrage of shameful and dark memories threaten to break through the levy holding them back.

"You don't know shit," I growl.

Planting my fists into the ground, I push myself off of her. A cold gust fills up the empty air between us. But I try not to linger on it as I storm for the door.

"Where are you going?" Rozalia asks, rising to her feet.

"To find Leander," I grunt.

Reaching into my pants, I go to tuck my raging erection back beneath my beltline.

But Rozalia stops me.

"Take me with you!" she demands.

My hand falls against the doorknob. Glass crunches beneath my feet.

"How could I trust you?" I ask, not bothering to turn around.

"You can't," Rozalia admits.

"Then why the hell would I take you with me?"

This time, I do turn around. To my surprise, there's a mischievous smirk drawn over Rozalia's pretty face.

It seems as if she's already forgotten about our short foray into her troubled past—or maybe she just doesn't feel so bad anymore, since she got a nice little jab in at mine.

"Because it would turn you on," she says, green eyes wandering below my waistline.

My hard cock twitches as she stares directly at the unavoidable outline.

"I'm already turned on plenty, thank you."

"Oh, I know. But imagine how hot it would be to watch me

kill the man who tried to take me from you."

"We aren't going directly to Leander," I tell her, immediately regretting my poor choice of words.

Rozalia's smirk turns into a full-on Cheshire grin.

I said '*we*'. Fuck.

"Then where are *we* going?" she teases.

"*I'm* going to visit one of Leander's friends. He and I are going to have a nice little chat."

"Hard to believe that fucker has any friends," Rozalia says, cracking her knuckles. "But I bet I can get him talking before you do."

I hesitate to play along.

"If you leave me here, I'll just escape," she casually notes.

I hate how right she is. How could I trust my men with such an important task? They've already failed me too many times—not that I want anyone else watching over my fallen angel. She's mine.

But how am I going to keep her by my side?

Thankfully, Rozalia lets me consider that conundrum in silence. As if on cue, I hear a muffled bark come from downstairs. It's the guard dog my men let inside.

It gives me an idea.

A cruel, naughty idea.

"Fine. You can come," I relent. "But only if you adhere to my conditions."

"Name them," Rozalia is quick to reply.

She eagerly steps forward, but I raise a strong palm.

"You aren't going to like them, angel," I tell her.

"Try me."

Now, it's my turn to smile.

16

ROZALIA

Could this be any more demeaning?

The dusty mirror by the club's entrance only reminds me of my shame—not that I need to see my reflection to feel the bulky shock collar fastened tightly around my throat.

"That fucker better be here," Rian grumbles next to me.

The bastard.

Of all the subtle contraptions a tech genius like him could have concocted to control me, he chose the most barbaric and obvious solution.

Shit. He wouldn't even let me leave that disgusting bedroom until his uncle had brought the thing up. And he definitely didn't let me put it on myself.

I don't blame him. I would have definitely found a way to disable the fucking thing if I'd had the chance, but that chance has long passed, and the last time I even reached up to scratch my nose, I got a quick shock. An infuriating reminder of who's in control.

Him.

The man who overpowered me back in that bedroom. The

man who pinned me to the wall, who wrestled me to the floor, who promised to kill anyone who dared try to marry me.

It's the same man I stupidly kissed.

Rian Kilpatrick.

My lion.

Hell, the shock collar hardly changes anything. Without it, I'd still be under his control. And it's not just because he can make my body squirm with anticipation, or cause my lips to tingle with electricity.

No. The moment he confirmed that he didn't actually want to marry me, I felt something I'd never felt for any man outside of my little adoptive family before.

Respect.

Hell, maybe even a little admiration.

If only that was where my new feelings ended.

But no. My life can never be so simple. Something else has appeared deep inside of me. Something more controlling than any shock collar or tracking device could ever be.

I'm starting to like the man.

I must be losing my fucking mind.

"If he doesn't show up soon, I'm not even going to let him talk," I murmur. "That fucker has kept us waiting for twenty minutes already."

"If you even go near him before I give you permission, I'm going to shock some sense back into you," Rian replies, lifting the remote to his face.

Fucking hell. Another remote.

I want to rip it out of his hands and crush it over his head. But not for the same reasons I have before.

This feels different than the tracking device he rubbed onto my clit. It feels kinkier.

Sure, It's still a cruel display of power, but this time, he's only doing it to appease one of my own desires.

I wanted to come, and he found a way to make that happen

—not that he really had much of a choice. We both know I would have escaped that cage by nightfall if he'd left me alone.

"Someone needs to pay for this shit," I hiss under my breath.

Without thinking, I reach up to the uncomfortable collar, but the second my fingers fall onto the heavy plastic, a light shock cracks through my body.

"Fuck!" I curse, flinching like a coward.

"Be a good girl," Rian says, nodding to a blinking red light on the ceiling. A security camera. "I'm sure he's watching. We need to make a good first impression."

"You fucking bastard," I sneer. I'm desperate to turn the tables on Rian again. Because even if submitting to him in the bedroom can feel like fucking heaven, I still haven't forgotten how good it felt to dominate him right back.

"Watch the language, angel," Rian smirks.

I ignore him. Instead, I push my attention towards that blinking red dot. My lion is right, someone is definitely watching us. Judging us. Trying to figure out if we're worth his precious time.

I want to raise a middle finger and give him the clue he needs to send us packing.

But my ire for anyone even remotely associated with Leander will have to stay hidden until we get the fucker behind closed doors. Because I'm desperate to fuck someone up.

Really, I just want to feel in control again. And if it can't be with Rian, then the friend of another one of my enemies is going to have to do.

"Monsieur Baros will see you now."

Looking down from the camera, I see a hulking ogre of a man step out of a nearby door. To my surprise, he's wearing a shiny multi-colored suit.

The sparkling material clashes so perfectly against his

Frankenstein's monster-like demeanor that I almost let out a laugh.

But then I catch a quick glimpse of my reflection again, and realize that I must look at least twice as ridiculous.

"Hurry up, angel," I hear Rian say. When I look back down the hall, he's already halfway up it, following the sparkling ogre towards the wall-rattling bass thumping up ahead.

I can already feel the headache coming on.

"I fucking hate clubs," I mutter, quickening my pace until I catch up.

"What was that?" Rian asks. But I can already barely hear him.

The further we walk, the louder the music gets. Soon enough, the floor is shaking too.

"Who the hell comes to a club this early?" I ask myself. It's late afternoon, and the sun was barely starting its descent when we were let in the front door.

Freaks.

"This way," I somehow hear the ogre grunt. He turns a corner up ahead and I clench my fists, ready for the crowd I'm sure is waiting.

But when I step around the corner, I'm not greeted by a throng of people. Instead, the pounding bass blasts over an empty dancefloor. The only people huddle around a sad-looking bar tucked away in the corner.

Other than that, there's no one.

My hackles rise.

What kind of club is this?

I'm given some kind of answer when Rian nudges me on the shoulder. I look over at him, and he gestures upwards.

This time, I can't help the laugh that slithers from my throat.

Hanging from the ceiling are more than a dozen gilded birdcages. Inside of each is a naked man or woman. They all mindlessly gyrate to the heavy rhythm as harsh strobe lights flicker over their masked faces. Glitter gleams off their skin. They don't stop dancing. Not even for a second.

I shake my head.

"I knew Leander was a freak..." I mutter.

In response, Rian nudges me again. This time, I follow his gaze to a dark balcony that overlooks the strange dancefloor.

A man I don't recognize leans on the railing. When I meet his watchful gaze, he offers a seductive wave and a flirty smile.

I hold back my sneer.

That must be Flavian.

The fool doesn't know what he's in for.

Following the shiny ogre up a set of stairs, we're led to the platform. Before we can reach Flavian, though, he turns around and struts towards a door; with one curious look back over his shoulder, he disappears behind it.

"The fucker thinks we're here to play his games," Rian grumbles.

"I'll make him pay for it."

"Not if I do first."

"Please enter," the deep-voiced ogre says when we reach the door. He opens it for us, but makes no attempt to follow us inside.

The moment I've crossed the threshold, the door clicks shut behind me.

"Welcome to my palace!" a voice announces.

The thumping bass is quieter here, but it still seeps through the thick walls like a faint but frantic heartbeat.

"Music's a little loud for this time of the day, don't you think?" I say.

In response, I feel a little shock pinch my neck.

"Behave," Rian whispers.

"Fuck," I curse, shaking the jolt away. "I swear to god..."

"I love it." The flamboyant voice carries through the dim

room like an air horn. Flavian steps out of the shadows, arms raised in the air. "The choke collar that is everything," he says, cupping his hand around his throat. "Very kinky."

The club owner is a thin, tightly-dressed man in his mid-to-late thirties. Handsome, in a way. His gel-spiked blonde hair stands at attention as he closely studies his two visitors. To my amusement, he's wearing the same type of shiny suit as the ogre.

"It does the job," Rian replies, and I can tell he's trying to keep his composure.

I like that he's going to have to suffer through this too.

"And what job is that, handsome?" Flavian asks, his question full of innuendo.

"It keeps the lady under control."

"Under your control," he points out. "And who wouldn't want a creature like that under their control."

Licking his lips, Flavian lifts his two hands to his face and claps twice.

The lights come on.

It instantly becomes clear what kind of man Flavian Baros is—not that it wasn't strongly hinted at before.

His office is essentially a sprawling sex dungeon: bubbling hot tub, sex swing, St. Andrew's cross and all. I wouldn't be shocked if the black leather chair sitting behind his desk had some kind of automatic clamps built into the armrests.

How delicious would it be if that's how we trapped him?

I can't help but bite down on the inside of my lip. The slightest pressure appears in my core. I'm past caring about whether it's my hormones acting up or not. I'm horny, so be it.

"Nice digs," I say, giving Rian a subtle side-eye.

For a man who can be so dirty, he sure looks stiff right now.

I like it. If I can make him half as uncomfortable as I am with this collar on, then I'll consider it a small victory.

"I'm so glad you like, beautiful," Flavian smiles. "But it looks so much better now that you're here."

"Easy there, Romeo," Rian warns him. "We're not here to play with your furniture."

"Ah yes," Flavian acknowledges. But even as he straightens out his collar in a show of professionalism, those slippery blue eyes crawl over Rian's body. "You're here to buy the place, correct?"

"We're here to make sure the place is worth buying."

I can't help but huff. That was the lie Rian came up with?

Pathetic.

... Even if it worked.

"I wish you'd had been able to come at a more desirable hour," Flavian says. Stroking his chin, he looks back and forth between Rian and me—like he's trying to decide which meal he'd prefer more. "Late afternoon isn't exactly our hottest time slot."

"You wouldn't be able to tell by the music," Rian snips.

"I like to keep a club atmosphere going around the clock," Flavian smiles. Lifting his hand to his lips, he acts like he's about to reveal some big secret. "Plus, all of the noise out there helps hide the sound of the fun we're having in here."

Rian shifts in place.

A grin washes over my lips.

"What kind of fun?" I poke, knowing that it will only make Rian even more uncomfortable.

Reaching into his pocket, Flavian pulls out a remote of his own. "Looks like mine is bigger than yours," he teases Rian.

"Much bigger," I agree.

Rian just rolls his eyes.

"Are we going to talk business or what?" he asks.

"I know they always say never to mix business with pleasure," Flavian sings. "But I just can't help myself."

Clicking down on the remote, he turns his attention to the St. Andrew's cross standing in the corner of the office.

Rian and I both tense up, expecting some kind of ambush.

But that betrayal never occurs.

Instead, we're treated to a slice of Flavian Baros' depravity.

To the sound of turning gears, the St. Andrews cross is turned around, revealing its backside.

"Fucking hell," Rian curses.

I join him. "What the hell is that?"

"One of my special friends," Flavian chuckles.

There, tied to the backside of the cross, is a naked man. A young man. Young enough that I'm not so sure I wouldn't categorize him as a boy.

He's passed out, head slopped to the side, eyes lightly shut.

"Is this some kind of joke?" Rian growls.

"Don't worry, he's eighteen," Flavian jokingly assures us. "And no, he's not dead or anything, just coming down from an ecstatic high. Consensual, of course."

Flavian winks at Rian, and my lion's hands curl into fists.

"Why are you showing us this?" I ask, trying to settle the tension somewhat.

Suddenly, I don't want to poke Rian too hard anymore.

If he snaps and kills Flavian, then I'm going to have to wait even longer to get my hands on Leander. I can't have that.

"As I said, I enjoy mixing business with pleasure."

"Is that a proposition?"

"I don't go into business with anyone I don't trust. And this is how I figure out if we're on the same 'page'."

When Rian steps forward, I grimace. The last thing I want is to have to physically stop him from doing something stupid. That's going to get me shocked.

Fucking hell, when did I become the reasonable one?

"Very well," Rian grunts. "Let's make sure we're on the same page."

To my utter shock, he starts to unbuckle his belt.

I can practically feel Flavian get hard in response. Not that I'm looking at that freak. When Rian takes off his belt, he has my full attention.

"I was hoping you'd say that," Flavian sings. "And you, princess. Will you be part of this deal?"

When I look over at Rian, I'm met by a stern glare. But I'm not sure if he's warning me to stay away or insisting I join.

It doesn't matter. I make up my own mind.

"How could I refuse?"

It's impossible to tell if that's the response Rian was waiting for. To find out, I start to approach Flavian, brushing by my lion's shoulder as he wraps his belt around his knuckles.

I don't get a shock.

I guess that means we're good.

"What a gorgeous couple you two are," Flavian says, unbuttoning the top of his dress shirt. "May I ask how you heard about me?"

"Through the grapevine," Rian is quick to respond. I've never heard my lion's voice so rigid before. It's like he's solely focused on the task at hand.

… Or maybe he's just jealous.

My thighs clench as I remember how good his angry cock feels. Getting hate fucked by Rian is the closest thing a girl like me will ever get to heaven.

Maybe I do want to poke him, after all.

"How fortunate for me," Flavian mutters, his greedy gaze fixed on my man.

My man.

My heart flinches at the thought. And the devil on my shoulder curses in my ear.

Fuck off, Roz. Don't be stupid. Rian isn't yours any more than you're his. And no matter what he says in the bedroom, you don't belong to him.

You don't belong to anyone.

Still, a small pang of jealousy cracks through me as I wrap a seductive hand around the club owner's shoulder. No matter how seductively I pull off his multi-colored jacket, the club owner's eyes stay fixed on Rian.

I mean, I don't blame him. My lion is a stud. But I'm not so bad either.

Right?

"Come here," I say.

Throwing caution to the wind, I wrap my fingers around Flavian's well-manicured jaw and yank his face into mine.

Even I'm shocked by what I do next.

I kiss him.

His lips are cold and wet. Mine are sloppy. There's no joy in it, but I kiss him with all the passion in the world.

No one is allowed to make me feel jealousy—especially not Rian.

He deserves this.

Flavian has hardly started to kiss me back when I feel a light shock ripple up from my collar.

That doesn't stop me. I'm almost used to the sensation by now.

Flavian's tongue digs deep into my mouth and his hands clasp around my waist. I kiss him back with disgust, half-hoping that Rian will end this before it goes too far.

I get my wish.

The next shock is so strong that I'm nearly blown off my feet.

"Fuck," I curse, jumping back.

Before my skin can stop tingling, Rian has pounced on Flavian.

The club-owner gasps as my lion wraps a strong hand around his throat.

"Rian, no. Don't—" I try to choke out.

But Rian doesn't rip Flavian apart. Instead, he does the last thing I was expecting him to do.

He kisses him.

Well, maybe not so much kisses as laps up what I've left behind.

Those blood-red lips push hard into Flavian's thin mouth as Rian licks every last trace of me from the club owner's mouth.

Rian is clearly pissed.

Meanwhile, Flavian looks like he's in heaven, and he quickly gives in, closing his eyes to faint into Rian's powerful grip.

But Rian doesn't close his eyes. No. He keeps them wide open, and glued onto me.

The pressure in my core expands. My cunt drips.

Why is this so hot?

How can I be so jealous and so turned on at the same time?

I can't take my eyes off the scorching scene. But the longer it goes on, the hotter my envy burns.

Then, just like that, I've had enough.

Rian is always going on about how I belong to him.

But who does he belong to?

The answer is clear.

Me.

Rian Kilpatrick belongs to me.

There's no ignoring it anymore.

And there's no way I'm going to stand here and let anyone else taste *my* man.

Reaching up to the shock collar, I consider trying to disable it while my lion is distracted. But those blue eyes are still trained on me, and Rian lifts the remote as he bites down on Flavian's lip.

That's one step too far.

Dropping to my knees, I find the belt Rian dropped when

he pounced on Flavian. With the thick leather strap in hand, I twirl around Flavian's backside and rise up behind him.

"Having fun?" I sneer, wrapping the belt around the club owner's throat.

Rian drops his hand, and I manage to tug Flavian into my body.

"Darling, I'm having the time of my life," Flavian chokes.

"I hope you like it rough," I warn him.

"Oh, I do."

Digging my nails into his spiky hair, I pull Flavian's head back until his Adam's apple throbs up to the ceiling. When I let go, it's to use that hand to pull Rian into my mouth for a steamy kiss of our own.

The faintest glacial fragrance lines his lips. That's Flavian's scent. I don't stop kissing him until it's gone.

"This is getting out of hand," I whisper, finally pulling back.

"You're right," Rian growls.

Wrapping his fingers back around Flavian's throat, he starts to push us both backward.

My knees immediately give out against the edge of the desk.

"Watch it!" I shout.

But Rian doesn't stop. With a strength so casual it almost scares me, he drags Flavian and me across the desk until we're falling off the other side.

Before we crash into the chair, I let go of the belt, rolling out of the way as Rian shoves Flavian down.

I don't waste a second. Crouching, I look for the control panel I know is there.

"Bingo," I smile, finding exactly what I'm looking for.

With a press of a concealed button, four hidden clamps spring up from the chair legs and arm-rests, restraining Flavian in place.

"Oh, how naughty," Flavian chuckles, hardly bothered by the strength and speed in which he's been captured.

The fucker is in for a rude awakening.

"We heard through the grapevine you like to hold naughty parties," Rian says, momentarily composing himself now that Flavian is tied down.

The sensual club owner raises a brow. His custom-tailored pants pitch an impressive tent. But before I can catch myself looking at his crotch, I feel the back of Rian's hand under my collar.

He lifts my gaze.

"I do many things," Flavian smiles. His spiky hair is already damp. Sweat drips down his golden skin. There's a mischievous twinkle in his eye.

I'll wipe that out soon enough.

"We're only interested in the things you do for Leander Onasis," I speak up.

Lifting my foot, I step down on Flavian's thigh, just below his erection. He shifts, pulsing with desire. But I keep my eyes trained on Rian.

The lion is seething with jealousy.

Still, he plays along.

"Leander Onasis," Flavian says, lifting his gaze to the ceiling, as if he's trying to figure out who that is...

Without warning, Rian slaps him across the face. Then, he digs his fingers into his jaw and forces him to look directly into his blue eyes.

"We heard you're the one who sets up his lavish parties."

"Oh, *that* Leander Onasis," Flavian smirks, clearly so turned on he's nearly lost all his senses. "That handsome devil gets whatever he wants."

In response, Rian spits in Flavian's face.

Feeling left out, I do the same.

"And what do we get?" Rian asks.

Inching my foot closer to Flavian's cock, I watch as he considers how much to reveal.

"I can set you up with him, if you'd like," Flavian tells Rian, before turning his attention to me. "I'm afraid he might only be interested in you, though, darling. Believe me, I've tried to sway him. He's like a rock."

"More like a pillow," I blurt out. "Extra soft."

That momentarily drags Flavian back down to earth.

"You've met the man before?" he asks, curious.

"He asked her to marry him," Rian says, a red-hot rage seething just beneath his surface.

"Lucky girl," Flavian chuckles.

"No," Rian says. Reaching down, he grabs Flavian's erection and twists. The club owner shakes with delight. "Lucky guy."

"Are you talking about me or Leander?" Flavian plays. His voice shivers with anticipation.

"Neither," Rian sneers. Looking at me, he pauses for a second before continuing. "I'm talking about me."

"Of course, I didn't—"

Flavian stops talking when I lunge forward to kiss Rian.

Shit. I can feel the club owner's cock twitching against my thigh as I use him as leverage. But I don't care.

Something has taken over me.

"Since when did you get so fucking sweet?" I hiss into my lion's mouth.

"That was a mistake," he grumbles, pushing me back. "It won't happen again."

"Can I just say one thing?" Flavian gulps. "I love you both."

"Shut up," Rian and I both say simultaneously.

"Yes, sir... Yes, ma'am... Whatever you say."

"Whatever we say?" I ask. Raising an eyebrow, I turn to our fresh captive.

"Whatever. You. Say."

"Get us an invite to one of Leander's parties."

"I'm afraid there are none on the schedule," Flavian sighs, looking particularly dejected.

"Then tell us where he holds them. We'll set up our own," Rian says.

"I'm afraid I can't do that either," Flavian tells us. "His privacy is of the utmost importance. But I can tell you where to find some of my other parties...."

"We aren't interested in other parties," Rian barks.

"Oh, then you don't know about my other parties," Flavian smiles. Nodding over to the young man tied to the cross, he bites down on his lower lips. "At my parties, I can get you anything you want. Younger. Older. Fresh. Experienced. I trade in them all."

Trade.

The word triggers a spark of rage in me.

Is Flavian a trafficker?

"You trade in little boys?" Rian growls.

Just like that, his hand clamps back around Flavian's throat. But the pretend playfulness is gone.

Rian is just as upset as I am.

"I trade in fun," Flavian chokes, not quite getting the point yet.

That ignorance won't last for much longer.

Lifting my hand, I wipe away any trace of him from my lips. I can't fucking believe I kissed that fucker. Even if it was just to prove a point.

"We've had enough fun," Rian snarls. "Now it's time to get serious."

"It's time to change the course of this interrogation," I agree.

"I'll go first," Rian nods.

Taking out his phone, he presses the audio record button before shoving it back into his pocket. Then, he bends over and pulls his pant leg up, revealing a switchblade tucked into his sock.

He grabs it.

To my surprise, he doesn't seem to notice as something falls from his pocket.

I do.

No matter what's just happened between us, I can't help but take advantage of the small slip-up.

Instinct forces me to react. This is my opportunity.

I grunt. My knees give out. Grabbing my stomach, I keel over. "Fuck," I mumble.

"Roz!" Rian shouts.

Concern whips around in his voice as he reaches down to touch me. I milk his fears for a little longer before letting him help me back to my feet.

"It's just cramps," I lie. "Lady problems. Let's get back to our interrogation."

"Interrogation?" Flavian catches on. The blood in his cock must finally be rushing back to his head. "What the hell is going on?"

He struggles against his restraints, but there's no point. He isn't going anywhere.

We've trapped him.

A familiar sense of power washes over me as I subtly slip the device I picked off the ground beneath my beltline.

"You're going to answer some questions," Rian says, flicking open his switchblade.

Flavian's eyes pop wide open.

"What questions? Who are you people?"

The growing panic in his voice is palpable.

A small smile comes over my lips. I'm slowly regaining control.

This is what I live for.

Not any man. Not any cock.

Not Rian Kilpatrick.

This.

Death. Violence. Power.

"You're about to find out," I tell him, leaning down nice and

17

RIAN

Something is off.

I don't know what, but I can sense it.

And it has nothing to do with Flavian.

Whatever sent Rozalia falling to the floor has changed her demeanor. How? I can't exactly tell, but I know I'm not about to turn my attention to anything else until I find out.

"You're coming with me," I say, turning to my Black Cat.

Grabbing Roz's arm, I pull her away from Flavian. She only resists for a split second, before giving in entirely.

That's equally strange. She usually puts up more of a fight.

"What?" she snaps.

"What do you mean what?" I ask, stopping us both before we can get too close to the office door. I'm sure that ogre in the multi-colored suit is standing watch outside, but I doubt he can hear much of what's happening inside. Not with that pounding bass shaking the walls.

"I'm fine," Rozalia insists. Pulling her arm away, she starts to turn around, but something stops her.

"What's wrong?"

"Hey, can someone tell me what the fuck is going on?" Flavian shouts from his chair.

We've barely even moved fifteen feet away, but the music outside is so loud I can barely hear him.

"Shut up!" Rozalia and I both shout.

That's the second time that's happened.

"Jinx," I hear myself say.

"Excuse me?"

"Never mind. Back to the–"

"You just said jinx..." she says, holding back a wide smirk. "What are you? Twelve?"

"You know damn well what I am," I growl.

Yanking her towards me, I push a hand up beneath her heavy collar.

"I thought I did," Rozalia whispers, not fighting back. "But the man I thought I knew would never have done what you just did..."

She looks down at my lips, and I immediately know what she means.

"You have a problem with that?" I ask, hating that I actually kissed a predator like Flavian—even if I didn't quite know the full extent of his depravity before I did it.

"Not if it was anyone else," Rozalia responds.

Shit. I can't believe I did something like that in front of her. Very few people know about that side of me. It's a quiet part. Hell, I'd even consider it a small part. But it's still part of who I am. I don't hide it on purpose, but I've never felt the need to go announcing it to the world either.

So, why the hell did I let it show in front of her?

"If someone else can do it, why can't?" I ask, almost ready to be judged.

"Because you belong to me."

My stupid stone heart cracks against her words.

"I don't belong to anyone," I say, doing my best Rozalia impression. "Plus, you kissed him too."

"Only to make you jealous," Rozalia whispers.

"And why do you think I did it?"

"Because you're a horny bastard."

I can't help but laugh.

"I'm only a horny bastard for you, angel."

Letting my hand drop from around her neck, I pinch her chin instead.

"You've got a real way with words," Rozalia sneers.

"You haven't heard anything yet." With that, I let go of her chin and splay my hand out across her chest. "Now, go stand over there," I say, pointing to the corner of the room. "Let that poor guy down from the cross."

"What? You're not going to let me interrogate Flavian? Why?"

"Because you're clearly not feeling well," I tell her. "I don't care if it's actually cramps or something else, you go stand over there until I tell you to move."

Fire jumps behind Rozalia's emerald green eyes as she fights an internal battle against my command. But it doesn't last long.

She's learning.

"Then what?" she grimaces.

"Then you can come help me clean up the mess I make."

"I'm not your fucking maid," she hisses.

"No. You're just mine. Period."

Giving her a nudge in the right direction, I make a big show of reaching for the pocket where the remote is stored.

Rozalia freezes up.

The reaction is so intense I actually start to feel a little bad about how hard I shocked her while she was kissing Flavian.

But who can blame me?

She's mine.

"Go, angel." With one last long stubborn look, Rozalia finally relents. "That's my good girl."

The look she gives me could burn a forest to ashes. But I take it head on. It's what I deserve.

The shock collar might have been overkill. But it was the only way to keep her under control while we left the house. And I wasn't about to sit around concocting some new device while a lead was just sitting at a club thirty minutes away.

"If you don't let me go soon, there's going to be trouble!" Flavian finally gathers the courage to speak up again.

Slashing my knife through the air, I turn my attention back to him.

"From now on, you only speak when spoken to," I growl, storming back towards him.

"Don't you fucking know who I am?"

Closing my hand, I crack the self-important club owner right between the eyes. His neck snaps back like a lever.

"You're lucky to still be alive. That's what you are."

Grabbing a fistful of his hair, I yank his head up. Flavian's nose is already crooked and bleeding. His blue eyes are hazy.

Shit. I might have hit him too hard.

Out of the corner of my eye, I see Rozalia unlatching the guy from the St. Andrew's cross.

"What... what do you want?" Flavian sniffles, choking back tears.

Typical human trafficker, I think. *Coward.*

With the back of my hand, I wipe away any last trace of him from my lips. Flavian is barely attractive. The only reason I kissed him was because I got lost in my game with Rozalia.

It won't happen again.

"I want answers," I say. "I want Leander Onasis."

"I... I don't know where he is," Flavian croaks.

"I don't care. You know about his secret properties. Tell me where they are."

To my surprise, Flavian doesn't just start blurting out addresses. The coward may be a little tougher than I thought.

"I... I can't," he finally sighs, flinching as I pull him up by the hair again.

"Yes, you can," I urge him.

"No," Flavian solemnly shakes his head. "Without my connections, I'm nothing... I can't lose them... I can't lose my connections..."

"Would you rather lose your life?"

"I wouldn't have much or a life after that..."

"You're being dramatic," I say. Lifting my knife, I press the blade's edge against Flavian's cheek. "Hey, maybe I won't kill you after all. Maybe I'll just carve something onto your face, or chop off a few fingers. Do you think your precious connections would stick with you after that? Or would all of that pain be for nothing?"

When Flavian starts to sob, I drop his head.

"Thank you..." he whispers.

I respond by plunging my blade directly into the back of his hand.

He screeches so loud I have to turn my back on him and cover my ears. For a moment, I even prepare myself for someone to come barging in through the office door.

But the music outside must drown us out because no one enters.

Flavian is fucked.

"I'm not going to give you another chance, Flavian. The next time you ignore one of my questions, I'm cutting off a hand."

"No... No... please, no..."

When I rip my blade from his hand, he lets out a pathetic whimper.

"Talk, you bastard."

I let him squirm for a little longer. Just when I'm about to impale his other hand, he gives in.

"... 775 Lemoine Street..." Flavian mumbles.

"Keep going," I tell him, not satisfied. "I know there's more."

Leander could be hiding out at any one of his secret properties.

"... 621 Baker Ave... 43 Hundle Road... 101 Baskerville..." Flavian starts listing the location off.

"Hey Roz, I hope you're taking notes," I say, turning to her. "I'm—"

I'm stopped cold.

The naked man who was tied to the St. Andrew's cross is splayed out on the ground, still unconscious.

But Rozalia is nowhere to be found.

"... 89 Bullosk Street..." Flavian continues to mindlessly rattle off addresses, but I'm not listening anymore.

Rozalia is gone.

Panicked, I start to search the entire office.

She's not here.

That fucking girl.

"... Those are the only ones I know of... I swear..." Flavian mumbles. His head bobs like a man on the brink of unconsciousness.

Grabbing one last fistful of his hair, I pull him up to face me.

"Are you sure? Those are the only addresses?"

"Yes... I promise... Please don't kill me."

"I'd be lying if I said this has been a pleasure," I huff. "But you're a human trafficker, and likely a pedophile too—but even if you weren't any of those things, I still like to tie my loose ends up in pretty little bows.."

"No—"

With a vicious slash, I tear open Flavian's throat. His skin might as well be butter, and that protruding Adam's apple of his comes tumbling out in a stream of blood.

"Asshole," I mumble.

Wiping my blade off on his shirt, I let him choke on his own blood.

Rozalia couldn't have gotten far.

She's going to pay for making me worry.

First, though, I quickly check on the unconscious man by the cross.

"Where did she go?" I ask, roughly slapping him awake.

"... What? I... What's going on?" he asks, slowly coming to.

Fuck. I'm not going to learn anything for this poor sap.

"Nothing. This is all a dream. Leave quickly, before it turns back into a nightmare.."

I don't wait around for him to get up.

Instead, I head straight for the office door.

When I open it up, I find the ogre who was waiting outside. He's lying in a pool of his own blood.

I lift his shirt. There's a holster, but no gun. There's also a bullet hole in his temple.

Rozalia must have shot him in rhythm with the pounding bass.

Clever girl. Too bad it won't work out for her.

Reaching into my pocket, I search for the remote to her collar.

It's gone.

My heart drops.

Slowly, a furious fire flickers up in its place.

Fuck.

FUCK.

She's actually escaped.

18

ROZALIA

He wasn't there.

The opulent private residence at 775 Lemoine Street definitely looked like the kind of place a cowering billionaire like Leander might hide out—a sprawling, countless-acre property with three separate pyramid-like mansions dotted along a cleared-out spot in the tree-covered hills—but I searched every last inch of it, and found nothing.

Hell, there was hardly any evidence to indicate that Leander had ever been there, let alone recently. From head to toe, the place was spotless, devoid of any clues.

But when I found a secret doorway, and saw that it led into a familiar-looking sex dungeon, I knew I was at least in the right place.

Flavian wasn't lying.

A warm tingle crosses my skin as I picture him tied to that chair, my hulking Irish lion leering over him.

I can't get that kiss out of my mind. Who would have thought that a man like Rian could ever do something like that?

It makes him far more interesting than I ever thought he could be. More alluring. More mysterious and complicated.

I can't get enough.

Hell, I almost regret leaving him in the lurch.

Almost.

Still, as soon as I realized Leander wasn't at 775 Lemoine Road, I left. And quickly.

There was no chance Rian wasn't on his way. And I didn't like how badly I already wanted to see him again.

Clenching my fists, I make my way through the darkness, hating that I don't know where to go looking for Leander next.

I had to get out of Flavian's office before Rian could notice I'd taken the remote. My opportunity arose while he was fist deep in the fuckers face. All I heard was the first address. 775 Lemoine Street. Then I had to take advantage of his slip-up and fucking skedaddle.

It's too bad, I would have preferred to confront Leander myself. Now, I might not get the chance.

Up ahead, I see a row of square yellow lights softly bleeding through the darkness.

Good, she's still up.

I desperately need someone to talk to. Someone who won't judge me for what I've done, for how I truly feel.

Babcia is just the person.

Shit got too real back in Flavian's office. The suppressed feelings I'd had for Rian momentarily exploded, scattering all across my insides before I could gather the strength to bottle them back up.

But there was no time to collect everything that escaped my padlocked heart. Red-hot remnants still flutter through my chest as I sneak around to the back of the little cottage.

The second I open the door, I'm greeted by an unexpected host.

"You've gotten bigger," I note, not daring to reach down.

To my surprise, Kaja doesn't hiss at me. Instead, the growing kitten brushes against my leg.

The contact sends a warm tingle over my skin.

"Does that mean I've won you over?" I ask. Bending down, I go to pet the purring cat, but she won't let me feel too good about myself—not for long, at least.

My hand might as well be venomous, and the stubborn creature avoids it at all costs, slinking away as I sigh and accept my position as an inanimate scratching post.

"I guess not," I mumble.

Still, Kaja looks back over her shoulder when I don't immediately follow her deeper into the house.

"Where's Babcia?" I ask, kicking the dirt off my shoes.

Kaja meows and turns back around. I follow her into the kitchen.

"Hello?" I call out.

No one responds.

Opening the fridge, I find it full of saran-wrapped meals. But I don't grab any of them.

Something is wrong.

"Babcia, are you here?"

She must be. The old woman doesn't have anywhere else to go.

My heart sinks a little as I make my way to the bedroom. The light in there is on too.

But there's no Babcia.

Back in the kitchen, Kaja meows on the counter.

"What is it?" I ask. "Where's Babcia?"

Kaja just looks up at a cupboard beside the fridge. Her yellow eyes glare at the wooden door so intensely it makes the hair on the back of my neck stand up.

"... Babcia?" I gulp, suddenly filled with dread.

My life has been filled with so much horror that I automatically expect the worst. Before I can stop myself, I'm reaching for the cupboard door.

"… Babcia?" I force myself to call out, a little louder this time.

Please, no.

When my hand falls on the tiny wooden knob, I freeze. For some terrifying reason, all I can think of is what happened to my parents.

From deep in the back of my mind, I see their charred corpses melting behind a wicked wall of flames.

Kaja meows.

I flinch.

When I look down at the black cat, I see those sharp yellow eyes on me. Slowly, she looks back towards the cupboard.

Cold sweat drips down my forehead.

What the hell is wrong with you? Why am I reacting so intensely?

It feels like I've been plunged into the tail end of a nightmare. And the longer I look down at Kaja, the less she starts to look like the black cat I rescued from Rian's coronation.

"Willow…" I whisper, my newly tender heart trembling.

The cat meows, and I'm transported back to a time and a place I never want to go back to.

I can feel the fire at my back. The horror in my heart. The fear of what's to come, and the dread of what's already happened.

I can almost see the bars of my cage… and a lone dark figure standing in the storm outside.

"Drago…"

Somewhere, a cat hisses, and I'm snapped back to reality.

A terrified laugh jitters from my throat.

I'm not back in that melting mansion. I'm not watching my parents being burned to ashes. I'm not desperately trying to save my only friend in the world.

I'm in a little cottage out in the country. I'm a grown-up. I'm a killer.

With a sharp breath, I tear the cabinet door open.

My aching heart stops.

There's nothing inside—at least, nothing gruesome. Only two dozen or so cans of tuna. Neatly stacked, as Babcia always does.

Another meow cuts through the quiet cottage. This time, when I look down, I don't see any ghosts from my distant past.

I just see Kaja. She stretches out, yellow eyes still fixed on the cupboard.

The poor little thing is hungry.

"Where's your grandma?" I ask. Taking out a can of tuna, I pry it open with one of my nails and place it down on the counter.

Kaja immediately digs in. The cat doesn't have a care in the world.

But a giant stone has appeared in my gut.

Fuck. This is why you never get attached to anyone. And it's definitely why you don't help out a kindly old lady when she gets evicted from her apartment. Because when something inevitably bad happens to someone you've allowed yourself to care about, all you're left with is sorrow.

And sorrow's awfully good at turning a person crazy— I've seen it happen.

Is that what's happening to me?

Pinching my nose, I push myself off the counter.

What the fuck is happening to me?

It's been years since I had a flashback like that. Am I just that worried about Babcia, or is it something more?

Somehow, I already know the answer. I just don't want to confront it.

Rian.

I actually like the fucker.

It's like he's managed to crack the cold shield around my heart. It's made me vulnerable. Weak. Stupid.

Afraid.

Shit.

Maybe I'm starting to do more than just like him…

A deep sigh escapes my lips as I remember what Rian said.

That he was lucky to have me.

Lucky.

To have me?

That doesn't sound like the kind of thing a hunter says about his prey, or a captor to his captive.

Not even I've ever felt lucky to have me before.

But when Rian said that, I lost control. My guard dropped, and I think my problem is that I haven't put those walls back up around my heart. Not yet. I just haven't had the chance.

And now I'm all worried about Babcia too…

Fuck. This past year has been a mess. The wall around my heart must have been thicker than I thought, because I haven't felt anything that sharp since Gabriel left us. And even then, I did all I could to ignore the pain. I went on the attack.

But now, it feels like I'm on the defense, protecting myself against a man who makes me feel like opening up—if even only just an inch.

He opened up to me…

"Babcia!?" I cry out. Trying to ignore my newfound vulnerability, I start speed-walking through the cottage.

The longer I go without finding Babcia, the heavier my dread grows.

Stupid old woman, where are you? Don't you know how worried I get?

For a second there, I really thought I might find the kindly old lady's head in the cupboard. But who would have done that? No one knows who she is. And even if they did, how would they have found her?

Only Tytus and I know about Babcia.

She's nothing special. No one of note. Just our adopted grandma.

But her irrelevance doesn't matter. She means something to me. And I'm nearly pulling my hair out when I return to the kitchen after searching every last inch of the cottage. There's no sign of a struggle. No sign that something went wrong.

There's no Babcia.

I want to call out for her again, but emotion clogs my throat, silencing me.

Get yourself together, Roz! The devil on my shoulder screeches. *You've been through worse before.*

That's no lie. But I also promised myself I would never care enough to be hurt so badly again.

Yet here I am, slouched against Babcia's kitchen counter, on the verge of tears. I'm getting weak. And there's nothing I can do about it.

What is wrong with me?

Before I can sink too low, I feel a warm presence brush against my shoulder.

Without ceremony, Kaja plops beside me, nuzzling against my trembling skin.

"Took you long enough," I say, wiping a tear from my cheek.

I'm about to take a chance and try to pick the kitten up when an unexpected sound breaks through my sad little haze.

The creaking of a door being opened.

In an instance, a feral instinct flares up in me, temporarily burning away my sorrow and evaporating my tears.

Reaching below my beltline, I pull out the pistol I stole from that ogre at Flavian's club. It should still have five shots left.

I don't dare call out as a pair of heavy footsteps approach down the hall. All I do is lift my gun and aim towards the doorway.

"I wouldn't do that if I were you," a familiar voice comes from around the corner.

My gun drops.

"... Tytus?"

"Your shadow," he says. Stepping into the kitchen, he nods down to the long black silhouette I'm casting on the ground. The light above the stove is on, and it's exposing my position.

Shit. That was sloppy.

Something really is wrong with me.

"Whatever," I mumble, putting my gun away.

Tytus does the same.

"I figured it was about time you showed up," he smiles. "Took you long enough to escape."

I'm surprised by how unsurprised he seems to see me.

"How did you know I was going to be here?" I ask.

"I didn't," he shrugs.

"Then why are you here?"

Joining me at the counter, Tytus runs a gentle hand over Kaja's back. The kitten purrs.

"Just feeding the cat, but it looks like you beat me to it." Before I can inquire further, he reaches up to his throat, all while looking at mine. "Are you alright?"

I'm well aware of the red mark burned into my skin. It's from the collar.

That fucking collar.

"Don't worry about it. I'm fine," I mumble, flushing with shame.

"Are you sure?"

Tytus turns his attention to my puffy eyes.

"Yes," I insist. "Where's Babcia?"

My adoptive brother hesitates to answer, and my raw heart winces.

"Ty..."

"She's at the hospital," Tytus says, before quickly adding,

"Don't worry, she's doing alright. Just had a little scare. When I came by to check up on her yesterday, she was on the floor, right by your feet. Says she got a little lightheaded. The doctors are doing some tests."

The sad daze returns.

"I wasn't here..." I whisper, bowing my head.

"You were busy."

"Take me to her," I say, forcing my chin back up.

"Of course."

"Now."

"Let's go then," Tytus chuckles. "You've already done what I came by to do."

Grabbing the empty tuna can, Tytus washes it off in the sink, then tosses it in the garbage.

"I'll come back tomorrow to give her more," he starts, but I stop him.

"No. She's coming with us," I insist, picking up the kitten. Surprisingly, Kaja doesn't fight back. "Who knows what will happen between now and then. The last thing I need to worry about is Kaja starving to death because no one is here to look after her."

"Where are you going to take her?"

"To the hospital."

"I don't think they allow pets, Roz."

Gesturing down to my gun, I hold Kaja tightly against my chest. "Let's see if they won't reconsider that policy."

"You're the boss," Tytus shrugs, before pursing his lips. "But I have to warn you... she's not alone."

19

ROZALIA

"Where is he?"

When I charge into the hospital room, it's with my fists raised, ready for a fight.

But Drago isn't there.

Instead, I only see kindly old Babcia. She's propped up on a hospital bed, a half dozen tubes winding around her poor little body.

For a moment, my fury flickers. Guilt and grief swirl inside of me as I approach the fragile grandmother. She's asleep.

At my back, I hear Tytus wander in. He closes the door behind him—Kaja meows from in his arms.

"Where is he?" I whisper, my voice shivering.

My anger returns with a vengeance. And by the time I turn back around, I must be seething, because Kaja jumps at the sight of me, squirming out of Tytus' grip.

"Don't go far," he tells the cat, as if it would listen.

Not that there's anywhere to go. This little room might as well be a prison cell. Kaja makes a beeline for Babcia's bed. Racing past me, she jumps up on the side table to check on her housemate.

"You said Drago was here," I remind Tytus, not sure if I'm more pissed that he's not than I would be if he were.

Either way, I still feel ready to confront my adoptive father, even after seeing Babcia like this. Hell, I spent the whole trip here practicing what I'd say, how I'd hit him, how I'd refuse to forgive his actions.

But the man never fails to disappoint.

"Shit. I thought he would be," Tytus responds. Furrowing his brow, he scans the room, as if half-expecting to find Drago hiding in some corner. "He was here when I left."

"Are you fucking with me?" I ask, unable to contain myself. I've got all this pent-up rage and no one else to turn it on.

"Roz, I'm telling you. He was here. And he was on his best behavior. I left him in charge of Babcia's while I went to feed Kaja…"

"Why the hell did you tell him about Babcia?" I snap. "Now he's got leverage on us."

"He doesn't want leverage on us," Tytus casually insists.

His flippancy only adds fuel to my fire.

"For someone who's supposed to be a strategic genius, you sure are acting like a fool," I huff. Shaking my head, I turn back towards the hospital bed.

Kaja is already curled up on Babcia's chest. The kitten looks comfy, like she's already back at home.

I find myself filled with envy.

"Roz. Drago's changed," Tytus says. When I feel his hand on my shoulder, I try to shake him away, but he doesn't let me. "I promise."

But the mini-breakdown I suffered earlier hasn't vanished entirely yet, and a ball of emotion clogs my throat.

"No. He hasn't. I don't care what he's said." Staring down at Babcia, I try to calm my racing heart. "He's barely been back in our life for more than a week, and he's already tried to marry me off to some sicko."

"It's different this time," Tytus sighs, knowing full well I won't believe him.

"How?" I ask, hating how much I want to believe him.

Kaja looks so peaceful on Babcia's chest. The simple kitten has managed to find a home in this old lady—it doesn't matter where they are, as long as she's with Babcia, she's comfortable. She's home.

Down inside, I realize I've always wanted that.

But I've never had it. Not even with Tytus or Gabriel—and definitely not with Drago.

So, why would I ever give him a second chance?

"Because this time, he was plotting on your behalf; for your own good, not for his," Tytus says.

My raw heart jumps, but my brain bashes it back down into submission.

"No. That's just an excuse," I mumble, shaking my head. "You weren't there when he told me about Krol."

"Oh, I've heard about Krol," Tytus sneers. "In fact, I've seen the fucker's tattered body. Believe me, he's in much worse shape than Babcia. And I don't believe for a second that the Greeks can actually help save him, but I do believe that Drago will do anything for his children."

"We aren't his children," I spit.

Tytus sighs. "We don't get to choose our family," he says. "Even when there's nothing to tie us together but our choices; when there's no blood binding us together; no law; we will always be family."

My vision blurs as a cold tear fills my eye.

"Why are you so sure he's finally on our side?" I ask, wiping the weakness from my cheek.

Tytus can only shrug. "Call it instinct."

"You've always had shit instincts."

That makes Tytus smile.

"Wait, how many times have you been captured or nearly killed again? Is it more than me? I think it's more than me."

I can't help but let out a broken giggle at his inappropriate confidence.

"It hasn't been from a lack of trying," I sigh. For a split second, I almost feel the kind of warmth I imagine Kaja is feeling right now. For all of our troubles, Tytus has always been there for me.

But the same could have been said about Gabriel—then he abandoned the both of us.

Taking a deep breath, I force a temporary calm over my tired body. It takes a moment to take hold, and I struggle to find any good thoughts to anchor it with.

But then a recent memory pops into my head, and a new warmth fills me from the inside out.

Rian said he was lucky to have me...

The warmth spreads.

"If only you knew the half of it," Tytus chuckles, seemingly unbothered. "Hell, I nearly joined you in a Kilpatrick cage when I returned that painting the other night."

My heart skips a beat.

"You what?"

"I might have been a little worried about you," he says, eyeing the mark around my throat. "I thought you might be treated better if I listened to that Irish bastard's least consequential demand."

I can hardly believe my ears. That doesn't sound like Tytus at all. Is he fucking with me?

"Where did you drop it off? Who did you give the painting to?"

An uncontrollable smile lifts my adoptive brother's strong cheekbones.

"I brought it right into the belly of the beast," he smirks, stroking his chin.

"Rian's place?"

Tytus nods.

"You didn't have to do that," I whisper, slightly irked that we gave up anything, even if it was something so utterly inconsequential. "Fuck. You *shouldn't* have done that."

"Don't worry, I didn't do it completely out of the goodness of my own heart," Tytus plays. "It's all part of a bigger plan. Hopefully, that sister of—"

".... Dragomir?"

Babcia's creaky voice cuts through our conversation like a serrated blade. Tytus and I are immediately done with our conversation. All attention turns towards Babcia.

"No," Tytus says, reaching out for Babcia's hand. "It's Roz and me."

"That monster is gone," I add.

Kaja is back up on her feet. The kitten licks Babcia's chin as the old lady slowly flutters awake.

Her hazy eyes search for something that isn't there, and when they don't find it, a momentary sadness takes over her.

It makes my heart contract.

Has Drago managed to fool Babcia too?

Maybe Tytus is right about him, after all...

"Where am I?" Babcia asks, trying to sit up. But Tytus places a gentle hand on her shoulder, preventing her from moving too fast. The old lady plops back down on the bed.

"You're at the hospital," Tytus explains.

"Oh, hello there, Kaja," Babcia says, a weak smile creasing her cheeks as her hazy gaze falls onto the cat. That smiles strengthens when she sees me. "And Rozalia, too. What did I do to deserve such a bountiful visit?"

"You fainted," I tell her. Reaching down, I take her wrinkly hand and squeeze.

"I'll have to do it more often," Babcia laughs, before a raspy cough quickly takes over.

"Don't you dare," I say, holding her as the fit passes.

"Yeah," Tytus adds. "Another inch to the left, and you might have cracked that hard noggin' of yours on the kitchen counter."

"it would take more than a counter to crack this old skull of mine," Babcia says. With a shaky hand, she softly strokes the side of Kaja's face. "Believe me, others have tried. My dear old husband especially, and it never worked out too well for him."

"That bastard is lucky he's already dead," I curse. My fingers curl back into fists.

"We all are," Babcia jokes, only coughing a little this time. "... Though, I would have loved for you both to meet his killer."

The words slip out of her like an old memory, carelessly shared for the first time. At first, Tytus and I are too shocked to respond.

Babcia has rarely ever spoken about her abusive ex-husband, other than to say he's likely rotting in hell by now. She's definitely never mentioned how he died.

"Someone killed the bastard?" Tytus asks, wickedly amused.

"Oh, yes. Very violently," Babcia nods. Her glazed eyes dim as she draws deep into her past. "It was done by the most interesting young man I'd ever met... up until I met you two, of course. He had eyes like a wolf and no mercy. Even when I begged him to stop, I think he knew I didn't actually want him to. He kept at it until Alan's head was mush. My only regret is that I never learned his real name..."

Tytus and I both share a concerned glance.

Then, something occurs to me.

"It... it wasn't Drago, was it?"

It's hard to tell if Babcia laughs or if she's just taken over by another coughing fit. Either way, I hold onto her hand until she's done.

"My goodness, no. Dragomir is not the type. Far too thin for something like that. This man was a beast. Much like you, Tytus, my dear—only if you had been born twenty years earlier."

"I wish I had been," Tytus notes. "Then I could have killed Alan myself."

"Yes, I know, dear," Babcia nods, kneading her knuckles under Kaja's ear. "You and the wolf share a kindred spirit. As does Dragomir. And you too, Rozalia. You are all such vicious protectors. My fallen angels..."

Fallen angels.

Without warning, Babcia's words send an invisible arrow piercing through my heart. I can't help but reach for my chest as a flash of pain cuts through me.

Only one other person has ever called me a fallen angel.

Rian.

Those ocean blue eyes sparkled with mockery when he first said it, but his words never faltered.

He said he was lucky to have me...

But he doesn't have me. No one does.

Right?

So why am I thinking about him at a time like this?

"The wolf?" Tytus mumbles, turning to me. "This guy sounds like mafia, do you think—"

Before Tytus can finish, Babcia raises a weak arm up at me.

"Are you alright, dear?" she asks, her creaky voice filled with concern.

It's like I'm the one in the hospital bed when I feel her eyes fall on my throat, on the red mark burned into my skin.

"Just dealing with a man problem of my own," I say, attempting to brush it off.

But those glazed eyes stay glued on me.

"Good or bad problems?" Babcia asks, her bushy eyebrows raising with a knowing curiosity.

"A bit of both," I sigh, before immediately regretting it.

Tytus is here. And I can feel him straighten up.

"What good is there?" he asks, his voice laced with suspicion.

"There was no good," I lie. "I'm just tired."

With all my strength, I try to keep my cheeks from flushing with a shameful pink fire.

Tytus seems to reluctantly accept my excuse, but Babcia isn't so easily wavered.

"Oh, my poor sweet Rozalia," Babcia smiles. Resting her head back on the pillow, she stares up at the ceiling with a puzzled look. I can't quite tell if she's smiling or frowning.

"I'm fine," I insist.

"I know. I know," Babcia whispers, her voice breaking. "But please promise me this. Don't deny yourself. Don't ever refuse what you want because it doesn't seem to fit into your life as you first expected. If there's one way I can repay you for all you've done for me, it's by begging you to please think only of yourself and no one else."

A thick blanket of silence falls over the room as Babcia's eyes glaze over again.

"What's going on?" Tytus cautiously asks, completely oblivious.

"Nothing," I say, shaking my head. But the gears are already spinning.

What does Babcia think she knows? Am I projecting something I'm not aware of? About Rian?

I want to know.

"Don't deny yourself, Rozalia, dear," Babcia quietly continues. "That's what I did with my first love, and it only led to sorrow. If only I had followed my heart, and not listened to what others said, I might have spent two years in heaven, instead of a lifetime in hell."

My limbs go limp as I realize what Babcia is saying.

"Roz, is everything alright?" Tytus asks.

"I think so," I say, not sure if that's true.

"My ex-husband was a rich man," Babcia mindlessly reveals. "Well, relatively rich. He owned a small business. A house. White picket fence and all. But behind it all was blood. Anger and resentment. People told me I would fall in love with the life before I fell in love with the man. But even back then, I knew it wasn't true... because I had already fallen in love with a man. And that man had no such life... only love to give... and that would have been enough... if only I had listened to my heart..."

I can only watch as a worrisome shiver rattles down Babcia's fragile body. It's significant enough that even Kaja reacts, jumping off the bed and scurrying onto the floor.

My twisting heart sinks.

"Babcia, what's wrong? Are you alright?"

Before she has a chance to respond, Tytus reacts. Racing to the door, he rips it open and steps out into the hallway.

"We need a doctor in here, stat!" he roars.

I stay by Babcia's side.

"Tell your brother I'm fine," she croaks, waving a weak hand in his direction. "... But you should also tell him about your feelings. He might not understand, but that doesn't mean you can't."

"I... I don't understand," I tell her.

What I don't explain, though, is how much I want to understand.

It feels like I'm on the cusp of something. Something that I can't quite grasp. Babcia shows me the way. Pointing towards my chest, she takes a creaky breath.

"Listen to your heart, dear, and everything will follow."

Her words echo around in my head as the doctors rush to her bedside. I'm pushed away, and. I'm too lost in my thoughts to fight back.

Listen to your heart, dear, and everything will follow.

It's only when Kaja hisses that I snap back awake. The kitten jolts from the commotion, sprinting through my feet towards the door.

No. I won't let her run off. I won't lose another one.

But I don't need to worry. When I turn around, Tytus is there, and he effortlessly swoops Kaja up.

"Let's leave the doctors to it," he says, gesturing for me to join him in the hallway. "I want you to tell me what's really going on."

"No…" I mutter.

Even with everything Babcia just said, I don't feel like explaining anything to Tytus—not until I actually know what's going on.

And there's only one way to find out.

"Hey, where are you going?" Tytus asks, calling after me as I brush by him and storm out into the hallway.

"Home," I whisper, not knowing exactly what that means.

Still, through all the confusion, one thing has become clear —and it's so clear that I find myself blushing as I run down the hospital stairs and burst out into the cool summer night.

Fuck. All I can see are those ocean blue eyes. The blood-red lips. The shallow dimples.

All I can think about is him.

Whatever Babcia was getting at, it's made one thing painfully obvious.

I need to see Rian again.

Fuck.

I *want* to see him again.

20

RIAN

"I've made sure everyone's on high alert. All we can do now is trust that our spies pick up the specifics before it's too late."

Maksim's focused gaze stays fixed ahead as we march down the hallway. The man's been through it all before, and a simple threat like this isn't going to ruffle his feathers. Not too much.

I'm not so sure I can say the same about myself.

"I don't trust our spies," I grunt, leading the way to the basement. "They didn't know about the plans for my coronation. They didn't know about Leander. They didn't know about Drago. How sure are we they aren't missing something now?"

"It's a king's duty to—"

"Enough of the king shit," I stop him. "Until the dust settles, I won't have it. For now, I'm a soldier. Just like I've always been."

"There's such a thing as a warrior king, you know," Maksim notes. "A man can be both." Lunging ahead, he opens the door to the basement for me.

I'm immediately hit by the scent of paint.

"How is she?"

"Fine," Maksim says, following me into the darkness below. "But you know your sister, sometimes it's hard to tell."

"She cares more about others than herself," I confirm.

"It's admirable," Maksim says.

"It's stupid."

Our footsteps must be loud, because we've barely hit the bottom step when Mel's head pokes out from behind a half-opened door.

"Who are you calling stupid?" she asks. But her banter is half-assed. She's not at full strength today, and it's completely understandable.

"You," I say, not bothering to hide my frustration... or my fear.

"That's mean," Mel says. Her voice is so quiet I'm not sure if she's playing up her innocence for sympathy points, or just fucking with me.

"I'm not mean," I insist, pushing my way into her makeshift studio. "The stranger you met the other night is mean."

"He didn't seem so—"

Lifting my palm in the air, I stop her.

"Where is it?" I ask. My eyes are still adjusting to the brightness as I look around the sprawling space. The path down here is so dark, yet the walls of the studio are white, and there's a miniature flood lamp in every corner, shedding a blinding light over the sprawling room.

"Over there," Mel shrugs, lazily pointing in an unspecified direction.

I follow her lead, but still have trouble picking out anything from the clutter of countless half-finished paintings and empty picture frames.

"It's a mess down here," I note.

"You should have seen it before we got rid of the cats," Maksim chuckles.

"I miss the cats," Mel sighs.

"What happened to them?" I ask. Buried under a mountain of painting supplies, I think I see what I'm looking for.

"We've shipped them across our empire," Maksim says. "They've gotten good homes, I made sure of it."

"Any sign of Mel's kitten?"

"No," Maksim says, shaking his head.

"She's not mine," my sister stubbornly points out. "She's supposed to be yours."

"I don't want a cat," I grumble.

But that's a lie.

There is one cat I want.

My Black Cat.

It's barely been over forty-eight hours since Rozalia escaped from me at the club, and I'm already desperate to see her again. To feel her. To fight her.

But I haven't been able to dwell on those desires. Not directly. Flavian gave me five addresses, and despite all of my hard work, I've only managed to explore three of them.

The last two on the list almost put me on a long flight, but then I heard about what happened back at home, and I knew I had to come back right away.

Now, I'm in the unenviable spot of trying to figure out just where the fuck to go from here.

Mel was put directly in harm's way.

And if I didn't trust anyone to look after her before, I definitely don't now. She's not safe with anyone but Maksim and me.

One of us has to be here at all times.

It's frustrating, but it's a necessity. My sister can't defend herself. She's innocent in all of this darkness. And I mean to keep it that way.

But I don't trust anyone to go out looking for Leander either. He's just as much my problem as Rozalia is—if only because he threatens what's mine.

She belongs to me, you bastard. And I'm going to make you pay for even thinking she didn't.

But first...

"Why did you hide it?" I ask.

Kicking aside two massive easels, a broad palette and three blank canvasses, I finally set my eyes on the reason I came racing home.

Mel's painting.

It's been returned.

"I didn't hide it," Mel mumbles.

When I look back over my shoulder, I find her mindlessly twirling a red paintbrush in her fingers and staring off into space.

"It's too good to stay hidden," I tell her, still feeling bad about my first reaction to the masterpiece.

"I didn't hide it," Mel lies again. "It just gets messy in my studios."

"Well, you better change that," I say, not pushing her too hard. "Your new master isn't going to like a messy apprentice."

"That's not happening anymore," she sighs. I can hear the heartbreak in her voice.

She's been looking forward to her apprenticeship for the last year. And now, it's in jeopardy because I can't control my empire.

Fuck.

"I'll figure everything out, I promise."

"It's fine," Mel whispers, waving me off.

But when her paintbrush drops, I know she's about to break.

I leave the painting and go to my sister. But not before giving Maksim a direct order.

"Take it to my office and check it for bugs," I tell him.

He just nods.

"I'll get you to Italy if it kills me," I tell Mel, placing a cautious hand on her shoulder.

"Don't say that," she snaps, finally turning around. Her eyes glimmer with barely restrained tears.

I knew she wasn't alright.

How could she be?

Two nights ago, my baby sister came face to face with a monster.

My hands curl into fists.

Tytus.

"Come here." Mel doesn't get a choice, I wrap her in my arms and give her an inescapable hug. "I'll make him pay for scaring you."

But first, I should make every last asshole on my security team pay for their failure.

After all, they were the ones who let Tytus sneak past them. Hell, I doubt we would have even known he'd been here if Mel hadn't stumbled out of her studio at three in the morning and come across the despicable beast.

It was only when she screamed that my men were finally alerted of a break-in.

But Tytus had already vanished, and he'd left his message in the form of a gift. A huge canvas that he somehow managed to smuggle past a small army's worth of security.

Mel's painting.

He returned it, alright. And he'd gotten close enough to my baby sister to scare the life out of her.

Thankful, that's all he seems to have done.

"Are you sure you're not hurt?" I ask, only letting Mel out of my arms so I can inspect her.

"I'm fine," she says, wiping a tear from her cheek. "It's you I'm worried about."

"I can take care of myself."

"But Tytus is so big..."

Hearing her say his name infuriates me. I've tried so hard to keep Mel from the worst of my world, yet here she is uttering the name of a demon.

Tytus is going to pay.

"You need to rest," I say, patting Mel's head as I try to keep myself from saying something vile.

Really, all I want to do is tell her every last brutal detail of what I'll do to Tytus for breaking into my sanctum and threatening her. But I know that won't help.

So, instead, I take her hand and lead her out of the messy studio.

By the time we're back upstairs, Maksim has dropped the painting off in my office and come back out to join us.

"Where did you put it?" Mel asks the second we see him.

"Somewhere safe," Maksim assures her.

"Don't worry about it, Mel," I tell her. "Here, let's go to your room. Watch something comforting on your laptop. I'll have someone bring up your favorite tea."

I'm so used to dealing with Roz that I'm expecting my sister to fight back.

But Mel isn't a fighter—at least, not in the same way Rozalia Dorn is.

"Alright," she weakly accepts. My heart sinks. I can tell she's emotionally exhausted. And even if I want to burn the world to ashes, I hold back my rage until I've seen her to bed.

"Have you been able to recover any security footage from the night Tytus broke in?" I ask Maksim, after I've gently clicked Mel's door shut behind us.

"No," he admits. "He did a good job of covering his tracks."

"Must have had help from Rozalia," I growl.

The thought makes my gut churn.

I didn't think she'd go that far, not after what we've been through. But I guess I was wrong.

"And what about the impending attack our spies informed

you about?" I ask, trying to get my mind off the betrayal. But I can't. And even the word betrayal feels wrong.

No matter what kind of feelings I'm developing for Rozalia, she's still my enemy.

How can your enemy betray you?

By making you like them...

"We still aren't sure where it might take place, or even who's going to carry it out. We've only heard rumblings that it's certain to happen soon. Someone has put the underworld on notice. They want everyone watching as they attack us."

"I can guess who's going to carry it out," I grunt.

Maksim nods.

"We should send more men to search Leander's last two properties."

I shake my head. "No. They haven't earned the honor. Either you go, or I do."

Maksim doesn't fight back. "Alright. Who's it going to be?"

Looking back over my shoulder, I think of how scared Mel must have been when she came across Tytus.

It makes my decision easy.

No matter how badly I want to kill Leander with my own two hands, I need to stay here and look after my sister.

"You go. Bring a team of your most skilled and trusted men," I tell Maksim. "I know you haven't completely lost faith in everyone yet. Here's your chance to prove their worth."

"We won't let you down," Maksim says.

Usually, my uncle takes an order and runs with it, sometimes even before I finish speaking. But not this time.

No. For some, he doesn't immediately leave. Instead, he hovers in place for a moment.

"Is there anything else?" I ask, slightly concerned.

In response, my uncle opens his mouth, but nothing comes out. When he shuts it again, a thousand alarm bells go off in my head.

"What?" I demand to know.

"... The Italians still want to meet," Maksim finally speaks. But it's clearly not what he was going to say first. This is just a distraction. I'm not going to fall for it.

"Tell them I'm busy," I brush him off. "What we're you going to say before that?"

"I... It's not my place," he says, pursing his lips.

"I give you permission to step out of line."

A subtle sigh escapes my fearsome consigliere as he looks around, as if to make sure the coast is clear.

My heart catches my throat.

What could Maksim possibly be this worried about? He's usually the one with the cool head.

"The girl," he sighs. "Is she worth the obsession?"

Fuck.

Of course this is about Rozalia.

I hate how Maksim can see right through me. But what I hate even more is that I already know the answer to his question, and I know it's not what he wants to hear.

Yes, she's worth it.

"It doesn't matter if she's worth it or not," I deflect. "The threat she and her brother pose is mine to handle. And I need to deal with it before they or their new ally decides to attack us."

"How will you do that if you're stuck here?" Maksim asks.

The implication is clear.

"You think Tytus returned the painting and scared Mel just to keep me housebound?"

Maksim sighs.

"They might be the biggest threat to our empire, but you're the biggest threat to them."

He's not wrong. But I'm also not convinced. Not entirely.

Roz doesn't want me to stop chasing her. She's just as lost in our game of cat and mouse as I am. So why would she want to keep me caged?

... Unless she's just been stringing me along this entire time, leading me around like a dog on a leash...

A stone drops in my gut. But it only exists for a moment before a visceral rage melts it away.

No. I've felt Rozalia's desire. It's just as strong as mine.

She wants me.

But does she need me?

Because it sure as hell feels like I need her.

"What are you suggesting?" I ask Maksim.

Before he can answer, though, both of our phones blare alive. It's immediately clear we aren't getting any ordinary call. The devices vibrate at an emergency frequency.

It's impossible to ignore.

"What the fuck?" My uncle curses as he looks down at his phone.

"What does yours say?" I ask, pulling out my own.

"It says, 'tell your king to look at his phone.' There's no number..."

I don't need to be told twice.

I'm sorry about what happened to your sister. Let me make it up to you. How about dinner at La Forcina? Tonight. Say 9 pm? Don't show me up.

"Fuck," I curse, my heart pounding.

There's no caller ID, but I know it's Roz.

It has to be.

But it's also clear what's happening.

She's leading me into a trap.

... Leading me by the leash...

My fury flares.

But so does something else.

"You stay here with Mel tonight, alright?" I tell Maksim. Shoving my phone away, I storm past him. "You can leave for

Leander's last two properties in the morning. Don't worry, I won't be late."

"Where are you going?" Maksim calls out after me.

Reaching under my belt, I check to make sure my gun is there. It is; tucked just above my swollen cock. I'm already half-hard.

Fuck it.

"I'm going to dinner."

21

RIAN

La Forcina isn't the type of place you set a trap—especially not one for Rian Kilpatrick.

The upscale restaurant borders on the edge of my territory, and is directly under my control, which means anyone trying to suck up to me is going to be coming here on a near-weekly basis.

Every night, famous athletes, celebrities, politicians, and police chiefs fill these seats. Their presence brings all kinds of paparazzi too. The streets outside are swarming with flashing cameras.

There's no room for stealth, no opportunity for reckless behavior. If you make a mistake here, it will be all over the news, right along with your face. And that's only after my men get through with you.

Causing a disturbance at one of my establishments is a big no-no. Hell, we even have a designated alley out back just for disgruntled customers. The cement is steeped in blood.

So, of all places Rozalia could have met me, why has she picked this one?

... Unless it wasn't her who sent that text.

Or Maybe she just wants a nice date.

"Here's your drink, sir."

The bartender serving me looks nervous. I can only imagine the manager put every employee on notice the second I called ahead—not that I needed to. Apparently, a reservation had already been made in my name.

"Thank you," I mumble.

The whiskey sour is acceptable, and I quickly down it before gesturing for another one.

For now, I'm waiting at the bar by the front. A dozen new guests stream in every second, and nearly everyone pauses for a second when they notice me. But I don't pay them any mind. Instead, my attention keeps turning back to the muted television at the corner of the bar. Just above its flickering screen is a clock. I've been looking at it religiously ever since I got here.

It's only 8:45 pm, and the table that's being held in my name is still empty. It sits atop a platform, slightly elevating it over the crowded floor like a velvet throne. Every once in a while, I spot someone taking a curious glimpse up at the best seat in the house. They're wondering who will sit there.

They'll find out soon enough.

At least, that's what I'm hoping.

When I receive my second whiskey sour, I take a small sip and look up. Above the stacked bottles of liquor at the back of the bar is a long mirror. In it, I can see everything going on behind me and everyone.

I spot some big-time athletes, and a few small-time actors I recognize from TV shows, but it's not who's already here that concerns me. It's who hasn't shown up yet.

At La Forcina, empty tables are an oddity. Tonight, though, there are two of them, not including mine. They stand out like big red flags, calling my attention to the danger that could be on the horizon.

Taking another sip of my drink, I crack my neck.

Bring it on.

"Don Kilpatrick? Is that you?"

The voice comes from all the way back in the coat check area. Placing my drink down, I brush the back of my hand over the gun-shaped bulge in my pants, then look over.

To my disappointment, I immediately recognize the face poking around the corner.

Leo Camporese.

"Fuck," I grunt, turning away from him.

The last thing I need right now is a distraction. And the last kind of distraction I want to suffer through is a pushy Italian don.

But Leo Camporese doesn't take the hint.

"Don Kilpatrick, I can't believe the coincidence. What an honor it is to see you here," the don grovels, coming up to bother me.

"I own the place," I remind him.

"Of course, I know that. It's why I always come. Not that you need my business, but rather because I trust that anything you're involved in will be of the utmost quality."

"Are you sure you didn't get a tip that I'd made a reservation?" I accuse, finally turning to face him.

The thin Italian is momentarily taken aback by my forwardness. Usually, I wouldn't be so direct. But I have too much on my plate to entertain this bullshit.

There's no doubt in my mind that Leo wants something. The Italians never talk to me unless it's to ask or take.

"If only I were that resourceful," Leo forces out a laugh. He's about to pat me on the shoulder, but he wisely thinks better of it. "No, I'm just here to treat my daughter for her birthday. Oh, there she is now. Would you mind saying hello? I know it would mean the world to her."

Looking over his shoulder, Leo gives an aggressive wave to the two women nervously shuffling into the dining hall. One of them I recognize as his wife. The other seems vaguely familiar as well. I figure I must have seen her at my coronation.

She looks young enough to have been one of those poor girls dressed in white. Too young to be put in such a situation.

"How old is your daughter?" I ask, looking back up at the clock above the flickering television.

8:50 pm.

"She's just turned eighteen!" Leo excitedly announces.

"Was she at my coronation?"

"Yes, and she was so disappointed that you two didn't get to meet before... well, before it ended."

"So, she was underaged when you tried to pawn her off on me?" The disdain in my voice is so sharp Leo winces against it.

"I... uh," he stammers, before his wife comes to his rescue.

"Don Kilpatrick. It's so nice to see you here. This our daughter—"

"Don Kilpatrick?!"

Like an echo, a new voice appears from back in the coat check area.

We all look over at the same time.

It's a waste of energy. Because all I see is Adriano Sabatino —that is, until he's joined by his wife and their daughter.

Adriana.

A sliver of guilt runs through my gut as I remember the last time Adriano tried to force her on me. The poor thing was terrified. And she looks even worse off now.

These animals just don't know when to quit.

"Adriano..." Leo grumbles under his breath.

It's not surprising he's upset to see the rival don. It just means more competition for him and his daughter.

Suddenly, the empty tables dotted around the dining room make a lot more sense. The Italians got wind that I was here. They set up last-minute reservations of their own.

It doesn't matter that I announced my fake engagement to their faces. They're all equally relentless and shameless.

Shaking my head, I down the rest of my whiskey sour and look up at the clock again. 8:55pm. It's about time I get to my table.

A subtle smile lifts my lips as I imagine the look on the Italians' faces when they see Rozalia for the first time. If I'm right, and she's who will be joining me, their reaction is going to be priceless.

Maybe it will even finally get them to stop pushing their daughters on me. But I doubt it.

Their ignorance on the matter is a sign of a deeper issue. They don't trust me. And it's showing in their inability to accept that I've decided to marry someone else.

It hardly matters that it's all a lie. Even if they knew the truth—and didn't just suspect it—their open rebellion against my wishes is a sign of disrespect.

I won't stand for it.

You better show up, angel.

Don't you dare disappoint me.

"Have a nice night," I nod, standing up from my seat. Leo Camporese and his family get a stern nod. Don Sabatino gets nothing.

He doesn't seem to like that.

I've hardly turned my back on them before I feel a hand on my shoulder.

"Don Kilpatrick, let me buy you dinner tonight, huh? How about—"

Adriano's voice is like nails on a chalkboard. Somehow, he's managed to sprint across the room and get to me before I could leave him in the dust.

Idiot.

Whipping around, I grab his wrist. "I own the place," I sneer, ready to teach the fucker a lesson.

But then I see how terrified his poor daughter is and I instantly regret my outburst. Fuck. Both kids look like they're about to crumble into dust.

They don't deserve this.

"Enjoy your night," I huff, throwing Adriano's hand down.

This fucking world. These fucking bastards. They're supposed to protect their innocent daughters, not whore them out to a monster like me.

I'm about to turn my back on them when something stops me.

Out of the corner of my eye, I see the bar clock strike 8:57 pm. But it's not the time that makes my stomach drop. It's what's on the television beneath it.

"... Dad?"

Adriano starts to apologize, but his words fade into the background as I concentrate on the screen.

Clear as day, I see my father.

It looks like he's on the steps of a federal courthouse. Cameras flash in his face. A dozen microphones are pushed towards him.

My chest flexes. My heart clamps up. The heavy pounding of my angry pulse quickens into an anxious rhythm.

Still, Dad looks completely composed—even as a strong wind blows back his salt and pepper hair and the black bar at the bottom of the screen races to keep up with all the questions he's being asked.

My fingers curl into fists.

Shit. Was his first official deposition today? I know my family has purposely been trying to keep me away from that shit, but how did I not pick up on it?

More guilt rages through me as I watch him calmly take on the world, doing whatever it takes to protect his family and his empire.

Anger rejoins my guilt. I want to jump through the screen

and wring those reporters around the neck. Don't they know who they're talking to?

That's the true king of the underworld. They need to show him some respect.

Fuck. I should have shown him some respect. At the very least, I could have tried to get hold of my dad before today. I should have wished him luck and reassured him that everything was going alright on my end.

I should have lied.

But I've been so stuck in my own head, fighting against my own problems, that I haven't—

"Cowardly feds," Leo Camporese hisses, snapping me out of my daze.

"Couldn't let one of us get too powerful," Sabatino agrees. "As if we were ever a real threat to the US government. Really, the fuckers should be thanking your dad for keeping the streets under control."

Both men are also glaring up at the TV. I can't quite tell if they're putting on a show for my sake, or if they're actually pissed at the treatment my father is receiving.

Neither option is exactly comforting.

Either they're secretly hoping for my father's downfall, or they actually respect him enough to defend his decisions.

But when have they ever defended my decisions? Hell, they still haven't accepted my very public decision to marry our sworn enemy, even though I announced it directly to their faces. It doesn't matter if they don't understand it, they should follow their leader.

I guess I haven't earned their respect yet.

My rage turns inwards.

That's my fault.

Ripping myself away from the TV, I stare out across the busy dining hall—I'm immediately met by another surprising sight.

My empty table isn't so empty anymore.

A stunning beauty in a sleek red dress fills one of our two seats.

Rozalia.

She's here. And when our eyes meet, she gives me a wicked grin and points down at her wrist. There's no watch there, but I get the message.

You're late.

With a quick glance back over my shoulder, I check the clock over the television.

9:01 pm.

Fuck.

Thankfully, Dad is gone from the TV, but that doesn't mean he's in the clear, and it definitely doesn't erase my anger and disappointment as I wordlessly leave the Italians at the bar.

Sure enough, they call after me. But I don't acknowledge them. I'll deal with them later.

My queen has arrived. And that blood-red gown makes her green eyes pop like cursed emeralds. There's no going back. I'm trapped in her alluring gaze.

Still, in the back of my mind, I can't forget about the balls on those pesky Italian fuckers.

They need to learn who's in charge. And I need to teach them.

Tonight is my chance to send a message.

Rozalia is mine.

My enemy. My prey. My problem.

My future bride.

Whatever trap she has brewing for me will come when it comes. But until she springs it on me, I'm not going to waste a second thinking about that.

Instead, I'm going to focus on what matters the most.

Her.

It's time to show off my fake fiancé.

Get ready for the night of your life, angel.

22

ROZALIA

Everyone watches as the king glides through the crowded dining hall. But those ocean blue eyes never turn away from me.

Even as the crowd murmurs and points, Rian stays focused. For a moment, I feel naked. Like he can see right through this slutty dress and into my soul.

It doesn't take long for the intensity of that attention to become overwhelming. I look away, ashamed of my weakness.

To make myself feel better, I stare out over the crowd. It helps my anxiety to look at each individual as they are, a cowed worshipper.

All the men here are obsessed with Rian's power. The women are consumed by his good looks. Between them all, though, I can sense the shared fear, and the common respect.

This is a monster who could burn your entire world down with the snap of his fingers; a man who could change your fortunes for the better, without even trying. He's a lover who could blow your mind.

Everyone imagines what he could do to them as he climbs

the stairs and walks toward me. I don't have to imagine. I've experienced all three.

The rumors are true.

He's a monster. A beautiful, brilliant, brutal monster. Yet no one knows how cruel he can truly be. Because no one's heart is beating as fast as mine. No one here has been made to miss him.

Fuck.

He's actually made me miss him.

The bastard.

"You're late," I snort, the moment he's within earshot.

To my surprise, the agitation I spotted on him at the bar seems to have mostly melted away.

"I've been here for half-an-hour already," he says, still not completely recovered.

Pulling out a chair, Rian sits down across from me. Those ocean blue eyes dig deep into my soul.

Under the table cloth, I use my foot to nudge a special package closer to me. The heavy crown doesn't make a sound as I nestle it between my ankles.

"I didn't see you."

"Liar."

Unfurling his serviette, Rian flashes it out like a matador before gently placing it on his lap.

I bite the inside of my lip.

How am I already horny?

"Would we like a drink for the table?"

I'm so distracted by my lion that I don't even hear the server approach.

My first instinct is to reach for the knife holstered to my ankle, but I manage to stop myself before I can make a scene.

"Not used to nice restaurants, huh?" Rian quietly taunts, taking a drink menu from the well-dressed waiter.

"Not used to being snuck up on."

"Distracted by something?"

Don't say anything about his eyes. Don't say anything about his eyes.

Waving away the server, Rian sets his deep gaze back on me. He seems to have shed the last bits of his agitation, and a suave, more relaxed demeanor is settling in.

It only makes me tense up even more.

What does he have up his sleeve?

"I'm just waiting for you to spring your trap," I tell him.

Rian huffs, the faintest smirk revealing those heart-pulling dimples of his.

"My trap? As if I had time to set up a trap. You're text only came in—"

"My text?" I interrupt, confused. "I never sent you a text."

Rian rolls his eyes.

"No need to be coy, angel. I know how much you missed me."

"You're the one who invited me here," I remind him, remembering the next I received two hours ago.

I'm sorry about your throat. Let me make it up to you. How about dinner at La Forcina? Tonight. Say 9 pm? Don't show me up.

"Are you fucking with me?" Rian asks. Leaning forward, he studies me carefully. I glare back at him.

"Are *you* fucking with me?" I snap back, turning away from his intoxicating gaze. "You sent me a text to meet you here at 9 pm. I know it was you, even if you were too cowardly to use your own number."

Rian doesn't immediately respond. Instead, he just continues to stare. Then, slowly, he reaches into his pocket and pulls out his phone.

Swiping down, he opens up the screen and turns it around.

"Did your text look anything like this one?" he asks.

My jaw drops as I read the near identical message.

"What the fuck is going on?" I mutter.

"You tell me."

"I don't know," I insist.

"You're saying you didn't send me this text?"

"Obviously not."

"Then who did?"

My mind spins as I try to come up with an explanation. Is Rian playing with me?

If not him, then someone else must be.

But other than Rian, who else knows about the mark on my throat? No one. I wouldn't dare tell a soul, and for some reason, I can't exactly imagine him bragging about it.

Still, I try to think up an answer as Rian stares me down.

Whoever sent that text to me must also know about what happened when Tytus returned Melina Kilpatrick's painting. But who the hell could know both of those things?

For a moment, I hit another dead end.

Of course, Rian and his sister would know about the encounter, and maybe a small group of their inner circle, but unless Rian is messing with me, then it couldn't have been any of them.

That only leaves Tytus.

A knot appears in my gut.

No. It doesn't just leave Tytus.

While I was under Rian's control, Tytus was with Drago. My adoptive father was supposedly at the hospital before I arrived. That would have given him plenty of time to hear about Tytus' little adventure.

Fuck.

If Drago knows, does that mean Leander could too?

A strike of fear flashes through me as I look around the crowded restaurant. We're vulnerable.

Dealing with an ambush devised by Rian Kilpatrick is one thing. I've learned my lion's habits. He won't do anything I can't handle. But Leander?

I have no idea what that fucker is capable of, and I definitely don't trust him. Same goes for Drago—no matter how hard Tytus is trying to change that.

My hackles rise.

"We need to leave," I say, standing up.

But Rian isn't having it. In the blink of an eye, he's reached across the table and grabbed my wrist.

"No. We're staying," he says, holding me down. "No more tricks, Rozalia. I don't care if you sent that text or not, we are having a nice dinner."

The chatty din of the restaurant momentarily goes silent as everyone watches us. I can feel the room collectively hold its breath.

Fucking hell.

I hate crowds.

"Why?" I mumble under my breath, refusing to sit back down quite yet. "So you can prove to the Italians that you actually plan on marrying me?"

Slowly, the chatter returns to the restaurant. But the eyes don't leave. The attention makes my skin crawl.

To avoid being at the center of it all, I finally fall back into my seat.

"I want them to stop sending their daughters after me," Rian confirms.

Even through all of the dread and uneasiness, I still feel a sharp pang of jealousy erupt inside of me.

"Why?" I sneer, remembering the girls that surrounded Rian at the bar. "They're pretty cute. How about you leave me alone and shack up with one of them."

"I don't want cute," Rian says. "I want corrupt and evil and disgusting. I want you."

That pang of jealousy is set on fire as a new sensation invades my chest. It's something I can't quite pinpoint. Something lighter. Something fluttery. Something unreal.

"You suck at giving compliments," I huff, calming down just a bit. Taking my own napkin, I hurriedly place it on my lap.

"You suck at receiving them," Rian smirks.

He's playing with me.

Why isn't he worried? Neither of us knows who brought us here tonight, yet he's acting like this is just some ordinary blind date.

"Keep telling yourself that," I mumble.

A cold shiver runs up my skin when Rian releases my wrist. I hadn't realized how warm his grip was. I quickly learn to miss it.

"A bottle of Bouley for the table," Rian orders, waving down a waiter

"Yes, sir."

"What are you doing?" I ask when the server scurries off.

"I'm wining and dining you—whether you like it or not."

Every part of me wants to stand up and storm out. But I know Rian's stronger than me, and all he'd have to do is make the smallest effort and every last eye in the place would be back on us—not that we aren't everyone's entertain for the night already.

"What's your angle?"

"No angle," Rian shrugs. "But if you want to answer for what your brother did the other night, I'll gladly listen."

"I don't control Tytus," I spit, contention rising in my voice.

But Rian stays surprisingly calm, especially considering his sister is involved.

"Does he control you?"

"No one controls me."

"I can only hope," he smiles, his blue eyes falling onto my throat. "I've tried. It didn't work out."

"So, what? Now you've decided to win me over with bribes instead of by force?"

"No, that's not it."

This time, I hear the waiter approach as he brings our bottle to the table.

"What is this, then?" I ask.

"It's called wine," he jokes. Waving off the waiter once more, he takes my glass and fills it up to the brim. "Drink."

"Are you trying to make up for that time you fed me raw chicken?" I push, unsure of how to feel about this.

"You loved that chicken," he smiles. "Almost as much as you loved what we did after you devoured it."

Rian practically shoves that memory into my face. There's no stopping the sweltering memory of what we shared in that bedroom. And there's no denying the effect it has on me.

My toes curl. My thighs clench. A familiar pressure appears in my core.

"I doubt I enjoyed it as much as you," I return. But that only draws me deeper into his trap.

My tongue flashes out across my lips. I can practically taste Rian's body. I can almost feel his thick cock.

"I hope you did," he says, leaning back in his chair.

Just like that, I'm overwhelmed by a very simple temptation. To sit back, kick off my shoes, and enjoy this night for what it appears to be.

An innocent dinner date.

But in our world, nothing is ever so innocent.

"What are you looking at?" I ask, but the venom in my voice isn't so strong anymore.

Still, I stay prepared for the worst.

But even that's hard to do as Rian stares me down. His ocean blue eyes twinkle with curiosity. He's looking at me like he can't quite believe I'm real. The crown hidden between my feet grows heavy.

"Tell me something you've never told anyone before," he says, ignoring my question.

"Stop it," I say, shaking my head.

I hate how domestic this is starting to feel. How warm and fuzzy and right. It reminds me of how I imagined Kaja felt cuddled up on Babcia's chest. But Rian isn't Babcia.

He's a killer. My hunter. My prey.

My enemy.

"Stop what?" he asks, playing dumb.

"Stop trying to make this a date."

"I'm not trying, angel. That's what it is."

"We don't even know who set this whole thing up."

Rian just shrugs.

"So, call it a blind date, then. Does that make you feel better?"

"No," I snap, almost standing up from my seat. The rational side of my brain is slowly fighting back against the heat in my heart. "How are you so comfortable with this? With all the enemies we have? The people we know don't just set up blind dates."

"You're right," Rian nods. Leaning forward again, he places his forearms on the table. "But I'm not worried."

"You've lost your mind," I tell him, unwilling to admit that his apparent tranquility is growing on me.

"Or maybe I just find your presence comforting."

"That's insane. I'm a killer."

Rian intertwines his fingers and leans further across the table.

"So am I," he whispers, like it's some big secret.

Still, despite the banality of his words, they seep down my tender throat and into my chest. My heart clenches, instinctually trying to fight off the warmth.

But it's a losing battle.

"So, what? You just want to sit here and drink champagne?" I ask, trying to hide any signs of the battle raging inside of me.

I've never been spoiled like this before. I've never wanted to be spoiled like this before.

So why is the idea of Rian doing it so alluring?

"It's not champagne. It's wine," Rian notes, smiling as he falls back in his chair. "And no, I don't want to just sit here, sipping on wine. I want you to talk."

"So, it's an interrogation?"

Now it's Rian's turn to get frustrated. Sitting up in his chair, his smile twists into an annoyed frown.

"Stop trying to make this something you're comfortable with, Roz," he says. "This has nothing to do with the underworld. This is about us, and us only."

To my surprise, I don't feel any satisfaction from finally breaking through his casual demeanor.

Instead, my stubbornness seems to bring a cold chill over our table. It only makes me realize just how cozy this has become. Despite my protests, I'm starting to feel almost as comfortable as Rian is pretending to be. And I don't want to lose it.

"And what are we?" I ask, almost afraid to hear the answer.

"That's what we're going to figure out."

I'm so tempted to play along. And not just because I'm curious about the answer too. But because I don't want to risk losing this sparkling warmth that surrounds us.

"Fine," I relent, slinking down into my chair. "Order me something expensive and start asking your questions."

That brings a smile back to Rian's stupidly handsome face.

"Not a question, just a small little dare," he says, gesturing for the waiter.

"Yes, sir?"

"What do you like to eat?" Rian asks me.

"Everything," I say, crossing my arms.

Rian's smile widens.

"Bring us one of everything, please," he orders.

The waiter doesn't even hesitate.

"Yes, sir," he nods, before quickly scurrying off to the kitchen.

It takes me a second to grasp what he just did.

"Rian, I wasn't asking for—"

But he isn't having it. Raising a finger to his lips, he calms me down.

"Just enjoy it, angel," he says. "Now, let's start. Tell me something you've never told anyone before."

"Why?" I gulp, terrified about the idea of opening up, but not quite willing to dismiss this warm little moment either.

"Because I want to get to know you. The real you."

"… What if you don't like the real me?" I hear myself whisper.

"Wouldn't that make you happy?" Rian chuckles. "A reason to start hating me again."

That piques my interest.

"Who says I ever stopped hating you?"

"I did. No more games, Roz. Only truths. Tell me something you've never told anyone before."

Reaching out across the table, Rian leans back onto his forearms. Those ocean blue eyes swim through my chest, crashing against my heart.

"Will you do the same for me?" I ask.

Rian's smile softens. His dimples deepen.

"I'll tell you anything, angel. But let's start with the truth."

23

RIAN

The first round of appetizers arrives before our conversation can get any deeper.

Plates of avocado bruschetta, crab palmiers, wagyu steak skewers, and spicy crab salad tapas fill the table as a private team fulfills my order.

"We're not going to be able to finish all of this food," Rozalia notes, her big green eyes popping at the feast being laid out before us.

"We'll take the leftovers to the nearest woman's shelter," I shrug, studying her reaction. "Then maybe the closest orphanage, after that."

Sure enough, the word 'orphan; triggers something in my reluctant date. "It will be past their bedtime…" she whispers, momentarily drifting back into the past, into *her* past.

"Think of how happy they'll be to wake up to so much food."

"No," Rozalia says, shaking her head. "This food is too good for them. They can't know what they're missing out on. It will only make them miserable. If you want to bring something to the orphanage, bring some basic bread and cheese. That's what

I used to like best. It won't get their hopes up. It won't make them pine for a future they'll never have…"

"Is that what happened with you?" I carefully prod. "Did Drago get your hopes up?"

Rozalia looks up from the food. "I'm not here for a therapy session," she sneers, realizing where this is going.

"How about a date?"

"I wouldn't know how to act on a date."

"You've never been on a date before?" I ask, flabbergasted.

"Who has time for shit like that?"

When I first saw Rozalia tonight, my chest was on fire. I was pissed off and frustrated beyond belief. But every step I took towards her calmed me, if even just a little bit.

By the time I sat down at this table, I felt like a new man. Cool. Collected. Curious.

But now my heart has started racing again.

This time, though, it's from excitement.

"A virgin," I smile. Grabbing a steak skewer, I dig in.

"You wish," Rozalia snaps back. Rolling her eyes, she hesitantly takes a fresh palmier.

"Don't be shy, angel. I'm popping your date cherry, aren't I?"

"You have a real knack for ruining the moment," she mumbles, swallowing her first bite.

The second the crab hits her tongue, her green eyes light up like Christmas decorations.

"Good?" I ask, reveling in her reaction.

Rozalia doesn't slow down for long enough to respond. All I get is a quick nod as she fills her pretty lips up with more food.

I finish another skewer, then I just watch.

The pace at which she eats is impressive… then almost concerning. What kind of grown-up eats like this? Even before Rozalia stole Gabriel's inheritance, she was a successful criminal. So, why is she eating like a ravenous orphan?

I guess some habits die hard.

"Slow down, angel," I insist, pulling one of her plates back across the table. "You're going to choke."

"Wouldn't you like that?" she mutters, her words muffled by a full mouth.

"No. I'm the only thing that's allowed to choke you."

That momentarily pauses her feeding frenzy. Those green eyes flash with fire. Her pale cheeks fill with a pink blush.

I can see her struggle over how to respond.

In the end, though, she decides to ignore it. There's more food to stuff her face with, after all.

"Why don't you start?" she offers, in-between bites. "While I take advantage of your generous offer, tell me something you've never told anyone before."

"I asked first," I recall.

"And I answered," Rozalia notes. "Do you think I'd ever told anyone that I'd never been on a date before?"

"Good point," I admit. "But that's not exactly what I had in mind."

"I'm sure. But that doesn't matter. If you want me to play along, then I'm going to need something from you too."

"And what do you want to hear?"

"What you promised. The truth."

Rozalia finishes off the bruschetta and moves on to what's left of the steak skewers. Something deep inside of me wants to give her exactly what she wants.

"Alright. I'll tell you something I've never told anyone before," I agree.

"Lovely. What is it?"

Before I answer, I let the waiting staff scurry up and carry away the empty plates.

"I'll tell you why I was on the west coast last year," I say, not quite ready to actually follow up.

Rozalia is hardly impressed.

"I know why you were on the west coast," she huffs.

"Enlighten me."

"You were exiled."

"And you know why?"

"Because you fucked up," Rozalia responds. Looking over her shoulder, she searches for more food. When she realizes there isn't more immediately on the way, she decides to take her disappointment out on me. "You killed a bunch of hard-working union reps because they pissed you off."

"I killed them because they were going to betray my family," I correct her, agitation rising.

"You didn't have any evidence of that."

"I did."

"Then why were you exiled?"

"... Because I lost the evidence," I sneer, a wave of bad memories washing over me.

That's a lie, but it's the only explanation I've ever given anyone.

Suddenly, I can feel everyone's eyes on us. They're watching. They've always been watching. The world knows all about my fuck-ups; about my shame. There's no escaping it.

"Is that what you've never told anyone before?" Rozalia pokes me.

"No," I growl.

Maybe this was a mistake.

No matter how comfortable I'm starting to feel around Rozalia, she still knows how to push my buttons. And that's even more dangerous than my attraction to her.

"Then lay it on me."

Over her shoulder, I see the kitchen door swing open. Our waiting staff is coming out with more food.

If I don't get this off my chest now, I never will.

"There was no evidence," I blurt out.

It's like throwing a mountain off of my back. For a moment, the impossibly heavy weight hangs in the air. And I'm not sure if Rozalia will catch it for me.

"You just said you lost the evidence."

"I was lying."

"Do you do that a lot?"

"Maybe we should end this night before it takes a turn," I grunt. I'm about to stand up when Rozalia raises her hand, stopping me.

"Don't go," she says. "At least, not until the next round gets here. I've got some good news."

The last thing I want to do is take her bait. I'm so raw and open right now that the slightest cut could make me bleed out.

But I'm desperate for Rozalia to catch my mountain.

"What good news could you possibly have?" I reluctantly ask.

"Plenty."

"Go ahead, then."

Taking a sip of her wine, Rozalia swirls it around her mouth, letting me stew in my self-inflicted wound before she finally decides to swallow it. Hell, she even waits until the servers have refilled our table with fresh food before continuing.

"You weren't wrong, Rian," she sighs, seemingly unimpressed with the wine. "Those union fuckers were on the verge of betraying you. The only reason they didn't get the chance was because you stopped them."

"... What?" I ask, stunned.

"You may not have had any hard evidence, but your only mistake was not looking hard enough for it. Because that shit definitely existed."

"How... how do you know that?" I ask, hardly believing my ears.

I've been carrying the weight of my mistake for so long now

that I never expected it to be lifted. Yet here is Rozalia Dorn, my enemy, dangling relief just above my head.

"Because Drago was the one who bribed them to betray you."

Picking up a spring roll, Rozalia considers whether or not now is an appropriate time to continue eating. To my surprise, she decides against it.

"Why didn't you tell me before?" I mutter, not quite sure how to feel.

"It never came up," Rozalia shrugs.

"You could have saved me so much pain..."

"And why would I have ever wanted to do that?"

She's right.

"Then why do it now?"

This time, Rozalia doesn't deny her appetite. "I don't know," she mumbles, gulping down a big chunk of the steaming spring roll. "Maybe because I'm starting to actually like you..."

I barely hear her, but somehow, that revelation is even louder than the last. It's so loud and bright that I can't even bear to confront it head-on. Not now.

"Tell me everything," I blurt out.

Rozalia seems relieved that I decide to ignore her slip up, but even as I beg for more information about my own past, I can't get my mind off what she just said.

Did Rozalia Dorn actually just say she's starting to like me?

"What's there to say?" Rozalia recalls, distracting herself with another handful of spring rolls. "Drago and Krol kidnapped Congressman Dean Olsen's daughter. Their plan was to use her as a test run for when you moved up to one of your cousins. But Krol got carried away. The poor girl died. The plan changed. Those two morons thought it might be even more beneficial to frame your family for her death. Get some federal attention on you. Spread your attention around and lower your defenses. But how were they going to blame the

Kilpatricks for the death of a congressman's daughter? No one was going to believe a couple of crooks..."

"The union reps..."

"That's right," Rozalia swallows. "Drago fabricated some evidence against your father, and paid those unions reps a hefty sum to take that evidence to the FBI, but before they could—"

"I killed them."

"That's right," Rozalia nods. "My question is: if you didn't have any evidence, then how did you know it was them?"

"It was a gut feeling," I remember. "A strong fucking gut feeling."

"But no one believed you. Not without evidence."

"I had to tell my father the evidence burned down in a warehouse fire."

"You set that warehouse fire," Rozalia smirks. "To cover your tracks."

"It didn't work."

"No, and it became your biggest failure. Your greatest shame. Prince of the underworld, future king, Rian Kilpatrick, exiled to the west coast for killing a handful of innocent men. I still remember the chatter in the underworld."

"It threw a wrench in your plans," I remind her, remembering how I'd helped my cousins out west thwart Drago and Gabriel's attempted coup.

"*Gabriel's* plans," Rozalia corrects me. "He was the one who was obsessed with destroying your uncle's west coast empire—well, him and Drago. I could have cared less."

"Do you have evidence?" I ask, my voice filled with far more desperation than intended.

"I don't, but Drago might."

Fuck. With evidence, I could clear my name. I could regain the respect I lost through my own foolish actions. I could show the world I wasn't so wrong, after all.

My heart drops.

But so much more has happened since my return from that shameful exile. The embarrassment of my coronation, for one. My reputation won't be so easy to salvage.

And Rozalia is partly to blame.

But so is someone else.

"Where is Drago?" I ask.

"I don't know."

Slowly, the mountain returns to my shoulders. There is no escaping from my past. The best I can do is try to redeem myself.

"I knew I was right..." I mutter. But there's no redemption in those words, just a heavy weight that sinks me down into my seat.

No one believed in me.

Rozalia must sense my defeat, because she offers me some sympathy, even if it is coated in fake sweetness.

"Aw, cheer up, buttercup," she pouts. "You should be happy, you were right."

"It doesn't matter how right I was," I tell her. "I fucked up, and my family paid the price. Instead of just sticking my father with the murder of congressman Olsen, the feds started chasing us over the killing of those union reps too. My dad forced me to the west coast not just as a punishment, but to protect me from their investigation. He took the brunt of it. Now, look where he is. On the courthouse steps, trying to defend himself in front of the entire country. I should be the one paying for my mistakes, not him..."

"Ugh, you're being so dramatic," Rozalia huffs. "Here, maybe this will make you feel better. I was only going to use it as a distraction—you know, since I was pretty sure you were going to ambush me—but since this is turning into some kind of weird date instead, I figure it's the least I could do."

I hardly even tense up as she reaches beneath the table.

"What are you—" My question is cut short when I see what Rozalia pulls out from under the table cloth.

"Good god, I keep forgetting how ugly this thing is," she teases, pushing aside a half-empty plate to make room for my crown.

"... You brought my crown back?" I ask, completely shocked.

Pilling some empty plates on top of each other, Rozalia makes more room for my ceremonial headpiece.

It glistens under the restaurant lights as she pushes it towards me.

"I figured our little game of hide and seek has gone on for long enough," Rozalia says, sitting back so I can bask in her gift.

But I don't give a shit about the crown.

"I haven't been chasing that thing for a long time now," I tell her, my self-pity slowly evaporating as the importance of her gesture dawns on me.

"Then what have you been chasing?" she asks, a small smile lifting her pretty red lips.

I know what she wants to hear.

The truth.

I give it to her.

"You."

An unmistakable sigh floats from Rozalia's lips. I lean forward, desperate to drink it in. I'm already starting to feel better when the waiter returns.

"There are more appetizers on the way. Would you like me to—"

Before he can finish, I wave him off.

"I'll call for you when we're ready for the next round," I say. "But you can take these plates. Thank you."

"Yes, sir."

When the plates are cleared, I pick up my long-lost crown and place it in the middle of the table, like it was always meant to be there. The centerpiece.

But it's not because I'm showing the thing off. It's not even that I'm glad to have it back.

It's a message.

Looking over my shoulder, I scan the dining hall below. Everyone averts their gaze.

Everyone except the Italians.

They're too shocked to look away.

Leo Camporese and Adriano Sabatino both gape at me, completely staggered by the sight.

They both must be thinking the exact same thing.

I'm their king—whether they like it or not.

And Rozalia is my queen.

I've done what I promised I was going to do.

"Don't you want to hear my confession?" Rozalia asks, when I finally get my fill of the two bumbling dons and turn back to face her.

"Your confession?" I ask, still half-lost in my own head.

"Something I've never told anyone before."

Slowly, I come back down to earth.

"You already did that," I remind her. "This is your first date, I was listening."

"No," Rozalia says, shaking her head. "Well, yes. That's true. But it hardly compares to your thing."

The main green gemstone on my crown sparkles against the chandelier above us. But not even the brightest diamond in the world could turn my attention away from the woman sitting across from me.

"Go ahead then, make my night," I nod, a familiar sense of comfort and warmth seeping back in through my pity and anger and dread.

"The crown wasn't enough to make your night?" Rozalia pokes.

"Don't spoil the moment, angel."

"Fine," she smiles. "But you better keep the food coming."

Lifting my hand in the air, I gesture toward the server waiting in the corner. He takes my cue and storms back into the kitchen.

"Done. Now, hit me with your best shot."

"I'm already regretting this," Rozalia mumbles, hesitating to continue.

"Hey, this was your idea."

Her pretty smile falters and my heart drops along with her lips.

"I'm guessing Gabriel has already told you plenty about my past," she starts, her voice lowering. "About the small village I grew up in. About how it was destroyed. About how I lost my parents, and my freedom. About how I was almost forced to marry the monster who did it all to me..."

"He did," I quietly confess, remembering how much more human it had made her seem. How much more fragile and tender. Back then, she was only the Black Cat to me.

Now, she's Roz.

"And he told you how Drago saved me from that nightmare?"

"Yes," I nod. "It helped explain your loyalty to him."

"I was far too loyal to that man for far too long," Rozalia snarls, but even that snarl slowly fades. "I won't let myself make that mistake again..."

"Drago doesn't deserve any of you," I hear myself say.

But I don't think Rozalia hears me.

She's too lost in her past.

"Gabriel knows all about that," she whispers. "So does Tytus. They know what I lost as a child. But no one knows about my final loss... about the friend I had to chase away..."

I keep my mouth shut as a new round of appetizers appear from the kitchen.

The waiting staff silently places them around my crown as we wait for them to leave.

When they're gone, I urge Rozalia to continue.

"I'm listening, angel. Who was this friend?"

"Willow..."

Roz's voice is so quiet that it's barely more than a squeak.

"Who is Willow?" I ask, leaning forward to hear her better. I'm completely invested.

What pain is my fallen angel hiding inside?

"Willow was my only friend," she says. "My first friend, and my last. She came whenever I called, but she didn't need me. So I pushed her away. It was the only way to save her..."

Reaching across the table, I gesture for Rozalia to give me her hand. To my surprise, she does just that.

Her warm skin curls into my palm as she continues to remember.

"Do you know where Willow is now?" I gently ask.

"That depends," she sighs. "Do you know how long cats live?"

Her question catches me off guard.

"I don't."

"Well, I do. About fifteen years. That means I've likely run out of time. Willow is probably dead by now..."

"Willow is a cat?"

"She *was* a cat," Rozalia whispers. "It's stupid, I know, but..."

"No. It's not stupid," I assure her, thinking of the only example in my life I can use to sympathize. "My sister feels the same way about the kitten that interrupted us in the throne room."

"Kaja?"

Just like that, Rozalia returns from the past.

"Kaja? Who's Kaja?"

"No one," she says, shaking the haze from her eyes. "... But your sister is worried about the kitten from your coronation?"

"She has spent way too many precious resources searching for that thing," I grunt.

"Well, she should stop."

"I know that's what—"

"Because I have the cat."

I've lost track of how many times I've questioned my hearing tonight.

"You what?"

"Well, not technically, obviously. But a good friend of mine is looking after her on my behalf. The kitten is safe."

"You took the cat too?"

For my count, that's Mel's painting, my crown, and Adriano Sabatino's sacrificial kitten that Rozalia stole from me on that fateful day.

"It just happened," Rozalia shrugs, slowly composing herself again.

"My sister wants her," I say, wrapping my fingers around her hand.

That's not entirely true. Mel just wants to know the kitten is safe. If anything, she wants *me* to have the black cat.

"Wasn't getting her painting back enough for your sister?"

"That was a gift for me. It's *my* painting now. Not hers."

"Alright. So now you have your crown back and the painting. Isn't that enough? At least for tonight?"

"No," I realize.

For maybe the first time ever, Rozalia doesn't try to pull away as I tighten my grip around her. But that might be because it's not a controlling grip.

It's a caring one.

And I think she can feel that.

I sure as hell can.

I've never held anyone like this before. It's intoxicating.

"You'd really rather have the cat?" she asks, raising a curious brow at me.

I shake my head.

And bite down on my bottom lip.

The warmth of Rozalia's tough but tender skin is turning my heavy heart light... and my soft cock hard.

"I'd rather have you."

24

ROZALIA

"Come with me."

With his hand squeezed around mine, Rian gestures to the waiter and stands up.

"What? Where are you going?" I ask, confused.

He doesn't need to speak to give me an answer. The second he steps around the table, I see the giant bulge in his pants. There's no hiding it.

I gulp.

When the servers arrive, Rian nods down to the crown. "Put this thing in coat check," he says.

"Yes, sir. Would you like us to pack up the food as well?"

"Don't bother. We're not—" Rian stops himself before I can. "On second thought, pack it up. Tell Carlos to send a truck filled with our finest dishes to the nearest women's shelter. Then cook a whole new round for every orphanage you can find. Make it a weekly thing too."

The waiter doesn't get a word in edgewise. With a stern tug, Rian lifts me from my seat and pulls me behind him.

I don't resist.

"Who's Carlos?" I mindlessly ask.

Rian doesn't seem to hear me. Every step we take through the crowded restaurant causes the chatter to rise. I can feel a hundred eyes burning through my skin.

But I don't care anymore.

There's a pressure in my core that's too hot to ignore; there's a bulge in Rian's pants that's too huge to resist. I'm turned on beyond belief. Fuck everyone else. All I want is him.

The second we push through the closest door, Rian slams me against the wall.

"Don't you dare ever speak another man's name when I'm this horny," he growls.

I can't tell if we're in a closet or a dark hallway, but that doesn't matter either. I'm possessed.

"I was just—"

He shuts me up with a vicious kiss.

The electricity in his lips sets me on fire, and I instantly melt.

If this is supposed to be the setup for some kind of trap, then so be it. He's already taken my pussy hostage.

And maybe my heart too.

For a split second, my racing heart freezes against the insanity of that thought.

How could he possibly have your heart? You don't have one, remember?

But when Rian's thick wet tongue slides down my throat, I'm shocked back to life.

Fuck all of this second guessing.

Wrapping my fingers around Rian's tie, I pull him into me. His massive bulge thrusts against my core. The pressure rises.

I need him to release it.

"You taste fucking delicious, angel," Rian grunts, pushing into my hips with enough force to momentarily stop my heart again.

"Better than that wagyu?"

Our tongues tangle and my legs wrap around Rian's hard waist as he smothers me with his massive body.

"Way better," he grunts. Grabbing my throat, he holds me in place and kisses me so hard I almost choke on his tongue.

"How can you say for sure?" I rasp, releasing his tie as my hands mindlessly wander down to his belt. With a blind fury, I start to unbuckle his pants. I need what's under that zipper.

"You haven't tasted all of me yet."

My desire is mindless. All I can feel is a primal urge. It needs to be satisfied, and he needs to be the one who satisfies it.

"Which part of you haven't I tasted yet?" Rian asks. Before I can answer, his fingers slip up my thighs. Passing over my holster and ignoring my gun, he finds my panties. "Oh, that's right. How could I forget?"

A brutal gasp tears up my throat as Rian rips my panties into pieces.

"Be gentle," I rasp, sliding off his belt. "... Or else my gun might go off."

"Only one gun is going off tonight," he growls, seamlessly unfastening my holster. "Mine."

When Rian sticks his tongue in my ear, the world goes silent. I don't even hear my gun hitting the floor. My back arches and my toes curl and I dig my nails into his back as I feel his pants fall down around his ankles.

"Don't shoot too quick," I demand.

In response, his giant fucking cock pushes under my upturned dress. I feel his swollen head pressing against my soaking lips. It pulls a high-pitched whimper from my lungs.

"I wouldn't dream of it, angel," Rian sneers. Pulling his tongue out of my ear, he reaches back down between my legs. "I'll make sure you feel every last drop before I end this."

With the swollen head of his thick cock pushing down against my clit, he dips the tips of two fingers into my leaking cunt. A warm shiver rages through my body. But I only get to experience two slow pumps before he carefully pulls out.

"You can do better than that," I breathlessly push him.

"You're right. Take a deep breath, angel. I'm about to defile all three of your tight little holes.."

I've hardly even opened my mouth to respond when Rian's dripping fingers slide down my pussy and over my asshole.

"Holy shit," I croak, my nails digging deeper into his powerful back.

His thick fingers break my virgin threshold. It feels like he's ripping me apart. But it's fucking amazing.

The deeper he slides those wet two fingers into my tight hole, the harder my ass cheeks clamp down around him. But Rian pushes through the resistance. Then, just when it feels like I might split in two, he pulls them back out.

"Open wide, angel," he smiles. Lifting those two fingers up to his face, he studies them for a moment before turning them to me.

I'm too aroused not to do exactly as he says.

"That's my good girl."

With his dimples deepening, and his giant mushroom head pressing hard against my clit, he paints my lips with his me-covered fingers.

When he gets to my tongue, I start to lick. His cock twitches against my cunt.

"Fuck me," I quietly beg him, gagging on his fingers.

"That's for dessert," he teases. Still, he closes his eyes and takes a deep, gravelly breath when I close my lips around his fingers and suck.

"I want my dessert now," I insist, spitting him out.

But Rian isn't hurried. Parting his lips, he taunts himself with his me-flavored fingers, holding them just inches from his face.

Finally, he slips them into his mouth.

"Delicious," he sighs, sucking my juices from his flesh. "All three courses."

"Will you put me on the menu?" I huff sarcastically. I'm tired of existing without his cock in my pussy.

He needs to start fucking me. Now.

"No," Rian sneers. "You are mine, and mine only. Understand?"

I can smell my own scent and feel the wetness he drew from me as his fingers close around my tender throat. The mark he's left behind burns hotter than ever.

"You're going to have to prove you deserve me," I snarl back, lifting my chin at him.

"Gladly."

With that, Rian impales me with his cock.

He's so big that every last bit of air is pushed out of my lungs. The gust escapes my throat in a high-pitched wail. My nails dig back in around his back.

The pressure in my core balloons.

"Is that all you've got?" I ask, my words shaking as Rian slides back out of me.

"You're going to regret asking me that, angel."

"Make me regret ever meeting you," I croak.

This time, Rian doesn't reply. Not with words.

Instead, he pounds his girthy cock so deep into my cunt, I can feel my organs shift. Then, he does it again. And again. And again...

By his fourth thrust, I've lost my mind. All I can do is hold on for dear life as he pounds me into oblivion.

"I want you to cum all over my cock, angel," Rian growls, his voice shivering from the effort.

"Make me," I hiss back.

Somehow, Rian picks up speed. His powerful hips jackhammer me without mercy. The darkness turns white-hot.

There's so much hate sizzling in the air between us. So

much loathsome energy clapping against my begging stomach. It's intoxicating.

But it's not the same kind of hate as before.

No. This feels so much better.

I don't hate Rian for existing anymore.

Instead, I hate that he's made me want him.

I hate that he's making me fall for him.

And I especially hate that I can sense he feels the exact same way about me.

This sex is just as angry as any we've had before, but the anger is so much different. So much more beautiful.

It's encompassed by this savage frustration that makes me want to tear out my own heart, just so I can choke Rian to death with it.

Look what you've done to us! I want to yell at him. *You've made me care about my worst enemy. You've made me sympathize with him. You've made me need him.*

If I wasn't so close to heaven, I might have the sense to dread the twisted beauty of it all. Instead, all I can concentrate on is the pressure in my core; each time Rian thrusts into me, it cracks just a little bit more.

"I'm going to cum," I heave, digging my nose into his broad shoulder.

"Do it already," Rian growls.

My thighs are spanked raw. My ass is red and tender.

The pressure in my core bursts.

"You bastard," I curse, screaming into his shoulder as I'm torn apart from the inside out.

"Tell me you love it," Rian grunts, not slowing down. "Tell me you want more."

"I want more," I whimper. "Give me more."

"Do you love it?"

When I hesitate to respond, Rian unsheathes his swollen cock from my dripping pussy.

"I... I love it," I say, the emptiness he's left behind threatening to eat me alive.

"That took you too long," he sneers.

Prying my legs off from around his waist, he shoves my feet back to the floor. But I've only hardly come down to earth when he wraps his hands around my waist and spins me around.

"We can't keep—"

Rian's bulbous head digs between my ass cheeks and I shut up.

"Have you ever been fucked in the ass before, angel?" Rian asks.

"That's none of your business," I weakly snap, my cheeks flushing.

"I'll take that as a no."

His cock is so lubricated with the juices he just fucked out of my pussy that it hardly takes any effort to open my asshole up. But that doesn't mean it's smooth sailing.

The pressure is immense. If I thought his two fingers might tear me apart, they were nothing compared to the size of his starving cock.

To my surprise, Rian doesn't immediately start to pound me from behind, though. Instead, he slides halfway in before stopping.

"You're so fucking tight," he growls.

His fingers dig into my red ass cheeks, spreading me apart as he pushes deeper into my stretched-out hole.

"Does it hurt?" he asks.

"No," I stubbornly insist.

"Good."

Making me regret my words, Rian starts to treat my ass like his personal pussy. Hell, he might as well set me on fire.

At first, the flames sting so hard I start to squirm, but then Rian reaches around and grabs my throat, pulling me back until his tongue slips into my ear again.

"You might not belong to anyone, angel," Rian whispers, his hips slamming into my raw ass as he rips me apart from behind. "But that doesn't mean I'll ever stop conquering your tight little holes."

The shattered pressure in my core returns, just so it can erupt again. It hardly lasts a handful of shallow breaths before it's smashed open again.

"I'm coming," I rasp.

A spasm-inducing orgasm tears through every last inch of my ravaged body as Rian's cock swells even bigger.

"Me first," he growls.

His grip tightens around my throat. His teeth close in around my earlobe.

"Fuck!"

When Rian explodes into my ass, my entire body begins to spasm. I've lost complete control. There's no room in me for anything but more of him.

Luckily, he fills me up to the fucking brim.

Thick globs of hot steamy cum burst from his cock. It doesn't take long before I start to leak. I can feel his seed dripping from my outstretched hole, down the inside of my thighs.

"That's how you end a date," Rian huffs. Slowly, his dripping cock slips out of my outstretched hole.

I feel empty. Yet so fucking satisfied.

"I guess that wasn't so bad," I hear myself mumble.

Reaching down through the darkness, I feel for my panties. But before I can find what's left of them, I feel something else.

My gun.

I pick it up, and a momentary heaviness fills the air. It wasn't too long ago that I would have taken this opportunity to end Rian Kilpatrick forever.

But now?

I don't even entertain the thought. Finding my holster, I slip it back up my trembling thigh and sheath my weapon.

Whatever tonight was, it's not the end. Fuck. It feels more like the beginning. Of what? I'm not—

Before I can finish that thought, a heavy knock comes at the door.

Then another.

It echoes through the darkness like a pounding heart.

"Sir! Sir! Are you in there?"

Even through the thick wall, I can hear the panic in the voice.

My hackles rise.

Is this the trap I was so worried about?

My fingers inch towards my gun.

"What the hell is that?" Rian grumbles. Picking up his pants, he buckles his belt and brushes past me. "Who is it?"

A name comes from the other side of the door, but I can't quite make it out. Whoever it is, he has enough of Rian's trust to get him to open up.

But before my Irish lion does that, he looks back over at me.

"Are you decent?" he asks, those blue eyes somehow cutting through the darkness.

"Never was and never will be. But I'm not hiding it either."

"Does that mean I can open this door?" he taunts.

"You can do whatever you want."

Those deep blue eyes look me up and down. That tongue flickers over his blood-red lips.

"I'll take that as permission the next time I want to fuck you."

With that, he opens the door.

A stream of light floods in, momentarily blinding me.

"Don Kilpatrick. Please, come with me. We have an emergency."

"What emergency?" I hear Rian growl.

"There's been an attack."

My heart drops.

It feels like the electricity in the room is immediately zapped away. My hand falls from my gun.

"Fuck," Rian curses. He starts to speak to the man at the door, but my ears rush with blood.

I don't know what the fuck is going on, but it sounds like bad news for me.

Looking over my shoulder, I search for the nearest escape route. Slowly, my vision refocuses. At the end of the hallway is a door. I start to make my way to it.

I've hardly taken three steps when I feel a strong hand on my shoulder.

"Where are you going?" Rian's voice is deep and stern. All Of his suave calmness from the date is gone. So is the savage charm he just fucked me with.

"I heard what happened," I say, not daring to turn around. "I'm not about to stay here so I can be blamed for it."

I try to pull away, but Rian digs his fingers deeper into my shoulder.

"Be honest with me, Roz," he says, the sternness in his voice breaking ever so slightly. My heart clenches against the hint of sincerity. He's suspicious. But he's also hurt. "You were sent as a distraction, weren't you?"

I shake his hand off of my shoulder.

"By who? I don't work for anyone anymore," I spit, finally turning to face him.

His beautiful face has turned to stone. The once electric air has become thick with tension.

"Why did you show up here tonight?"

"Because you sent me a fucking text!"

"No, I didn't," Rian sighs, shaking his head. "And even if I did, why would you do anything I say? In what world does Rozalia Dorn respond to a text from Rian Kilpatrick?"

"In this world," I tell him.

"Why?"

"Because the message said you wanted to apologize," I huff, hanging my head.

It sounds so dumb when I say it out loud, but there's no denying that was part of my decision.

"And you believed it?"

"No... but maybe I wanted to."

"And I want to believe you're not involved in this," Rian sighs, some more of the sternness melting from his voice.

"You think I'm going to stick around and try to convince you?"

I can still feel his cum in my ass. My hole throbs. My thighs are stained with his seed. I don't want to leave.

But what choice do I have?

"You think I'm going to let you leave?" Rian says, stepping forward.

I grip down on my gun.

"Try and stop me."

He pauses. Those blue eyes stare right through my soul.

Then, just like that, his broad shoulders drop, and he turns from me.

"No. I won't. If you want to help, you can come. Otherwise, you're free to go."

I've barely even processed his offer before he disappears into the light.

The door shuts behind him.

The room becomes dark again, and unbearably cold.

"I was always free to go!" I yell after him, emotion clogging my throat. "Fuck this!"

Whipping around, I storm towards the door on the opposite end of the dark hallway.

It leads out into the alleyway out back. I burst through it with cold tears in my eyes.

"Fucking asshole," I curse.

I hate how emotional I'm getting, but there's no denying what just happened back there.

Fuck.

I went on my first date.

Rian spoiled me. I'd never been treated like that before. It felt fucking special.

The vulnerable warmth that fell over that table still lingers on my skin as I stumble through the dark alleyway.

Somehow, for the briefest moment, that stupid table felt like home.

Then, it was all ripped away.

Reaching behind a dumpster, I find the jacket I left out here earlier. It's heavy, filled to the brim with the dozen or so devices I brought in case I had to fight my way out of a trap. They all feel so useless now.

Pushing them aside, I search for my phone.

I want to figure out what's actually going on.

But when I pull up my home screen, I don't find answers. Instead, I'm immediately confronted by a slew of new questions. And a huge stone of dread.

My home screen is overflowing with unread texts.

With great hesitation, I open up the first one. Then the second. And the third...

They all say the same thing.

It's all going to be alright. Just go back to where it all began. That's where you'll find your answers. I promise.

Just like the text I thought Rian sent me, there's no ID, no number. And while I don't know who sent it, I do immediately understand what it means.

It's all going to be alright. Just go back to where it all began.

My chest tightens at the implication.

Home.

Someone's trying to get me to go home.

My pounding heart sinks.

I have no home.

Not in a place, and definitely not in a person.

But that doesn't mean I'm not desperate to be proven wrong—anything to rekindle the warmth I just experienced... and lost.

Fuck it.

What else do I have to lose?

25

RIAN

"They did what?"

My tires screech across the pavement as I make a sharp turn down an empty street.

"They razed the place to the ground. Trapped everyone inside and took a torch to union headquarters," Maksim repeats. "Then they spelled out the Kilpatrick name on the sidewalk out front—from the photos I saw, it looks like they used blood."

"Fuck!" I curse.

Punching my steering wheel, I kick down extra hard on the gas pedal. My engine roars like an angry lion as I speed through a red light.

"I'm still trying to figure out exactly who did it, but that's kind of hard to do without being out there. Rian, I—"

"Don't you dare leave Mel alone," I order. Another sharp turn sends me careening onto a slightly more crowded avenue. I weave between the cars, my mind racing with possible solutions to our big fucking problem.

Still, in the back of my mind, I see Rozalia.

She stands there in her elegant red dress, a blank look on her face. I can't stop trying to decipher that fucking look.

Did she use me? I haven't been able to decide yet. And my heart won't cooperate with my brain.

"I'll do whatever you say," Maksim assures me. "But if you want my advice, it's this: stem the bleeding immediately. We need to do whatever we can to stifle this story before it gets out. It might be too late to keep the underworld from knowing what's just happened, but there's still hope we can keep the Kilpatrick name out of the news cycle. If we do that, then at least your father has—"

"Have you talked to my father yet?" I interrupt, blasting by a pair of slow-moving cars.

"No. And I'm not sure I should. The last thing he needs is for me to tie him to this incident with a phone call."

"A phone call is the least of our worries," I think out loud. "Whoever did this isn't worried about how it will affect Dad. They only want to embarrass me. Why else would they strike a union stronghold?"

"The implication is obvious," Maksim agrees. "They want everyone to remember why you got exiled. They want people to doubt that you've changed. They want our allies to question their loyalty to you. They want our empire to crumble from within."

With my speed-o-meter nearly topping out, I swerve onto the highway.

"We both know who wants to do that."

For the first time since I called him, Maksim hesitates to speak.

"… We can't do anything without evidence," he finally mumbles. "Not this time. Not with the whole world watching, waiting for us to fuck up."

My gut lurches at the accusation. Maksim doesn't know what I just learned from Rozalia. But even if what she said was true, it doesn't change much—at least, not externally.

For anything to change, Rozalia's going to have to help me present proof. But that's the least of my concerns right now. For all the shit that's just popped off, there is one silver lining.

I trust my gut again.

I wasn't wrong. Those union fucks were going to betray my family. They deserved to die. I needed to send a message. It didn't save my family, but it sure as fuck bought us a few months to prepare for the storm to come.

We needed all the time we got.

"I'll find the evidence we need," I growl. With a quick glance down at my dashboard's IVI screen, I take note of a blinking red dot and its ever-changing location.

That's what I'm trying to catch up to.

"Be careful, it could be another trap," Maksim warns.

"If they kill me, I want you to nuke the entire area," I foolishly demand.

"You know I won't do that," Maksim wisely responds. "We're already walking on thin ice. Hell, I don't even think it's a great idea to send back-up."

He's right. A firefight could make this mess a whole lot worse and way more public.

Fuck.

Speeding towards an exit ramp, I try to calm myself.

But even as one wave of fury fades, another grows.

I can see Rozalia. That red dress drifts across a black void, revealing her pale thigh... and holstered gun.

I bite down on my tongue. There's no figuring that girl out. Is she on my side? Is she playing the middle? Or is she just playing me?

Does it matter?

My brain can't make sense of it. My gut pulls both ways. My cock is not trustworthy.

But through all the chaos, one part of me doesn't budge. It's a part of me that's crystal clear. It knows what it wants, consequences be damned.

My heart.

Part of it remains at that cozy table back at La Forcina. The warm blanket we were shrouded in is somehow still holding on through the gale force winds blowing me down.

"Fine. Don't send any backup," I accept. "But don't try to stop me either. Wherever these fuckers end up, I'll go in there quietly. But the message I leave behind will be loud and clear."

"I understand," Maksim says. "Just make sure you get as much out of them before—"

I try not to make a habit out of interrupting my consigliere, but when a new caller ID pops up on my car screen, I know my conversation with Maksim is done.

"My dad's calling me," I murmur.

"Really?"

My uncle sounds just as shocked as I am.

"I'll call you back if I need more help. Look after Mel."

"With my life," Maksim affirms, hanging up before I can.

But I don't answer my dad's call right away. First, I try to further compose myself. Dad doesn't need to know about all the chaos swirling around in my head.

He's probably just calling to hear me tell him everything's under control.

It's not, but I can't let him know that. He's got enough shit on his plate.

"Hello?"

When I answer his call, he talks first.

To my surprise, there's no concern in his voice. No rage or frustration either—at least, not that I recognize.

"I'm guessing you've heard the news," I say, trying to keep the concern out of my reply.

"Several times now, and from several different sources."

"You don't sound too worried."

"Why would I be? I have Rian Kilpatrick on the case. He's never failed me before."

The implicit trust doesn't have the effect I imagine he wants it to have. Instead, it feels like a sharp blade digging through my chest. I've lied to him, and my lie hasn't made his problems go away. Not yet. I'm still steeped in dishonesty and failure.

"I've failed so many times before," I quietly remind him, rage clashing with doubt as I veer off the highway.

"No. You haven't," Dad insists. "You've made mistakes, sure. Everyone has—me included. But if you'd ever truly failed, our family wouldn't exist anymore. Our empire wouldn't exist."

"Don't jinx it just yet."

"I'm not worried. I just wanted to check in to see how you were handling everything."

"With as much patience as I can muster," I admit.

"What's the game plan? I hear an engine. Where are you headed?"

This time, when I come across a red light, I at least slow down a little. The blinking red dot on my screen is on the other side of a residential complex. I don't want to draw too much attention to myself before I can catch up.

"A few of my men were in the area when the explosion went off," I explain. "They didn't know what happened, but when they went to check it out, they were confronted by a heavily-armed group fleeing the scene."

"The perpetrators?"

"It could only be them. They slaughtered most of my guys. But one managed to survive. He's still chasing after them. I'm locked onto his signal."

"That's a brave boy," Dad says.

"He's doing his job," I nod. "But only after fucking up his first duty."

"What was his first duty?"

"To protect that fucking union building," I snarl. "For a

moment, my fragile composure breaks. My rage comes spilling out. "That's what they were doing in the area, after all."

"You sent them over there?"

I shake my head. "No," I explain. "Ever since I returned from my exile out west, I've been half-expecting someone to take advantage of the fuck up that sent me out there. What better way to do that than to go after the same union I got in trouble for busting up? All anyone would have to do was frame me for the attack, and I'd be in a world of shit. To prevent that future, I set up small teams of men to constantly watch all union buildings around the city. They were supposed to stop anything like this from happening."

"How small of a team are we talking?" Dad asks.

"Half a dozen men. Maybe a few more, depending on the night. There are a lot of union buildings in the city. I'll admit, we were spread thin."

"So, you only had half a dozen men at the scene," Dad points out. "And how many men did they go up against?"

"The info wasn't clear, but it sounds like at least twice that."

"So your men were outnumbered? They fought to the death? And the sole survivor is risking the life he just barely escaped with to chase down the fuckers who just steamrolled him and his friends?"

"... Yes."

To my frustration, I come up at another red light.

The night has turned silent. I'm all alone.

"So, why are you angry at them?"

"Who said I was angry at them?" I snap.

"I know my son," Dad insists. "Your voice is different when you're angry at yourself."

"They failed me," I tell him.

"But not because they didn't try their best."

"Their best wasn't good enough."

"it often isn't."

"If we're going to survive, it has to be."

My engine crackles as I roll through the red light. Part of me is expecting to hear police sirens. Anything to add insult to injury. But nothing comes. I speed up again, just in time to hear my father's heavy sigh.

"These men aren't you, Rian," Dad says. "They weren't raised the same way. They don't live the same way. They didn't grow up learning from infamous advisors, or receive training from the deadliest killers out there. They don't have access to the best weapons or the finest technologies. They do what they can with what they're given. And it sounds like they do it to the best of their ability. Cut them some slack."

That's the last thing I was expecting to hear my dad say. He's notoriously strict.

"Slack? How can I cut anyone slack at a time like this? Our entire way of life is on the line."

"And it might remain that, even in victory. If you don't win over the men who work for you, you'll have no one."

"I lead by example," I snip.

"A king can't always do that. Sometimes, he just needs to prove himself to be a man worth fighting for."

"I can do all the fighting myself," I grumble. But at this point, it's just stubborn instinct.

Dad is right. He always is.

"Clearly, that's not true," he harshly points out.

"If I had been there, there would have been no explosion."

"Oh, then why weren't you there? What kept you, the almighty king, from being in all places at once?"

"I was busy."

"Doing what?"

"Retrieving my crown."

"Fuck that crown," Dad barks, a splinter of anger lashing through the speakers.

"I agree," I fume back.

Hell, I hardly even made an effort to get it taken care of before I pulled Rozalia into that dark room...

My pants tighten at the recent memory, no matter how hard I try not to think about it.

"I knew you would," Dad says, easily calming himself. "But that's because none of this was ever really about the crown, was it?"

My heart freezes.

"What does that mean?" I ask.

Staring out into the night, I spot another red light ahead. It flickers through the darkness like a flowing dress.

Rozalia.

My frozen heart starts to pound. I can taste her on my lips.

I can feel her in my chest.

"It means I understand," Dad sighs. "Loving an enemy isn't—"

"Who said anything about love?" I furiously interrupt.

"You don't seem like the type to marry someone out of spite," Dad chuckles.

The sudden levity in his voice is surprising. And I hesitate to fight back.

He still doesn't know that my proposal was a sham.

... Or does he?

"I did what I thought was right."

"Do you regret it?"

"No."

The answer comes spilling from my lips before I even have a chance to consider it.

That's how I know it's the truth.

Fuck. Is that what this has all really been about? All of this time and energy, spent just to get close to a thorn in my side? My enemy. The bane of my existence.

Rozalia Dorn.

The truth is obvious, even if I don't want it to be.

She was worth it.

Hell, that dinner alone was worth it all.

Love definitely wasn't the right word before, but maybe it is now.

No. It's not possible. She's your enemy. The sex is amazing, but it's the hate that makes it great. And that's it.

"I know what you're going through," Dad sympathizes. "You may think I don't, but I do. I went through the same thing with your mom."

"This is nothing like what you and mom went through," I reply, hoping it's true. But I don't dare consider the comparison. Not right now. Not when all I can think of is how good Rozalia tastes. How light her laugh is. How black her soul is.

How much I love it.

Fuck.

"Maybe, maybe not," Dad says, and I can practically hear him shrug. "But if you never listen to anything I tell you ever again, I want you to listen to this."

"What?" I huff.

Taking a soft turn, I finally reach the edge of this residential complex. Slowly, my foot pushes down onto the gas pedal.

"Follow your heart. Do that, and you'll never fail, no matter what happens."

The advice careens around my thick skull as the sound of my engine grows. But no matter how hard I fight back against it, the words only get louder.

Slowly, the doubt raging inside me fades, and a wave of clarity laps over me.

"I'll do what I can," I mutter, blazing down the empty street ahead.

"That's my boy," Dad says. "Oh, and one more thing. This brave young man who's helping you chase these fuckers down, what's his name?"

My brow furrows.

"I... I don't know," I realize.

"You should learn it. Good luck, son."

I know a goodbye when I hear it. But I'm not ready to be on my own again. Not with all the conflict burning inside of me.

"Wait!" I call out.

"Yes?"

I'm not sure what to say.

"I saw you on the courthouse steps today," I stall. "... How did it go?"

"Everything will be fine," Dad assures me, his voice filled with confidence. "As long as I keep following my heart, everything will be fine."

With that, he hangs up.

The silence that follows is suppressed by the roar of my engine. I roll down the windows and burst ahead. Through the rumbling wind, I hear the sound of tires screeching in the distance.

I'm close.

Looking down at my dashboard screen, I set my gaze on that blinking red dot.

"Text Maksim," I boom, initiating my car's AI.

What would you like to text to Maksim Smolov? The computerized voice quickly responds, initiating the voice-to-text feature.

When I turn down the next street, my hackles rise. Through an alleyway up ahead, I'm given my first glance of what my blinking red is tracking.

A swerving convoy blares through the night—a flash of danger among the quiet darkness.

I grip down on my steering wheel until my knuckles turn white.

"Maksim. Get me the name and number of the man chasing these fuckers," I growl. "I want to speak to him."

26

ROZALIA

I didn't expect it to be so quiet.

It's naïve, I know. But when I look at the place where my village once stood, I can't help but listen. Part of me still expects to hear the sounds that once made it home.

Fuck.

There's no bottling up the memories that leak from this cursed place.

When I look across the overgrown grass, I can almost see my family's shack. I can almost picture my mother standing there; almost hear the dinner bell in her hand as she rings us in for supper.

But no matter how hard I listen, I don't hear her. I don't hear anything. No children laugh. No adults talk and drink and complain about how hard life is.

There is only a soft breeze. It brushes over my shoulder, rustling the bushes and the weeds and the buried ashes.

My stomach fills my empty chest. My heart is in my throat.

What the hell am I doing here?

It's surreal to finally be back in the place savagely ripped from me all those years ago. I didn't think I'd ever have the guts to return.

Yet here I am, standing alone in the dead place that once gave me life.

It's horrifically sad.

But that's no surprise. I've avoided this place for years because I knew there'd be no avoiding the trauma that came with it.

At least out there, I can ignore it.

Wiping away a cold tear from my cheek, I trudge forward.

It's like I'm being controlled by a greater force—or maybe just an irresistible desire. Every step I take through the ruins of my old home sends a chill across my skin.

It's not a pleasant feeling. So, why do I keep moving forward?

It's hard to say, but part of me can't avoid the most blatant explanation.

I'm searching for some warmth. Something that will remind me of what it feels like to truly be home.

Still, the further I wade forward, the clearer it becomes that I will find no comfort here. No. The only warmth in my cold life was left at that dinner table. It was left on Rian's lips as he left me to the darkness.

A hint of that heat still clings to me. And I imagine it's all that's keeping my heart from freezing over right now.

The further I venture away from that dinner, the fainter it grows.

Rian.

What has he done to me?

Turning towards the former center of my village, I step through a clump of tall weeds and almost trip when my toes hit something solid. The metal clangs through the empty night, rolling forward to reveal a blackened cup, or maybe it's a pot. In the darkness, it's hard to tell. And I don't care enough to investigate.

I step over it and continue forward.

When I hit the edge of where my village used to be, I reach into my jacket pocket and pull out my phone. The program I devised to track down the number that texted me is still running.

Whoever called me here isn't an amateur. Hell, the cloaking technology they're using could rival my own. Who the fuck is capable of that?

As far as I know, only Rian and I could have concocted something like this. And there's no way he sent that text.

Slipping my phone away again, I carefully continue forward. The flattened ruins loom tall behind me as I close my eyes and search for a sound. Anything to tell me I'm not alone.

I don't hear anything.

Behind my shut eyelids, though, I do see something.

The warm orange glow of La Forcina's. That red table cloth, covered in half-empty plates. The glasses of expensive wine we barely even tried.

Those ocean blue eyes.

I rip my eyes back open. The warmth fades away. My heart is pounding in my chest.

Ahead, I see the silhouette of a giant weeping willow.

Shit.

"Willow..."

The whisper barely leaves my lips before it's lost in the soft breeze.

My chest constricts.

I shouldn't have come here.

Pinching the bridge of my nose, I pause for a moment. Tears trickle down my cheeks. The soft breeze blows back my hair.

For a moment, I just stand there, quietly sobbing. But it's not all sadness. And it's not all regret. Even without any trace of warmth, this almost feels like where I should be. Alone, amongst the ghosts of my childhood. I belong in the dirt, right along with everyone else, right with the—

Suddenly, my brain freezes.

My pitiful thoughts pause.

A tiny sound carries on the breeze, perking up my ears.

Unclasping the bridge of my nose, I reach for my gun. But my hand halts before I can feel the cold steel.

Please...

Leaves rustle. Branches creak. But the sound I think I just heard remains elusive.

Then, I hear it again.

My pounding heart stops dead in its tracks.

A meow.

"... Willow?"

My voice is hardly more than a silent croak.

Am I going crazy?

"Willow?" I rasp again, louder this time, not caring about my own sanity. That ship has long sailed. "Willow!"

As if heeding my calls, the cloud-filled sky momentarily breaks, and a slice of pale moonlight illuminates the dark world ahead.

Still, I don't see anything. The tall grass that surrounds the weeping willow dances in the breeze. I search it intensely, looking for any signs of—

Meow.

My gaze rips towards the sound.

No way.

There, perched on a black rock, barely twenty feet from me, is the silhouette of a cat.

The air is ripped from my lungs. Blood rushes into my ears.

"... Willow..." I can barely breathe. My feet feel like anchors as I try to take a step forward. But my advance is interrupted by something protruding from the earth. It trips me.

This time, I don't catch myself. I fall to my knees, nearly face planting in the mud.

"Willow!" I cry out.

My view is shrouded by the tall grass. I push myself back onto my feet. But the second I get a glimpse of that heart-stopping silhouette again, a thunderous clap rips through the night.

It snaps me out of my daze. Reaching for my gun, I whip around, weapon drawn.

But when the blood rushes from my ears, that thunderous clap quickly becomes a pathetic clang.

Someone's kicked that same ashen can I did.

"Who is it?" I shout. My gun is just as shaky as my voice.

Wiping the tears from my eye, I look back over my shoulder, towards the rock.

My heart drops.

The silhouette is gone.

"... Willow..."

Did I imagine her?

There's no time to think about it. And there's definitely no time to grieve.

The pale moonlight disappears as clouds blanket the sky once more. The clanging can echoes through the night.

Turning back around, I put both hands on my trembling gun.

"Show yourself!" I command.

"I come in peace..."

The familiar voice might as well be a bullet. It rips through my aching chest, leaving a hole where a smidgeon of hope briefly existed.

"... Drago?"

Squinting my eyes, I peer through the darkness.

That's when I spot him.

The dark figure is like a flash from the past. Only now, what was once a broad and intimidating frame has shriveled down into nearly nothing.

"Easy there, Roz," Drago quietly insists. His gravelly voice cuts through the quiet knight like a jagged knife as he raises his hands into the air.

"You brought me here?" I ask, just confused enough to momentarily let my guard down.

"What? No. I thought you were the one who texted me?"

My fingers clamp down around my gun handle. Fucking hell. Not this again.

"I didn't do shit," I mumble.

Even with my barrel pointed directly at his head, Drago continues his steady approach.

To my disgust, I react by backing away. Before I can stop myself, the same soft mound I tripped on early catches me in the back of the heel.

I stumble, but I don't fall.

"Are you alright?" Drago asks, his old voice filled with fake concern.

"I'm fine," I curse, looking down.

I don't find any relief on the ground. Instead, I see what keeps tripping me.

A skeletal hand reaches out of the mound I nearly tripped on. It's a grave. The bones are too small to belong to an adult.

"Fucking hell," I grimace, flinching away from the horrifying sight. Traumatic memories threaten to pound me down into the earth. I try to ignore them.

It's impossible.

My gun drops to my side. My eyes close. I see the fire that engulfed this village. I see the frightened silhouettes of the women and children as they run from the flames. I see them fall as they're shot in the back.

No one was allowed to escape.

No one but me.

Guilt weighs me down. I fall to my knees, new tears filling up my eyes.

Then, I feel a pressure on my shoulder. It's not warm, but it's not cold either.

A hand wipes the tears from my cheeks.

"I'm sorry, Rozalia. I truly am. You never deserved any of this."

I don't resist as Drago helps me back to my feet. I can't.

"I didn't want to come back here," I tell him, wiping my nose.

"I know. It's the only reason I came armed," Drago says. I follow his gaze as he nods down to his waist. A huge silver Glock sits on his hip. "You would never voluntarily want to come back to this place. I figured it must be a trap of some kind."

"Then why did you come?"

Drago sighs.

"Just in case it was you."

My fallen heart shrivels.

"You betrayed me..." I whisper.

"I've failed you so many times," he agrees, his brows furrowing in pain. "But you have to believe me. I'm done with that. I've learned my lesson. I'm trying to help. Please believe me."

An awkward tension swirls in the air. I don't know what to say.

"Tytus seems to believe you," I weakly huff.

"That's because he wants to," Drago acknowledges. "He misses what we were."

"I don't," I'm quick to reply. But I'm not sure how true that is.

"That's alright. I don't expect things to go back to how they were. The past is done. But I can't rest until I help you control your future."

"How is pawning me off on Leander supposed to help me?" I snap.

A sliver of moonlight finds its way through the clouds above. I see Drago look around, searching for danger. When he doesn't find it, he sets his gaze back onto me.

That pale dead of his looks right through my soul.

"I wasn't pawning you off on him," he whispers, deep and low. "I was pawning him off on you."

My tears threaten to return as I pull myself from the man I once foolishly considered my adoptive father.

"I've heard all of your tricks before," I say, looking back towards the empty rock. "They won't work on me."

"This is no trick," Drago insists. "Not on you. I've set everything up. I've infiltrated Leander's mercenary army. I've whispered in the ears of all his seedy associates. Behind his back, I've done what he desired to do. I've built an army. But this army isn't for him. It's for you, my dear. Repayment for all I've made you suffer through."

His words bash around my insides like falling boulders.

"And what do you get out of it?" I stubbornly question.

"Nothing."

"I don't believe you."

"You don't have to," Drago sighs, shaking his head. "But believe your brother. Believe Tytus. He's been helping me lay the groundwork for your takeover."

"Is that what he's been doing?" I mumble, remembering how focused he'd seemed at the hospital. Fuck. He'd trusted Drago enough to let him around Babcia. Tytus has never been an easy sell on anything, and he's too smart to fall for any of Drago's tricks.

There must be some truth to what the old dragon is telling me.

"What happens to Tytus in all of this?" I ask.

"He'll be right there with you, ruling."

"And you?"

"I'll vanish. I'll never bother you again. But if you never need help, I'll come running."

"And if I want you dead?"

"Then I will personally hand you my gun and give you permission to end me."

"I don't need your permission."

No matter how hard I try to hiss at Drago, all that comes out is a jittery sob. I'm getting way too emotional. But there's nothing I can do to stop it.

"I know," Drago sniffles.

To my surprise, he seems to brush a tear from his scarred cheek.

"Drago... I..."

I don't know what to say. My heart hurts.

Drago fills in the silence for me.

"I know the truth about your army, Roz," he says. "There is none. Whatever those Polish priests fed us, it was full of lies. There may have been a fortune waiting for you and Tytus, but there was never going to be anything else."

My shriveled heart drops further.

"Tytus told you that too?"

"He didn't have to. I've spent the last year doing whatever I can to make up for my past. And part of that was figuring out your weaknesses—but only so I could strengthen them. If you and your brother are going to survive—if you're going to thrive like I always promised you would—then you need to trust me. You need an army, and I've made one for you. Please, Roz. Believe me."

"I want to," I hear myself admit, breaking down. Globs of hot tears race down my cheeks as I hang my head. "Stupid hormones," I sob, trying to brush it all off.

Drago isn't having it. He lends his shoulder for me to cry on. I soak his shirt.

"It's going to be okay," he assures me, sucking back his own tears. I feel his rough hand gently pat me on the back of the head, just like he did when I was a little girl.

Just like he did at the end of the night he saved me, all those years ago.

A pinprick of warmth appears inside of me.

Even with all of his faults, there's no denying what this man has done for me.

After my village was razed, the only time I'd ever felt anything close to the warmth of a home was when I was with Drago, Gabriel and Tytus. Hell, even Krol was almost like a hated older step-brother or creepy uncle.

Krol.

"What about Krol?" I sniff, reminded of Drago's cryptic words on the slimy half-dead bastard.

"Don't worry about that," Drago says. "Whatever happens with him, I'll make sure it doesn't affect you. I promise."

I so badly want to believe him; to let my tears sink deeper into his shoulder; to be his daughter again. My shriveled heart begs to be refilled with the warmth I felt at dinner—even if it is a slightly different warmth.

I just want to give in.

"I didn't bring you here," I stubbornly remind him. Reluctantly, I push myself off his shoulder.

This is getting too raw. Too emotional. I can't be this vulnerable around Drago. It's not smart. He always finds a way to take advantage.

"I know," Drago nods. "I believe you."

"So, who did?"

"I don't know. And I don't care. I'm just glad you're here with me. Now, can we leave together?"

With a grace I didn't know he possessed, Drago reaches out his hand to me.

I let it hang in the air.

"And go where?" I ask, wiping away the last of my tears.

"To take control of your army," Drago says, a stifled smile shining through his sadness.

"Already?"

Drago nods.

"Like I said, Tytus and I have been working in the background. Everything is ready, all we have to do is go to Leander and take it."

My shriveled heart kicks.

Leander.

"Do I get to kill the bastard?" I sneer, my cheeks still rosy and stained with salty tears.

"Only if you don't want to watch me do it myself," Drago smirks, the sadness slowly fading.

I mull that offer over for a second.

"Let's play it by ear."

Drago laughs.

"Sounds like a plan," he says. "Does this mean you'll come with me?"

The hope in his voice is so sincere I can't help but huff.

But there's no resistance left in me. Not towards him.

With one last deep, shaky breath, I take his hand.

Drago's skin is cold, but when I close my fingers around his palm, the pinprick of warmth inside of me grows... but only to a point. Something holds it back from getting too big.

"I'll come," I softly agree. "But if you try anything stupid, I won't hesitate to end you."

"I wouldn't have it any other way," Drago smiles. "That's how I raised you, after all."

He's right.

When Drago turns to lead the way, our hands fall apart. I don't immediately follow after him.

Instead, I peer back over my shoulder, towards the rock. It's still empty.

I remember how I told Rian about Willow. I remember how good it felt to be vulnerable—if even only for a second.

The warmth inside of me grows a little more.

Then, the dread appears. It's accompanied by a wave of doubt.

Willow fades from my mind, and I can only think of Rian.

What am I going to do with him?

Shit. What am I going to do with an entire army?

It's been an entire year since Tytus and I found out that there was no secret Polish force waiting for us in the shadows. That the mythos we'd been fed all our lives was a lie. That the inheritance we stole from Gabriel only included riches, and no inherent power.

I'd long since resigned myself to the fact that I was never going to be some great commander. If we were going to take power, and our revenge, we'd have to be sneaky about it.

But now the question has re-emerged.

What will I do with an entire army at my command?

For years, the brutal answer to that question was clear as day.

Destroy. Everyone.

Go scorched earth. Leave no survivors.

Now, though, I hardly even know what I want to do with Rian.

Do I want to destroy him?

... Or join him?

My shriveled heart flickers.

Fuck.

Turning away from the empty rock, I step over the shallow grave at my feet and slowly start to follow after Drago's silhouette.

With a concerted effort, I push Rian from my mind. I'll deal with him later. Right now, I only need to focus on one thing.

How to kill Leander Onasis.

Apparently, he's all that stands between me and the army of my dreams.

My fingers tighten around my gun handle.

That fucker is going to pay.

The real question is, will I end him quickly or make him suffer?

Gazing ahead, I watch as Drago walks through the overgrown ruins of my village. For just a split second, I swear I see his thin, sickly silhouette grow back into that dark, intimidating figure I first saw all those years ago.

The devil in the storm.

My savior in that burning castle.

The warmth inside me grows a little more.

Maybe I don't have to think about what I'll do to Leander.

Maybe, when the time comes, I'll just let my dad decide.

27

RIAN

It takes all of my willpower not to pounce.

The fuckers who tried to frame me are barely a hundred yards away. They've parked at the other end of this dark alley. I can see the lights on their phone screens as they sit around, waiting for further instructions.

They think they've gotten away. They think they're in the clear.

They're dead wrong.

"Speak to me," I grumble from the driver's seat of my quiet car. The engine has been turned off. The lights dimmed. I might as well be a shadow.

"I have eyes on them."

The fresh voice comes through my phone's speaker. I reach towards the ignition.

"Tell me when."

"Just let me get into a better position," Deacon says. I can hear the focus in the young man's words. He's all in.

A swell of pride rises up behind my chest. It's joined by a pang of guilt.

This kid chased these fuckers down after they slaughtered

his entire crew. He's got the bravery of a lion and the loyalty of a wolf. And until just a few minutes ago, I didn't even know his name.

Now, we might as well be blood brothers. Because I've entrusted my life to him, and he's entrusted his life to me.

"When you give me the word, I'll flick my high beams on," I remind him. "So don't worry if you can't find any good lighting."

"Oh yeah, shit," Deacon curses. "Alright, then I'll set up here. Give me a second."

My fingers twitch over the ignition. I'm starved for blood. I've never been a patient man, but I'm trying my best to change—if even only for the moment.

Dad was right.

I never gave my men a chance.

I have good soldiers working for me. Deacon is proof of that. I've just been too lost in my own head to see it.

That's my fault. And it's going to change, starting tonight.

Deacon and I came up with this little plan of attack together. It's not complicated, but it's not like we had much time, either.

"Maksim says you have a hell of a shot," I say, trying to distract myself from the wait.

"That's just because I learned from the best," Deacon confirms.

"Maksim taught you how to shoot?"

I shouldn't be surprised. But I am. How does that man find the time to teach on top of everything else he does?

"Yep. The old man's got some skills."

"Couldn't agree more," I nod. "Let's do him proud."

"Yes, sir." Deacon's voice becomes more hushed as he approaches our targets. "Ready," he whispers.

"Showtime."

Transferring the call to my earpiece, I finally press down on the ignition. The engine roars alive. Before I can flick the high beams on, I see the lights on the phone screens ahead vanish as the men jump at the sound.

Get ready to meet the devil, assholes.

I kick down on the gas pedal and my car lunges forward, picking up speed until the alley walls become nothing more than a blur.

The high beams flick on just as the first bullet hits my armored windshield. It barely even makes a dent.

Ahead, I spot my targets. They're squinting against the light. If they had any sense, they'd already be running away. But the idiots don't budge. Instead, they just stand there, guns raised and blindly firing forward—lambs for the slaughter.

"Light them up!" I order.

Somehow, through the chaos, Deacon is able to hear me. In the blink of an eye, the fuckers ahead start to fall, shredded by Deacon's high-caliber bullets.

Thankfully, he leaves a few standing for me.

"You fuckers!" I roar, blasting into the line without slowing down.

Half a dozen bodies crash into my hood and roll over my windshield. I hear the fresh corpses tumble over the roof of my car before falling behind the bumper.

That's when I take my foot off the gas pedal. But I'm not done yet. Throwing my car in reverse, I come to a screeching stop.

"I'm not done with you assholes yet," I grunt.

Their bones crunch under my heavy wheels as I back up. I don't stop until I see their flattened bodies in my headlights. Then, I shove an elbow into my door handle and jump out into the action.

Lifting my gun, I go to shoot the first asshole I see. But before I can pull the trigger, his head explodes.

"Hey!" I shout, pressing down on my earpiece.

"Oh, sorry, did you want to kill him?" Deacon apologizes. "Oh shit, watch out."

The second I open my mouth to respond, I feel a bullet whizz past my shoulder. A split second later, someone falls at my feet.

"Careful!" I curse. "That almost hit me."

"Oh, boss, I would never dare. Trust—"

This time, I beat him to the draw. A bullet rips from my barrel, slicing through some poor fucker's throat just as he lunges at me through the smoke.

"Make sure we leave a survivor," I remind Deacon, stepping over the fresh corpse.

The next asshole who comes at me gets a bullet through the gut.

"I've already taken care of that," Deacon says. "The first asshole I shot got a bullet right through both of his shoulders, then two more through his shins. He's not going anywhere, but he'll able to do plenty of talking—that is, if we can clear out everyone else before he loses too much blood."

"I'm on it."

"Me too."

Three quick shots rain down from above. Three bodies hit the floor.

Through the smoky aftermath, I spot someone trying to make a run for it.

He doesn't get far.

"Coward," Deacon curses, putting a bullet in his back.

"Not everyone can be as brave as you," I play, watching as the fucker hits the ground, squirms for a moment, then goes still.

Turning back around, I search for any stragglers. There are none. We made quick work of these losers.

"I'm not brave," Deacon replies. "I'm just pissed off."

"Welcome to the club," I grunt. "Now, get down here. We have an interrogation to start."

"Yes, sir."

Smoke drifts through the shattered tail lights as I survey the scene. All I see are corpses.

These fuckers hardly put up a fight. If they hadn't gotten the jump on my men earlier, then I doubt they would have even made it this far.

But their weakness only makes the mess they caused so much more infuriating. Lifting my gun, I empty my clip into the nearest cadaver.

This was my fault. I knew something like this was bound to happen. I should have committed myself to stopping it and sent more men to the union strongholds months ago. If I had, none of this would have happened.

Fucking hell.

Another mistake.

... But not a failure. No. I won't allow this to be a failure. I'll learn from my mistake. I'll—

Suddenly, my train of thought is interrupted by a loud battle cry. Through the high beam haze, I spot a figure running frantically towards me. His arms are raised. A sharp blade glimmers in his hand.

He jumps at me.

I don't even bother to shoot the fucker. Instead, I just step aside and grab his collar.

"Idiot," I growl.

Pulling him into my body, I grab his knife-wielding hand. He's not strong enough to stop me from pushing the blade into his throat.

Blood spills from the widening gash as he tries to cry out again. But all he manages is a gurgle. It's the last thing he ever does.

"Fucking pathetic," I spit, pushing his dead body to the ground.

His skull cracks against the pavement. I bend down and pick up his scarlet-stained knife.

Through all of the rage, I'm almost disappointed.

These aren't mafia men. Underworld soldiers fight like demons. These grunts barely did enough to earn their paycheck.

My chest tightens.

I've fought men like this before. At the beachside mansion where I first took Roz.

That must mean...

"Hey, boss!" I hear Deacon shout from behind me. "We should probably start our interrogation. This guy isn't going to last much longer."

Wiping the blade of my new knife off on my shirt, I turn around. But I'm not so desperate to get answers anymore.

I feel like I already know everything.

These aren't mafia men.

These are mercenaries.

And I'd bet they were hired by Leander fucking Onasis.

"Step aside," I tell Deacon. Twirling the knife in my hand, I approach the poor sap bleeding out against the alley wall.

His eyes are already starting to get hazy. I decide to shock him awake.

Deacon steps aside and I crouch down. Without saying a single word, I crack the fucker's nose open with a vicious punch.

His head snaps back. I grab his hair and force him to look at me.

"Where is he?" I ask, as calmly as possible.

"... Wh... Who?" the idiot whimpers.

Sucking on my teeth, I reach down and pull up his shirt. Using my jagged blade, I slice the fucker's right nipple clean off.

He howls into the smoke-filled night as blood gushes from the open wound. I shake some of the blood off my blade and let his shirt fall back over his squirming body.

"Where is Leander Onasis?" I ask, once more, tightening my grip around his sweat-drenched hair.

"Just fucking kill me," the bleeding man begs. "Please. Just fucking kill me!"

"Only if you answer my question."

"And.. And if I... if I don't?"

He's not going to last much longer. Each new breath he takes is shallower than the last. If I'm going to get answers out of him, I'll need to be quick.

"Then I'll keep you alive as long as I can," I tell him. "And I'll make sure every last second is utter hell."

Reaching down, I drop my knife and take his hand. He's not strong enough to resist as I take his index finger and bend it backward until I hear a snap.

"Stop!" he whimpers.

"Where is Leander?"

"I... I don't know..." I grab his thumb next. "No!" he cries out. "Listen. Listen! The best... the best I can do is tell you where to find someone... find someone who should know where Leander is... I swear... please...."

"I've already been down that road before," I grunt. "I'm sick of it."

Grinding my teeth, I start to bend his thumb back.

"His name is Tytus!" the fucker squeals.

That stops me dead in my tracks

"... Tytus Ryzdon?"

The dying man nods.

"I... I know where he hides out..."

The fucker's head bobs as blood pours from his wounds. He's on death's door.

I slap him back to life.

"Tell me," I demand.

But suddenly, I'm not so worried about Leander.

"Please... kill me..." he whispers.

"Tell me!" I roar.

My heart is pounding. I can't think straight.

Tytus.

Fucking hell.

What the hell is he doing with Leander?

My pounding heart drops.

Does Roz know?

... Or is Tytus working against her now?

"I... I..." the dying man starts to fade again. Panic grips me.

If Roz is in trouble, I don't have a moment to spare.

"Where is Tytus Ryzdon!" I shout. Grabbing the man around the throat I try to shake him awake again. But his eyes are quickly glazing over. "Fuck!"

"Here, wait, try this." Suddenly, Deacon is at my side. Crouching down, he shoves his phone into the dying man's face. A smart map is opened up on the screen. "Point to where he hides out. Just point, and this will all be over."

To my surprise, the dying man seems to understand. With his mangled hand, he reaches for the phone. A pinky finger gently taps down on the map, pinning a location.

Through all of my panic, I still find room to be impressed by Deacon's ingenuity. It feels like something I would have done, if I were thinking straight.

But there's no time to think straight.

Roz might be in trouble.

"Are you sure this is the spot?" Deacon asks.

The man nods. "I've been there before... He... He's building an army... I was going to be part of it..."

"I'll make sure to send all his soldiers to the same part of hell as you," I growl. Standing up I press my gun against his forehead.

"Kill me..."

"Fuck you."

I pull the trigger. His brains splatter against the alley wall.

I turn my back to the carnage.

"Let's go," I grumble.

I'm already at my car when Deacon catches up.

"You don't think we should call for backup?" he asks.

"I'll do it on the way. Are you coming with me or do you want to wait for them?"

That draws a laugh from the young knucklehead. "As if I'd pass up on a chance to ride with *the* Rian Kilpatrick."

"My grandfather was *the* Rian Kilpatrick," I say. "I'm just Rian."

"The king."

"... Only if our empire survives."

Slamming the driver's door shut behind me, I wait for Deacon to jump in the passenger's seat. Then I take off.

Without being told to do so, Deacon starts entering the coordinates into my car's GPS.

He also starts talking, but I barely hear a word he says. Blood has rushed into my ears. All I can focus on is what's ahead.

Tytus.

Fuck. Has he betrayed his sister? Is he working with Leander?

My pounding heart kicks as I consider the worst.

No. I won't let Roz get hurt. I can't.

That's how I lose her.

No matter what it takes, my fallen angel will be safe. And she will be mine again.

I'll make sure of it.

... Even if that means killing her own brother.

28

ROZALIA

"Remember what we talked about," Drago says.

His scarred hand hovers above the door handle as we exchange one last knowing glance.

"I'll be ready," I nod.

"I know you will."

I take a deep breath and Drago opens the door. I'm still not sure how to feel about all of this. But I do know one thing.

It's too late to turn back now.

"Nice of you two to finally join us."

Leander's voice slithers through the darkness ahead, curling into my ears as we step into the sweltering greenhouse.

"... What is this place?" I mutter, sniffing up into the fragrant air.

The seemingly endless structure is filled with all types of exotic trees and plants and flowers. They rise up from the hidden corners of the impressive structure, expanding outwards like suffocating clouds. A thin smoky haze drifts along the floor. Pale moonlight drifts in through the glass ceiling above. I swear I hear crickets chirping.

A wide path cuts through the canopy. In the middle of it all is a single silhouette. A loathsome figure.

Leander Onasis.

"I'm not sure. This is my first time here," Drago whispers. "Just stay ready."

"Care to share your whispers with the classroom?" Leander teases. His voice is coated in a sickly-sweet charm. I already want to gag.

"We're not here to play games," Drago rumbles. Stepping in front of me, he takes a protective stance. "Where's Tytus?"

"Right here."

My brother's voice comes from the shadows. For a moment, my hackles rise. But when he steps into the light, I can't help but breathe a sigh of relief.

I'm not alone.

Even if Drago might betray me, Tytus would never do such a thing.

"Is everything alright?" I ask. The implication in my words is clear. I don't give a shit about this shady meet-up.

I just want an update on Babcia.

"Everything is fine," Tytus assures me. The glint in his eye calms me a little. He knows what's coming. We all do.

Still, I can't shake a suspicious twitch. Something doesn't feel right. There's a heaviness in the air that can't be explained away by all the plants.

Stepping around Drago, I take note of Leander's security detail. As far as I can tell, there are only six men. They stand just behind Leander, blocking off the exit, Ak-47s held tightly between their white fingers.

If we act swiftly, they won't be much of a problem. I know what kind of company Leander keeps. His mercenaries are no match for us.

If he was smart, he would have brought some of those mafia

troops he's supposedly been cultivating. Then, we might actually have a fight on our hands.

But I doubt Leander knows any better. He's a stranger to our brutal world, after all. His unearned confidence is going to be the end of him. I'll make sure of it.

"What a charming little reunion this is," Leander chuckles. "No need to thank me, though."

"Why would we thank you?" I hear myself ask. There's too much venom in my voice. I try to dial it back by forcing a small smirk onto my lips, like I'm joining in on the banter.

Leander can't know how much I still despise him. He's supposed to think I've come around on his offer.

"For helping you escape, of course," Leander explains, hardly fooled. Furrowing his brows, he gives Drago a confused look. "Didn't you tell her who set that union building on fire?"

"Union building?" My heart clenches as I glare over at Drago.

But Drago doesn't flinch. Instead, he just gestures toward the Greek billionaire.

"Leander lent us some men to set a distraction. I told them to burn down union headquarters and paint the Kilpatrick name in blood on the street outside. It was the most sure-fire way to grab the lion's attention."

A sharp gulp cuts down my throat as I remember how Rian looked at me when he learned about that attack.

My clenched heart twists.

"Why the hell did you do that?" I blurt out. My words don't carry far before they're engulfed by the thick foliage surrounding us.

"To help you escape his grip," Drago says, his confidence wavering.

Clearly, he can hear how upset I am. It confuses him.

"I had already escaped by the time you attacked," I sneer. "How didn't you know that?"

Pulling my glare from Drago, I fix it on Tytus.

My brother knew about my escape. He was with me at Babcia's cottage. He was with me at the hospital. Why didn't he tell Drago?

"It didn't come up," Tytus shrugs. "But that doesn't matter. An attack on Rian Kilpatrick is never a bad thing. Right?"

The glint in his eyes suddenly isn't so reassuring.

I gulp.

Does he know about my feelings for Rian? Did he overhear what Babcia and I talked about in her hospital room?

Is this some sort of punishment for caring about our enemy?

My hackles rise.

My heart drops.

Who the hell can I trust anymore?

My eyes dart back and forth as I realize there's nowhere to go.

"You fucked up," I say, biting my tongue. "Now, every Kilpatrick soldier on the east coast will be after us."

I don't dare utter the real reason I'm so upset.

My chest feels hollow as I remember the relief in Rian's ocean blue eyes when I absolved him of his sins.

He wasn't wrong about those union fucks. But now his past will come back to haunt him... and possibly destroy him.

And that's partly my fault.

"That works too," Tytus responds. "We'll be ready for them."

His flippancy is starting to get on my nerves, even though I know it shouldn't—in a sane world, I would be happy to make Rian Kilpatrick suffer.

But I've lost my damn mind.

"That's right," Leander confirms. "All we have to do is tie the knot, and the army I've worked so hard to gather becomes yours too. Then we can take on those Irish bastards in a real war. No more pussy-footing around this conflict."

"What do you know about war?" I grumble, fingers curling into a fist.

"Not much. Not yet," Leander admits. "But I can't wait to find out all about it. And I'm even more thrilled to share the experience with you."

"You maniac," I whisper through gritted teeth.

The insult isn't meant to be loud enough for Leander's ears. But he seems to hear it anyways.

"Sounds like we were made for each other, then," he grins, his white teeth sparkling against the moonlight.

I want to punch him square in the nose. But before I can even take a step forward, I feel Drago's cold hand on my shoulder.

"Easy there," he soothes me, his raspy voice so low it's barely audible. "Remember what we talked about."

I'm oddly eased by his reminder.

Leander is going to pay. I just have to be patient.

Still, it's hard to trust anyone right now.

"I promise I won't be so bad," Leander taunts, almost like he's trying to provoke me. "As long as you're an obedient little wife, I'll be a loyal husband."

Fucking hell.

No army is worth this.

… But the promise of ridding a man like Leander from my life is just enough to keep me from lashing out.

Unfurling my fists, I brush the back of my hand against the thigh holster hidden under my dress. We had to pass through a metal detector to get in here, and Leander's terms stipulated that no weapons were allowed.

But his men were lazy—or they were ordered not to molest me. Because I wasn't searched.

If they had patted me down, they probably would have

found the stone-carved knife Drago gave me. It's as sharp as any steel and fits perfectly in my empty holster.

All I have to do is get close enough to stick it through Leander's throat. Tytus and Drago will take care of the rest. How? I'm not sure, but I need to trust them.

I *want* to trust them.

"I'll do whatever it takes to bring the Kilpatricks to their knees," I say, forcing back my sneer.

"I've heard," Leander smirks. "In fact, I've heard you'd go so far as to get on your knees for them first."

His words reach out through the sweltering heat and slap me across the face. My cheeks flush red. A burning anger erupts in my core. A whirlwind of shame whips up beside it.

My brother and father are here.

They don't need to hear this shit.

I'll make him suffer.

"Don't worry," Leander continues, before I can bite back. "I'm not angry. I understand what needs to be done. I never expected you to be some unsullied rose."

This time, not even Drago's cold hand can keep me from advancing. His fingers fall down my back as I take a cautious step forward. Then another one.

I can feel myself seething. Leander must see it. But his stupid grin doesn't waver.

Why the hell is he doing this? Is he just that dumb, or is he trying to make me do something stupid?

Why?

"Enough!" Drago booms from behind me. "Watch your tongue, *boy*."

Leander hardly flinches against the dragon's rage. Instead, he places a light hand over his chest, and tauntingly bows in our direction.

"I'm sorry," he says, clearly not meaning it. "I'm just excited. It's not every day a man like me gets to reclaim his roots. My family hasn't been in the mafia for so long. But ever since I learned of our history, I've been dying to change that. Now is my chance. It just feels so right, you know?"

The hot air thickens. I look over to Tytus. He's privately fuming, but we're both desperately trying to play it cool.

We both know what's at stake. Neither of us can blow our tops. Not until I make the first move.

And I'm not close enough to make the first move. Not yet.

Taking a step forward, I try to change that.

"You've proven yourself worthy of a place in our world," I lie to Leander, barely holding back my disgust. "First you build an army, then you make a fool of the king. When we destroy what's left of Rian Kilpatrick's empire, no one will doubt who to follow next. You... and me."

Swallowing my rage, I strut down the stone path that cuts through the heavy foliage. Somewhere behind all the leaves, I hear a waterfall; it swirls around the growing choir of crickets.

"I'm glad you think that too," Leander's grin grows. Seemingly taking the bait, he lifts his hand into the air, reaching out to me. "This whole night might have been spoiled if I had to force you into anything."

As if you're strong enough to force me into anything, I want to snap. But I bite my tongue and continue my advance.

"Careful, Roz," Drago's hushed voice brushes over my shoulder. He's still filled with anger. But he's doing his best to control it too.

"I agree," I say, ignoring Drago for Leander. "There's no need to be at each other's throats when we could be—"

"... At each other's lips?" Leander finishes for me. Spreading out his raised hand, he motions for me to stop.

"That's not quite what I was going to say," I mumble, reluctantly slowing down.

"Please, then, don't come any closer. Not until it's time."

I don't have a choice. Taking one last strategic step forward, I pause.

"You don't think we've waited long enough?" I seductively purr, trying to lure him towards me.

Leander's light blue eyes fall lazily down my body. When he reaches my thighs, he cracks his neck and sighs.

"We have," he says, subtly licking his lower lip. "But that doesn't mean we can't wait a little longer, just to make sure we get things right."

Recoiling his outstretched hand, Leander signals to the armed men behind him.

I tense up.

But they don't charge forward. Instead, the two closest to the exit disappear behind the door.

"What's going on?" I ask, holding my breath.

"I have something for you," Leander replies. "A wedding gift."

"The army will do just fine."

"You don't like surprises?" he asks, lifting his brow.

"No."

That makes him chuckle.

"Well, then I'll spoil it for you."

When he reaches into his pocket, every muscle in my body flexes. Out of the corner of my eye, I can see Tytus getting ready to pounce. I imagine Drago is doing the same behind me.

But Leander doesn't pull out a gun. And when I see the black fleet box in his hand, I immediately feel foolish for being worried. The billionaire would never get his well-manicured hands dirty.

"Is this your way of proposing?" I taunt, taking one more subtle step forward.

"oh, we're far past that stage," Leander chuckles.

Behind him, the exit door is pushed open. The two men re-emerge.

My breath catches in my throat.

One of them is carrying a long, frilly, blindingly white wedding gown. The other has his gun pressed into the back of a man who is dressed an awful lot like a priest.

My pounding pulse quickens.

Fuck.

It doesn't matter that I came here knowing full well Leander intended to marry me on the spot. The two blaring symbols of my most feared fate trigger a deluge of nightmarish memories.

I swallow a jagged whimper.

This isn't the first time I've had to do something like this— but I'm determined to make it my last. I just need to stay in control of myself for a little while longer.

Taking another quiet step forward, I get ready to make a run for Leander's throat. To my dismay, he's quickly joined by his two guards. They momentarily block him off.

"Bring the dress to my bride," Leander orders. "You, priest, prepare as you must."

"… Yes, sir," the frail old man whispers. His eyes are so sunken I can't tell if they're black from bruises or from the shadows they cast. They get even darker as he reaches into his breast pocket and pulls out a book.

"According to Greek mafia tradition, it is the bride's father who first presents the wedding band to his daughter," Leander lectures me. "Or so I've heard. But since you don't have a dad, then—"

"I have a dad!" I mindlessly interrupt.

My declaration vanishes into the thick greenhouse air just as quickly as it left my mouth. But the impact doesn't disappear as swiftly.

It's like I've been punched in the chest.

Did I just say that out loud?

"I didn't think you two were on the best of terms," Leander admits, a subtle confusion scrunching his nose.

"That doesn't matter," I realize. "He raised me. He is my father."

My shallow breaths become deeper as a wave of emotion swells over me.

It's the truth—even if it took me this long to figure it out.

For all of Drago's faults, he is my father.

"Very well," Leander smirks, his confusion quickly dissolving. "Dragomir Raclaw, would you please step forward and accept this ring from me to your daughter?"

Drago hardly hesitates.

"I will."

His voice overflows with pride, momentarily breaking in the middle.

This must mean the world to him.

I want to cry. But I do everything I can to hold back the tears as he approaches.

"Thank you," he whispers, brushing by me; his once powerful voice reduced to a grateful murmur.

My tense heart unspools just a little.

I want to reach out and hug him. But I don't think either of us actually know how to give a proper hug. And even if we did, this isn't the time. We'll have to wait until this is all over.

Fuck.

My heart tenses up again at the thought of what will happen when this is over.

The decisions I'll have to make...

After Leander is dead, and we have his army, what will we do about Rian? What can we do? There's no way he'd ever agree to work with Drago, a man who's set him up twice.

But I don't want to hurt Rian. And suddenly, I'm not so ready to discard Drago.

He's my dad, after all.

"Give it here," the once fearsome dragon says as he approaches Leander and the priest.

Before he can take the black box from Leander, though, the shady billionaire leans forward and grabs his wrist.

"Hey!" Tytus and I both shout out at the same time.

But we can only watch as Leander pulls Drago towards him and whispers something into his ear.

"Let him go!" I shout.

"It's alright," Drago soothes me. Pushing himself off Leander, he turns around and lifts the black box in his hand so Tytus and I can both see it.

"Stay here until your daughter is ready," Leander orders. Then, with a subtle glance, I catch him gesturing to his guards. I watch with horror as they tighten their grips around their guns.

My hackles rise.

"I'm ready," I hiss. But when I take another step forward, Leander lifts up an open palm and stops me.

"No," he says, shaking his head. "You're not ready. Not yet." Turning to the bodyguard on his right, he nods.

The armed goon steps forward, wedding gown in hand. When he's halfway between Leander and me, he stops.

"You still need to get dressed," Leander explains.

With that, the guard throws the wedding gown at my feet. I let it fall onto the ground.

"I'd rather not," I spit, unable to hold back my disdain.

"I'm afraid there's no choice," Leander says. "It's tradition."

His guard retreats, and I quickly realize the real reason Leander called Drago to his side.

To act as a human shield.

Fuck.

I should have seen that coming. But I underestimated the Greek billionaire. Does he know what's coming? Does he know what we have planned for him?

If he does, we might already be fucked.

"We'll start a new tradition," I say, hand sliding down my

thigh. A knife won't do much good in a gunfight, but it's all I've got.

"I'd rather stick with the old ways," Leander smirks.

"She's not wearing the dress," Drago growls. He must realize what's happening. I can hear the frustration in his voice.

Shit's about to unravel, and fast.

Out of the corner of my eye, I give Tytus a quick glance. His back is already arched.

"Like I said, I'm not giving her the choice," Leander grumbles, clearly fed up. "If you want this deal to happen, if you want your life's work to be fulfilled, you'll tell your daughter to be a good girl. You'll tell her to strip down right here and now. You'll tell her to change in front of her new king. You'll tell her to forsake that beastly Irish devil she's clearly fallen for, and you'll order her to do as I say, forever."

My heart drops.

Leander isn't even trying to hide his hate anymore. He's talking like a man who's in complete control. And suddenly, I can't tell if it's because he's just naive, or if he actually has something else up his sleeve.

"Never," Drago growls. His pale face turns a deep red as he shakes with anger.

Easy, I mouth to him.

But Drago just shakes his head.

I can tell he's getting ready to do something stupid.

My fallen heart disappears into a black abyss. I haven't completely forgiven Drago yet. But I know it's just because I need more time.

Neither of us is allowed to die yet.

"Well, then what good are you?" Leander huffs. With a resentful eye roll, he reaches into his breast pocket and pulls out a knife.

He doesn't give Drago a chance to turn around. Without another word, Leander plunges his blade into Drago's back.

"Dad!" I scream.

It's like the air is sucked out of the room. Blood rushes into my ears. Drago's dark eyes go wide as he falls to his knees.

I reach for my knife.

But before I can grab it, Leander gestures to one of his guards. The man presses the barrel of his AK-47 against Drago's temple.

Somewhere, in the distance, I hear Tytus roar.

"You fucking bastard," I cry, lunging at Leander.

I don't make it on time.

The gun goes off and Drago's skull is blown into a thousand tiny pieces.

"No!"

The horror of it all sends me falling to the ground. It feels like I've been plunged back beneath those heavy black waves I first fell into near Drago's island cave hideout.

But who will jump in after me this time?

A storm of gunfire erupts around me as I fight back burning tears and try to scramble onto my feet.

"I'll kill you," I shout at Leander, but I can barely even hear myself over the chaos, let alone anyone else.

Still, as I look toward the wicked Greek billionaire, I can read his slimy lips.

"Shoot her. Kill him."

A split second later, I feel Something sharp pinch into the back of my neck.

Almost immediately, a flurry of big black dots spot my tear-filled vision. My eyelids become so heavy I can barely keep them open, and my body becomes so numb I don't feel any pain as I fall.

My cheek cracks against the hard stone ground. I can't even whimper. I'm paralyzed.

My racing pulse starts to slow. My vision fades. All I can do is watch as an army of ghosts seeps out from the thick green foliage that surrounds us.

No...

This whole time, we've been surrounded. There was never any hope. We were tricked.

Leander outmaneuvered us.

My skull burns. My vision worsens.

Somewhere nearby, a flashbang goes off. Out of the corner of my eye, I can just barely make out Tytus fighting for his life.

I try to call to him, but nothing comes out.

Any warmth I'd ever felt is erased from my body. The world turns freezing cold.

Everything goes black.

29

RIAN

"Fuck, this place is well hidden," Deacon remarks.

"And well protected," I grumble.

Pushing the barrel of his rifle through a tangled wall of hanging vines, he cautiously moves them aside.

We both tense up, ready for another trap.

To our relief, nothing comes.

That's a first.

"Well, it looks like we may be past the worst of it now."

"Never assume that things will get better," I teach the young hotshot.

"If only I could be so pessimistic."

"You'll learn."

Brushing past him, I carefully stumble into the above-ground sewer that was hidden behind the vines. Stale water drips from the leaking ceiling. A rancid river flows at our feet.

I try not to breathe in the toxic fumes as I charge forward. But it's no use. I'm exhausted, and I need all the air I can get, no matter how tainted it is.

"Do you see anything?" Deacon asks, following behind me as we wander deeper into the darkness.

"There should be a door up ahead," I note, remembering the digital blueprints my drone scanned earlier.

"Thank god. I'm already getting nauseous."

"Don't get distracted."

Keeping my gun trained forward, I step around a tall corner and prepare myself for yet another surprise.

But once again, nothing appears.

The absence of any obvious trouble is suspicious. Something is off. There's no way we're in the clear yet. If I've learned anything since we got here, it's that Tytus is almost as devious as his sister.

Over the past four hours, we've had to work our way through acres of expertly laid traps. It's how I know we're in the right place—because while most of them clearly weren't made by Rozalia, a few had her handwriting all over them.

Tytus must have borrowed some of her contraptions to beef up his security. For most, that would make this place an instant death trap. But I've decided I'm not allowed to die.

Not yet.

"Is that the door?" Deacon asks.

Pointing the flashlight on his rifle over my shoulder, he illuminates a large black door.

"Must be. Stay ready."

"Yes, boss."

Our wary footsteps splash through the shallow water as we make our approach.

"Wait. Stop." I grumble, spotting something unusual.

"What is it?"

Nodding up, I gesture towards a wire hanging from the ceiling above the door.

"Oh, shit," Deacon curses. "Wait... that kind of looks like the trap we saw out at the front gate..."

"...*After* we disabled it," I note.

"You think it's disabled?"

"Let's find out."

Reaching into my pocket, I pull out one of the pebbles I picked up on the way in here. I toss it forward.

To my surprise, it clangs harmlessly against the door, before falling into the shallow water below.

Still, I wait until the echo fades before taking another step forward.

"Fuck. It is disabled," Deacon curses, hardly relieved. "What does that mean?"

Getting closer, I spot something even more troubling.

"There's blood on the handle."

"Fresh blood?"

"Looks like it."

Shit. Did someone beat us here?

My grip tightens around the handle of my gun as I tip my head and search for more blood. But even if there had been more, it would have been instantly washed away by the running water.

My hackles rise.

"Wait outside," I tell Deacon.

Reaching out, I place the tip of my barrel against the heavy door and push.

It creaks open.

"Boss, I can't let you go in there alone," Deacon says, pulling up beside me.

'That's an order, soldier."

My voice is stern and loud enough to make Deacon pause.

"What if there's an ambush waiting inside?" he asks.

"I'm more worried about an ambush coming from out here," I tell him. "You saw the blueprints. The halls upstairs are tight and winding. There's nowhere to hide an army. There's no room to spare in a fight. If we go together, we'll just get in each other's way."

Deacon chews on his tongue as he considers my explanation.

"Fine. You're the boss," he finally agrees.

"Don't forget it."

I've hardly taken a single step inside before he's at my back again.

"So, What?" he asks, already restless. "I just wait here and call you if I see anyone coming?"

"That's the idea."

"Sounds boring."

"It's better to be boring and safe than reckless and sorry."

Fuck. I'm starting to sound like my father.

… That's not exactly a bad thing.

"Alright. Alright. I'll be your eyes out here," Deacon says, retreating back into the tunnel. "Just promise me you'll be safe, boss. I don't want to leave here alone."

"You won't," I promise him.

Still, I can practically feel the heat of the conflict raging inside him as I step through the doorway.

He's a good kid. I'll make sure he's rewarded for his loyalty.

"Fuck…"

The second I step inside, I try to take a much-needed deep breath, but the air in here is hardly any better than the air outside, and I'm immediately met by a stale gust… and the metallic scent of more blood.

What happened here?

Leaving Deacon behind, I find the set of stairs I know is nearby. Then, I begin my ascent.

It doesn't take long before I reach the next door.

My chest tightens.

It's already half open.

Someone is definitely here.

… So why don't I see any more blood?

With all the caution in the world, I push my way into a

creaky hallway. It's quiet enough that each step I take sounds like thunder. But there's no going back now.

Looking down, I search for bloody footprints.

There are none.

There's no blood on the door handle either.

Lifting my chin, I sniff the air. More blood. I sniff harder.

Part of me is desperate to smell that spicy rose scent that has captured my heart—anything to indicate that I'm getting close to Rozalia.

I already miss her.

But her intoxicating fragrance is nowhere to be found.

She isn't here.

Has she ever been?

My gut churns at the thought of what might lie ahead. The idea that Tytus could betray his own sister makes me sick to my stomach.

It's a concerning feeling.

A squabble between two of my enemies would normally be a good thing. But Rozalia hasn't felt like a true enemy for a long time now. Even if our passion still teems with rage, something else has appeared in the meat of it all.

Something warm and wonderful. Something horrifying. A four-letter word that could change my life forever if uttered out loud.

It's a word that's too intense to even consider right now.

I need to focus on the task at hand. I need to find Tytus. I need to protect Rozalia.

Everything else can wait.

My pulse deepens as I peel around a tight corner. Somewhere up ahead, I swear I hear the echoes of a distant commotion clang through the walls.

My focus wavers. My mind wanders.

No matter how hard I try to zone in on Tytus, all I can really think about is Rozalia.

I can't let him hurt her.

It hardly matters that his treachery would only push her deeper into my arms. That's the last thing I want. She can't be forced to want me. It needs to be a choice.

That's why I let her go after dinner.

I wanted her to chase after me again. To prove she feels the same way

But she left.

Now, I'm back on the chase. But my goal isn't to capture her. It's to give her the freedom to choose me over everyone else.

Somehow, I know she will.

I just need to give her the chance.

If that means killing her brother, then so be it.

Keeping my gun locked ahead, I forge forward. The mansion isn't nearly as decrepit as I was expecting. From the outside, it almost looks like an abandoned castle. On the inside, though, there's a cozy lived-in museum vibe that's clearly been created on purpose.

Antique paintings and busts line the tight hallways. Fine Persian rugs fill out the floors. Sconce lights flicker with electric candlelight.

I take great care not to bump into anything as I make my way through the twisted maze. But it's not because I'm worried about shattering some priceless relic. My only concern is staying as quiet as possible.

Someone is here. And I can't let them get the jump on me.

When I turn the next corner, though, my vow of silence is tested. It looks like I've come across the scene of a murder. But there's nobody. Only blood.

I want to curse, but I just barely manage to stop myself.

The bloody footprints I lost earlier have reappeared, seemingly out of nowhere. They surround a crimson pool. I try to find where they've come from, but they seem to have walked out of the walls.

My lips curl into a sneer.

Looking around, I spot an old renaissance painting. It's crooked. When I cautiously step towards it, I feel a cold draft.

A hidden door.

Fucking hell. That's where the blood came from.

Now, where did it go?

My pulse slows as I follow the bloody footprints. They stumble around a dark corner up ahead. Cocking my gun, I take a deep breath and chase after them.

Tytus is here. He has to be. This is his hideout, after all. Who else would know about that hidden doorway?

"Is everything alright in there?"

Deacon's voice crackles through my earpiece just as I reach the dark corner. Resting my back against the wall, I place a finger against the device and click it off.

I can't allow myself to be distracted, and I definitely can't risk giving my position away.

Tytus is dangerous, and I'm on his turf. Really, I should be waiting until backup gets here, but I have a bad feeling something is seriously wrong.

And after what Rozalia told me at dinner, I've decided I won't ever ignore my gut again.

Not about my feelings for her, and definitely not on anything business related.

The attack on that union building was clearly a distraction. My worry now is that it was a distraction to separate Roz and me.

My heart sinks.

I just want to feel her again.

Closing my eyes, I picture her in that elegant red gown one last time. The stale mansion air tingles with electricity.

With a final deep breath, I rip my eyes back open. A sneer twists my lips.

Let's do this.

My gun whips around the corner first. When nothing attacks it, I follow. The hallway ahead is darker than the one I just came down, but it's just as empty.

Looking ahead, I search for more bloody footprints.

But they disappear just a couple of yards ahead. A pair of bloody handprints stain the walls, just below a bent sconce. Then, there's nothing.

The stale air thickens. My fingers curl tightly around my gun handle. There must be another hidden door.

Cautiously, I approach the bent sconce. When I pull at it, though, it hardly budges. When I pull harder, it rips off the wall.

"Fuck..." I mumble, jumping back.

So much for being quiet. The metal fixture clanks against the creaky floor as I rip my gaze ahead, half expecting to see Tytus charging at me from the darkness.

But all I get is silence.

... Until I hear the faintest dripping sound.

What the fuck is that?

Turning around, I hold my breath and listen for it again.

The next drop is louder than the last.

My gaze drops to the floor. There, right next to my feet, I find a spot of blood that I swear wasn't there before.

My hackles rise.

I'm already lifting my gun to shoot at the ceiling when a huge weight falls on me. My knees buckle under the force. I hit the ground with a heavy thud and the wind is momentarily knocked out of me.

My gun goes flying across the floor.

"What the fuck are you doing here?" A growl comes from on top of me.

The voice is red with anger. It lashes into my ear as I fight to push myself up. But before I can get to my knees, a thick forearm wraps around my throat and shoves me back to the ground.

"Fuck off," I rasp, scratching at the impossibly powerful grip strangling me.

"You first," the voice barks. Black spots pop up in my vision as I scramble to reach for the knife taped to my ankle. But whoever's on my back has me pinned down so hard I can barely move.

"I swear to fucking god," I curse. Closing my eyes, I touch my chin to the fucker's forearm, then plunge the back of my skull directly into his forehead.

I hear a crack. The grip around my neck eases just enough that I can wrestle my own forearm through the chokehold.

"You fucking asshole," the fucker shouts, falling backward.

I reach down for my knife and turn around. But before I even see my attacker, I'm greeted by a fist.

The punch lands right between my eyes, and I'm sent flying onto my back. Stars replace the black spots in my vision. A wave of pain snaps through my skull.

Fighting it all away, I roll onto my side.

I don't get far.

"You shouldn't have come here, asshole," the stranger swears, jumping back on top of me.

"You shouldn't have killed my men."

Somehow, I manage to give myself enough space to knee the fucker in the groin.

He grunts and temporarily recoils, giving me the space I need to reach up to his throat and throw him to the ground.

Now, I'm on top, and I finally get a good look at my attacker.

"You…"

"Who the fuck were you expecting?" Tytus spits up at me.

He's covered in blood, but that face is unmistakable.

"Where is she?" I ask, fury rising. "What did you do with her?"

"Why the hell do you care?" Tytus sneers.

Grabbing his collar, I pull him up just enough to slam his head back into the ground.

"She's mine," I tell him, blood dripping from my nose. "And you're not allowed to hurt her."

Something snaps behind Tytus' already wild eyes. With incredible quickness and strength, he wrenches his arms between my vice grip and rips me off of him.

I jump to my feet, stumbling backward until I catch myself against the wall.

"I would never hurt my sister," Tytus growls. Grabbing onto a sconce light, he pulls himself up. But the beast is wounded, and he wobbles against the wall as blood drips from an unseen wound.

Crouching down, I pull the knife from my around my ankle.

But I don't attack. Not yet.

Tytus is injured. Badly.

"What the hell happened to you?" I ask, almost not wanting to hear the answer.

Did he confront Roz? Did they fight?

Fuck. Tytus is strong as hell. If he looks like this, how does Roz look?

My stomach drops.

"That's none of your fucking business," Tytus wheezes. Gripping his abdomen, he tries to straighten himself up. But it's no use. He's too weak.

He falls to the ground.

Before his knees can hit the floor, though, I jump forward and grab him.

"What the fuck is going on," I grumble. Helping him down, I push him against the wall and place my knife against his throat. "You better start talking."

"I have nothing to say to you."

"That attitude is going to get you killed," I warn him.

To my surprise, Tytus chuckles. Blood dribbles from his split lip as he looks up to the ceiling.

"I almost had you there," he says. "Catching you off guard was my only chance—but only because of the circumstances. In a fair fight, I could take you. Easily. But not like this, not after what they did to me…"

"What who did to you?" I ask.

A stubborn part of me almost wants to let him back up, to tie an arm behind my back and make this a fair fight. Tytus is right. I only won this easily because he's injured.

But that doesn't matter. Honor doesn't mean shit while Rozalia is in danger.

"You need to let me go," Tytus grumbles. With a pain-filled grunt, he tries to stand up. I don't let him.

Placing my hand on his shoulder, I shove him back down onto his ass.

"Fuck," he grimaces. "You're lucky they got to me first, or else I'd make you pay for that."

"*Who* got to you first?"

I'm still hoping beyond hope that Tytus' wounds aren't the result of a battle with Rozalia.

Not unless they mean she's won.

"As if I'd tell you."

"You better start telling me, or else I'm going to put you out of your misery."

A deep sigh lifts Tytus' powerful chest.

"As nice as that sounds, I can't die yet."

"Want to try me?"

"No. If you kill me, you'll never find her. And I won't be able to save her…"

My knife drops from his throat.

"… Roz is in trouble?"

It's what I've already suspected, but to hear it confirmed like that is even more heart-wrenching.

"Like you really care."

This time, when Tytus tries to stand up, I'm not so gentle. Lifting my knife again, I slam it into the wall just above his shoulder and grab him by the throat.

"You have no idea how much I care," I sneer.

"Is that why you're here?" Tytus asks, his hazy eyes studying me carefully. "Because you care about her?"

There's a caution in his voice that I don't quite understand. But I'm in no mood to sit around and try to figure the fucker out.

Ripping my knife out of the wall, I place it back against his throat.

"I'm here because I caught up to the men you sent to burn down that union building," I explain, leaning in nice and close. "I'm here because one of them squealed. I know they were Leander's men. I know they were working with you. I also know that Roz would never work with Leander. To me, that leaves one explanation. You've betrayed her. You set that building on fire and killed those men to draw me away from her. You know where she is and you know what's happening. You're going to force your sister to marry that slimy Greek fucker just so you can benefit from the alliance, aren't you? Fucking answer me!"

My rage spills out as I press my blade deeper into Tytus' throat. He barely even flinches as the first bits of blood start to trickle out from behind my blade.

"Interesting..." he mumbles, shifting his jaw.

"What's interesting?" I demand to know.

"You keep calling her Roz."

"So what?"

"Does she know you call her that?"

"She likes it."

Tytus laughs.

"Are you sure?"

"Positive."

He seems to chew on something substantial before another heavy sigh leaves his bleeding throat.

"I knew it," he quietly whispers, more to himself than to me.

"You knew what?"

Shaking his head, Tytus slowly lifts his right arm.

"Help me up," he says, presenting me with an open palm.

"Fuck no," I instinctively react.

"Help me the fuck up," Tytus growls, not budging. "If we're going to save my sister, it will have to be together. I'm in no shape to do it alone."

His arm stays raised. His hand remains offered.

But I hesitate to respond.

A million conflicting thoughts whirl around inside of me.

Tytus is my enemy. How can I trust him?

The same way you've learned to trust Roz, an inner voice whispers.

But do you really trust Roz, another voice responds, *or do I just love her?*

My pounding heart freezes.

Fuck.

... Did I really just admit that to myself?

"I'm not working with you," I mumble. Still, I retract my blade from his bleeding throat and stumble backward.

"So you don't really care about her that much, I guess, huh?"

"You have no idea," I snarl, still reeling from that single thought.

Love.

Do I really love Rozalia Dorn?

It seems impossible. But my gut begs me to believe it.

How can I love someone I don't even entirely trust?

When I first heard about the attack, my initial reaction was to assume Rozalia had something to do with it. It didn't matter that we had just shared the best night of my life. She was still a femme fatale. *The* Black Cat.

But fuck me if I don't love that.

She isn't just any black cat anymore.

She's my Black Cat.

"I have some idea," Tytus huffs. His outstretched hand remains offered to me as I straighten myself back up.

"What does that mean?" I ask, not ready to take his offer just yet.

"It means I understand my sister well enough to know when something has changed. Believe me, Roz doesn't change easily. But something has changed. Someone has changed her."

"Who?" I foolishly ask.

"You."

My frozen heart starts to pound again as I come to my senses. I look down to the floor. It's covered in blood.

My pounding head aches. My chest too.

"Where is she?" I ask, my voice shaking.

I need her to be alright. I need to see her again.

I need to hold her and never let her go.

Fuck it.

I'm in love.

"I'm not 100% percent sure," Tytus coughs. "But I know how to figure it out. My big problem will be rescuing her from that Greek asshole. He's got an army of mercenaries on his side."

"Leander has her?"

"Who else?"

"I don't fucking know. You. Maybe Drago?"

Suddenly, Tytus' outstretched arm drops. His hand crashes into the floor like a thousand-pound weight.

"Drago..." the beast of a man whispers.

Are those tears welling up in his eyes?

"What the fuck happened?" I ask, my desperation growing alongside my suspicion. "How did a pathetic fucker like

Leander Onasis manage to capture a woman like Rozalia Dorn?"

"We got cocky," Tytus sighs, those hazy eyes drifting off again.

"You were with her?"

"We all were."

My heart squirms against the idea that Roz had gone directly back to Tytus after dinner.

The man who helped tear that wonderful night away from us.

"Who else was there?"

"Leander, obviously," Tytus snips. "Then there was me, Roz, and Drago... We were just going to play with that fucker until we could get close enough to cut his throat... But he isn't as helpless as he seems. The bastard was ready for us... or maybe he wasn't, and the plan was always to stab us in the back..."

"He ambushed you?"

Tytus nods.

"Doesn't feel so fucking good, does it?" I can't help but jab.

Tytus' big broad chest heaves as he chokes out a laugh.

"I guess not," he chuckles. "But you got back what was taken from you. All of it. No matter what happens, we'll never get back all of what Leander stole from us."

"What does that mean?" I ask, panic suddenly rising.

"Roz is fine," he says with an understanding sigh. "She just got hit with a tranquilizer dart. She'll be alright... as long as we get to her before Leander can do something irreversible."

My fingers curl into fists as I search the floor for my gun. It's over by the fallen sconce.

"How the hell did you and Drago get away and Roz didn't?" I ask. Keeping my eyes on Tytus, I slowly step over to my discarded weapon.

"Drago didn't get away," Tytus quietly says. His voice is thick and heavy. I swear I see his eyes fog up again.

"But *you* did."

"Just barely."

Reaching down, I pick up my gun.

"... And you left Roz behind?"

I can't tell if the sound that tears up his wounded throat is another chuckle or a silent sob.

"It was my only chance," he whispers. "I couldn't save her if I was dead..."

"No. You couldn't," I admit.

I can feel the pain in his voice. The guilt and the regret.

I feel the same way.

Wiping the blood from my fingers, I holster my gun. Then, I reach down and offer my hand out to Tytus.

This time, he's the one who hesitates.

"Are you sure?" he asks, his brow furrowing in a mixture of suspicion and pain. His foggy eyes are filled with uncertainty, like he's not quite sure what's happening, or what's going to happen next.

That makes two of us.

"I'd do anything for Roz," I say. "Even work with you."

"Sounds about right," Tytus weakly smiles.

With great effort, he lifts his arm up again. I lean forward and take his hand, helping him to his feet.

"Let's go hunting."

30

ROZALIA

The idiot doesn't even realize I can see him.

Fuck.

That just makes this all so much worse.

How the hell did an amateur like Leander Onasis get the jump on us? It hardly makes sense. Sure, the ambush could have been planned by any one of his mercenary lackeys, but that doesn't excuse what's happening now.

The first lesson any good criminal learns about kidnapping a person is that when you take them, you put a bag over their head, or at least a blindfold over their eyes—even if you think they're unconscious.

It keeps them from learning the layout, recognizing the location, and gaining even the slightest bit of an advantage.

But Leander hasn't done that to me. And none of his hired guns have tried to fix that mistake.

It makes me feel like even more of a failure, and it takes a concentrated effort to not let my anger and frustration seethe from my limp face as I try to pretend I'm still knocked out.

Still, I can feel my cheeks twitch every time I think of what happened. I'm desperate to sneer. To spit. To rage.

Leander should have killed me when he had the chance. He should have stabbed me in the back, just like he did to Drago.

Drago.

My heart lurches as I fight away the sharp grief cutting through my chest. I've cried enough for one lifetime. I don't want to feel bad anymore.

But that's easier said than done.

Growing tears blur my vision as I stare ahead through half-closed eyelids. I'm not sure where Leander dragged me while I was still unconscious, but I have a great view of the inside.

It's a hell of a lot comfier than any place I'd have brought him to.

The carpet at my feet is thick and luxurious, and the paintings on the walls are modern and grand. There isn't much furniture, but there is a window. The blind hasn't been closed all the way. In the dark slab of glass, I can see Leander's reflection.

That golden skin has turned white.

He's pale as a ghost.

Squinting, I try to make out more of his blurry reflection. I want to see why he's so pale. Is it fear? Disgust? Nerves?

God, I hope it's fear. I hope he's shitting his linen pants right now.

But what could he be scared of? Drago is dead. I'm bound to this chair. He's not in any danger.

… Not unless Tytus escaped.

My aching heart twists with dreadful hope.

My head is still pounding from the tranquilizer, but I can remember exactly what I saw before I passed out.

Tytus. Fighting for his life.

He was ripping Leander's mercenaries to shreds.

But there were so many of them…

"Are you awake?" a deep voice asks, stepping up from behind me.

I don't answer, not even as the cold barrel of a rifle dips beneath my chin and lifts my head. I keep my neck limp.

Pretending that I'm still unconscious is my only advantage right now.

My hands are tied behind my back. My ankles are bound to the legs of some thick chair. I can't see the other men in the room, but I can feel them.

If I had to guess, I'd say there were about four guards. They watch me as Leander's reflection talks to someone I can't see or hear.

"Give her a little slap," someone barks.

The barrel drops from beneath my chin and I let my neck snap back down.

"Boss said not to touch her," a closer voice warns.

"Fuck the boss," the other voice snaps. "Her little friend killed my friends. I'm not going to stand around—"

"Stop," a hushed voice urges. "He's coming."

In the distance, I hear footsteps. They clop over a wooden surface before being muffled by the carpet.

Leander is finally coming. But I wish he wasn't. I want these buffoons to keep talking. They're bolstering my hope.

Is Tytus still alive? Do they want to punish me because they didn't get a chance to punish him?

Please.

"Is she awake?"

Leander's voice is like nails on a chalkboard. The hairs on my forearms rise.

This is the man who killed my father.

Fucking hell.

I want to thrash and squirm and break out of my restraints so I can tear his throat out with my teeth. But I know it's no use.

I'll only give away my sole advantage.

"Doesn't look like it, sir," the deep voice beside me says.

"Call the doctor, then. I want her awake."

The fear I spotted in his face has leaked into his words. His voice is shaky with a barely contained concern.

I need to know what he's so worried about. Is it that Tytus is still alive?

... Or is it that Rian already knows about what's happened?

My clenched heart flutters.

"Yes, sir."

A radio crackles as the deep voice follows Leander's orders. I try to hold back my sneer and steady my broken heart.

Someone might be coming to save me. But right now, I'm on my own.

"Wake up, my beautiful bride," Leander's hot breath sends a cold shiver up my spine. I can feel him leering over me. I can sense the heat hiding just beneath his pants. He's placed his crotch in my face. I should make him pay for it.

"The doctor is on his way."

"Good," Leander says. Crouching down, he brushes the back of his hand against my cheek.

"But maybe we won't need him quite yet. I'm sure I could wake my sleeping princess with a simple kiss."

Just try it, you bastard.

It takes all my self-control to keep from lashing out as I feel him getting closer.

The sickly-sweet stench of his cologne fills my nostrils. He places a hand on my thigh. His cold fingers run up my leg. His lips get dangerously close to mine.

I've had enough.

Ripping my eyes open, I cock back my neck and slam my forehead directly into his nose.

A gut-wrenching crunch follows. Leander squeals like a pig. His hand tears off my thigh as he falls to his knees.

I pull back for another crack. But before I can lunge forward again, someone catches a fistful of my hair.

I'm tugged backward. My chair tips, and I start to fall with it.

Then, suddenly, I'm stopped.

"I thought I told you not to touch her?"

Leander's voice is wet with blood.

Looking down, I see that he's grabbed one of my chair legs. His hand wraps around the ornamental wood, just beneath my restrained foot.

"I'm sorry, sir," that deep voice says from behind me. "It's just that—"

"I don't want to hear it," Leander interrupts. "If you assholes were any good at following orders, then maybe this bitch's brother wouldn't have killed so many of you."

Pulling out a handkerchief from his breast pocket, he tries to wipe up the blood spilling from his nose.

"He'll pay for that," a voice growls.

My eyebrows perk up. My heart jumps.

Tytus is alive. He must be.

They're talking about him like he escaped.

Leander must see me come to that realization, because with a shaky grunt, he pushes himself to his feet and turns to the reckless voice.

"You idiot," he gurgles. "Now she knows her stupid brother is still out there. That's a piece of information I could have used to get something from her. Don't you know how any of this works? Fucking hell. All of you, leave. Now!"

A disgruntled grumble passes over the room before the armed men finally decide an argument with Leander isn't worth their time.

"Do you really think you're safe in here with me alone?" I ask, finally letting a sneer twist my lips.

Leander spits a glob of blood onto the thick carpet.

"I'm not worried," he huffs. Turning his back on me, he watches his men file out. "You aren't going anywhere. And we better both get used to it. If all goes as planned, you'll be stuck to me for the rest of your life."

"Sounds like a nightmare," I hiss back.

That makes Leander chuckle.

Wiping away some more blood, he walks to the door and clicks it shut.

"You have no idea how true that is," he smirks, turning back to face me. His crystal white teeth are stained with blood. "Your nightmare is just beginning."

"I can't imagine anything worse than being stuck in here with you."

"You have a better imagination than that. Don't you, kitten?"

"Untie me and find out just how imaginative I can get with turning you into a corpse," I snarl, trying to ignore how much the word kitten reminds me of Rian.

My heart pumps full of blood as I remember how we left each other at dinner. Fuck. It was a mistake to leave. I was being stubborn.

I need to see him again. I need to feel his warmth.

The desire is unexpectedly emotional.

"Are you hitting on me?" Leander smirks.

"I'll start hitting you, alright."

I want to smirk right back at the monster, laugh at his broken nose. But I can't bring myself to find any joy in this situation, no matter how small.

All I can think of is how much I want to see Rian again. All I can see is Drago's head exploding before my very eyes. All I can feel is the hopelessness of watching Tytus fight for his life alone.

No matter what happens here, Drago will still be gone. The connection we were mending will stay severed. That part of me will remain empty.

He'll join Willow at the pit in my stomach. One of the

ghosts from my past that appears when I'm at my lowest. A memory that can still make me feel pain, but I can never touch.

Will I ever feel whole again?

"No," Leander says. Shaking his head, he wipes away the last bits of blood from his upper lip. "You're never going to hit anybody ever again. I'm about to make sure of that."

"What the fuck is that supposed to mean?" I rasp, holding back a soft sob.

I hate feeling sad. So, I do my best to replace that sorrow with rage.

Curling my fingers into fists, I finally test the resolve of my restraints. They're fucking tight.

"It means I'm glad you're finally up, because I want you to be awake for every insufferable, horrifying moment of what I have in store for you."

"I've been up for a fucking hour already," I bark, gesturing to the dark window on the wall. "I've been watching your reflection. I saw how scared you were. You aren't made for this world. You fucking coward. Leave before I make you pay for trespassing on my turf."

For a second, it looks like Leander short-circuits. But then something snaps in him, and a cold fire flickers up behind his pale blue eyes.

"You stupid fucking bitch," he curses. With the backside of his bejeweled hand, he slaps me across the face.

It's stronger than I expected.

The moment I taste blood on my tongue, I start pulling on my restraints again. It doesn't matter that I won't get out. I just want to fucking explode.

He's not allowed to touch me.

"You piece of shit," I snap. "I'm going to make you pay for that."

"No. You're not. You're not doing anything ever again. Not

without my direct involvement. Oh god, I'm going to make you suffer so horribly…"

The hate in his voice is so vicious I almost flinch. Where the hell is this coming from?

"What the fuck is wrong with you?" I croak. "Huh? What the fuck did I ever do to you?"

Leander doesn't hesitate to answer.

"You rejected me," he barks, his voice cracking. "No one rejects me. No one chooses another man over me."

The fire raging behind my chest fizzles when I realize he's talking about Rian.

An empty hole appears in place of the flames.

I miss him already.

Fuck.

"I was never going to choose a loser like you," I tell him. But even if it's the truth, there's no power in my claim. I can't even look at Leander. My eyelids feel heavy as my gaze drops to the floor.

Rian.

"And it cost you dearly."

With all my strength, I try to force Rian from my mind. Whatever we have, it will be worthless if I don't get out of here alive.

"What does that mean?" I ask, forcing my glare back up to Leander. His lifeless blue eyes are a pale imitation of my lion's ocean blue gaze.

"Your father is dead," Leander callously reminds me. "Your brother probably is too. My men think he might still be alive, but I saw the wounds he escaped with. No one is surviving that."

The empty hole in my chest grows larger.

Tytus is hurt.

Fucking hell. He's not coming to rescue me. If anything, I should be going to save him.

But how am I going to do that?

Clenching my fists, I try to brute force my way out of this stupid fucking chair one more time. I'm not strong enough.

My mind drifts back to Rian.

Fuck.

He's my only hope.

Never in my life have I even thought about relying on anyone outside of the small dark little circle I was forced into as a child.

Now, I have no choice.

The empty hole in my chest starts to throb.

Why the hell does that excite me so much?

"You weren't going to kill Drago before I rejected you?" I ask, trying to focus on something else.

I don't need anybody, I chant to myself. *I don't need anybody.*

But that doesn't mean I don't *want* Rian.

Fuck. I want him so fucking badly—and I don't even hate that I do. Not anymore.

"No. I was," Leander chuckles, like he's reliving a moment in his master plan. "But only because he cared about you too much. He would have never let me do any of this to you."

Two weeks ago, I would have laughed directly in Leander's face. *Drago doesn't give a shit about what anyone does to me*, I would have said. *As long as he gets what he wants he's happy.*

But that's not what I think anymore. Tytus was right. Drago had changed. He actually cared about me.

And Leander killed him for it.

"What are you going to do to me?" I rumble, involuntary tears welling back up in my eyes. "Spit it out already!"

Tucking his handkerchief away, Leander turns and walks towards the window. With a quick tug, he lifts the blinds, revealing the waking world outside.

The bottom half of the window is still black, but the first bits of dawn are starting to peek over a silhouetted treeline.

"Maybe I should tell you," Leander thinks out loud. "Maybe that will make it even worse."

"Either start explaining or shut the fuck up."

I'm so sick of the fucker's voice. I'm so tired of his tough guy act. I wish he'd remember whatever was scaring him early. I want to see him shaking in his boots again.

"Fine," Leander shrugs. "Have it your way." Staring out the window, he presses two fingers against his temple and starts. "My ancestors were criminals," he explains. "All of them. Hundreds of years ago, they formed some of the first mafia families in Greece. The Onasis clan wasn't exactly the biggest of them all, but we had our fun. For hundreds of years we had our fun... until my *father* decided that fun was too dangerous..."

The vitriol in Leander's voice when he mention's his father is nearly strong enough to crack the window.

"That doesn't explain shit," I sneer.

Turning from the view outside, Leander's pale blue eyes fall back onto me. There's a heaviness in his gaze that weighs down his eyelids.

"Each Greek mafia family had their own unique traditions," he notes, ignoring me. "My favorite was how a certain clan would take care of their unwilling brides."

"With sunshine and rainbows," I snidely guess.

"With fire and a hacksaw," Leander smirks.

He takes a step forward and I shake at my restraints.

"Back off," I warn him.

Leander doesn't seem to hear me. He's lost in a past he never lived.

"It wasn't uncommon for the leaders of Greek families to take unwilling wives. Often, they'd grab a woman from a rival family to claim. But Greeks breed fiery women, and keeping such a prize in good shape was risky. So, this is what they'd do: First, they'd tie their unwilling bride down onto a bed... or a chair. Then, they'd bring in a doctor. The doctor would provide the hacksaw and the fire, as well as a little morphine to keep the subject from dying of heart failure before the procedure was completed. In a perfect world, I'd do everything myself. But with something like this, there's a fine line between success and failure. The subject needs just the right amount of morphine to be kept awake. More than that, and you might fall asleep. A little more, and that nap might last forever. The process requires an expert."

"What the fuck are you on about?" I rasp, my throat getting dry. Dread has started to curl around my neck. I know where this is going.

"Sometimes, they'd put a gag in the lady's mouth. But I won't do that. I want to hear you scream as your limbs are chopped off."

A deep primal shot of fear shivers through me.

"You fucking maniac… " I croak, still desperately trying to get out of my restraints.

"My father squandered our underworld connections for the sake of going legitimate," Leander says, hardly listening to me. "It made life boring. I don't like boring. I want to go back to my roots. I want to be a villain. I want to be evil. I want to be irredeemable."

"You don't have the guts," I bark.

He steps closer to me.

"You're about to see how wrong you are," he says. "You're about to feel it. I'll bathe in your screams. And when your stumps are cauterized and your tongue is cut out and your teeth are pulled, I won't even have to tie you down. I'll just take you whenever I want. I'll fill you up with my cock until you're bloody. I'll drench you in my seed until you're big and swollen. Then I'll take the child and do it all over again, and again, and again…"

Fear grips me like a frigid hand. My limbs go limp. I stop

trying to break from my restraints. Leander takes advantage of my lapse.

Lunging forward, he grabs me by the jaw.

"Fuck off," I grumble, trying to pry myself out of his grip as he squeezes my lips closed.

"Do you know what my name means?" Leander whispers, shoving his face into mine.

"Coward," I squeak out through my shut lips.

"It means 'lion man'. Isn't that nice? I can be your lion, kitten. And believe me, I'm so much more fearsome than that fool you've fallen for."

Before I can respond, Leander forces a rancid kiss onto my captive lips.

I nearly gag.

"A lion would never be as scared as you are right now," I spit when Leander finally releases me.

But I'm not just talking about any lion. Only one matters.

Rian.

My lion.

"Who says I'm scared?" Leander tsks.

"You're pale as a ghost," I point out, trying to distract from my own paleness. All the heat has been drained from my body.

I didn't think Leander even had it in him to imagine such depraved cruelty. But he keeps on shocking me in the worst way possible.

"I'm just tired," he mumbles in response. Pushing himself back, he leans over to catch his reflection in the window. The vain fucker. "it's been a busy week."

"No. You're scared," I keep pushing, afraid of what will happen if I give him a chance to breathe. "You're worried you aren't as evil as you want to be."

"No. Idiot girl. That's not it," Leander sneers, looking back at me.

"What is it then?"

"None of your fucking business."

"... Maybe I can help."

By now, I'm just buying time—anything to save myself from the horrid fate he just described.

It doesn't sound like there's any chance Tytus is going to come to my rescue.

But that doesn't mean Rian won't.

Still, doubt invades my mind.

How will he know where I am? How will he even know what's happened?

A knot forms in my gut as I realize what's going to have to happen.

Shit.

Rian is going to have to find Tytus, or Tytus is going to have to find him. They're going to have to find a way to work together. That's my only hope.

Fuck.

How the hell is that going to work?

The knot in my gut tightens... before being crushed by a heavy warmth.

They'll make it work.

They both care about me. They'll do whatever it takes. I believe it. I know it.

I just have to hold out long enough for them to make it here.

"How could you possibly help me?" Leander asks. "By lunchtime, you won't be able to walk or eat or talk without my help. You don't—"

"You can take every last one of my limbs, and I'll still have a hundred times more experience than you in this twisted world," I sneer.

Leander's icy gaze drifts up and down my body. I can see him considering my proposal.

Fool.

"An experiment of mine has broken free," he eventually admits. "It's dangerous and unhinged… and it's not happy that I killed its father."

At first, the words pass over me like a gentle breeze. I don't understand what he's saying, or the importance of it.

But I can practically feel the gears turning in the back of my mind. Something deep inside my brain is desperately trying to connect the dots. My hackles rise, and a primal instinct screams up from the darkness.

You know what he's talking about.

Then, suddenly, it clicks.

My jaw drops.

"… Krol," I whisper.

Leander purses his lips.

He's about to say something when a knock comes at the door, interrupting him.

"Don't move," he taunts, turning to answer.

Dread threatens to drown me when I see who's in the doorway.

A pale bald man in a white lab coat. He's carrying a big black briefcase by his side.

It's a fucking doctor.

The numb fear evaporates from my limbs. I begin to shake and rattle and pull at my restraints.

They don't budge.

"Over there," Leander nods, gesturing to a small table at the far side of the room. The doctor nods and shambles towards it.

"You're making a big fucking mistake," I screech, my voice like broken glass.

Leander just shrugs. "So what if I am. If I lose you, I'll just go after some other mafia bitch."

"You won't ever get my army!" I heave.

"Stupid girl, I know there's no army. I'm just doing this for the thrill."

My racing heart twists into a knot as Leander makes his way over to the table. The doctor is already getting set up.

"Tytus won't let you," I shout after him. "Rian won't let you. I won't let you. You may have killed Drago, but that won't save you from their wrath."

"You don't have a choice in the matter," Leander responds. "And Tytus is likely already dead. Rian... well, if he's taken my bait. He should be meeting his end soon enough—if he hasn't already."

My twisted heart drops into the abyss.

"You don't fucking touch him!" I yell.

A new wave of terrible energy comes over me, but even with the fresh strength, I can't break out of my restraints.

"I'll do whatever I want," Leander snidely remarks.

No. I can't lose Rian. I won't.

I've already lost too much. Gabriel. Drago. Now, it looks like Tytus might not make it either.

It's like there's a sharp seesaw cutting through my heart. Every time I find something to latch onto, something warm and hopeful, the other end comes down and a new wound opens up.

Gaining love only gives you something more to lose. No matter how hard I've been trying to deny it, Rian has given me that something to lose.

He's given me love.

Fuck.

Why don't I hate him for that?

"You fucking leave him alone!" I cry, tears welling up in my eyes.

Leander ignores me. Walking up behind the doctor, he stares down into the now open suitcase.

I can't see what's inside. But I can imagine.

"Boss!"

For a split second, not even one of Leander's guard's barging into the bedroom can rip his attention away from whatever's in the doctor's suitcase.

When he does eventually look back over his shoulder, it's with an annoyed reluctance.

"What?"

"We have company."

My fallen heart freezes into place.

Leander's entire face contorts in disgust.

"Who!?"

That finally tears him away from the table, and I'm given a brief glimpse of what's inside the briefcase.

I don't see much, except for the tip of a long syringe...

"I don't know, sir. It looks like they're—"

"What do you mean you don't know!" Leander's roar draws my attention away from the doctor's morbid lab.

I see the guard who came barging in. He's holding out a tablet. Leander rips it from his hands.

"I've never seen this person before," the guard mumbles, stepping back.

Staring down at the screen, Leander starts to pace back and forth. I stretch my neck, trying to get a good look. But it's impossible.

"How the fuck did they find us?" Leander grumbles, furious.

"It's Rian, isn't it," I rasp, desperate to know.

"No," Leander instinctively sneers. "It's not your precious lion."

"... Tytus?"

"It's not your dead brother either."

"Then who is it?" I quietly ask.

With a blue fire burning in his cold eyes, Leander rips his gaze off the screen and turns it onto me.

Without another word, he storms forward and shoves the tablet in my face.

"You tell me."

31

RIAN

"Why did I agree to this again?"

From the drone footage on my phone, I can't see the look on Deacon's face, but I can imagine it.

"Agree to what?" Tytus grunts. The beast of a man is lagging behind. His injuries are severe. But he wouldn't let me come here alone, no matter how much I insisted on it. "You're the one who volunteered to be bait."

"I can be an idiot sometimes," Deacon mumbles. "Shit. Here they come."

Planting my back against a thick tree trunk, I zoom in on the screen. Sure enough, a wall of soldiers has exited Leander's secluded mansion. They've got their guns drawn and pointed towards Deacon.

"Don't make any sudden movements," I warm him.

"I wouldn't dream of it."

"Give that to me," Tytus says. Reaching out an unsteady hand, he gestures for my phone.

I hesitate to give it to him.

He's still my enemy, after all—that isn't going to change just because we both care about Roz.

"Why?" I ask, wondering if he has the same technological gifts as Rozalia.

"Because I want to feel useful," he coughs. "And I don't know how many of those fuckers I'm going to be able to kill while I'm like this."

"You put up a pretty good fight against me."

"I'm still recovering from that," Tytus grimaces.

He grabs his abdomen and leans against the trunk beside me.

"Fine," I huff, handing him my phone. "Be our eyes in the sky. I'll contact the troops."

"Thank you."

Turning away, I press a finger into my earpiece and look through the trees ahead. The first bits of morning sunlight are starting to light up the property, but the forest surrounding it is still draped in darkness. It provides the perfect cover.

I pull out my radio.

"Maksim, do you copy?"

A rush of static hisses over the airwaves until my uncle's voice appears.

"I hear you, loud and clear. Everyone's set up. Wish I was there to help."

"You are helping," I assure him. "How is Mel?"

"She seems alright. We're in her studio now. I've got one eye on her and one eye on the escape hatch, just in case."

"Hopefully it won't come to that."

"Hopefully."

Pushing myself off the trunk, I check each of the four pistols I have holstered around my body. Each one is locked and loaded. I'm ready for action. My ammo is hot. My pulse is calm and steady.

My focus is clear.

Staring out into the clearing ahead, I glare down Leander's tacky mansion.

Rozalia is in there.

I'll do whatever it takes to get her out.

Glancing back over my shoulder, I see that Tytus has slid down the trunk of his tree. He's bleeding again.

"You stay here," I tell him. "I'll take care of Leander and Roz."

"No," he mumbles. "I can help."

But when he tries to stand up again, his knees give out on him.

Fuck. It's like staring at a wounded bear.

"You'll just get in my way," I tell him, holstering my gun.

"I'll get in the way of you dying," he huffs. A small coughing fit follows.

I roll my eyes. "Are you really trying to convince me that if it came down to it, you'd try to save my life?"

"Hardly," Tytus replies, slapping his own cheek to wake himself up. "I'm just pointing out the obvious. The more targets those bastards have to shoot at, the less likely they'll be shooting at you."

I just shake my head.

"You should have let me take you to the hospital," I grumble.

"Why? So you could chain me to a bed? I'm not my sister. Caging me isn't going to make me fall in love with you."

His words shatter my focus.

"That's not why she fell in love with me," I mindlessly bark, not even bothering to deny the obvious anymore—no matter how intense the truth is. "

"Ah, so you think she's in love with you, too..." he chuckles, sliding back down onto his ass. "That makes four of us."

"Four?"

"Me. Leander. Drago, and you. We all see it."

"That's some shit company."

"It will get a whole lot shittier if I don't come in there with you," Tytus coughs. "Unless you want to end up like Drago…"

His voice drops as it trails off. A spark of sadness undercuts his words.

"is Drago in there?" I ask, pointing through the trees towards the mansion.

"No. Drago's dead," Tytus sighs.

"Good riddance."

"You wouldn't be saying that if you really cared about Roz," for the first time since we got here, Tytus allows his chin to drop to his chest.

"Shows what you know. She hates him."

"She *hated* him. Past tense. They were fixing their problems. By now, their scars could have healed… if only Leander hadn't stabbed Drago in the back." A shiver runs through my chest when Tytus' voice breaks. "Fuck. It was my fault. I didn't see it coming. I thought controlling the Greek mafia was enough to ensure our safety. But I forgot that mercenaries only care about money. And Leander has so much more money than I do… But not for long."

My focus splinters further at all of Tytus' confessions. But one thing in particular latches onto my reeling mind—even more so than Rozalia's ever-changing relationship with her adoptive father.

"You control the Greek mafia now?"

To my surprise, Tytus laughs. That costs him. Another coughing fit grips his shattered body. It doesn't last long, though, and when it's done, he looks up at me, his silver-blue eyes sparkling in the growing light.

"We're going to lose our cover," he grunts, not even bothering to stand up anymore. "Start the attack. Save Roz. I'll do what I can to help from here."

I hesitate to agree. He's clearly trying to divert attention away from what he just accidentally revealed.

But I've already wasted enough time standing here chatting with him. Taking a long step towards the fallen beast, I gesture for him to return my phone.

He sighs, then reluctantly gives it up.

"I'm giving you control over the drone," I explain, locking every program on my phone but one. "You can drop smoke bombs by tapping here. There aren't many. Choose your timing wisely."

When I hand the phone back to Tytus, a wry smile comes over his bloody lips.

"Smoke bombs..." he nods. "I love a good smoke bomb."

Without responding, I turn back around.

Through the trees, I can see movement. Leander's men are taking our bait. The guards standing watch by the side door have already started to wander to the front, towards Deacon.

They don't know what's going on.

Idiots.

Lifting my radio back up to my mouth, I press down on the push-to-talk button.

"Maksim?"

"Yes, boss?"

"Everyone's in position?"

"That's right."

"Tune them into my signal. I'm ready to give the order."

Static cracks and pops as Maksim gets to work.

"Done," he quickly replies. "Everyone is listening."

Taking a deep breath, I stare ahead and think of Roz.

I want to hold her again. Feel her. Hear her. Smell her.

I'll do anything to get her back.

"Team One, save Deacon's ass. Team two, wait for my word."

I've hardly even started running when I hear the first gunshot go off. It crackles through the crisp morning air like a splintering tree. A dozen more follow in its wake.

Then, just like that, chaos erupts.

I'm already pushing out of the trees and towards the now unguarded side door when I hear Deacon hollering in my earpiece.

"Come get some!" he shouts. When he starts shooting, I click my earpiece off.

"Maniac," I mumble to myself, jimmying the locked door.

It comes open easily enough. An alarm bell follows. But I was expecting that. Reaching into my pocket, I pull out a little black ball and throw it directly above my head. When it hits the ceiling, a flash of red-light bursts from its seams, spreading in all directions until the alarm goes out.

The lights turn off.

Perfect.

"Now, where are you, angel."

Planting a finger on my temple, I play with my earpiece until it connects with my phone.

"Tytus?" I ask, hoping he can hear me.

"Did you find her?" he asks, hope cutting through his drooping voice.

"Not yet. I need your help. There should be a button on the lower left screen of my phone. A blue rectangle. Do you see it?"

"Yeah."

"Click on it. It should bring up the drone's thermal camera."

"Okay, I clicked on it, but I can't see shit."

"That's because it's too high up," I explain. "But now that everyone is distracted you can fly it lower. Do that until you can see inside, then lead me towards Rozalia."

"On it."

As Tytus figures out the controls, I start to make my way through the darkness. Outside I can hear the roar of a battle raging on. I decide to give my men some relief.

Grabbing my radio, I give the rest of my soldiers the go-ahead. "Team Two. Team Three. Team Four. Annihilate."

A split second later, the muffled roar outside gets louder.

Upstairs, I can hear hurried footsteps rush through the halls. Men shout. I find my way to the nearest set of stairs.

"Ah, there we go," Tytus mumbles into my earpiece. "Now, where the hell are you, Roz?"

I wait at the top of the dark stairwell, ear pressed against the door as I wait for Tytus to find her.

"Look for a red blob that's not moving," I whisper, trying to help. "If Leander has any brains, he'll have tied her up."

"Oh, just wait until she hears you called her a blob," he chuckles, weakly.

"Snitch," I quietly bite back.

"Hey, you should be thankful I don't—oh shit, is that her?"

My heart kicks.

"Where?" I growl, immediately dialed back into the hunt.

"Hmm. I'm not used to this thermal imaging shit, but if I'm seeing this correctly, it looks like she's in a room at the far end of the hall on the top floor. That's the only red blob that isn't moving."

"Is she alone?"

"No," Tytus coughs. "There are three other blobs in the room. They're pacing back and forth. It looks like there are at least a dozen in the hallway outside, too. And two dozen more on the way there."

"I'll take care of them all," I sneer. "Just lead the way."

Their blood will be my reunion gift to Rozalia. That and a kiss. A kiss that says what I was too cowardly to admit, even to myself.

I love that fucking girl.

"Wave for me," Tytus says. "I need to know where you are."

Putting my radio away, I pull out the first of my four guns and swing it in the air.

"Can you see me?"

"Ah, there you are," Tytus mumbles. "You're going to want

to make a sharp right. But watch out, there's a group of four blobs barreling down the connecting hallway."

"I'll paint the walls red with their blood."

"Do it then."

Bursting out in the hallway, I make that sharp right. It leads me down a long open hallway. Up ahead, I can hear approaching voices. I slide up against the wall, just before the hallway turns down a corner.

The few seconds it takes for them to catch up feels like an eternity. But the second I see that first pale face, I go blind with rage.

Three quick shots rip from my muzzle. Three bodies hit the floor. The fourth one gets a shot off at me before I can get to him. But the bullet races harmlessly over my head.

"Big mistake," I growl. Lunging forward, I manage to land a single shot in his gut, right before my shoulder digs into his chest.

A rush of blood spills from his mouth as I tackle the fucker to the ground. I don't stick around for a wrestling match. Pushing myself off his convulsing body, I aim my gun down and fire.

Chunks of skull and brain matter splatter against my pant legs. I trudge forward.

"It looks like there's a set of stairs just up ahead. To your left," Tytus points out.

I find them quickly enough.

"Any surprises up there?"

"Oh, a whole lot. You're going to have to go up against a mini-battalion. Bet you're going to wish I was there."

"I'd rather keep working like this," I grunt. Cracking my neck to the side, I get ready to put my life on the line.

I'm not scared.

But I am nervous.

I'm not allowed to die. Not until I've felt Rozalia again. Not until she's heard that four-letter word come rushing from my mouth.

"If I were you, I'd go now," Tytus suggests. "They all seem to be turned to a window. My guess is that they're trying to help their buddies outside."

"How is that battle going, by the way?" I ask, starting up the stairs.

"It's hard to tell," Tytus notes. "All I see are a bunch of red blobs."

"I guess so," I grunt. Lowering my voice, I reach the top of the stairs. Behind a closed door, I hear muffled gunshots. Snipers, it sounds like. That's good news. They'll be slow and distracted.

"Left or right?" I ask.

"Right."

"How many men?"

"Six in this section. But the second you start shooting, six more will come running from the west."

"I like those odds."

I'm so close to Rozalia I can almost smell her. Nothing will stand in my way.

"Good luck," Tytus says.

With that, I click open the door and jump into the chaos.

Sure, enough, six snipers are set up along a stretch of open windows. I pick the first two off before any of them even realize I'm here. The third falls shortly after that. But I have to duck back behind the doorway when the last man in line manages to pull out a pistol.

"Fuck," I curse.

A hail of bullets rip into the wall where I just stood. When the barrage pauses, I hear shouts and footsteps coming from the other direction.

Shit. That means I'm up against nine soldiers now.

"Need a smoke bomb?" Tytus offers.

Before I can answer, a gun-wielding arm foolishly reaches around the corner. I immediately grab onto the wrist and plow a fist into the back of his elbow. A howl cuts through the gunfire as his bones snap in half.

Before he can finish crying out, I pull the fucker into the darkness and put a bullet in his head.

"Yeah, now would be a good time for a fucking smoke bomb," I grunt, stepping back a few more steps.

"Way ahead of you."

In the blink of an eye, a flashbang erupts on the other side of the wall. Shouts fill the air as the first bits of smoke seep through the doorway.

"Nice shot," I admit.

"I've only got three more," Tytus reminds me.

"Hopefully, that's all we need."

After a quick reload, I jump back out into the room. The smoke is thick, but I can still make out the confused silhouettes stumbling around. I sneak up behind the first fucker and snap his neck.

He falls, and I move on to the next.

It's not until I get to my fourth victim that the rest of them catch on. A new flurry of gunshots rip through the smoky air. I don't snap the fourth fucker's neck. Instead, I fling him around, using his body as a human shield.

It works, but the force of the barrage is still enough to send me flying back against the wall.

"Five more," Tytus tells.

"I know," I spit, wiping blood from my lips. "Left or right?" I ask. Lifting my gun into the air, I wave it.

"Left," Tytus quickly reacts.

In response, I lower my gun and fire an entire round ahead. In response, I hear a chorus of grunts, and at least one thump as a body hits the ground.

I drop to the floor right alongside it. A second later, a stream of bullets rip over my head.

I roll away beneath them until I hit another wall.

"Right," Tytus shouts.

I empty the rest of my clip into the fog.

"How many are left?" I heave, tossing aside my empty gun for a new one.

"You got them all," Tytus says. "Good job."

"The job's not finished yet. Tell me where to go."

"Oh shit!" Tytus curses, his weak voice crackling against the strain. "They're on the move. Someone is dragging Rozalia away."

"Where. Do. I. Go?" I growl.

"It looks like they're heading up to the third floor. Push ahead. Straight ahead. I'll shoot another smoke bomb in there. Don't bother fighting. Just get to them. Get Roz."

I don't need to be told twice.

Pushing myself back onto my feet, I start to race forward. Behind me, a window shatters. Another flashbang erupts into the room. I stumble, but manage to keep my feet.

The fog thickens until I can barely even see the countless silhouettes storming toward me. Jumping against the wall, I hold my breath and let them pass.

To my relief, they all do.

I have to cough into my forearm as I peel myself off the wall and continue forward.

"When you pass through the next doorway, take a right."

"What doorway?" I wheeze. "I can't see shit."

"Just hug the wall."

That's exactly what I do until I feel a door-latch. When my fingers brush across the cool metal, I make my right turn.

"How many people are with Roz?" I ask, feeling for another door latch or opening.

"Just three others. One of them is Leander, I'm sure of it."

I don't ask how Tytus knows. The second I feel an opening

in the wall, I burst through it and up the stairs.

"Am I going the right way?" I ask.

"Yeah, they should be—wait, stop!"

Before I can heed his warning, I'm blindsided by a fist. It hits me directly in the temple, nearly knocking me back down the stairs.

"What the fuck…" I curse, stumbling into a wall. Pain throbs through my skull. I try to turn around. But before I can do that, a bullet rips through my shoulder. Then, another one slices across my calve.

An excruciating heat rips through my body as I fall to my knees.

"Rian!"

Rozalia's voice cuts through the agonizing pain like a scythe. My aching heart jumps. But when I force my gaze up to search for her, I'm only met by the barrel of a gun.

The cold steel presses into the skin between my eyes.

"Say goodnight."

32

ROZALIA

"What the hell do you think you're doing?" Leander snaps.

The needle he has pressed against my throat digs into my skin as he seethes behind me. I hold my breath. Anything to keep that morphine from seeping into my veins, from making me useless.

Rian is in trouble.

I need to help.

Outside, I can hear a battle raging. It rattles the windows like an earthquake.

"I'm putting an end to this fucker," the guard sneers. "Once and for all." He wants to pull the trigger so badly.

But he's just a lackey. A servant. And he won't do anything unless his master tells him to.

"He's mine to kill," Leander spits. His hand is shaking. I can't tell if it's from rage or fear.

It doesn't matter anymore.

My heart is ready to implode.

"... Rian..."

He's been shot. Twice. It doesn't look like his wounds are fatal, but if someone doesn't stop the bleeding, then that's not going to do him much good. He'll bleed out on the floor in front of me.

Then, I'll be alone again.

I don't want to be alone again.

"Does that mean you're going to let the girl go?" the guard asks. The snide remark gives me hope that I might be able to pit the two men against each other.

Anything to get closer to Rian.

Anything to save him.

I just want to see those ocean blue eyes again. They're trained forward, fixed on the barrel pinning him to the ground.

I can see him waiting for an opening. He's shaking with anticipation. He wants to look at me too. I can feel it.

"I... I..." Leander stutters, stumbling over his own thoughts. I want to send my heel into his crotch and my teeth into his hand, but I can't risk it.

One prick from this oversized needle and I'm done for. I'll be a slobbering mess until it's too late to do anything. The doctor said so himself.

That fucking doctor.

Out of the corner of my eye, I can see him cowering in the corner. He looks like a scared child, when just minutes ago, he was ready to tear me from limb to limb.

Pitiful.

"Fucking speak," the guard curses at Leander. "Make up your mind or I'll make it for you."

"How dare you speak to me like—"

Before Leander can finish, Rian takes advantage of the distraction. With a roar that shakes the room, my lion grits through his pain and grabs onto the guard's gun.

My heart jumps.

... Then plummets into the abyss.

A shot fires from the threatening muzzle.

"No!" I scream tears, watching in horror as Rian is flung

back against the wall. A burst of blood splatters against the white paint.

My whole world collapses. But when he lifts his hand, a sliver of hope slices through it all.

Rian hasn't been shot in the skull. His palm took the brunt of the bullet. For a moment, we both just stare at the wound in disbelief.

Then, he looks over at me.

Those ocean blue eyes sparkle with a wild furry, and an endless passion.

My fallen heart perks back up.

Kill him, I silently plead.

Rian's blood-red lips twist into a snarl.

Tearing his gaze from me, he pushes himself off the wall and lunges at the guard. The fucker doesn't even get another shot off before my lion's big broad shoulder dig into his gut. The two men go flying to the floor.

I follow Rian's lead.

Lifting my tied ankles off the ground, I gather as much momentum as possible. Then I throw my heels back into Leander's limp dick.

I make direct contact.

"You bitch…" he grunts, crumpling behind me.

But he doesn't let go. And before I can bite down on his hand, I feel the tip of his sharp needle break the skin on my throat.

"Fuck!" I cry out.

Almost immediately, I feel a heavy warmth fill my veins.

"Rozalia!"

Rian's voice cuts through the thick heat.

My vision flickers. When I look over at him, I see that he's gotten on top of the guard. But he's not looking down at his victim. Those ocean blue eyes stare at me, endlessly gorgeous.

For a moment, everything slows.

I can picture all that we've been through together. I can feel all that we've done. I can imagine all that's still to come.

Then, just like that, the moment is over.

The guard plummets a fist down into Rian's injured hand, then chops at his forearm. It sends my lion falling to the ground. The guard jumps to his feet and scrambles for his gun.

A heavy dread joins the warmth weighing me down. I want to help so badly, but it feels like I'm back beneath those black waves, drowning.

"... Rian..." I whisper, calling on the last bits of my strength.

His name floats from my lips like a soft summer breeze. It's the last thing I say before I feel my soul leave my body.

I watch as Rian crawls through his own blood, trying to catch up to the guard before he can reach his gun.

He fails.

"You're dead," the mercenary growls, pointing that bloody barrel back down at my man.

Before he can pull the trigger, though, I hear a loud click. The jarring sound sucks my soul back into my body. The needle is dropped from my throat. A gun is lifted in its place.

"He's not yours to kill!" Leander shouts, pointing his pistol at his own guard.

"Are you fucking crazy?" the mercenary barks back.

"There can only be one lion in the underworld," Leander snaps. "And that's me..."

"You aren't paying me enough for this shit," the guard grunts. His gun straightens.

Leander does the same. My head is too heavy to think straight, but I don't need to think. I just react.

Calling on whatever strength I have left, I pry my tired mouth open and gnash down on Leander's forearm.

"You fucking bitch!" he cries, dropping his gun.

When he jumps backward, I fall to the ground. My temple smacks against the carpet. I don't feel any pain.

But I do hear one last gunshot.

It rips through the room like thunder.

A body hits the floor. I can't tell where.

My vision blurs. But ahead, I can see smoke billowing from the guard's gun. I blink. My vision blurs further.

Where's Rian?

I just want to see my lion. One last time.

Not even the warmth of the morphine can rival the warmth he's made me feel. My mind wanders. I see the soft lights at La Forcina. I feel his intense gaze. I sink into his passionate kiss.

My hazy mind flips back the pages. I see it all. I feel it all. The hate. The admiration. The crush. The disgust. The sex.

I remember the butterflies I tried to ignore the first time I saw him in person, back in that little throne room.

I remember how he played with me.

Rian Kilpatrick wasn't fooled by the hologram. But he let me go anyway. Because he wanted to chase me. And I didn't run because I wanted to lose him. I ran because I wanted to feel like I was worth chasing.

He made me feel that ten times over. He made me feel worth the pain and the anguish.

He made me feel worthy of love.

My lion.

"... Rian..."

I whisper out into the growing void.

"... Roz..."

His voice is raspy and distant. But it's unmistakable.

The morphine flickers. An easy bliss lightens my heavy load.

For a moment, I can see again. Through my blurred vision, I watch as a massive figure drags himself off the bloody floor.

The mercenary who just shot Leander stares blankly ahead, stunned. Rian plunges his shoulder into his abdomen. The gun drops from the man's hand. A roar fills the room.

The two giant figures barrel towards me. I try to cry out, but nothing escapes my lips.

A heel catches against my thigh. The force flips me around. For a moment, all I can see is Leander's pale face. Then, a body falls over his corpse, tumbling into the window behind us. The glass shatters. The body disappears.

A howl grows and then fades as the chaos outside seeps into the room.

I hardly even react. I can't. My body is growing numb. My mind is heavy. My gaze drops back onto Leander.

The dead Greek billionaire lays on the ground next to me. His pale blue eyes have rolled into the back of his head. There's a bullet wound in the center of his skull. Blood pools below his cheek.

I try not to look. Leander's dead body is the last thing I want to see before I slip into the abyss. But I don't have the strength to look for Rian. I barely even have the strength to hope he wasn't the one who just fell out of the window.

"... Rian..."

Suddenly, a heavy body drops to the floor, right between Leander and me. It hits the ground with a thud. My empty chest stirs.

At first, I only get to see the back of his head. But that wild dirty blond hair is unmistakable. When he rolls around, the air is stolen from my lungs.

Those ocean blue eyes wipe away the fear. They eat up the dread. They spit out my sadness.

It doesn't matter that they're just as glossy as mine. They're still moving. We're both still moving.

For now, we're alive.

For now, we're together.

It's all I want.

"Rozalia Dorn..."

Rian smiles at the sight of me. Those dimples fill with blood.

A weak laugh sputters from my numb lips. My insides feel frozen, but a small flower of warmth spurts up beneath it all.

"Rian Kilpatrick…"

"I love you."

The flower explodes in a bouquet of fireworks. Through all the numbness, I can feel a hot tear trickle down my cheek.

"I… I love you too," I quietly admit.

"Let's never get married."

That draws an even stronger laugh from me. But it must sound like a sob, because Rian's brows tent as he lifts a heavy hand and gently pinches my chin.

"Never," I silently repeat.

Those dimples deepen.

"You said you loved me," he smiles, like he's won some big game.

"You said it first."

"I'm delirious from blood loss," he rasps. "What's your excuse?"

Somehow, I manage to lift my chin half an inch in an attempt to reveal where Leander's needle broke my skin.

"Morphine," I whisper.

"That is a good excuse," Rian nods. With a great deal of effort, he shimmies close enough to touch me. "But I want to hear you say it when you're sober."

Before I can answer, he kisses me.

It's a soft kiss. A kiss unlike any I've ever experienced before. It melts away everything bad, and leaves only the good.

An electric warmth sizzles away the numbness on my lips. For a beautiful moment, my mind swims above the black waves I was once plunged beneath.

"It's going to take a long time before I'm sober enough to say that again," I sigh, ready to pass out.

"We have until the end of time," Rian whispers. "I'm never

letting go of you again, angel. Never."

His arm falls onto my shoulder and I sink beneath his weight.

"Promise," I say. Closing my eyes, I let the warm heaviness win. It's the most comforting sensation I've ever felt. The dark world fades away.

I don't even flinch when I hear someone burst into the room. It sounds like they're a million miles away.

"Are you a fucking doctor?" someone demands to know.

"Yes... I... I am..." another voice answers.

"Well, don't just fucking stand there. Help me with these two."

The commotion that follows hardly phases me. My mind has left my body. It floats in some warm dark endless pool.

Rian floats beside me.

It feels like home.

"It's going to be alright, angel," I hear him sigh. "I promise."

"I know," I reply, though I'm not sure if the words ever leave my lips. "I know."

33
RIAN

At first, all I have are nightmares.

I see myself passing out beside Rozalia's unconscious body. I feel myself sink into a dark abyss. I sense the foreboding of what's to come.

Even after I wake up in a hospital bed, surrounded by friends and family, my dread remains.

I'm too weak to speak, to ask about the only thing that matters.

Her.

What was in that needle? What happened to the girl I chased beneath those dark waves?

I need to know.

But I'm not strong enough to ask.

Tubes pump me full of fake warmth. I slip in and out of a deep sleep. Every time I close my eyes, I see Rozalia in that red dress. I see her stunning green eyes.

But I can't reach out and touch her. I can't recapture that blissful warmth we found at La Forcina. It's always just out of reach, blocked off by that dreadful possibility. She's dead.

No!

My eyes snap open.

Someone is standing over my bed. I struggle to make out who it is.

"... Dad?" My dry lips finally part. I feel a strong hand on mine.

"You're going to be alright," he promises. "Everything is going to be alright."

"Roz..." I croak. "Where is she?"

My vision is hazy. But I still understand my dad loud and clear when he nods to the bedroom wall.

"She's next door," he assures me. "Don't worry. She'll be back on her feet before you are."

"I need to see her."

The IV stands that surround my bed rattle as I try to push myself up. But my left shoulder is numb and the rest of my body is quickly engulfed in fire.

My blurry vision is overtaken by blackness.

The next time I open my eyes, no one's at my bedside.

No. Wait. There is someone.

"I brought your painting," Mel quietly says.

I'm just able to turn my head. In the corner, I see a tall canvas. It rises to the ceiling. Somehow, the abstract artwork makes more sense now.

Even through the blurriness, I see where my heart is supposed to be. I see where pride got in the way. I see my destiny. I see my true mistakes.

"I'm sorry," I whisper to my little sister. "... For leaving you..."

"I understand," Mel sighs. "I was never really alone..."

Her sweet innocent voice fades with the room as I'm dragged back into the darkness again. This time, no nightmares wait to greet me. Pinpricks of warmth jump around like jolts of electricity.

Still, the emptiness is overbearing. I sink further and

further... and then, I hit something. A solid floor. It's so warm I never want to leave.

My heavy eyelids flutter back open.

"You look like hell."

That voice.

That sweet, sweet voice.

A painful laugh rattles from my throat as a beige ceiling blurs in and out of focus.

"Turn my head so I can see how bad you look," I carefully rasp.

A sharp set of fingernails trace a gentle figure eight over my stubble before spreading out across my jaw. A warm palm is rested on the back of my hand.

Roz turns me by the chin.

Those stunning green eyes come into focus.

"Do I look as bad as you thought?" she asks, raising a brow at me.

"More beautiful than I could have dreamed."

"You're so cheesy when you're hurt," she laughs, rolling her eyes.

For a moment, we just stare at each other. Then, I remember something. Something mind-blowing. Something that fills my aching heart with a morphine-like calm.

"You said you loved me."

"Only because I thought you were about to die," Roz is quick to reply.

"And now?"

"I stick by my words," she admits, hardly hesitating. "But I'm not saying it again until you're strong enough to beat me in an arm wrestle."

"That won't take long," I cough, my lungs pounding painfully with every heave.

Releasing my chin, Roz gives my cheek a gentle slap.

"Well, I'll leave you to it," she says, some reluctance finally seeping out of her calm façade.

She goes to pull away, but before her hand can leave mine, I wrap my weak fingers around her wrist. It takes all of my strength just to tug her a little, but Rozalia doesn't resist.

"Don't go far," I tell her.

She smiles down at me, her lips pursing.

"I'm not sure your family will let me."

"They're keeping you here?"

"They're strongly suggesting I don't leave."

Stars dot my vision as I try to think clearly. My eyelids start to get heavy again.

"And you're listening to them?"

Scrunching her nose, Roz looks down at her feet. A subtle pink shade flushes her pale cheeks.

"I'm listening to my heart," she mumbles.

I get to laugh one more time before my eyes fall shut again.

This time, though, I'm not greeted by an indifferent void. No. This time, I'm embraced by a beautiful warmth.

No nightmares haunt me. No emptiness threatens me. No dread drags me down.

The horrors of the past fade away.

A lightness takes its place.

I dream of my future.

A future with her.

It will be there when I wake up.

She will be there when I wake up.

I'm sure of it.

Even before I open my eyes, I know it's her.

My bedroom window slides open. A cool breeze drifts in. It carries a spicy rose scent.

"You're making a house cat out of me," Roz grumbles. Her impossibly light footsteps sweep across the rug. I'm just barely able to roll over before she jumps on top of me.

"You were gone too long this time," I say, slowly letting my eyes reopen.

The sight of her steals my breath away. She straddles my waist, green eyes seductively staring down at me.

"I was gone for as long as I needed to be."

Reaching up, I palm Roz's tits. She lets out a deep sigh and starts to sway her hips.

I'm already hard.

"This is going to last as long as I need it to," I say. Dropping my hands around her waist, I flip her onto her back.

The act makes me grimace. But my lust overpowers the pain in my shoulder and hand.

"Easy there," Roz gasps, her hot breath washing across my neck. "You're still not fully recovered yet."

"It's been over a month," I mumble, kissing the edge of her jaw. "I'm tired of resting."

"Fine. I'll give you a little workout, then."

Wrapping her leg around the back of my knee, Roz uses that leverage to flip me onto my back again.

"Fuck," I wince.

A sharp pain flashes across my shoulder.

Roz's shoulders drop.

"You're still too weak," she sighs.

"Try me," I sneer, pressing my hips up into her cunt so she can feel my hard cock.

"Wouldn't you just love that?"

With my good hand, I reach up and grab her around the throat. She doesn't resist as I twist her back onto the bed.

Suddenly, I just want to hear her say one thing.

"Arm wrestle me," I say, grabbing her hand. "Even with a bad shoulder, I'll destroy you."

"You wish."

Our fingers clasp around each other's palms, forming a single fist.

"Three, two, one..." I count down. Before I can say go, Roz starts.

But I wasn't kidding around. Even if I'm still healing, there's no way she's going to overpower me—especially not with this much on the line.

"Fuck!" Roz curses, as I slam her entire arm down onto the mattress. "Fuck," she quietly swears again, covering her mouth with her other hand.

"Don't worry," I huff. Looking over my shoulder, I stare at the closed door. "My family is coming around to you. You don't have to hide anymore."

"Then why am I still sneaking in the window?" she asks.

"Because you like to," I remind her. Tightening my grip around her fallen hand, I stare deep into those deep green eyes. "I won. Say it."

With a defiant fire lighting up those emerald green eyes, she glues her lips shut and shakes her head.

I tighten my grip around her hand. She doesn't give in.

So I do the one thing that makes her melt every time.

I kiss her.

The glue gives way. Her lips part. But before she can start to kiss me back, I teasingly pull away.

"Fine," Roz huffs, rolling her eyes. "I love you. Happy?"

"Yes."

This time, when I kiss her, I don't pull away until precum is leaking from my cock.

"Are you going to say it back?" Roz asks, rubbing her thigh between my legs.

"Not until you beat me in an arm wrestle."

With the quickness of a cat, Rozalia jumps up from the bed.

The cold breeze blowing in from the window wraps around my begging body.

"If that's the case, I'll get back to work," Rozalia snips.

Reaching out, I grab her wrist and pull her back into bed, biting back the pain the whole way through.

"I love you," I whisper into her ear.

"Good."

Our lips have only barely touched again when I hear a knock come from my bedroom door.

"Fuck," I grumble.

"Are you up?" Maksim's voice comes from the other side of the wall.

"Yes."

"Can I come in?"

"No."

A short, understanding silence follows.

"You have a visitor," Maksim eventually says. "He's waiting downstairs."

"Who is it?"

"Adriano Sabatino."

"Double fuck," Rozalia whispers.

With a frustrated grunt, I reluctantly pull away from Rozalia and push myself out of bed.

"I'll be down in a moment," I grumble.

Shuffling over to the closet, I find a shirt and start to get dressed.

"What's he doing here?" Rozalia asks. Standing up, she comes to join me.

"I guess he's finally decided to answer one of my fucking calls."

"You should be punishing him for ignoring you so blatantly," she suggests, resting her chin on my shoulder. "It's disrespectful."

"No," I say, buttoning up my dress shirt. "I'm done being

combative with my own allies. I don't want to end up like Leander."

"You and Leander are nothing alike."

"I know. But I still have to prove it. Every single day, I have to prove it."

"Poor you."

With a teasing kiss on the neck, Rozalia steps away again.

"It's a king's duty."

"How mature."

I can't help but laugh.

"Don't jinx it, angel. This is the first time I'll be talking directly to an Italian since I called off our wedding and announced my intention to rule as an unmarried king."

"You think they're still pissed? Why exactly? Just because they can't force you to marry one of their daughters?"

"I'm sure we'll exchange some heated words," I nod.

"You think you can handle that alone?"

"Yes. You've calmed me."

"Maybe," Rozalia laughs. "But only outside of the bedroom."

"Just how you like it. Would you like to come downstairs with me?"

"I was planning on it," she immediately replies. "We're supposed to be partners, after all."

"More than partners," I smirk. Turning around, I gaze up and down her perfect body. For the first time since she snuck in my window, I spot the blood stain around the neckline of her black turtleneck. "How was your day? Any luck finding Tytus?"

Rozalia's steady spirit falters at the mention of her missing brother.

"No," she sighs. "No one's seen him since you left him in the woods." A heavy pause fills the air. "Rian, I'm worried about him."

Dropping her chin, Rozalia goes to hug herself. But before

she can, I do the job for her. She sinks into my embrace, and I hold her tight.

This is a vulnerable side of her that only I get to see. For someone so tough, Rozalia can be surprisingly fragile when it comes to those she cares about.

I've decided to commit the rest of my life to protecting this side of her, as well as every other side, at all costs—even when she doesn't need my help.

"I'm sure he's fine," I insist. "We've both heard the rumors. Some old Greek mafia families have been reappearing, causing trouble. Someone has to be behind that. I bet it's Tytus. It has to be. Wasn't that the plan all along? To take what Leander had started and use it for your own benefit?"

Rubbing her forehead against my chest, Rozalia considers the theory before positing her own.

"I still think it's Krol."

A cold shiver runs up my spine.

"There's no way he's still alive," I tell her. "Leander must have been fucking with you."

"Maybe," Roz sighs. "I don't want to think about it right now, anyway."

"What do you want to think about?"

Brushing her cheek against my chest one last time, Rozalia looks up at me. A mischievous spark glints behind her fiery green eyes.

"How we're going to deal with that pissy Italian downstairs."

A big smile takes hold of my face.

"You're not worried that my family might see you?"

"I hear they're coming around to me," she smirks back.

"It's true. Though, I think they're still trying to wrap their heads around our, um, 'uncommon partnership'."

"How hard are they trying?"

"A lot harder ever since you helped fabricate the evidence that implicated Leander in the union building fire—as well as half the charges my dad was facing," I shrug. "One day, you'll have to tell me how you did it. Shit. Because of you, the feds had to throw out their case against my dad. I'm sure they'll try to find another reason to come after him. But you've bought us a whole lot of time. And in this business, the only thing more valuable than power is time."

"Even more powerful than love?" Roz teases.

I take her hand.

"Love is only powerful when it lasts forever," I tell her. "And this shit right here, it's going to last forever. I'll make sure of it."

"I'll help," Roz lilts. "I mean, if I have to."

"I insist." Intertwining our fingers, we head for the bedroom door. There's little I want to do more than pin her against the wall and fuck her until we're both leaking, but I know there's no hurry anymore.

Rozalia is mine. And I'm hers. Forever.

They'll be plenty of time for each other after we've dealt with our responsibilities.

"How's Babcia, by the way?" I ask, when we step out into the hallway.

"Good," Roz nods. "At least, she's healthier than you are right now."

"And Kaja?"

"I'm taking her to visit your sister tonight," she says.

To everyone's surprise, Roz and Mel have been getting along progressively well over the past month. It's almost worrying. How long will it take until my sister wants to be just like my Black Cat?

"Good," I note. "Mel needs something to pick her up. She's been so cold to me lately. I worry she hasn't actually forgiven me for leaving her here while I went out chasing you."

"I'm sure she will," Rozalia comforts me. "Eventually. You're family, after all."

Stopping at the top of the staircase that leads downstairs, I let us bask in the morning light seeping down through the large sunroof in the ceiling.

"And what are we?" I ask, taking Roz's other hand too.

"We're something weird and unexplainable," she smiles.

"Try your best."

"To do what?"

"To explain it."

Those perfect red lips curl as she thinks on it for a second. My full heart jumps when I see a lightbulb go off in those impossibly beautiful green eyes.

"It feels like home," she says, a happy sigh lifting her chest. "No matter where we are. When we're together, it feels like home."

"And it always will, angel," I say. Rubbing my thumbs over the back of her hands, I lean down and kiss her.

"Promise?" she whispers into my mouth.

"I promise."

EPILOGUE
ROZALIA

Three months later...

"It's not happening."

I don't know how many times I have to tell Rian that before he gets the message.

"It will be good for you," he insists.

"No. it won't be."

"How do you know?"

"Because I've already been back once now, and the person who met me there is dead because of it. That place is cursed."

With a shallow sigh, Rian reaches past me and takes the handle of the tall ballroom door.

His other hand wraps around my palm.

"Drago isn't dead because you two went back to your old village," he whispers.

My heart dips.

"A curse is a curse," I mumble.

"I don't believe in curses. But I do believe in second chances. I believe in revisiting the emptiness of your past. I believe that's the only way any one of us can truly be full. It's what helped me turn into a real king. I'm convinced it can help you too."

"Are you full?" I ask, sinking beneath his strong grip.

"Yes," he nods, a soft smile bringing out his heart-stopping dimples. "I'm overflowing."

Those ocean blue eyes don't flinch. I feel so safe beneath his gaze.

But Rian is right. I'm not completely full. Not yet. Not even with all the love he gives me.

Something is missing.

Closure.

He thinks I'll find it back at the village where my story started. I don't know why. But I'm not entirely convinced.

Too much pain remains there. If I go back, then it could seep out of the ruins and corrupt the life I have now. It's a nearly perfect life—at least, it's as close to perfect as someone like me is going to get.

There's only one thing missing.

Well, maybe two.

"Why ruin a good thing?" I shrug.

"Since when has my guardian angel ever been satisfied with what she has?"

My dipping heart perks back up as I remember all that I've gained over the past year.

A partner. A home. An empire.

A warmth to help fill the cold emptiness inside.

"Since I got you," I sheepishly admit.

It's true. Even with all the uncertainty still swirling around us, the past three months have been the best of my life.

There's no pressure to be anything but exactly what I want to be. And I know that's not going to change any time soon. Rian is my protector. Any time there's even an indication that someone might start pressuring us to follow a path we don't want to go down, he steps in the way. He takes my hand and pulls me to his side. We walk together. Everywhere.

"I love you," Rian says. Leaning down, he kisses my forehead, then lets go of my hand. "Are you ready?"

"As ready as I'm ever going to be."

"Such a brave girl," Rian teases.

"Don't test your luck," I gently bite back.

"You love it."

"I love you," I remind him.

But he's not wrong. I love our banter. I love our playfulness. I love how we jump from job to job, fixing the cracks in our growing empire, getting our hands dirty, leading by example.

I love how we're here today to bargain with the Italians because they're still pissed Rian has chosen never to marry. I love that I've made such a powerful man choose me over tradition. I love what we have, whatever the hell that is.

I love how special he makes me feel.

"I know," Rian smiles. Stepping aside, he pulls aside the big wooden ballroom door. "After you, my queen."

"Be careful saying that around the Italians," I chuckle, seductively brushing by him. "They might think you want to marry me."

"Angel, I want to be with you for the rest of my life. And I want every second of that life to be filled with happiness. I know you well enough to know that a ring will only get in the way."

"A ring is nothing more than a pretty cage," I remind him.

"And I'm never locking you up again," he says, nudging me forward. "At least, not outside of the bedroom."

My back furls as I brush by him. A warm pressure appears in my core.

No matter how many times I've had this man, it's never enough.

But now is not to think about wanting more.

I need to concentrate.

"Behave," I whisper.

Together, we walk into the lavish ballroom. The walls seem to stretch up into the cloud. Room-sized chandeliers hang from the ceilings. Ahead, I spot a long wooden table. It sits in the middle of it all.

Even from a distance, I recognize the lone man at the head of the table.

Adriano Sabatino.

His hate practically seethes through the warm air.

He hates me. And I hate him. A year ago, I would have killed him without a second thought. But doing something like that now would only hurt the man I love.

So, instead, I've come to help Rian negotiate with the unhappy don.

"Rian. Rozalia." Adriano nods as we approach his table. There are two empty seats beside his. We don't take them. Not quite yet.

"Adriano," Rian replies, his voice rigid and stern. "I'm glad you've finally decided to talk to us."

"Yes, I'm glad you accepted my invitation," he says. "The other dons will show up momentarily. But first, I'd like to talk to you privately and apologize for my past insolence. You must forgive me, I—"

"He doesn't have to do anything," I hear myself interrupt. With a subtle side step, Rian places himself between me and the infuriating don.

Fuck. I promised myself I wouldn't cause any trouble. But sometimes, that's still hard to do.

Old habits die hard, after all.

"Yes, of course," Adriano quickly agrees. "The king does as he pleases, with whomever he pleases."

Despite his obedient words, I can see the Italian just barely holding back a sneer.

He'll never forgive me for ruining his plans. The idiot still thinks I'm the reason Rian didn't want to marry his underage daughter.

Moron.

A man this stupid shouldn't be afforded a position in our empire. But Rian insists that the Italians are too important to cast aside. So, we must learn to work with them—or, at the very least, we must try.

It's not going to be easy.

"What are your terms?" Rian asks. Pulling out a chair, he rests his powerful hands on the crest rail. His sleeves are rolled up, and his thick veiny forearms bulge with strength.

I bite my bottom lip.

Sometimes, I just want to beg Rian to leave this royal life behind and run away with me. Then, we could spend all day fucking.

Adriano starts talking, but I don't listen. Gazing around the grand ballroom, I let my mind wander.

I picture a cottage in the hills, like the one Tytus and I bought for Babcia in the countryside. I imagine an entire litter of kittens making a mess of the place. I imagine a sturdy bed and all the privacy anyone could ask for. I imagine keeping some of our underworld connections, just so we could slip into the city and have a little fun every once in a while.

All of my life, I've wanted to be powerful beyond belief. I've wanted to be richer and stronger than everyone else. But I only wanted that so I could finally be free.

Now that I have all that at my fingertips, I realize freedom doesn't come from power.

It comes from love.

A quiet existence could be enough now.

… Or it could be boring as fuck.

Shit. Who the hell knows?

"Where's he going?" I ask, slowly coming back down to earth.

Adriano has turned his back on us and started to walk away from the table.

My instinctively hackles rise.

What did I miss?

"Apparently, he has a gift for us," Rian casually responds.

"It better not be a wedding gift," I grumble, curling my fists. "That fucker is obsessed with marriage."

"If he wants to keep his head, he'll never bring up marriage around us again."

"Bastard."

We watch as Adriano disappears behind a small door at the far side of the room. When he's gone, Rian turns to me.

"I hear Gabriel's heading back out west tomorrow," he says, his ocean blue eyes searching mine. "Do you think you're going to be alright?"

"I'll be fine," I huff. Though, it's only half true. "Our little reunion was nice, but he's got a family to raise and an empire to run. If there's one thing I hate more than a quick goodbye, it's feeling like I'm holding someone back."

"That's something we've got to work on, angel."

"What?"

"The idea that you could ever hold anyone back."

Reaching out, Rian takes my hand. The warmth of his grip calms a growing anxiety I didn't know I had.

"Your sweet talk isn't going to work on me," I lie.

"There's nothing sweet about it," Rian insists. "If anything, I'd call it tough love. No one's allowed to doubt you, Roz. Not even yourself."

"And if I do?"

"Then you'll be punished."

With a gentle tug, Rian pulls me into his massive body. I hit his hard chest with a warm thud. His pulse is slow and steady.

"Always giving me what I want," I play.

For a moment, Rian's powerful warmth lulls me into a state of peace. But peace has never been able to stick to me for long. Even now.

A thread of darkness curls around the calmness.

I reluctantly push myself off of Rian.

"We have to remember to ask Adriano about Tytus," I remind him.

"I haven't forgotten."

How could he?

Tytus is still missing. And I've brought it up nearly every day since he disappeared.

We've had a few tips, here and there. Hell, we even get a sighting every now and then, too. But it's hard to say how credible it all is.

At the very least, I'm past thinking my brother is dead, but an even worse fear has wormed its way into the back of my happiness.

What if Tytus isn't dead? What if he's simply decided that I'm dead to him?

Fuck.

This isn't the first time I've had the thought, but it still hits me like a ton of bricks.

Rian told me about the tentative truce he and Tytus had come to before coming to my rescue.

But I can't imagine he reached that deal willingly.

If he could have ambushed Leander's mansion himself, I'm sure he would have. But his injuries prevented that. So, it sounds like he put aside his hate for Rian and his family for just long enough to make sure I was safe.

What came after that?

Gabriel and I talked about it last night. Neither of us could decide for sure.

Tytus' fate remains a mystery, an empty pit that prevents me from feeling completely full.

That pit throbs in my belly as I think of my two brothers. Shit, Gabriel hasn't even left yet, and I already miss him.

The idea of losing Tytus forever hurts even more.

Has this fear always been there? Or has accepting Rian's love just softened me up?

"Where the hell is that fucker?" Rian grumbles, breaking my concentration.

As if on cue, the door clicks open again.

Out steps Adriano.

He's carrying a large, gift-wrapped box.

The hair on my arms instantly stands straight up.

That's no ordinary looking box.

"What took you so long?" Rian asks, clearly sensing the same disturbance I do.

Adriano only takes a couple of steps forward before stumbling to a stop. His dark eyes dart back and forth as he considers how to respond.

Instinctively, I reach for my gun. But I don't pull it out just yet. I'm supposed to be on my best behavior.

But something is wrong. I can feel it.

"He asked you a question," I shout to Adriano. "What took you so long?"

A sudden calm comes over the Italian's face. His shoulders drop.

To my shock, a cocky grin comes over his chubby face.

"I just had to make sure the cameras were set up."

Before either of us can react, Adriano reaches under the gift-wrapped box. Rian seems to understand what's happening even before I do. Twisting around, he tackles me to the ground.

I just barely see the bullet ripping out from behind the wrapping paper.

A thunderous gunshot blasts through the ballroom as we hit the floor.

The realization is immediate. We only need to share a quick glance to confirm the obvious.

This is a trap.

We need to act. And quickly.

There's no time to coordinate—not that we need to. Rian rolls one way, and I roll the other. Another thunderous fills the air. I feel a bullet whizz past my ear.

"Finally," I spit towards Adriano as I push myself onto my feet. "You don't know how long I've been waiting to kill you."

Pulling the gun from my thigh holster, I aim at the treacherous Italian. But just as I'm about to pull the trigger, the door at the far end of the room bursts open.

It distracts me just enough. My bullet goes flying above Adriano's head. He ducks to the floor, and a stream of heavily-armed men rush into the room behind him.

"Maksim. Deacon. Get the fuck in here," Rian yells into his earpiece. "And bring the troops. It's a trap. We need—"

Rian is cut off by a hail of gunfire. The deafening boom is so loud it sends me onto my ass. A smoky residue fills the air. I search for my lion.

My heart jumps when I spot him.

He's taken cover behind one of the chairs at the table. The wood is splintered from the bullets. But he's still breathing. I follow his lead and scramble behind a chair of my own.

"No! Stop!" Adriano shouts. "I need to be the one who kills them! That's what the fucking cameras are for! Make sure they're recording!"

For a moment, the chaos pauses. I pull my gun up to my cheek and gaze beneath the table.

"Are you alright?" I ask Rian.

"Never been better," he growls. "Now we finally have an excuse to kill this fucker."

I can't help but laugh.

"That's exactly what I said."

Reaching down to my ankle, I pull out a smaller pistol. The two guns fill my hands with a familiar weight. My heart starts to race. My pulse quickens with excitement.

Fuck. How could I ever abandon this shit? A quiet life would never suit me.

This is my heaven. Fighting next to the man I love.

"You idiot," Rian shouts out to Adriano. "You've signed your death warrant. We have men outside. You really think we'd be stupid enough to come here alone?"

"No. But that doesn't matter. I have men outside too. They'll buy me enough time to kill you and then escape."

"Moron," I mumble.

"Hey, angel," Rian calls to me. "I count eight men. That gives us four each. Do you think we can handle that?"

"I bet I don't even break a sweat," I respond, loud enough for Adriano to hear.

"You cocky assholes!" Adriano shouts. His voice is shaking, but I can't tell if it's from anger, frustration, or fear. "Come out here and fight me!"

"As you wish," Rian smirks, looking over to me.

Those ocean blue eyes sparkle with the same excitement I feel. We both know that Adriano's made a grave mistake. Eight men aren't enough to bring the two of us down. Especially not if we're fighting together.

"You go left. I'll go right?" I smile back at him.

"Meet you in the middle."

"Don't keep me waiting."

"I wouldn't dare."

We let our gazes linger for a little while longer before my trigger finger gets too itchy to ignore.

"Love you," I say.

"Love you."

With that, we get to work.

Spinning around my chair, I fire three quick shots. Two bodies quickly hit the ground, dead on impact. A fourth bullet catches Adriano in the leg. He joins the corpses on the floor as his goons fire a return volley my way.

I'm too quick for them. Bullets flash over my head and upend the expensive carpet at my feet as I zigzag towards them.

Lifting my smaller pistol, I start to pick off the stragglers, one by one. They don't stand a chance. Whoever Adriano has brought with him, they aren't used to fighting against killers like Rian and me.

By the time I reach the squirming don, the battle is won. Rian fires one last bullet for good measure, then joins me.

"You've got a lot of explaining to do," he says, pointing his barrel into the back of Adriano's skull.

"You fuckers!" he screeches, rolling on the ground like a pig in the mud.

Blood pours from his shin. I find the bullet wound and step down on it, pinning him in place.

He howls up to the chandeliers.

"You idiot," I hiss. "What the hell did you think you'd get out of this?"

Adriano starts to cry from the pain. But when he doesn't answer my question, I dig my heel deeper into his gash.

"Stop!" he pleads.

"Then fucking answer me," I tell him. "What the hell did you think you'd get out of trying to kill us?"

"Answer the lady," Rian echoes, tracing his muzzle over Adriano's tear-stained cheeks. "Were you looking for revenge?"

"No," Adriano grits. He tries to reach for his leg, but Rian grabs his wrist and stops him.

"Then what? What was your master plan here, moron? What did you think you were going to gain from killing us?"

"... An ally."

Sneering, I kick away Adriano's injured leg and crouch down so I can stare into his terrified eyes.

"What the fuck does that mean?" I ask, grabbing his collar.

To my disappointment, there's hardly any fear in his beady little brown eyes. Instead, I spot something far more disturbing.

"It means you will never find peace," he wheezes.

Rian cracks the butt of his gun against the back of Adriano's skull.

"Who's your new ally?" he growls. "The Greeks? Krol?"

"You wish," Adriano spits, the life in his eyes flickering as he looks over to me.

"Then who?" I demand to know, furious.

When Adriano doesn't answer right away, I shove my barrel into his mouth. I can feel his teeth chattering against the cold steel.

This bastard just tried to slaughter us, and for what? To make a good impression?

It reminds me of the stunt he attempted at Rian's coronation. But this time, instead of slaughtering an innocent cat to show his loyalty, Adriano tried to kill us.

And I thought he couldn't get any dumber.

"Answer her!" Rian orders.

I rip my gun back out of the Italian's mouth.

"Just give me a chance to fucking breathe!" Adriano coughs.

"No," I spit, slapping him with the back of my hand.

His head snaps to the side.

A sickening laugh gurgles from his blood-filled mouth.

"Who were you trying to impress with this shit?" I repeat, increasingly irate.

"A man you know well," Adriano coughs.

"Who?" I ask, one last time.

Just outside of the ballroom walls, I can hear our men trying to fight their way in. I tune out the noise. I only care about one thing.

I'm completely obsessed with finding out who Adriano would throw away his life for.

"Talk," Rian barks. "Or I'll make sure you suffer a hell of a lot more before you die. Now fucking tell us, who the hell were you trying to impress with this shit?"

Adriano's fading gaze sharpens as he stares deep into my eyes. I can see his anger. I can feel his disappointment.

I can taste his hate.

"Your brother," he rasps, his bloody lips twisting into a bloody frown. "Tytus Ryzdon. He recruited me. He wants to overthrow you. He wants you dead."

Just like that, the world goes silent.

My pounding heart stops beating.

Without thinking, I shove my gun back into Adriano's mouth and pull the trigger.

The silence is invaded by a harsh ring. It grows until I feel Rian wrap his arms around me.

Still, it takes a moment before everything comes rushing back into focus.

"What's going on?" I ask, still shocked at what I just heard.

"I don't know," Rian says. Dropping his embrace, he stands up and offers me his hand. I mindlessly take it. "Are you alright?"

"I... I think so," I mumble, not sure if it's true.

Tytus...

Why?

"Good," Rian growls. Pulling me up onto my feet, he lets me lean on his searing body. "Because we're not resting until we find out what just happened. No one gets away with trying to hurt my girl. No one. It's time we track down your brother, Roz."

"Rian, I—"

"Shush, angel," he interrupts, placing a gentle finger on my lips. "Let's go hunting."

EPILOGUE
RIAN

1 month later...

Maybe this was a bad idea, after all.

I may not believe in curses, but this place feels cursed. The earth is black. The ruins are charred. And under the dim moonlight, it's hard to tell the difference between the rocks and the bones.

Yet through all the darkness, there's one redeeming quality—an unmistakable light.

This is where the love of my life grew up.

It's also where we'll find the last piece of her puzzle. The one that finally allows her to feel as complete as she makes me feel.

At least, that's what I hope.

Now, I'm not so sure.

"Are you alright?" I ask.

When I place my hand on Roz's shoulder, she flinches. Her entire body is stiff.

The knot in my gut tightens.

"Why are we here again?" she asks. There's a vulnerability in her tough voice that would be imperceptible to the average person. But I know her well enough to hear it loud and clear.

"We're looking for Tytus," I gently remind her.

"And you think he's here because of the coordinates he left you?"

"Yes," I sigh, knowing how foolish it sounds.

The last time anyone saw Tytus was when I left him in the forest outside Leander's mansion. Two weeks later, when I was lucid enough to ask after him, I found out that he had disappeared.

But not without a trace. He'd left one thing behind.

My phone.

It took another two weeks before I decided to take a closer look.

That's when I saw the primitive carving.

Coordinates.

Tytus had etched a small set of directions into the back of my phone case.

When I finally had the strength, I followed them.

They brought me here, to Roz's old village.

Why?

I still don't know. But ever since then, I've been trying to get Roz to come. Part of me can't get past the idea that Tytus might be trying to help his sister.

Another part of me worries he might be trying to do the opposite.

There was only one real way to find out.

"I'll start looking," Roz says, shaking my hand off her shoulder.

I don't let her get far. Grabbing her wrist, I pull her in for a hug.

"if it's too much, just tell me and I'll take you home."

"I'm already home," Roz whispers, nuzzling her nose into my chest.

I take a deep breath. Her well-being is a heavy responsibility. I don't take it lightly. But I also know I can't hold her too close. Even after all we've been through, she's still a feral cat. It's part of what I love about her. She makes me feel free. And I try my best to make sure she never feels trapped.

"Be careful," I say, kissing Roz on the forehead.

For a brief moment, we just stand among the ruins and hug. I do my best to keep the darkness at bay.

"You know I never am," Roz sighs.

With a light kiss on my shoulder, she pushes herself out of our embrace.

I reluctantly let her go.

"I'm still not convinced this isn't a trap," I mumble, watching as she starts to pace through the ashes.

"Neither am I," she agrees. "But I'm too curious to turn back now."

"Curiosity killed the cat," I mumble.

But Roz doesn't hear me.

Giving her one last long look, I turn and slowly make my way to the other end of the small village. There isn't much to see that isn't already clear from the center point.

The land is flat. The ruins are short and overgrown. Only small pockets of elevated earth interrupt the leveled fields. Shallow graves.

I try not to think of the horrors hiding beneath my feet. Kicking my way through the thick of it, I quickly find myself at the edge of the faded village.

"Do you see anything over there?" I ask, turning around to look for Roz.

But she's not there.

"Roz?" I call out.

There's no answer.

Furrowing my brows, I step back into the ruins. Almost immediately, I nearly trip over one of the shallow graves.

"Fuck," I grumble, catching myself.

Over the past four months, I've come out here a dozen or so times by myself. But I'm still not used to the jagged terrain. It seems to change with every visit.

"Roz!" I call out through the darkness.

By the time I reach the center of the village again, I'm starting to panic.

A soft wind rustles the long grass. But other than that, there's almost no sound.

"Where the hell—"

"Rian!"

Roz's shout cuts through the silence like a scythe. Before I can even process the sound, I'm running.

"Roz?!" I yell back.

"Over here, quick!" she responds.

I follow her voice until I hear the sound of running water.

"Where are you?" I ask, reaching down for my gun.

"This way."

Beside a modest stream rises a giant weeping willow. Roz's voice comes from the darkness beneath the hanging leaves.

"What's wrong?" I ask, joining her in the darkness.

Instead of answering, Rozalia presses a finger to her lips. Her big green eyes shine through the darkness.

My hackles rise.

When I hear a commotion in the branches above, my instinct is to attack. Tearing my gun out, I lift it to the sky, but before I can fire, Roz jumps on my arm, knocking the weapon from my hand.

"No!" she pleads.

A split-second later, something jumps from the branches. It lands on the leafy ground by the trunk, then flashes across the stream, following a spotted bridge of stones.

By the time the black figure disappears into the woods on the other side of the water, I understand what's happening.

"A cat," I mumble, picking up my gun.

"Not just any cat," Roz whispers. "Willow..."

"Roz, I... listen," I'm not sure what to say.

There's no way that was Willow.

"Do you think that's why Tytus brought us here?" Roz asks, the hope in her voice is so innocent it carves a hole in my chest.

"No," I grunt, shaking my head. "Tytus doesn't know about Willow. No one does. Don't you remember?"

"I... I..." Now it's Roz's turn to stumble. "I wanted your help getting me up into the tree," she finally says. "But I think I scared her away."

"I don't think that was Willow," I carefully remark.

"How do you know?"

"Wouldn't she be almost sixteen years old by now?"

"So what?"

"How is an old cat going to move that quickly?"

I can see the realization dawn over Rozalia's pretty green eyes. But before her hopes are dashed, a brightness flickers in her gaze.

"Maybe she had kittens," Roz says.

"Maybe," I mutter. "But that's not why we're here. Roz, we need to—"

"Rian, please."

When Rozalia squeezes my hand, I know I can't refuse.

Her emerald green eyes glisten against the moonlight. My heart flutters.

She needs this.

So do I.

For as happy as we've been, something has been missing. Something small. But something vital.

For a moment, all I can think about is how I sometimes catch Roz staring off into space, like she's looking for something that isn't there. I think of how I'll wake up in the middle of the night, and roll over in bed to find her staring up at the ceiling.

I think of how she brings Kaja over to play with Mel, and how they both just sit there watching the cat play.

Mel...

My sister's also been distant lately. Something is wrong there, too. I don't know what. But I need to find out and fix it.

First, though, I need to help fix what's right in front of me.

"Let's go catch that cat," I say.

Roz squeezes my hand extra tight before letting it go.

"You go left, I'll go right," she nods.

"No," I tell her. "I'm not leaving you alone again."

Those big green eyes sharpen as a fiery determination takes hold of my Black Cat.

"Rian, listen. You want me to be whole, right? This is a piece of me that's been missing since I was a child. Help me recover it, please."

I don't have the strength to push back. At least Roz is telling me what she wants now.

Mel won't even give me that.

"Fine. But keep your phone in your hand and keep your eye out for danger. I haven't been to the other side of the stream yet. We don't know what's hiding in those woods."

"Hopefully a kitten," Roz says, a small smile lifting her lips.

"Hopefully."

Without wasting any more time, we follow the cat's path over the stream, stopping at the forest's edge.

"Love you," I tell Roz, knowing full well that there's no point in asking her to be careful.

"Love you back," she says.

Then, just like that, she vanishes into the forest. My chest tightens, but only slightly.

This is just another adventure, I tell myself. *Another adventure with the girl of my dreams.*

Unholstering my gun again, I step into the black woods. It takes a second for the flashlight on my scope to start working, but the second it does, I immediately realize the futility of our search.

How the hell are we going to find a cat in all of this?

Ahead, dark trees stretch off into an endless forest. Fallen trunks litter the ground, overgrown with moss and plants. There are countless places for a tiny animal to hide.

If this cat doesn't want to be found, then we aren't going to find it.

Fuck.

I'm already about to give up when I remember something that Roz once told me.

Willow always came when she was called.

I still don't think we just saw Roz's old cat, but maybe a descendant of hers will have a similar reaction?

"Willow?" I call out into the darkness.

At first, it feels foolish, but then I remember why I'm doing this, and it becomes the most important thing in the world.

Love.

I'm doing this for love.

"Willow!" I call out again, louder this time.

Far in the distance, I can just barely make out Rozalia calling out too.

I start to hope that she's right.

Willow could still be alive, right?

"Willow," I repeat, at various volumes, over and over again as I venture deeper into the woods.

The longer I go without getting a response, the less hopeful I get. Soon, I can't even hear Roz in the distance. There's only a deafening silence. I puncture it with Willow's name.

But soon, the darkness begins to eat up my words, too.

And then I hear something that stops my heart.

A meow.

I whip around, pointing my flashlight where I think I heard the sound come from.

A pair of yellow eyes greet me.

"... Willow?"

Immediately, I know it's not the old cat. It looks far too young. But when I call the name out again, it ventures closer towards me.

Crouching down, I reach out my hand and let it sniff my finger.

"Do you have a mom anywhere nearby?" I ask. "Maybe a grandmother? Or great-grandmother?"

Shit. How many generations of cats could there be after sixteen years?

I feel the vibrations of a purr as the cat softly brushes against my finger. But when I try to pet it, the creature slinks from my touch.

When it turns away, I take out my phone and call Roz.

"Anything?" she quickly answers.

"I found a black cat," I tell her. "It's too young to be Willow, though."

"Doesn't matter. I'm locking onto your location. See you in a sec."

Roz hangs up. The cat looks back at me. When our eyes lock, it almost seems to nod.

Then it turns around again and starts to strut away. There's no time to wait for Roz, I have no choice but to follow it.

"What the hell am I doing?" I grumble to myself.

With careful steps, I follow the cat through the tangled forest floor until we reach a small clearing. At the edge of the clearing is a fallen log. Its bark is mossy. Its inside is hollowed.

The cat disappears inside of it.

Curiosity pulls me forward. I hear a meow.

Then another.

And another.

By the time I shine my flashlight inside the trunk, a chorus of cats are singing at me. A dozen yellow, green and blue eyes shine through the darkness.

"Not again," I mutter, remembering the mess in my basement when we were searching for Kaja. The place was filled with strays for a week before we managed to rehome them all.

This time is different, though.

Immediately, I know I won't be getting rid of these kittens.

Not when Roz shows up and sees them.

"My place is much nicer than this," I tell the cats. "You guys will like it there. You'll like my sister, Mel, too. She'll be in heaven. Same with Roz."

Shining my light through the hollow trunk, I search for more cats. It doesn't even register how crazy I must sound, talking to a bunch of strays like this.

"What is that?" I mumble, when my flashlight comes across their makeshift nest. The bed of the trunk is filled with leaves and twigs. Some small bones are sprinkled in there too.

In the midst of it all, though, is something far more unnatural.

Wires.

Black ones. Red ones. Blues ones. Yellow ones. They almost match the cats' eyes. Some are twisted into the fabric of the cozy nest. A few others hang down from the slits in the trunk, like toys.

It's too curious to ignore.

"Mind if I take one of these?" I ask.

No one stops me as I reach over and grab one of the dangling wires.

It doesn't immediately come sliding out. And I quickly realize that's because it's attached to something. Reaching through the slit it hangs from, I find what I'm looking for and pull.

One of the kittens hisses as the bark gives way.

"Sorry," I apologize, pulling back out of the trunk. "Now, what the hell is this?"

The strange black box doesn't look like it belongs in the middle of these dark, isolated woods. And it definitely doesn't look like something that we'd have found in Roz's old village.

Running the tip of my finger over the edges, I search for a ridge or an opening.

I find a button.

"What do you do?" I ask, pressing down on it.

A first, nothing happens. But then, I hear a small engine whirl alive inside the box.

Suddenly, a slot flips open and a bright light bursts out of the little machine, blinding me.

I drop the box and jump back.

I'm still trying to recover my vision when I hear a voice that sends a shiver up my spine.

"Took you long enough."

It's Tytus.

My vision is still spotty as I draw my gun and lash around.

"Don't fucking move!" I order, blinking away the flashing white light.

"You may be wondering what this is," he continues, undeterred by my threats.

Slowly, my vision refocuses.

Sure enough, I see Tytus. He's standing right where I just was, in front of the log.

But something is off. His image seems to flicker.

I rub my eyes. But it doesn't take long to realize what's happening.

"A hologram," I curse.

"Well, let me explain…" Tytus' bright silver-blue eyes glow in his unsteady projection. His image flashes and pauses, but the audio remains surprisingly clear. "I thought this might be our safe place," he says. "Our hidden little secret away from prying eyes. I engraved those coordinates on the back of your phone in case I ever wanted to get a message to you. I figured no one would ever show up here, not voluntarily—least of all Roz. But you would. Anything to solve the mystery of my disappearance. Anything to protect your empire... and your girl."

Tucking away my gun, I begin to circle the hologram. It quickly becomes apparent that it's a recording. Tytus must have left this somewhere in the ruins of Roz's old village.

The cats probably dragged it back to their nest.

"I'm not as tech-savvy as Roz," Tytus keeps talking. "I won't be able to hack into your systems. But I do still have access to some of her devices. And I plan to make full use of them. If you ever need to talk to me, just come back here. If you ever think I need to explain myself, come back here. Leave your own message. I'll return the favor. But I must warn you, don't you ever try to catch me. Don't set up an ambush. Don't bring anyone else. This is a sacred place. A cursed place, sure, but sacred nonetheless. I may not be as tech-savvy as my sister, but I have my own specialties. I can make you pay for breaking the rules. All I ask is that you treat this place with as much respect as it deserves. This is the birthplace of the woman you love, after all."

With a mischievous wink, the hologram disappears.

I'm immediately back on my knees, reaching into the hollowed-out trunk, looking for more wires.

It sounds like Tytus would have returned to the village and left more messages. How many has he left over the last five months?

In the span of a few minutes, I pull out four more black boxes. I find the freshest looking one and press down on its button.

A new hologram flickers up into the clearing.

Tytus looks a hell of a lot more pissed than he did in his first message.

"I don't know what the fuck is going on, but this is the last message I'm going to leave. If you're trying to play games with me, stop. It won't end well. I don't want to hurt you. Not physically, at least. So, here's the deal, I'm going to—"

Suddenly, the image disappears. The recording stops, and I'm engulfed by a near deafening silence.

A cat meows. And then, the hologram flickers back to life.

I can immediately tell this isn't another recording. Tytus is wearing a different outfit.

He's live.

"You," I growl, hackles rising.

Tytus furrows his brows as he tries to make sense of what he's seeing.

"Hello there," he smiles, when the lightbulb goes off. "I guess I was wrong to accuse you of stealing my devices. It looks like some animal was dragging them into the woods."

"How observant of you," I sneer.

All I can think of was the last line I heard before that last recording went dead.

I don't want to hurt you. Not physically, at least.

What the hell does that mean?

"Well, that's a relief. I thought you might be angry at me," he teases.

"I am angry at you," I spit back. "Furious. You almost got Roz killed."

Suddenly, Tytus doesn't look so playful.

"I heard about that," he snarls. "If you haven't heard my messages, let me update you. I did not tell that greasy Italian fuck to kill you. And I definitely didn't send him after Roz. Don't you ever dare accuse me of that again."

"Bullshit," I spit. "If you didn't tell him to come after us, then why the hell did he do it?"

"For the same reason he brought Kaja to your coronation,"

Tytus says. "Because he's an idiot. A small-minded, vicious little idiot."

Part of me wants to believe him. Everything would be so much better if he hadn't actually sent a hit out on Roz. But how can I trust him?

"Where have you been?" I ask, not letting the sneer drop from my lips.

"Preparing."

"Preparing for what?"

"War."

My grip tightens around the handle of my gun.

"With who?" I ask, already knowing the answer.

"With you, of course. Who else is worth fighting?"

"So you do want us dead?"

"No," Tytus says, shaking his head. "I just want your power. Well, most of it anyway. I'll leave enough to you and Roz so you two can retire to some tropical paradise."

"And let you destroy the rest of my family?"

"I don't have any soft spots for the rest of your family," Tytus callously points out. "Well, that's not true. There is—"

"What the fuck…"

Looking over my shoulder, I see Roz stumble into the clearing.

"Hey, sis," Tytus smirks.

"You… You're alright," she mumbles, staring up at the hologram. The relief in her voice is tentative.

"I'm better than ever,' Tytus assures her. "Though, I do miss you. And our brother. How is Gabriel, by the way?"

"He… He's good," Roz stutters, stepping forward.

I take her hand. Those sharp brows are twisted with confusion.

"Tytus has been leaving messages in the village for me to find," I quickly explain. "The cats have been dragging them out into the woods to use as nesting and playthings."

"... The cats? Plural?"

As if on cue, a pair of yellow eyes stick out from the hollow trunk behind Tytus' flickering image. A pair of green eyes pop out to join them. More follow.

"Enough about the cats," Tytus interrupts. "You've got some shit to catch up on."

"Like how you tried to kill us?" Roz whispers, her confusion slowly turning into anger.

"I did no such thing," Tytus hits back. "If anything I gave you new life."

"How's that?" Roz challenges.

"By setting you up with the love of your life."

The self-impressed smirk on Tytus' face sends me reeling.

"What the hell does that mean?" I ask.

"It means I knew that my sister was developing feelings for you," he responds. "It means I knew she deserved to be happier than me, and as happy as Gabriel. It means I set up that wonderful little date for you at La Forcina's..."

"You sent that text?" Roz and I both blurt out at the same time.

Her jaw drops. I quickly pick mine back up off the floor.

"You did that as a distraction," I remind him, still trying to make sense of what he's saying.

"No. Drago and Leander wanted a distraction. I wanted you two to fall in love. Well, deeper in love."

"Why the hell did you want that?"

"Aren't you listening?" Tytus' smirk deepens. "I did it because you deserve the same happiness and security that Gabriel found with Bianca. That's why I sent you back here to meet with Drago, too. I wanted you to see that he'd actually changed. That he actually cared for you. That you were worthy of being cared for."

Roz's shoulder brushes against mine as she sways on her feet.

"I don't believe you," I growl, stepping in between her and the hologram.

"That's because you don't know me," Tytus spits.

"I know you…" Roz mutters.

"And do you believe me?"

"Yes…" she sighs. "But my happiness can't be the only reason you did what you did."

"It's not," Tytus confirms. "Sure, I foresaw how happy Rian could make you, but I also foresaw my own path to power. I'd have a lot more of it if I didn't have to share it with anyone."

"So you pushed me away?"

"I pushed you towards love."

"And what about you?" Roz asks. "Do you not need love?"

"All I need is power."

"What power do you have?" I snap.

"So much more than I did just a year ago," Tytus chuckles. "The Greek mafia that Leander was secretly rebuilding is now under my control, as well as a good chunk of his mercenaries. Would you like to guess which Italian families I've corrupted, too?"

"The Italians wouldn't dare. Not after what I did to Adriano."

"No. What you did to Adriano only helped push them further towards me. Call it a happy accident. Honestly, I'm a little ashamed that the final straw wasn't something I orchestrated—if only the Italians had decided to finally abandon you after what happened at La Forcina. That's why I sent them there, after all. So that they could see how little you cared about them and their daughters."

Fucking hell.

"How will starting a war with us make Roz happy?" I ask him, pointing out the contradiction.

"Oh, how little you know her," Tytus chuckles. "What's the one thing my sister loves more than anything?"

"Me," I blurt out.

"Alright," Tytus laughs. "That's true enough. But what's the second thing?"

"Fighting…" Roz mumbles.

"Correct. A boring life isn't for you, Roz. So, I've decided to make it a little more exciting. You're welcome."

Before either of us can respond, the hologram vanishes.

For a brief moment, neither of us talk. We just bask in the mindfuckery of what just happened.

Then, a cat meows, and we come hurtling back down to earth.

"What the hell do we do now?" I ask, turning to Roz.

She's already started to walk towards the hollowed-out trunk.

"We go home," she says. Crouching down, she entices the cats to come out to greet her. One by one, they do just that. One even curls up in her lap.

I sigh.

"And I'm guessing we bring the cats with us?"

Those sharp green eyes flicker up at me. There's a new life in them.

And a new hate.

Fuck. Here we go again.

"You're damn right we do."

"What do you mean she's missing?"

Three cats brush by my feet as Maksim gives me the horrifying news.

"Mel managed to sneak away while you were out," my uncle says, his usually calm voice spiking with panic. "I've sent a hundred men to find her. Deacon's leading his own crew. But no one's sure how long she's actually been gone for."

Blood rushes to my ears as a wave of dread pounds me into the floor.

I know Mel's been unhappy lately, but I would never expect her to do something this drastic.

"How the fuck did she get out?" I demand to know. "We've been on lockdown for months. This place is surrounded."

"This way!" Roz shouts.

She's at the other end of Mel's studio. Pushing aside the giant painting my sister gave me for my coronation, she reveals the escape hatch built into the wall.

The door behind it is open.

"That's right," Maksim confirms. "That was the first place I looked. We still have men in the tunnels. But I haven't heard back from any of them yet."

"How did she know about the escape hatch?" I question, growing increasingly numb.

How could this happen?

How could I let it happen?

"I'm still not sure," Maksim admits. His voice is full of shame.

"I think I have an idea," Roz calls out again. "Someone hit the lights."

"What are you—" I start, before being interrupted.

"Hit. The. Lights."

"Do as she says," I grumble. There's a wild look in Roz's eyes. She's found something important.

"Come here," Roz insists. The lights shut off. The studio goes dark.

Taking out my phone, I light the way.

Every step I take is like a punch to the gut. Mel will never survive out there. Especially not with Tytus on the hunt.

We need to bring her back home. And fast.

"Look at this," Roz says. She's pulled out a lighter and flipped my coronation painting around. Pressing the flame against the back of the canvass, she illuminates a hidden message.

Your artwork is beautiful,
And so are you.
If you want to be free,
Then I can show you what to do.
At the far end of your studio,
Beneath the very last light,
There's an escape hatch you can use,
To take your very first flight.
Yours truly,
The shadow.

My heart drops.

"There's more," Roz says. Leading the flame beneath the poem, she finds a much more rudimentary message. It's painted in white just beneath one of the wooden wedges.

I'm sorry. I need to be free—if only just for a little while.
Love, Mel.

"That fucking bastard," I curse, ready to explode.

"Tytus must have written that message before he returned the painting," Roz points out. "I wonder if he tipped your sister off when they ran into each other?"

"Mel is smart," Maksim says. "She could have figured it out herself."

"She's more than smart."

The hairs on my neck stand up at the sound of Tytus' voice.

It appears out of the darkness behind us, raspy and distant like the devil.

Roz drops the painting and her lighter, and we all whip around, guns immediately drawn.

But we're met only by darkness.

"Turn the lights back on!" I yell.

A second later, I get my wish.

The lights snap back on. But Tytus is nowhere to be found.

"Where are you?" I demand.

"I assume we're in your sister's studio?"

"There," Roz hisses.

I follow her green eyes down to the floor.

"Hi there," Tytus says. His voice crackles up from one of the cats.

"What the fuck is going on…" I mumble.

Am I having a fucking nightmare?

Before I can act, Roz bends down and picks up the black cat. A quick search through her fur reveals a small black device. I instantly spot the speaker on it.

"How the hell did you get this on the cat?" Roz asks, unable to keep an impressed lilt from cutting through her rage.

"I didn't do it," Tytus says. I can practically hear his smirk. "It must have latched onto the creature's fur when it was destroying one of my message boxes. Another happy accident."

"I'm going to fucking kill you," I roar. "If anything happens to my sister, you'll be held directly—"

"Easy there, lion," Tytus interrupts. "The message I left on your sister's painting was written well before we came to our little agreement."

"We haven't agreed on shit," I spit.

"Fine. Be stubborn," Tytus taunts. "Either way, I promise you this: I'll find Melina Kilpatrick. I'll make sure no one else gets their hands on her. Call it an apology gift for what happened with Adriano."

"Leave her alone, Tytus," Roz begs, sternly. But her voice cracks just enough to send a cold shiver skating up my spine.

Is she scared?

Fuck.

What is Tytus capable of?

"You two better start treating me with a bit more respect," Tytus says, playing with us.

"Or what?" I sneer, wishing I could send my fist flying through his icy silver-blue eyes.

This is bad. Mel is in trouble.

A beast is after her.

I have to find her first.

"Oh, I'll still find her," Tytus promises. "But if you don't start playing along, I might just decide to keep that pretty little sister of yours for myself."

"You wouldn't dare," I growl, fists clenching until my knuckles turn white.

"Watch me."

TYTUS IS NEXT. HE'S HOT, WILD & DANGEROUS BEYOND BELIEF. CAN MEL HANDLE HIM? FIND OUT IN SINFUL LORD!

ALSO BY SASHA LEONE

RUTHLESS DYNASTY

Ruthless Heir

Lethal King

Sinful Lord

BRUTAL REIGN

Merciless Prince

Brutal Savior

Cruel Knight

Wicked Master

Twisted Lover

Savage Don